SPIKED

JON McGORAN

HOLIDAY HOUSE New York

To my siblings Maeve, Alison, and Hugh,
who have given me a lifetime of
love and support.

Library of Congress Cataloging-in-Publication Data

Names: McGoran, Jon, author.
Title: Spiked / by Jon McGoran.
Description: First edition. | New York : Holiday House,
[2020] | Sequel to: Splintered. | Audience: Ages 14 and up.
Audience: Grades 7-9. | Summary: In her fight for
human rights for chimeras—people who alter themselves with
animal DNA—seventeen-year-old Jimi Corcoran and her
chimera boyfriend Rex are drawn into a whirlwind of secret
identities, shocking experiments, and an apocalyptic
plot that threatens the future of humanity.
Identifiers: LCCN 2019044186
ISBN 9780823440917 (hardcover)
Subjects: CYAC: Genetic engineering—Fiction. | Survival—Fiction.
Toleration—Fiction. | Love—Fiction. | Science fiction.
Classification: LCC PZ7.1.M43523 Sp 2020 | DDC [Fic]—dc23
LC record available at https://lccn.loc.gov/2019044186

PROLOGUE

Even with the sun directly overhead, the Wells Tower cast a long shadow. The headquarters of Wellplant Corporation was the tallest building in the city. It represented everything that was wrong with the world, but to be honest, at that moment, I was grateful for the shade.

I was headed to the Independence Seaport Museum, down on the waterfront, a half-hour walk from the Levline hub. I could have taken a bus or a cab, but I liked walking in the city, even in the summer heat. Plus, I needed to clear my head and steady my nerves.

It had been a while since I'd been in the Tower District, and I took a moment to glance around. From far away, the buildings that dominated the city skyline were quite a sight. They were majestic, especially at night, but thin and glassy and delicate. They looked like they'd break if you touched them. Up close, they were dizzying, even awe-inspiring, especially the Wells Tower, which soared into the blue sky behind me. As I watched, a lone cloud crashed into the top floor and was neatly sliced in half by the tower's edge, creating two smaller clouds, which slipped past it on either side.

My neck was starting to ache from gazing up so high, and when I looked down again I was greeted by scowls from the business-types walking toward me, then *around* me—kind of like that cloud, but more clearly annoyed.

I rolled my eyes and resumed walking. I was pretty sure that whatever stress they were feeling about the afternoon ahead would pale compared to mine. I was about halfway to the museum, and as I approached the city's Historic District, the Thursday lunchtime office-worker crowds of a few blocks earlier were increasingly replaced by tourists. It was late June in Philadelphia, and the surge of Independence Day visitors was ramping up.

I glanced at my watch. I had ten minutes to get there. I put my head down and hurried along, not looking up as I passed the Liberty Bell, as a mail drone whizzed by overhead, or even as a white van pulled up beside me. Not until a black hood dropped down over my head. And by then, it was too late.

ONE

When Reverend Calkin had called me at home a few days earlier, I was sure it was a joke. I knew it wasn't my brother Kevin—he's terrible at voices—but I thought maybe he had put one of his buddies up to it. Because why would a member of the Board of Advisors of Humans for Humanity, the biggest chimera-hating organization in the world, be calling *me*? Yes, Calkin had a reputation as a moderate, but he had still supported H4H's efforts to pass the Genetic Heritage Act. And that meant he supported defining anyone with a splice—meaning pretty much all my friends these days, including my boyfriend, Rex—as a nonperson.

So, yeah, you could say I was surprised when he called.

"Hello. Is this Jimi Corcoran?" he'd said, after I'd picked up.

"Yes," I'd said. "With whom am I speaking?" If I feel at a disadvantage because I don't know who I'm talking to, I like to throw a little grammar at them.

Calkin explained who he was while I mentally flicked through Kevin's friends, trying to decide which one was pranking me, wondering if maybe it was some new knucklehead from college. It had only been a few weeks since he'd left to start freshmen preseason training, but Kevin made friends quickly, if not always carefully.

"Jimi," Calkin said, "I'm calling you today because I sincerely believe that you and I have more in common than you might think." He went on to say that he did not hate chimeras and was open to other viewpoints. He was concerned about the future of humanity, and that with splicing and whatever other physical alterations might be coming our way, he simply thought we needed to be very careful about the changes we allowed ourselves to make to our bodies. "I don't believe people who have gotten spliced with animal DNA are less human, necessarily," he continued. "Or people who have been spiked, for that matter. In fact, an argument could be made that Plants have made similar choices to chimeras."

That was interesting. By "Plants," he meant people who had gotten a Wellplant computer implant "spiked," or inserted, into their craniums. Both terms were pretty new slang, so he was probably just trying to prove he was cool, but I was impressed that he mentioned them at all because I happened to agree. Plants *were* just as altered as chimeras, maybe even more so, though of course, they insisted otherwise.

"But," Calkin said, "both groups are on a slippery slope toward a future populated by beings who *are* much less human, where humanity has lost its distinction, or where artificial intelligence or what have you, could claim to be human and end up ruling over us, with superior intelligence and an utter lack of compassion."

By this point, I believed he was who he said he was, or at least that he was not one of Kevin's friends.

"Well Reverend," I said, "that's great. But it seems to me we're already halfway down a different sort of slope, where you have one group of people labeling another group as nonpersons and trying to take away their rights. And it seems to me like that shows there's already an 'utter lack of compassion.'"

I didn't understand why this was so hard for H4Hers to get. The Genetic Heritage Act had been passed by the state legislature and signed by the governor months earlier, with rabid support from H4H. Earth for Everyone, the pro-chimera-rights organization, had filed a dozen lawsuits challenging GHA and was making some headway in the courts; but the law was still on the books, and H4H had introduced similar legislation in dozens of other states, and a national version, as well. E4E was scrambling to keep up. I knew this because I was interning for Marcella DeWitt, one of the E4E lawyers working on the lawsuits.

Calkin went quiet, then he said, "Indeed.... And that is why I'd like to invite you to a luncheon I'm hosting before next month's convention."

If I'd been drinking my coffee, I would have spat it out. I was disgusted that Philadelphia was hosting the first national Humans for Humanity convention, although the location made sense. Howard Wells was the head of H4H, and of Wellplant, his massive technology and medical corporation. Both were based in the city. I was actually planning on being at the convention, or near it, to protest alongside my friends.

I was so taken aback by Calkin's invitation that before I could reply, he continued.

"We'll be meeting off-site, discreetly if not secretly, a quiet get-together of clergy, scholars, lawyers, and activists, chimeras among them, including some young people and Earth for Everyone's national vice president and regional chair. I'm hoping we can have a thoughtful conversation to find common ground, as we move forward into humanity's uncertain future."

I'd been ready to slap him down with a snarky retort and hang up the phone, but I didn't. I seriously doubted I could find common ground with anybody involved in the efforts to dehumanize my friends, but maybe dialogue would help them see the error of their ways.

"Why are you inviting me?" I asked.

"Well, you've gained a certain notoriety—"

I laughed. "You're inviting me because I was on a T-shirt?"

"You have a unique perspective.... Indeed, you've seen up-close some of the less-fortunate consequences of our endeavor to achieve clarity on the questions surrounding the manner and criteria through which humanity is defined."

"Indeed," I said, "if, by 'less-fortunate consequences' you mean that your *endeavor* has already caused the deaths of several people I care about, and almost killed *me* more than once. You know I'll be outside the convention, protesting against H4H. And against your buddy Howard Wells."

"Ind—" He stopped himself and laughed. "Of course. I know you've been working with E4E, and I gather you're involved in Chimerica, as well, whatever that means."

I didn't comment on that one. Chimerica was a secretive organization dedicated to protecting chimeras. Rex had recently been a part of Chimerica in some way that was a mystery even to me, and pretty much all he could tell me about it was how he didn't know what anyone else was doing. I'd had a brief encounter with them myself, but I wouldn't say I was *involved*, even though a few months ago I had found out that my long-lost Aunt Dymphna—my namesake, whom I hadn't seen since I was four or five—was actually the head of Chimerica. I was still trying to make sense of that, wondering if I should try to connect with her through the group, or, since I was living right where I'd always been and she hadn't gotten in touch with me, if I should just leave it alone and pretend to forget about her.

"As I said," Calkin continued, "we want a variety of viewpoints—from Plants, chimeras, and others—and a dialogue. We all come at this issue from different places, from secularists who think splicing is detrimental to public health to fundamentalists who think chimeras are harbingers of the end of the world. And you should know that while Howard Wells and I agree on some things, we disagree on many more. I certainly wouldn't say we're buddies."

I thought about that for a few seconds, then told him I'd have to think some more. I spent the next hour at the library, reading up on Reverend Calkin.

Then I called Rex.

TWO

What?" Rex said when I told him about the call.

I could hear him sipping tea over the phone, and I'm pretty sure he *did* spit it out.

"So, what did you tell him?" he asked when he was done sputtering and coughing.

"I told him I had to think about it."

"You're *thinking* about it?"

I wasn't surprised that Rex was surprised, or that he disapproved, at first. I had disapproved at first, too. But from what I'd read, Calkin didn't seem too bad. I disagreed with most of what he said, but he at least seemed thoughtful, like he was trying, looking for a solution. The more I thought about it, the more I realized that if there was a chance to ratchet back tension, and to help the people at H4H to see how wrong they were, I had to support that however I could. Of course, realizing I should go to the luncheon was a lot different from *wanting* to go. I pictured myself sitting there feeling totally inadequate and out of place in a room full of "clergy, scholars, lawyers, and activists," half of them chimera-haters who probably hated me, too, and the others pro-chimera types—and chimeras, themselves—wondering what the hell I was doing there.

But despite all that, I said, "Yes, Rex, I am."

"Do you think it's safe?"

I told him what Calkin had said about quiet and discreet if not secret. "I think it'll be at least as safe as standing out there protesting with E4E."

Rex and I decided to meet at New Ground after work the next day to discuss it further.

Work, for me, was my internship with Marcella DeWitt. She split her time between a private office that, as far as I could tell, she hardly used, and an office at E4E headquarters, where she spent most of her time, and where I worked for her.

We'd actually had a bit of a rocky start. We first met the previous winter, when she represented Doc Guzman against a bogus murder charge. DeWitt and I disagreed about how best to defend him. I thought she was short-tempered and stubborn, and I'm pretty sure she thought similarly about me. But it was a desperate time, and neither of us was at our best. In the months since, we'd gotten to know each other better. And she'd actually gotten me thinking seriously about my future.

A year ago, the extent of my long-term goals was to attend Temple University with my best friend, Del Grainger. But Del was dead now, killed by his own father, Stan, who couldn't deal with his son being a chimera. And as it turned out, Del had abandoned our college plans anyway.

Since he died, I'd found solace and some meaning in the fight to preserve chimera rights. And I'd found true friends in the chimera community. But I'd also been moving forward without a *real* plan, a long-term goal. I wanted to finish high school, of course. And go to college, probably. But beyond that, I didn't have a clue—at least not until a few months ago, when the FBI had come by the house to question me about a militant chimera group called Chimera Liberation and Defense, or CLAD.

For some reason the FBI thought I had some connection to CLAD, which I totally did not—CLAD's violent tactics disgusted me. But DeWitt had acted as my attorney, and I had been impressed by and grateful for her help. A few weeks later, she was arguing a chimera-rights case in federal court and a few of my friends and I went to watch and show our support. Truthfully, a lot of it went over my head, but DeWitt was a force of nature: smart, tough, sincere, and morally right.

Seeing her in action inspired me to consider a path like hers.

After her court adjourned, I asked a few vague questions about her career choices. DeWitt, being DeWitt, knew exactly what I was getting at.

"Jimi," she said, "why don't you intern for me this summer? You won't get paid much. But you'll get a sense of what a career like this entails."

In the few weeks that I'd been her intern, between all the filing and collating and answering the phone, I was able to shadow her and ask questions about her work—the E4E cases in particular. As we got to know each other better, I grew to respect her even more.

When I arrived for work the day after Calkin called, she looked up from her desk and immediately said, "Hi, Jimi. Something on your mind?"

I was kind of taken aback. "Why do you ask?"

She fought off a smile. "There is, isn't there?"

I hated the thought that she could read me like that, and I made a mental note not to try to ever get anything past her. Then I told her about the invitation from Reverend Calkin.

"He asked you to attend his luncheon? That's interesting," she said. "Well, he's not the worst of them."

"No, but he's still one of them. I don't know what I'm supposed to do."

She sat back with a smile, tapping her chin with her pen. I realized I had just stepped into a teachable moment.

"What are your pros and cons?" she asked.

"Well, I'd feel nervous and awkward being there, but more important, I wouldn't want to do anything that would make H4H look good, or make E4E look bad. I wouldn't want to do anything that could be used to hurt the pro-chimera movement somehow."

"I don't see how simply talking with people trying to find common ground could do that. Do you?"

"No," I said, feeling my shoulders relax a little. "I figure dialogue is probably good…right?"

"In general, yes, I should think so."

"If the chimera-haters meet some chimeras and their supporters, maybe they'll realize we're not so bad."

She nodded slowly. "It's possible, although I wouldn't get your hopes up."

"No, but I figure I should do whatever little thing I can to help support the effort."

She shrugged. "Sounds like you've made up your mind."

"Not quite."

"Then what else is there?"

I bit my lip, trying to think of a way to say what was on my mind that wouldn't sound pompous or stupid. "Well…I know some other people from E4E have been invited."

"Yes, I'm aware. Myra Diaz and Davey Litchkoff. The national vice president and the regional chair. They're great. Do you know them?"

"Not at all."

She shrugged. "So, what's the problem?"

"Well, I didn't go looking for this or anything. And I worry that people might, I don't know, resent me going, like I'm trying to be something I'm not, or trying to represent E4E, or something like that."

"I see." She nodded slowly, thinking. "Well, I must say, I'm impressed that you considered that possibility. But did Calkin say anything about you *representing* E4E?"

"No."

"So he asked you to attend because of things you've done and seen, right? He wants your perspective as an individual, right?"

"Well, yeah, I guess. But people aren't going to know that. What if they think, I don't know—"

"Jimi," she said, leaning forward and cocking an eyebrow. "I was under the impression you were the type of person who does what she thinks is right regardless of what other people think."

"I guess. I mean, I hope so."

She sat back again. "Seems like you have your answer."

I didn't, but I was closer. I nodded. "Thanks."

Then she reached behind her with both hands and hoisted a thick stack of manila folders. "Happy to help," she said as she held the stack out to me. "Now, can you log these by date and file them in the archives?"

▬ ▬ ▬

The filing and logging was almost, but not quite, the kind of work you could do while your mind pondered larger issues. I pondered anyway, but it did slow me down. DeWitt was right, as she usually was, but when I walked out of her office four hours later, I still wasn't entirely convinced.

After work, I talked it over with Rex some more on our way to the coffee shop. I was looking forward to hearing what some of my other friends thought about it, too.

Reactions varied.

Pell and Ruth were sitting at the counter when we walked in. Pell actually worked at New Ground, but she was apparently off the clock, because Jerry, the owner, was behind the counter and he wasn't giving Pell grief for not being back there with him.

Jerry wasn't a chimera, but he was a solid supporter. His pale white skin was decorated with piercings and gauges and lots of tattoos—including a prominent E4E logo on his forearm.

Ruth and Pell were best friends, and they'd become two of my closest friends, too. They had gotten spliced together, with the same bird splice, so they looked alike, with the same fawn-colored feathers framing their faces. They were similar in a lot of ways, but different in others. When I told them about the call from Reverend Calkin, their differences became more pronounced.

Ruth beamed, her eyes wide. "That's great, Jimi!" she said. "I mean, surely if these anti-chimera people would just get to know some chimeras and their supporters, they'd see the error of their ways." She squeezed my hand. "This could be the dialogue that changes everything, and you could be a part of it!"

Pell snorted and rolled her eyes. "*Or*," she said, "it could be a fat waste of time for Jimi and E4E, and a giant public relations boost for chimera-haters."

Jerry laughed behind the counter and shook his head. "Why the hell did they invite you?" It wasn't like I hadn't been wondering the same thing, but it stung a little to hear him say it.

I pretended to ignore him.

Luckily, at that moment, Doc Guzman walked in, looking dazed.

He held his back as he eased himself into a chair.

"You okay there, Doc?" Rex called over to him.

"What?" Doc said, vaguely confused. "Oh, yeah. My back's acting up. But that's not it. I just got the strangest phone call."

When it turned out that Doc had also been invited to Calkin's luncheon—and was planning on attending—people began to think differently. Pell acknowledged that maybe the whole thing did make sense. Jerry said that if Doc were invited, then something might actually get accomplished.

Doc felt the way I did—if there was a chance to engage and try to change people's minds, you had to at least try. Besides, he said, Calkin was far from the worst of the H4Hers. He was right. In fact, thinking about the worst of them—Stan Grainger—was probably what cinched it for me. If there was a chance to be a part of something that might prevent tragedies like Del's murder, I had to attend.

And the fact that Doc would be there helped a lot. Doc was smart and savvy, and if he thought it was a good idea, it probably was. Plus, I was hugely relieved to know there would be a familiar face there, and I'm pretty sure Rex was, too.

So I was pretty disappointed a few days later when Doc called—an hour before the luncheon—to tell me his back had gotten worse instead of better, and he wasn't going to make it after all. I'd be there completely on my own.

I thought about asking Rex to come with me, or even my mom, but they both had work, and my mom was my *mom*. If I was already expecting to feel out of place there, I could only imagine how much worse it would be if I showed up with a parent.

Mom was still dubious about the whole thing, anyway. I had played it down, said it was no big deal, but she only relented when I suggested that, combined with my internship with DeWitt, participating in the luncheon would look great on college applications.

In the end, I figured if I was grown up enough to have done the things that got me invited—helping to end the horrors in Pitman and Omnicare, making a spectacle of myself so Rex could escape the police, being on the news, and even ending up on a T-shirt—I was old enough to go on my own. It was just lunch.

Or at least that's what I told myself as I emerged from the underground Levline hub and stepped out into the sunlight and the oppressive heat rising from the asphalt.

The Lev hub was underneath the Convention Center, and the steps let me out half a block from the protest areas. Tomorrow, when the convention officially started, the anti-chimera H4H people would be cordoned off on one side of the street, and the pro-chimera E4E folks would be cordoned off across from them. I would be there with Rex and Ruth and Pell, and a bunch of other people I knew.

For the moment, the only visible sign of what was to come were the stacks of dismantled police barricades leaning against light poles, waiting to be assembled and put into place. But there was also a vibe on the street, a kind of nervous energy, excitement and trepidation. The calm before the storm. The convention was a big deal, and not in a good way.

Or maybe that was all in my head.

The sun beat down as I headed down Market Street, toward the Seaport Museum. I edged closer to the shade and tried to picture myself at the luncheon, being confident and eloquent instead of awkward and out of place. But I couldn't conjure the image. So instead, I focused on what I planned to say, if I got a chance to say anything: Coming together was all well and good, but if we were looking for common ground, we weren't going to find it anywhere near the idea that chimeras were nonpersons. And if Calkin and his pals actually believed that they were, then we were all wasting our time.

I hung my head as I hurried along, depressed at the thought that I had to be prepared to say something that should have been so obvious.

It was going to be a strange afternoon, and I was wondering exactly how strange when the white van pulled up beside me. As the hood fell over my head, I realized it was going to be even stranger than I could have ever imagined.

THREE

Before I could scream, a hand clamped over my mouth. I was grabbed by my arms and lifted, firmly but gently, into the van.

I kicked and thrashed and tried to bite the hand covering my mouth. A voice next to my ear said, "We're not going to hurt you. We just want to talk."

My wrists were taped together behind my back as the tires squealed and the van surged away.

We turned a corner, sharp and fast, then turned again a half-minute later. We zigged and zagged through the city for a while, long enough that I was totally disoriented. And furious. I hadn't actually had time to get scared, or at least not until the van stopped and the hood came off of my head.

There were no windows in the back, just a cloudy sunroof. A metal partition blocked the driver and the windshield.

I was on a bench seat and three of my captors were sitting across from me on another one. They all wore masks.

"Who are you?" I demanded. "What do you want?" I was trying to sound defiant, but by now, the fear had hit me. I could hear it in my voice. The van turned again, and I slid in my seat, unable to stop myself with my hands taped behind me.

"We just want to talk to you," said the figure in the middle. "You can call me Cronos."

His voice was hoarse and raspy, like a very old man. And he seemed to be over-enunciating each word. The effect sounded alien but somehow familiar, as well. He was bigger than the others, and his mask was more elaborate. Theirs were simple, similar to the hood I had been wearing, but with holes for the eyes and mouth. The mask on the guy in the middle was fitted, not tight, but stitched and seamed to match the contours of his face. The fabric over his mouth was some kind of mesh, and his eyes were hidden by a pair of mirrored shades.

"Who's *we*?" I demanded.

"That's not important now," he said. "What is important is that you are about to make a mistake."

"*You* made a mistake," I shot back. "I don't know what you want, but you can't just grab people off the street. Kidnapping is a federal crime."

He laughed, but it sounded like a cough. "We don't care about federal crimes," he said as the van turned another corner.

"Is this good?" called a voice from the driver's seat.

Cronos turned toward the front and said, "Not yet." Then he turned back to me. "What we do care about is that you're planning on meeting with the enemy, and I can't allow that."

"I beg your pardon?"

"You mean well, Jimi Corcoran, we know that. But you're mistaken if you think the people you're meeting with mean well, too. Reverend Calkin. H4H. They hate chimeras. They *kill* chimeras." I had wondered if my kidnappers were spliced, but with the hoods and masks there was no way to tell for sure. "You'll never change that about them," he continued. "All you'll accomplish with your presence there is to give them the appearance of moderation, the political cover they need to continue their campaign against us."

"You don't know that," I shot back. "Calkin has said publicly that he seeks common ground, ways to accomplish their goals without hurting chimeras or anybody else."

Cronos laughed again, softly. "After all you've seen, how can you still be so naïve?"

"I'm not naïve!" I snapped back. I knew I sounded juvenile, but something about the way he said it brought it out in me. He was obviously a jerk, but he sounded like a cartoon bad guy, like a James Bond villain from an old movie. He was scary, and I was scared, but he was also ridiculous in a way.

"Well, it doesn't matter," he said. "As I said, I cannot allow it."

"You can't tell me what I can and can't do."

He sighed, a raspy scraping sound. "Yes, I can."

He knocked on the partition separating us from the driver. One of the other two quickly leaned over and tugged the hood back over my head.

"No!" I yelled. "Dammit!" I jerked my neck from side to side, but he pulled it down over my face. Then a pair of hands clamped each of my arms and the van screeched to a stop. I would have gone sprawling if not for their grip. I heard the door slide open, and something metallic brushed against my hands as I was hoisted out of the van and placed on my feet.

The door slid shut and the van sped off. I filled the hood with curses and tried to free my hands. I expected to struggle, but my hands came apart easily. The tape had been cut.

I ripped off the hood as the van disappeared around the corner. I was standing underneath a mass of ancient blue steel trestles. I realized I was under the Vine Street Smartway, the highway that separated the Tower District from the expensive residential neighborhoods to the north. Right above me was the spot where it turned into the Benjamin Franklin Bridge, which crossed over the river to New Jersey. I was about a mile from the museum.

I looked at my watch. It was five after twelve. The picture I had been trying to conjure—me sitting in the luncheon, calm, self-confident, and mature, and the others nodding sagely as I shared insights that changed people's minds for the better—was an image that had never fully materialized. But now even the vague outlines of it were obliterated as I pictured myself bursting into the room—late, sweaty, traumatized from being abducted off the street—as E4E's national vice president and regional chair shook their heads with disgust, along with everyone else there. I considered not going, rationalizing that I could actually do more harm than good. But then I decided that was a cop-out, and obviously what my captors wanted.

Plus, it was only a mile. I smiled, thinking this Cronos character and his buddies didn't know me as well as they seemed to think they did. I started running, through Olde City, down Third Street, back to Market Street, and east, toward the waterfront. I dodged and weaved around the tourists gawking at the old buildings the way I'd been gawking at the new ones just a few minutes earlier.

I made it to the promenade at 12:10. As I ran along the water, the museum came into view. It looked out over the river, a squat, concrete building, like a bunker except for the colorful posters and all the decks and balconies. The meeting was on the second floor. At least there'd be a nice view.

I was about fifty yards away from the museum entrance, when I heard a loud, rumbling *boom!*

The deep-set windows of the museum blew out, shooting jets of fire and glass, like an old battleship firing its guns.

On the promenade ahead of me, a woman jogging by was sent cart-wheeling into the river.

I stopped so suddenly that I stumbled to my knees, and for half a second I watched the debris tumbling across the pavement as the first tendrils of smoke curled up from the windows. Then I staggered to my feet and sprinted forward.

FOUR

n the seconds it took me to run to the burning museum, people who were there before me were already backing away, abandoning their attempts to reach any survivors in the rapidly intensifying fire.

Broken glass was everywhere, some blackened, some red. The smoke grew thicker and darker. I started up the concrete steps to the second-floor entrance, feeling a wall of heat ahead of me, but before I could take more than two steps a hand grabbed my shoulder, holding me back.

A figure appeared at the top of the stairs above me, blackened and smoldering. He coughed and took one step, then collapsed and tumbled down, coming to a stop, unmoving, right at my feet. His face was sooty, red, and blistered, and he smelled of burnt hair. I'd had CPR training, but I didn't know if that was even relevant here.

Luckily, as I knelt down beside him, an older woman gently edged me out of the way, saying, "I'm a doctor."

I stepped back, grateful to let her take over and do what she could. I looked behind me to see the jogger being helped out of the water, scraped and bloody, but looking mostly okay.

The sky overhead filled with the buzz of drones, like a cloud of gnats. News and police copters approached from the west. Sirens wailed, getting louder and closer. A crowd had formed in a circle around the museum, all of them standing a good twenty feet back from where I was.

The doctor stood, looking grim, and stepped away from the man on the ground. Now, with some of the soot wiped away, I recognized his face from the photos I'd seen. It was Reverend Calkin. He was dead.

Even with all the noise in the background, there was a strange muted quiet, and an audible hush fell over the crowd.

No one else came out of the museum.

A sob burst from my mouth and I took another step back as a firefighter in full gear ran past me up the steps, into the inferno, followed by another.

More of them showed up, pushing the crowd farther and farther back.

Suddenly, we were surrounded by fire trucks. Hoses materialized, crisscrossing the ground, some leading up the steps and into the museum, some snaking up truck-mounted ladders and arcing through the sky, onto the roof and into the windows.

The farther I moved back from the fire itself, the more the magnitude of what had happened sank in.

Those people were all surely dead. Everyone in the museum. Everyone at the luncheon. Some of them were likely people I'd had nothing in common with, who I might have considered enemies. Others were probably friends of friends. All different people, but with one thing in common: their willingness to try to find common ground.

Doc and I could have been in there, too. Doc had been saved by his bad back, and I had been saved by three creeps in a van.

For the tiniest fraction of a second, I thought that someday I'd have to thank them. But then, a cold rage seeped into my bones as I realized they were probably *responsible* for this.

They had tried to talk me out of going, and when that didn't work, they'd left me where they knew I wouldn't get to the museum in time to be caught in the blast.

You couldn't call it saving me if they caused the blast in the first place. They had chosen not to murder me when they murdered all the others. And I had no idea why.

For several long moments, I stood there amid the chaos and destruction, briefly oblivious to my surroundings as I pondered that question. I realized I was shaking—from shock or fury, I didn't know. But I did know that as the crime scene got bigger and bigger, I was more and more in the way.

News of the blast would travel quickly. I needed to get to a phone and call my mom, find Rex, let them know I was okay, that I hadn't been inside. I also needed to talk to the police, to tell someone about this Cronos person, about what he had done and said.

My stomach twisted at the thought of how that might look. After everything that went down at Omnicare, the thing the FBI had cared about most was finding out whether I had any connection to CLAD.

That's when it hit me. CLAD had no problem with using explosives to make a statement. They'd never killed, but they were known to plant bombs. Maybe it was CLAD who did this. Maybe the people in that van were with CLAD. And if the FBI suspected I was connected to CLAD before, the fact that its members had intervened to make sure I wasn't there for the bombing was going to make them even more suspicious.

I could feel a storm of trouble gathering on the horizon, and I knew that before anything else, I needed to talk to DeWitt. She had helped get Doc Guzman out of jail. I might need her to do the same for me.

Unfortunately, when I turned to get out of there, those storm clouds I'd been worried about had arrived.

"Is that Jimi Corcoran?" asked the woman walking up behind me, sounding surprised. She held up her badge. "I'm Special Agent Ralphs, FBI. We met after the events at Omnicare in Gellersville."

"Yes, of course," I said, my heart still pounding. "I remember."

"Events" was putting it mildly; what happened at the Omnicare hospital in Gellersville was horrifying, a concoction of greed and hatred and xenophobia and evil on almost every level. My involvement in exposing it was part of the reason I had been invited to the luncheon.

And by "we met," Ralphs meant she had grilled me for hours on six separate occasions about CLAD.

As she took a step closer, I noticed two other agents flanking her, looking tense, like they were ready to spring into action if I bolted. And I'd be lying if I said the thought hadn't crossed my mind.

Ralphs slipped her badge back into an inside pocket of her blazer. "We need to talk."

Crap. I wanted to talk to the authorities, but I wanted to be going to *them*, voluntarily, not having them find me at a crime scene. As a minor, I probably could have insisted on waiting until my mom was there, but I wanted to tell them what I knew as soon as possible. I didn't want to do anything else that would make them think I was somehow involved, but I also didn't want to go in there alone and say something I'd regret later.

"Yes, we do," I said. "But not without my lawyer."

FIVE

alphs rolled her eyes and nodded when I said I wanted my lawyer there, as if I had just confirmed some unpleasant suspicion. I started to explain why, but she stopped me with a raised finger and said, "You can tell us back at the office. When your *lawyer* is present."

Ralphs turned and the crowd parted as she and her minions escorted me through the police perimeter to their car and we sped off. Ralphs and I sat in the back, while her two silent underlings rode up front.

I gave her Marcella DeWitt's name and phone number, and Ralphs nodded in recognition before radioing ahead and asking someone to call her. "What's your mother's name?" she asked.

"Why?" I asked, defensive, wondering if it was some sort of trap, or if they were going to question her, as well.

Ralphs rolled her eyes again. "So we can tell her you're safe, and where you're headed."

"Oh," I said, feeling stupid. "It's Christine."

Ralphs shook her head as she asked them to call Mom, as well.

"Um," I added timidly, "can you ask them to call someone else, too?"

Ralphs furrowed her brow. "Who?"

"My boyfriend, Rex. He's going to be worried."

She paused, staring at me dubiously, but I guess she figured since I was being cooperative, she could be, too. "Okay. What's his number?"

I told her and she asked whomever she was talking to if they could call Rex, also.

The Federal Building was on Market Street, just past the Liberty Bell, halfway between the waterfront and the Convention Center. In the shadow of Wells Tower.

DeWitt's office was just a few blocks away.

As we drove up, people streamed past us on foot, first a few, then a lot, a thickening crowd, all rushing to the site of the bombing to see what had happened.

Calkin had said discreet, if not secret. I wondered how many of the people on the street knew about the luncheon, how many opposed it, and how many half-informed rumors and conspiracy theories—or conspiracy facts, for that matter—were swirling around. I wondered if there would be more violence.

We turned off Market Street and drove down a ramp, into the bowels of the Federal Building. Ralphs hustled me onto an elevator to the eighth floor, then down a short corridor and into a conference room, where she left me alone for what felt like ages.

I could feel the minutes ticking by and that white van getting farther from the city, or being painted or dismantled or hidden. It was incredibly frustrating.

For a while, I stared out the window—unfortunately out the rear of the building, so I had no view of whatever was going on down by the waterfront. The room I was in was totally different from the dim and dirty interview room at the Montgomery County police station, where I'd been interrogated last fall, out in the zurbs. It felt like a lifetime ago. This room looked more like something from a lawyer's office than a police station: a richly stained wooden conference table and seats that were plush and comfortable, swiveling and reclining. The table had a Holocon setup in the middle, for remote holographic conferencing. Or maybe for monitoring the interviews in the room, since there didn't seem to be any two-way mirrors.

Finally, Ralphs returned, and with her was Marcella DeWitt.

DeWitt rushed across the room, the concern plain on her face. She put her hands on my shoulders, not a hug, but not too far from it. "Jimi, are you okay?"

DeWitt was generally kind of brusque, no-nonsense. This was the most unguarded I'd seen her.

I smiled and started to tell her I was okay, but my voice caught on a swell of emotion as the reality of the past hour or so hit me. Suddenly, I was in tears and it caught me totally by surprise.

"It's okay, honey. You're okay," she said, guiding me toward one of the chairs.

Ralphs put tissues, a pitcher of water and a stack of reusable plastic cups the table. "Your mother's on her way," she said with a quick, tight smile. "You sure you don't want to wait?"

DeWitt cocked an eyebrow at me.

I nodded, wiping my eyes. "Yes, I'm sure. I think time is a factor."

"I agree," Ralphs said, filling three cups with water and placing one in front of me. She put a notepad and a pen on the table and sat in front of them. "So, I find it interesting that you were on the scene when this bomb went off. When we questioned you a few months ago, you said you had no interaction with CLAD, no idea why they might have been talking about you. Is that still your story?"

"It's not a story," I said, "and no, I'm not sure."

"You're not sure?" she echoed pointedly. "You mean you're not sure you want to protect them any longer, now that they've escalated their tactics and people are getting killed?"

"*Really*?" DeWitt said. "My client is here of her own free will, a *minor* willing to proceed without her legal guardian here because she wants to share information with you, and you're coming in like that?"

Ralphs looked back and forth between us for a moment, then said, "Okay. Ms. Corcoran, could you clarify what you meant by that?"

"Has CLAD claimed responsibility?" I asked.

Ralphs nodded and sipped her water. "They issued a statement to the press. All the press, actually, locally and nationally, saying they 'struck a blow against those who seek to dehumanize chimeras, and the false allies who would legitimize that effort.' So, are you ready to change your story?"

I rolled my eyes. She seemed smart—too smart for an idiotic question like that. "No, I'm not *changing my story*. I'm trying to share information that could be very relevant, but you seem like you'd rather be a jerk than listen."

DeWitt looked down and pursed her lips, like she was trying to hide a smile.

Ralphs glanced at the Holocon module, which was probably recording us. "Okay," she said, putting her pen to the notepad. "Share it then."

"I was at the scene of the bombing because I was supposed to be *in* the bombing. I was invited to be at that luncheon by Reverend Calkin."

She wrote a few words on the pad, then paused, her eye twitching. "You were?"

"Yes, I was." I guess Reverend Calkin had been pretty discreet after all. "I was on my way there when I was abducted."

"Abducted?" She raised an eyebrow, as if she found this hard to believe. With everything that had been going on, I'd forgotten exactly how much I had disliked her when we'd met before. It was all coming back to me.

"Yes. They put a hood over my head and pulled me into a van."

"And when was this?"

"I don't know, forty minutes ago? An hour? Ten minutes before noon. They drove me around for, like, fifteen minutes telling me why I shouldn't go to the meeting."

"And why was that?"

"They said it would make H4H look good. It would make them appear reasonable, willing to talk."

"So then what happened?"

"When I refused to skip it, they dropped me off under the Ben Franklin Bridge. By then it was five after. I was already late, and I knew it would be even later by the time I got there, but I didn't want them to keep me from going. So I ran to the museum. The bomb went off just as I was approaching it."

"The people who abducted you. How many of them were there?"

"I think four. Maybe five. Three in the back with me, one or two in front."

"What did they look like?"

"I don't know, they had masks on."

She looked at her notes. "Wait, I thought *you* had a hood on…."

"Yes, but they took that off me."

"I see." She wrote for a few seconds, then cocked her head. "Seems like a bit of a coincidence, doesn't it? They 'abduct' you, and just happen to make you late enough that you just happen to miss the bombing?"

DeWitt gave me a questioning look, letting me know that she would end the interview if I wanted, if Ralphs continued to be a jerk.

"No, of course not," I said. "It's not a coincidence at all."

"Meaning what?"

"Meaning I think they knew about the bomb. I think maybe they were the ones who planted it." I took a deep breath, knowing that what I was about to say was likely to make Ralphs more suspicious that I was somehow involved. At the same time, in my mind's eye, I saw the explosion again, vivid enough that it made me flinch. I was hit by another wave of intense emotion, like a delayed reaction, as I thought about all the people who had died in the blast—both E4E and H4H, chimeras and those who had persecuted them. Reverend Calkin. My eyes welled up again, and I felt a pang of intense guilt that they had been in there and I hadn't. "For some reason," I said quietly, "they didn't want me in there with the others when the bomb went off."

Ralphs slid the box of tissues toward me, waiting as I dabbed my eyes and wiped my nose, got my emotions under control again.

"Are you okay?" she asked, in a tone that seemed too gentle coming from her. It was almost apologetic.

I took a deep breath and nodded. "Do they know yet if there were any survivors?"

Ralphs shook her head. "I'm sorry. No word on that yet. Did you know others there?"

As I shook my head, I heard DeWitt sniff and I turned to look at her, saw her wiping away a tear, and I remembered she knew the national vice president and the regional chair. I put my hand on hers and gave it a squeeze.

"I'm sorry," I said softly, and she nodded in reply.

Ralphs let out a sad sigh. "Look, I know this is hard right now. For both of you. Do you want to take a break?"

DeWitt seemed to re-solidify back into her usual self. "I'm okay." She turned to me. "Jimi? Do you need a break?"

More than anything, I thought. But I shook my head. "He told me his name," I said. "Or at least a name that he was using."

Ralphs had started writing, but at this, she stopped. "Who did?"

"The one in charge."

"He did?" she said, surprised, looking at her notes, as if she couldn't believe this hadn't come up already. "What is it?"

"Cronos."

She stared at me intently for half a second, then she hit a button on the Holocon box and said, "Tell the boss we've got something in here."

SIX

Within seconds, the room was filled with several other agents, including one named Agent Griffin who came armed with a huge tablet and a stylus. She drilled me for information about what I had seen, every detail about the van, the people in it, the masks they wore, everything. I didn't remember all that much at first, but she prompted and cajoled me: What were the seats made out of? What did the dome light look like? Did you see the handles on the doors? What kind of bumper? What kind of fabric were the masks? What was his voice like? I was surprised at how many details came back to me, and I wondered how much of it was memory and how much was imagination. But every detail went into the sketches she was creating, and she seemed pleased with the progress.

DeWitt stayed next to me but didn't say a word.

Ralphs retreated, leaning against the wall, letting her colleagues do their jobs. But when the van on the screen began to take shape, she stepped forward to get a better look.

"Ford," she said. "Late-model Econoline DVX."

Griffin tapped the stylus onto the upper right corner of the screen, and a keyboard appeared. She typed with one hand and an image of a truck appeared, three-dimensional, floating in front of a white background. With her stylus, she grabbed one of the fenders and moved the vehicle around, rotating it so I could see all the angles. Then she looked up at me. "Does that look like it?"

"I think so," I said. "But I can't really say for sure."

I wondered again about memory versus imagination, but Ralphs seemed sure of herself as she snapped her fingers and pointed at two of the other agents. "Get that picture and description out there," she said. "Now."

They both bolted for the door and a new agent stepped in to whisper something in Ralphs's ear.

She nodded, her face solemn, and turned to the remaining agents. "Please clear the room," she said, and they filed out, so it was just Ralphs, DeWitt, and me.

Ralphs sat in the chair to my left and put a hand on my wrist. I knew that meant there was bad news, but before I could predict it, she said, "We got official word. I'm afraid there were no survivors from the blast."

DeWitt stiffened and put a hand on my other wrist.

"I'm sorry," Ralphs said softly. "For both of you."

We sat quietly while DeWitt and I got ourselves together. Ralphs didn't try to rush us, which was nice of her. After a minute, I said, "Okay, what now?"

Ralphs cleared her throat, once again all business as she resumed questioning me, mostly asking over and over, but in slightly different ways, what exactly Cronos had said to me. Each time she jotted down notes, but as time went on, she jotted less and less frequently, until finally, she put down her pen and rubbed her eyes.

"Are we done?" I asked. My brain felt wrung out, like a sponge. I stifled a yawn.

Ralphs nodded. "For now we are. I'd like to follow up with you again in the next day or so." She collected her things and stood.

I nodded back, relieved. DeWitt and I stood, as well. "So who is he?" I asked. "Cronos, I mean. Do you know him?"

"No, I don't," she said, her face hardening as she moved to the door. "But I look forward to meeting him. According to our intelligence, he's the head of CLAD. We've busted several CLAD cells in Connecticut, Boston, Baltimore, and DC, which we hope puts a sizeable dent in what we believe is a relatively small organization. But none of them will talk, and we haven't been able to get close to this…Cronos person." She thought for a moment, then added, "I don't know what your plans are for tomorrow, but you might want to stay away from those protests. I don't expect the convention will be cancelled, even after what just happened. Things could get a lot uglier."

Ralphs led us out of the interview room and into the hallway, where Rex and my mom were waiting, looking agitated.

I smiled at the sight of them, incredibly glad to see each of them and amused at the thought of them sitting there together. They both shot to their feet when they saw me, Rex towering over my mom, making her look tiny.

DeWitt glanced at her watch, and for an instant her face was suffused with stress. "I've got to go," she said close to my ear. "You did great in there, Jimi. Why don't you take a few days off, okay? With everything that's happened, the news about Myra and Davey…the office is going to be…" She paused for a moment, collecting herself. "Anyway, you've just been through a lot and I think it would be good if you took some time to process it. I have to take some depositions in DC on Monday anyway, so I won't even be in the office until Wednesday. But call if you need me. I'll be checking in for messages. Take care of yourself, okay? And stay out of trouble."

Before I could reply, she had turned and said hello to Mom and Rex as she hurried past them toward the elevators.

I bear-hugged Mom first, because I knew she'd feel hurt otherwise, but I locked eyes with Rex and held them the whole time.

"Oh, Jimi," Mom said. "I was so worried."

"I'm okay, Mom," I whispered. "I'm fine."

Rex managed an impressive imitation of patience as he waited for my mom to let me go.

I pulled away from her before she was quite done—I got the feeling that otherwise she would have just kept holding on. My eyes were still on Rex's, right up until we kissed and I closed them, absorbing the comfort and relief from his arms as they wrapped around me. I pulled him tight and pressed myself against the mass of his body.

"You okay?" he said into my hair.

"I'm fine," I said. "Really." My eyes watered as I said it, though, as thoughts and images of the bombing came back to me.

"I was so scared," he said.

"I was, too," I said, softly enough that I hoped my mom couldn't hear me.

We got onto the elevator, the two of them crowding me, one on either side. As we walked through the lobby, I told them both what had happened. My mom blanched, and Rex's face turned stony when I told them about being abducted.

"*Abducted*?" Mom said, actually putting a hand over her mouth in horror.

"Holy crap, Jimi," Rex said. "Who—"

"No, no—not actually abducted," I backtracked, trying to tone down the seriousness of the conversation. "Waylaid, whatever. I don't know who it was. It was only for like, ten or fifteen minutes."

I kept talking, trying to downplay my kidnapping to get them past that part of the story, but when I got to the part about the explosion, and they realized how close I'd come to being in it, their reactions became even more extreme.

"But I'm fine," I said, reassuring them both as we stepped out onto the street. I was shocked that the sun was still high, burning bright and hot. So much had happened, I had somehow assumed it would be almost evening.

"I need to call Doc," I said suddenly. "I need to let him know I wasn't there."

"I told him," Rex said. "He knows. I let everyone know."

"We need to talk about all this, Jimi," said my mom shakily. "You need to tell me what happened. But first, I think I should take you to see Dr. Simmonds. You've been through hell today."

"I'm fine, Mom. Really." Dr. Simmonds was great and I'd known her forever, but apart from the fact that I really was fine, she was a pediatrician, and the last thing I wanted was to be treated like a little kid.

"Well, we need to get you some food, then," she said, determined to find relief in focusing on the safe and mundane.

"Mom, no. No thanks," I said. "I'm really just tired."

She reached up and cupped my cheek, seeming to snap out of it a little. "Of course. You must be exhausted. Let's get you home and we'll deal with everything else after you rest, okay?" She turned to Rex. "Maybe you'd like to come over in a bit? I'm making dinner. Trudy's coming, too."

Rex smiled and opened his mouth, almost certainly about to politely and charmingly accept the invitation. But before he could, I said, "Um, Mom? Actually, think I want to go to Rex's now." I turned to Rex. "If that's alright with you."

My mom's expression froze for a second, and Rex's mouth hung open.

"Um, yeah—yes, of course," he said, looking back and forth rapidly between my mom and me. "I mean…if…sure."

I felt bad. I knew how worried Mom was, but I really didn't want to go home and have her fuss over me. I wanted to be with Rex. I *needed* to be with Rex. I'd witnessed death and loss, up close and personal, and I wanted to feel life up close and personal, too. I knew going home and having dinner with Mom and Aunt Trudy would be comforting in a way—and I was glad Mom would have Trudy to comfort her—but I also knew the two of them peppering me with questions wasn't going to be restful at all.

I could tell Mom was unsettled by my decision, and sad. I was sad, too, and not just because of death and loss. Because of time.

Time passing is sad. Growing up and growing old and dying, there's sadness in all of it. And realizing you aren't your kid's go-to for comfort had to be hard, too, and I was sorry about that. But it's also a part of that kid growing up.

"Oh," my mom said, trying to hide her dismay as she accepted what I was telling her, and maybe what she could and could not control.

Rex and I had been together a while now. We were both seventeen. My mom knew we were no longer just holding hands. She and I had had plenty of "safe sex" talks over the years, and she knew how seriously I took that. We'd also had one excruciatingly awkward and roundabout conversation where I had to reassure her once again that chimera splices were somatic, not germline, meaning they didn't affect the genes that were passed down from generation to generation. She had already known everything I told her, but she needed reassurance that if Rex and I slipped up—or even if we just held hands for ten years then got married—there wouldn't be any grand puppies in her future.

But as much as she must have known the status of my relationship with Rex, I knew she didn't want to have to acknowledge it—particularly on top of everything else that had happened today.

"Okay I'll see you at E4E tomorrow, though, right?" she said. Both my mom and Trudy had become regular volunteers at E4E, which was really great. The next day was Saturday, and Mom, Trudy, and I were all signed up to stuff envelopes.

"Absolutely," I said. "Especially considering what happened today. We'll be at the protests beforehand, but then we'll be there."

"Okay," she said with a tight smile. "I wish you wouldn't go to the protests, Jimi. But I understand. You be careful out there, okay? Both of you."

I kept Ralphs's similar admonishment to myself and gave her a peck on the cheek. "We will."

She cupped my face once more, then looked around for her car.

"Where are you parked?" Rex asked. "Can we walk you to your car?"

She looked up at him and smiled, "No, that's okay, sweetie. It should be here any second." She turned to me, having regained her composure. "You kids just…be safe. And take good care of each other." That's what her mouth said, but her eyes were reminding me to be careful, in every way.

I nodded and she nodded back.

Her car pulled up next to us, empty. She started opening the door, but paused, like she was going to say something else. "Hey," she said as she got in the car. "Why don't you hop in and I'll give you a ride. Silver Garden is practically on the way home."

"Um…" I wanted to say no, to bring this whole awkward scene to an end, but realized it made sense. It *would* be safer, given how crazy the day had been so far, and it would make my mom feel better, as well. I glanced at Rex, and he shrugged, making it clear this was my call. "Sure, Mom. That would be great."

I got in the front and Rex stretched out across the back seat. We didn't talk much on the way, except for Rex giving Mom directions. I felt relieved when we pulled up outside Rex's apartment.

"Is this it?" Mom said, looking around, checking out the neighborhood. It was far from ritzy, but it wasn't dangerous. She seemed more or less satisfied that at least there weren't any suspicious white vans around.

"Yup," Rex said. "I'm up on the third floor."

I felt Rex inhale, as if he was going to speak again, and for a terrible moment I knew he was going to invite my mom in. I totally appreciated the impulse, but I couldn't imagine anything more awkward.

"Okay, well, thanks Mom," I said quickly, to cut him off.

"Of course, Jimi." She sat back and I leaned over to give her a hug.

As we got out, Rex said, "Thanks for the ride, Mrs. Corcoran."

She gave him a smile, then turned back to me. "Be careful, okay? And I'll see you tomorrow."

Then she waved and drove off.

I grabbed Rex's arm and we started walking toward the door.

"Well, that wasn't awkward at all," Rex said sarcastically.

"Sorry."

"No, it's fine. And I'm glad you're coming over, I just...I didn't know. And I didn't know she was, um...cool with it."

"'Cool with it' might be an overstatement. But she's getting there. I think the bigger issue right now is that she wants to take care of me."

I felt sad saying it out loud, and I felt bad for Rex, not having a mom to worry about him. I mean, yeah it could be a pain, but it was also nice. He was taking his keys out of his pocket but he seemed to notice me looking at him. "What?"

"You okay?" I asked.

He laughed. "Me? Why do you ask?"

I shrugged, not wanting to bring it up if he wasn't already thinking about it.

He kissed the top of my head. "I'm not the one who was abducted and almost blown up. If you're okay, I'm okay." He paused, serious again. "...Are you okay?"

"Yeah. I think so. It's not like I knew Calkin or any of the others, really. But still." I swallowed hard, trying not to picture Calkin lying dead at my feet. "I'm still processing it, I guess. All those people."

"I know," he said softly. Then he opened the door and we went inside.

SEVEN

Rex's apartment was warm but not unbearable. He didn't have an air conditioner, but it was essentially one room and the solar fans on the windows made a decent cross breeze.

He put the kettle on without asking if I wanted anything. I sat on the sofa and stared out the window, looking over the rooftops, in the direction of the Church of the Eternal Truth. It was the spiritual home to H4H. The pastor there, a guy named Kern, was the person who gave H4H's hate-mongering a spiritual seal of approval, working hand in hand with Howard Wells to give all that toxic anti-chimera sentiment a veneer of respectability.

The open air I was looking out at had once been dominated, briefly, by a massive cross on top of the church. It had been controversial because any church that preaches hatred like that is controversial, but also because the center of the cross had been emblazoned with the H4H logo, which many in the religious community—including Reverend Calkin—said bordered on blasphemy.

Another local minister had caused a stir calling it a case of the tail wagging the god.

Rex and I had been sitting right there on that sofa just a few months earlier when the cross had come down. Part of a series of bombings committed by CLAD—the group's first terrorist action, as far as anyone knew.

It had made things worse at the time, as violence usually did. But no one had been hurt in those bombings. Unlike today.

My vision clouded with tears as my mind returned to the vision of Reverend Calkin. Throughout the day, memories of what I had seen had been increasingly interspersed with imaginings of what it must have been like inside when CLAD's bomb went off. By now, a cinematic loop was playing in my brain: a handful of young people, some of them chimeras, standing on one side of a long table, and Calkin and a bunch of older 4H4 types on the other side. As they all move to their seats, there's a flash and a bang, and everything is turned to chaos and carnage and fire. I wince when it happens, trying to stop the film, trying to stop my imagination. But I can't stop it, can't look away. I see Calkin, burned and battered and covered in blood. Then the loop starts all over again, interspersed with images I really had seen.

I couldn't make it stop until I felt Rex lifting me up off the sofa, and I realized only then that I had fallen asleep. I smiled at the sight of him looking down at me, as he crossed his tiny apartment in a few steps.

"Your mom was right," he said softly, his voice a deep rumble I could feel through his chest as clearly as I could hear it. "You should be in bed."

He lowered me onto the bedspread, but as he tried to take his hands away and step back, I hooked an arm around his neck. "You should be, too," I said.

His smile widened as he eased himself down beside me. We lay facing each other for a moment and he rested his hand on my hip, sliding it up until it was cupping my face.

"You sure you don't want to rest?" he said. I could see in his eyes the same longing that I felt.

"I've never been surer of anything," I replied, kissing him. Then I put my hand on his face, too, and for a while at least, the thoughts and images of the day, horrors both real and imagined, were finally banished from my mind.

━ ━ ━

When I woke up again, the sun had moved, and the far end of the apartment was filled with orange light. I was tangled in sheets and Rex was sitting on the edge of the bed, his broad back turned to me, his silhouette clear against the light. He turned to look at me.

"You're awake," he said, brushing my hair from my forehead. "Hell of a day."

"Yeah, it was," I replied. I took Rex's hand in mine, spreading my fingers wide to fit around his, and hefted it, lifting his arm so I could press my lips against the back of his hand. "Thanks for taking care of me."

He smiled, and then the doorbell rang and I shot upright, pulling the sheet around me. "Are you expecting someone?"

He smiled and cocked an eyebrow. "Some *thing*. Round. Covered with cheese and sauce."

I laughed. "Man, you are good."

As Rex thumped downstairs to get the pizza, I pulled on one of his T-shirts that I had appropriated as mine. It came down to my knees and was pale blue and worn soft from age. On the front was a picture of planet Earth made into a vaguely sarcastic smiley face—with tiny people crowded on the top of it, like a head of hair—poking through a guillotine, with the blade suspended menacingly above. Underneath were the words HOW ABOUT LET'S *NOT* KILL THE PLANET AND EVERYTHING ON IT?

Rex never wore it—he said the sentiment was too dark—but I thought it was just about right. And it *was* really soft.

I reassembled the bed—not as precision-neat as Rex would make it, but close enough that he wouldn't feel compelled to remake it, or to stare at it side-eyed trying to resist the urge to do so. As I flattened out the last major wrinkle in the bedspread, I felt the apartment shake with the vibration of his footsteps as he thumped back upstairs.

I smiled to myself, feeling bad for the neighbors. When Rex came in the door, carrying the pizza, he looked at me and said, "What?"

"Nothing," I said. I kissed him on the cheek and got plates from the cupboard as he put the pizza on the coffee table. Then we both sat on the sofa and each took a piece.

Rex grabbed the remote and turned on the holovid. "Movie?"

I nodded as I took a giant bite. Romance time was over. I was ready for some brain candy. And dinner.

Unfortunately, before Rex could find anything suitably mindless, the holovid picture from a local station assembled in front of us: a three-dimensional talking head, Talia Chen, who had been on the local news since we were kids, and next to her, a two-dimensional aerial shot of the Seaport Museum. It looked like a police video that had been AI-enhanced.

Rex's thumb jabbed the buttons on the remote, but before the holovid shifted to the free movie channel, I saw the words across the bottom of the screen: WIDESPREAD CONDEMNATION IN PRO-CHIMERA BOMBING.

I growled and sighed, but then it was gone, replaced with an old-fashioned movie intro. Part of me wanted to ask Rex to switch the channel back, and when I looked over at him, he was staring at me expectantly, like he was anticipating the question.

"Let's take a break from it, okay?" he said.

I didn't want to take a break, but I knew he was right. "Yeah, okay. What's the movie?"

"*The Empire Strikes Back.*"

"Perfect."

And it was. I'd seen it at least twenty times, but it was still a favorite. I used to watch it with Del regularly—enough that we could recite pretty much all the dialogue. Del was particularly fond of the Darth Vader lines. Whenever we watched it, for days afterward, he would randomly break into, "I'm your father, Luke"—which we both knew wasn't the actual line, but was funny anyway. And when his own dad was being awful, which was most of the time, he'd follow it up with a mordant, "Darth, I wish you really were."

It was rough humor, but he would laugh his butt off, and I'd join right in.

I smiled at the memory, then felt teary. Taking another slice of pizza, I pretended to watch the film as, despite my best efforts, my mind once again replayed the events of the day. I cringed at the horror of it and scoured my memory for examples of things I should have done differently or better, ways I could have changed the outcome, ways I could have handled the questioning—or my mom—better.

And I wondered why I'd been spared. The fact that I had been was gnawing at me in a way that made me think it would continue to do so for a long time to come.

Judging from his frequent, furtive sidelong glances, I think Rex was mostly distracted with wondering how I was doing.

Periodically, I'd look back at him and say, "I'm okay."

He'd nod and say, "Good," then we'd both go back to pretending to watch the movie.

It wasn't just the day behind us that was on our minds. I think we were both worried about tomorrow, too, the first official day of the week-long convention. After the bombing, tensions would surely be escalated. Howard Wells's keynote was going to be incendiary to begin with, but who knew how much gasoline he was planning to pour on the fire now.

The credits began rolling up the screen. The movie was over, and I hadn't even noticed.

I turned to Rex and said, "I think we should still go tomorrow," just as he turned to me and said, "Maybe we shouldn't go tomorrow."

We had a good laugh at that.

"Oh, you do, do you?" Rex said when we stopped, his eyes sparkling in the dim light.

I kissed him, just because, then I said, "Yes. Especially now, it's important to let the world know that whoever did this, CLAD or whoever, that's not us, and we're not going away. And that *we* lost people, too."

"It could be dangerous." Rex worried a lot about things being dangerous. To be fair, he was usually right to be worried.

"It's a dangerous world, right? We're protesting to make it less dangerous."

"I guess we are," he said, but he didn't look convinced.

——— ——— ———

I hadn't spent the night before.

It felt nice. It felt cozy and domestic, and I loved the idea of sleeping next to Rex. And he didn't even snore, which could have been a serious problem.

But it was also weird. I wasn't used to it. I couldn't sleep the way I usually slept—which apparently involved my arms and legs sprawled in all directions. And even without snoring, Rex kept me awake just by the sound of his breathing, not to mention the occasional mattress tsunami whenever he changed position.

It gave me more time for reliving traumas and stewing in guilt, regret, and second guesses. Good times.

I tossed and turned until two a.m., but I woke up at seven anyway, exhausted but apparently done with sleep. Rex awoke almost immediately, opening his eyes with a soft, surprised snort. He looked vaguely bewildered at first, but he glanced at the clock, and when he looked back at me, his gaze was crystal clear.

"Good morning," he said with a smile. "How'd you sleep?"

"I slept."

"Did I snore?"

"No, you didn't."

"Well, thank God for that."

"I already did."

He laughed. "Do you want a cup of tea?"

"Got any coffee?"

He gave me an awkward, apologetic grin. "Sorry.…I could go out and get some."

"No, don't do that," I said. "I can get some when we go out. I'd love a cup of…tea." I do love a good cup of tea, but I'd gotten into the habit of having coffee first thing in the morning, and hadn't realized until that moment how much I'd come to depend on it.

As Rex put the kettle on, I went into the bathroom. I was standing at the sink, realizing I didn't have any of my stuff, when Rex called through the door, "You can use my toothbrush."

It was hanging in the toothbrush holder, alone, over a tube of toothpaste. I felt momentarily overwhelmed by the intimacy of it. I mean, we'd been intimate, but sharing a toothbrush was *intimate*.

But I plucked it up and put some toothpaste on it. "Thanks," I said as I ran it under the water.

When I came out, Rex was waiting for me with two mugs of tea and a grin on his face. "How'd it go?"

I grinned back, wide enough to show my teeth. "Minty fresh."

He handed me one of the mugs and I got dressed while he was in the bathroom. He got dressed quickly afterward, and we agreed to get breakfast when we got coffee.

I was sorry to go, sorry to leave our little bubble and go out into the world. But, seeing as it was the first time I'd stayed over, and it had been just about perfect, considering, I kind of also wanted it to end before anything ruined it.

I knew I could count on Rex not to ruin anything, but I was a little less sure about myself.

As we descended the stairwell to the street, I felt not only relieved, but fortified by our time together. And hopefully ready for whatever was next.

EIGHT

We emerged onto the street from the Levline hub under the Convention Center and headed for the protest area. It was at least as hot and way more humid than the day before, but the towers were gray, reflecting the overcast sky. The two groups were cordoned off, facing each other across Market Street. Hostility radiating in waves between them as they glared through a phalanx of cops on bicycles.

We angled left, crossing the street toward the pro-chimera, E4E side.

Rex pointed above us. "Guess they're expecting a show." The sky was speckled with police and media drones and copters. Behind them, Wells Tower loomed ominously. I wondered if Howard Wells was up there in his penthouse office, looking down at us like ants or amoebas under a microscope.

As we approached the cordon, I saw a lot of faces, both spliced and not, but I didn't recognize any of them. They were grim, seething, staring daggers at the H4Hers, who were staring daggers right back.

As we joined the pro-chimera group, Rex exchanged nods with a couple of people I didn't know. He looked at his watch. "I'm surprised to see so many H4Hers out here. Wells is supposed to be delivering his keynote inside any minute."

From the corner of my eye, I saw a pair of hands waving in the air and I turned to see Ruth and Pell, making their way through the crowd toward us.

"Jimi!" They said in unison, both practically tackling me as they pushed past the last people between us.

"I'm so glad you're okay!" Ruth said. "When I heard about the bombing, and I knew you and Doc were supposed to be there, I thought…" Her voice caught and her eyes filled with tears.

"We're devastated about it," Pell said, her jaw tight, as if she were willing back her emotions. "But we're really glad you and Doc are okay."

"Hey," said a voice behind us. "Were you invited to that secret meeting, too?"

I turned to see a thin guy with a scraggly beard and red, sunken eyes that might or might not have been a result of his splice, which I couldn't quite identify.

"What?" I said, getting a bad vibe. "Um…yeah."

"Well, good for you for not going," he said. "It's a shame about those people and all, but they got what was coming." He shook his head. "Secret meetings with damn H4Hers."

I took a deep breath, filling my lungs for the tirade I was about to unload on this idiot. Rex put his hand on my shoulder and squeezed, his way of trying to give me patience and tolerance and reminding me that maybe things were too tense to tear into this guy.

He failed on all counts, but he did make me pause, and in that moment, a collective gasp rose from across the street and all the H4Hers turned their backs to us.

Overhead, a massive video screen came to life, a bright red field with the H4H logo. It flashed to a live feed of Howard Wells, ascending an indoor stage in front of thousands of cheering, chanting followers.

The protestors across from us joined in with the cheering, drowning out the beginning of my rant, which trailed off anyway as we all focused on the spectacle across the street. I could see the pro-chimera protestors booing all around us, but their voices were completely drowned out by the cheers.

"Thank you, thank you!" Wells called out over the cacophony. His eyes twinkled under the small silver glass disk of his Wellplant. Incredibly, his skin looked even more fake tan and his teeth more fake white than usual.

"What an amazing crowd," he said, earning a boost in the already deafening sound. "I am honored and humbled that so many of you have traveled so far, from around the country, around the world even, to be a part of this week's historic event, our first ever International Convention of Humans for Humanity! It is incredibly powerful that so many of you have come to join in protecting that which is most sacred." Dramatic pause. "Our humanity!" Even more cheers.

"I had prepared remarks," he said, sliding a sheaf of papers out of the inner pocket of his jacket, then tossing them onto the floor. "But in light of recent events, I think it's better if I speak from the heart, don't you?"

The H4H crowds went wild, both on the screen and on the street, willfully ignoring the fact that the remarks he'd just discarded were surely uploaded to his Wellplant.

"These are dark, desperate times," he said, his face somber. "It has been left to us, to all of us, to cherish and protect that which makes humans unique in this universe, that which God gave to us, and trusted us to protect: our humanity. We've been working hard these past years. You"—he pointed at the crowd, swinging his arm to encompass everyone—"*you* have worked hard. Mobilizing, organizing, doing the hard, necessary work, and weathering the attacks from those who seek to undermine our mission." He laughed and shook his head. "Oh, I know what they say. That we are peddling fear and hatred, that we are being unfair to our mixie brothers and sisters.... Or I guess half brothers and half sisters." He grinned at that, letting the crowd know the line was supposed to be funny. After an awkward half second, they roared with laughter.

"And they say worse than that," he continued, "making up lies about us, about you and about me, the God-fearing, rule-abiding Americans. They're making up stories about the terrible things that happen to the mixies, making up stories about how we are responsible for it all, for all the bad things that happen to them. But it's all lies. All of it. The mixies do these things to themselves. They render themselves unemployable, they leech off of society, and I know we're not supposed to say it, but they bring with them diseases. Is it a coincidence that the great flu epidemic coincided with the first mixies? I don't think so, do you?"

The crowd roared in agreement, and Wells waited until they had fully quieted down before he began again, his voice almost a whisper, then growing again in volume. "But the worst thing they've done, the saddest, most damaging, most tragic thing, is that they have turned their backs on God, who made them in his image. They have turned their backs on the humanity the Lord gave them!"

His voice grew to a thunderous climax, and the crowd roared again, this time in a rapturous frenzy. Across the street, some in the crowd of H4H protestors turned to glare at us.

"But, of course, the forces of darkness are fighting back. E4E, CLAD, Chimerica"—he used air quotes when he said Chimerica—"it doesn't matter what you call them. They're all the same. They don't *want* to prove our point, with their savagery and violence, but they can't help themselves. They try to disrupt our meetings, like this one. They've desecrated our houses of worship, they've murdered our friends, and they're not going to stop. They are not going to stop. It's not just about the natural order, it's about *law* and order, as well. And it's up to *us* to stop them. Am I right?"

More rapturous cheers.

"Now, I know we've been working hard to do that," he said, his voice going quiet again. "But we haven't been working hard enough." The crowd went silent. "I"—he jabbed a finger into his own chest—"*I* haven't been working hard enough. But that is going to change.…Because I am announcing to you today, that we are taking our mission to the next level. I am announcing, right here and now, in front of you, the people I love, the people who will make us victorious, that I have formed an exploratory committee, and with your hard work and support, I will be…the next President of the United States of America!"

For a brief moment, the crowd across the street was pulsating, jumping up and down, roaring approval, some even weeping, while around Rex and Ruth and Pell and I, there was utter stillness, a shocked, immobilized silence.

On the screen, Wells was grinning and clasping his hands over his head, basking in the adulation of the crowd inside. For a moment, the image cut to a wider view, showing the adoring throngs waving their arms and holding up signs as Wells walked across the dais, shaking hands with his beaming lieutenants. As he reached one end of the stage, the camera picked up a row of serious-looking bodyguards in identical gray suits, tinted glasses, and Wellplants.

As Wells reached the edge of the stage and turned to walk back, the camera picked up the guard at the very end. My brain registered that I recognized him, and a chill ran through me as I realized who it was.

"That's Stan Grainger," I said to Rex, pointing up at the screen.

"What?" Rex said, trying to follow my finger. But the camera had already panned away. The view cut back to a close-up of Wells.

"Who?" Pell asked.

"Del's dad," Rex said. "Jimi, are you sure?"

I hadn't seen Stan since Pitman, since he shot Del, since he murdered my best friend after making so much of his life miserable. Stan had disappeared after that. He quit his job as a cop out in the zurbs and his house had been siting empty next to my mom's ever since.

Hatred quickly burned off the chill I had felt. "I'm sure."

Then someone from our side threw a large cup of soda toward the screen. It was a good throw, a high arc that hit right in the middle of Wells's face, splashing those below as it fell to the ground. Nervous laughter rose around us.

A moment later, the cup came back, but on a much different trajectory. It didn't arc through the air, it came in fast and low, in a way that no empty paper cup would behave.

It disappeared into the crowd, and I heard the sound of broken glass, accompanied by a scream. I saw a flash of red through the crowd. The bicycle cops were all looking around, confused. A bunch of the E4E protestors surged against the cordon, then climbed over it and rushed across the street toward the other protestors.

The crowd briefly thinned out behind them, and I caught a glimpse of a girl with long black hair and blood streaming down her paper-white face, being led away by two cops. I guess other people saw it, too, because suddenly half of the people in our cordon were running across the street.

Those remaining behind, including Ruth and Pell and Rex and me, all shouted, "No! Don't!"

But the first group reached the far side of the street, viciously punching and kicking the H4Hers. The drones in the sky all swooped down, clustering in the air above our heads, recording as the bicycle cops tried to restore order, first with whistles, then truncheons, and then stun batons.

Rex froze for a moment, torn, then he said, "We need to get out of here. Come on." He grabbed my hand and I grabbed Ruth's—she was already holding onto Pell—and we ran away from the violence.

More and more police flooded onto the scene, batons raised as they plunged into the melee. I was surprised by how many of them had Wellplants.

Rex stopped and looked back. I knew he still wanted to do whatever he could to protect the other chimeras back there. In all the chaos, I couldn't see what was going on in the center of the throng, although with his height, maybe Rex could. I knew it was likely that the chimeras were bearing the brunt of the brutality, but I also knew that all Rex would accomplish from going back there would be to get himself beaten and arrested.

I gripped his hand tighter and pulled. "No," I said. "You're right, we do need to get out of here."

"She's right," Ruth said, and Pell nodded, reluctantly.

Rex resisted for a moment, then he nodded, as well. We hurried away, putting another block between us and the violence before we stopped to consider our next move.

We were just a few blocks away from E4E's offices, and I was supposed to be meeting Trudy and my mom there soon anyway. I suggested we go there to regroup.

E4E headquarters was in an old, three-story building above a print shop in Callowhill, just on the other side of Chinatown. As we hurried along, Rex and I checked in with each other, quietly asking if the other was okay. Ruth and Pell did the same thing.

"I can't believe Wells is running for president," Ruth said, then held up a hand and as the rest of us all started to weigh in, saying how we totally saw it coming. "I know, I know," she said. "I'm not surprised, I just can't believe it."

"He's been running for years," Rex said. "All that riling people up. It's not about chimeras. He's just using us as a tool to get what he wants."

"Do you really think he's that cynical?" I said.

Rex raised an eyebrow at me, like I should know the answer to that question.

And I did. "Man," I said. "I don't know what would be worse: to actually have that much hatred in you, or to *pretend* to for political purposes."

"I hate him either way," Pell said. "And I'm not pretending."

NINE

I had thought E4E would be a safe, friendly place where we could process what had just happened and decide what, if anything, we needed to do about it. It hadn't occurred to me that, of course, everyone there would be processing things, as well.

We entered through the door on the street and climbed the narrow stairs to the third floor. Through heavy glass doors, I could see most of the people standing and staring intently up at a holovid unit mounted on the wall. Behind them, through an open office door, I could see a trio of senior staffers clustered around a speakerphone. It could have been my imagination, but it seemed like a palpable sense of sorrow hung in the air. A lot of the people in that office had been friends with Myra Diaz and Davey Litchkoff.

At the far end of the room, through a glass wall, I could see the bullpen, where the volunteers worked. There were a dozen people, half on the phones and half folding papers and stuffing envelopes, as if maybe no one had told them what had happened at the protests or that it was there on the holovid. Mom and Trudy were stuffing envelopes, chatting quietly with an older woman sitting next to them. I felt a wave of warmth. They had come to feel strongly about chimera rights, but I knew the main reason they were there was to support me and the things I thought were important.

No one looked up as we pushed open the glass door and entered. They were paying close attention to the newsfeed on the holovid mounted in the corner of the room.

I turned toward the bullpen, to let Mom and Trudy know we were there and to tell them what had happened, but stopped as the holovid cut to footage of the violence we had just fled.

It was surreal to be watching it just minutes after having been there, knowing that I was in that crowd on the screen. The holovid showed the beginning of the brawl—with the soda cup sailing one way, then shooting back the other—then the surge from the pro-chimera side and the mayhem that followed.

A male voice intoned from off-screen, "Once again violence has infected the debate about chimera rights, only this time, by all accounts the blame lies squarely with the pro-chimera camp...."

"What!?" I said, as a murmur of groans rose from the room, accompanied by lots of shaking heads and downcast looks.

Someone in the room said, "Idiots."

"In the wake of yesterday's devastating bombing by the pro-chimera terrorist group that calls itself CLAD, a peaceful protest and counter protest at the inaugural Humans for Humanity Convention was marred by violence that quickly escalated after a soft drink was thrown from the group of anti-Humans for Humanity protestors. When the beverage container was thrown back, a sizable portion of the anti-Humans for Humanity protestors launched a vicious attack on the H4H supporters."

"*What?!*" I said again, in disbelief about how one-sided the reporting was. But watching the holovid feed, all I could see was the soda cup flying one way, then back the other—a different trajectory, yes, but still looking like a soda cup, and with no sign of the girl whose face was bloodied by the bottle hidden inside the cup. Then the pro-chimera protestors surged across the street in response, punching and kicking and looking like a crazed mob. And the protestors on the H4H side did...nothing. Some covered their heads and hunched over, some stood up straight with their hands at their sides, but none of them hit back.

The feed went from a wide overhead shot to lower angles, a montage of different close-up views of E4E types beating up H4H types, who suffered like martyrs as the fists and boots rained down on them.

Then the feed cut away from the protestors back to the studio, as the newscaster talked with a legal analyst about how the violence, both the bombings and the riots, could negatively impact the legal challenges to the Genetic Heritage Act. The newscaster was a white guy in his sixties, with a Wellplant. The legal analyst, a younger African American woman without a Wellplant, was outlining the political pressures on the judges hearing the different cases, as well as their predispositions.

"Judges on the state level are elected," she said. "And that means they want to be reelected. So, when public opinion is impacted, sometimes legal opinions are, too. And with Howard Wells announcing his candidacy for president, that adds a whole new level of pressure."

The newscaster nodded. "Excellent point, and an excellent segue to our other big story: Howard Wells is running for president. Our own Max Rivera spoke with Wells just after his announcement."

The camera cut to a Latinx man in his thirties holding a microphone in front of Wells, surrounded on all sides by H4Hers. He asked Wells a couple of questions about how his candidacy would impact the other candidates, and got non-answers in reply, sound bites that meant nothing.

Then Rivera pressed a little harder. "Mr. Wells, you frequently claim that chimeras leech off of society—"

"Yes!" Wells said, cutting him off. "Ours is an era of dwindling resources. Scarce resources. And it's unconscionable that the hard-working men and women of this nation are being asked to support these mixie freeloaders. And that is what they are, a drain on our economy, on our world."

"Right," a sarcastic voice called out from the group watching. "As if rich bastards like him weren't the ones making those resources scarce."

The rest of the group murmured in agreement as the interview continued.

"But your group has produced no figures to back that up," said Rivera. "And your claims that chimeras spread disease have been refuted by experts time and ag—"

"Well, you have your experts and I have mine, and my experts say there is very clearly a link. And it stands to reason: If you make yourself half chimpanzee or half panda bear or half lemur, you've not only rendered yourself unemployable, you've made yourself a vector for disease, a convenient stepping-stone for pathogens to jump from animals to mixies to innocent people. It's happened in the past and it killed hundreds of millions."

"Once again, if you're talking about the great flu pandemic, scientists have said there is absolutely no link between that and the chimeras."

Rivera was right. My biology teacher had to spend an entire class going over this exact point just a month earlier, explaining how a link between chimeras and the pandemic, while a legitimate theory, had been conclusively disproved. Yes, he said, it did make some theoretical sense that blending species through splicing could possibly induce a pathogen to jump species, but it had never been proven. And in the case of the pandemic, the first cases of flu occurred long before the first chimera, and were a variant of a flu that had been around for decades.

It was a lesson my classmates and I had learned many, many times before, but our teacher had had to repeat it because of the disinformation being spread by Howard Wells and Humans for Humanity.

"Just because they haven't found the link yet," Wells told Rivera, "doesn't mean it's not there."

"Experts say the timing of it is impossible. The pandemic was already underway long before the first chimeras got spliced."

"Well, we'll have to agree to disagree."

With that, Wells turned away and raised his arms over his head, bringing more cheers from the crowd around him.

The feed cut back to the anchor, who welcomed a new panel of experts, which seemed to consist mainly of hosts from other shows on the same network. I didn't hear much of what they had to say, because at that point, Mom and Trudy emerged from one of the rear conference rooms.

"Jimi!" they both called out, causing everyone in the room to turn and look at them, and then turn and look at me.

"Oh, thank goodness you're okay!" Mom said, holding my shoulders.

"We just heard about the fight at the protest," Trudy said, brushing the hair away from my face.

"I'm fine, I'm fine," I said. "Are you two okay?"

"We're fine. We were in the back, stuffing envelopes when someone turned the news on," Trudy explained. "We saw the violence in front of the Convention Center, and we were so worried about you." She smiled at Rex then reached up and patted him on the shoulder. "You too, Rex."

"We're fine," he said.

"When did you get here?" Mom asked.

"A minute ago," I told her. "We just walked in."

She pulled me in for a hug, then pushed me away, holding me at arm's length.

"You can't keep doing this," she said, crying now, both angry and upset. "First that bomb and now this? Every day, you're putting yourself in danger."

"I'm not putting myself in danger," I said, trying not to snap. "I can't help it if maniacs and boneheads are doing stupid, crazy things around me."

"You *can* help it!" Mom shot back, her voice rising before she got it under control. "You shouldn't be where these maniacs and boneheads are. That's the point. I know it's not your fault, Jimi, but, well, it kind of *is*."

I didn't want to have an argument with my mom at E4E headquarters in the middle of a crisis. Luckily, before we could continue, a voice called out, "Hey everyone, can you all listen up for a moment?"

It was Donna Bresca, the regional director of Mid-Atlantic E4E. She had dark hair and pale skin, with faint gray-and-white tabby stripes on the sheen of fur that thinly coated her face. She wore a slate-colored suit that perfectly complemented the stripes. I knew she was in her mid-thirties, but the way her face was creased with sorrow and stress and fear, she looked closer to sixty.

"Okay, folks, it's been a tough couple of days, and I think we need to take a breather and get back to it tomorrow. Senior staff, I'd like you to stay for a strategy meeting, but everyone else, I urge you to go home, spend some time with your people, and come back tomorrow refreshed and ready to take on the next chapter of this fight. Okay?"

No one said anything, but a few people nodded.

Bresca clapped her hands. "Okay. Thanks for all you're doing. We've had a couple of bad days, but hopefully tomorrow will be a better one." She turned as if she was finished speaking, but then turned back and said, "One more thing." She paused, collecting herself. "We lost two of our own in yesterday's bombing. Some of you knew Myra Diaz, our national vice president, and Davey Litchkoff, our Mid-Atlantic chairman. They were friends. Good people. Both of their funerals will be family only, but there's going to be a memorial service for *all* the victims, non-denominational, from both sides of the issue, next Wednesday, in front of the Art Museum." She paused again, this time to collect herself. "Most of the senior staff will be going, and everyone is welcome to join us, *encouraged* to join us. If you want to go but need a ride, or just don't want to go alone, let us know and we'll figure it out."

Mom and Trudy were both looking at me with tear-filled eyes, and for a moment I wondered if maybe they had known Diaz or Litchkoff, or someone else in the bombing that I wasn't aware of. Then I realized, of course, they were thinking about me, about how close I had come to being in that museum, how close they had come to planning a funeral for *their* loved one.

"It's all right," I said, "I'm okay," gathering them both in a hug. "Let's go home."

TEN

Mom invited Rex for dinner again. This time, before he answered, he paused and looked at me, making sure I didn't have other plans. I gave him a slight nod, and he said he'd love to. He had to do a quick job for Jerry, unloading a pallet of sheetrock, but he'd come out afterward. Ruth and Pell went to the coffeehouse, to be with friends and friendly faces. I kind of wanted to be there, too, but today I felt ready for the comfort of Mom and Trudy and home.

It was sweet watching them all saying goodbye: Mom and Trudy both reached up to hug Rex, then hugged Ruth and Pell. Ruth and Trudy lingered for a moment, talking quietly, and I realized they had become friends—not just through me, but on their own—and it made total sense. They shared similar types of sweetness and wisdom.

I was touched that Mom and Trudy had made an effort to get to know my new friends and my new world, and also that my friends were cool enough that they were open to that, that they welcomed it.

As the car drove us home, Mom and Trudy in the front, me in the back, I told them what had happened at the protests. Then Trudy started asking me questions about the day before, about the bombing. It seemed like a long time ago, so much had gone on since then. When I got to the part about the abduction—pulled off the street, a hood over my head and my hands taped together—they both turned to look at me, horrified and sympathetic, yes, but also a little accusatory. It took me a second to figure out what that was about, but my mom's expression gave it away: she might not have been so cool about me going to Rex's if she'd known *just* how creepy the kidnapping had been.

Before she could say anything, I switched gears. "Mom, I saw Stan Grainger." That was legitimately newsworthy, even though I'd brought it up then to change the subject.

My mom's face froze. "You saw *Stan*? Are you sure?"

Trudy looked back and forth between us. She knew who Stan was, but she didn't *know* him, hadn't experienced him and or shared any of that history.

I nodded. "Pretty sure. When Wells was giving his speech, right before the brawl, they showed it on a big screen outside. Stan was onstage, part of Wells's security team."

"Are you serious? How did he look?"

"He's alive. He looked good, I guess. For Stan. He got spiked."

"Spiked?" Trudy asked.

"Yeah." I pointed a finger at my forehead. "He got a Wellplant."

Trudy screwed up her face. "Is that what people are calling it?"

"Wow." Mom shook her head. "I guess they must be paying him well enough then."

"They all had them. The whole security team. A lot of the cops, too. I guess it's one of the perks of the job, if you can call having a spike drilled into your brain a perk."

"Oh, I get it," Trudy said. "When was the last time you saw him?"

"Not since Pitman," I said, mentally stiff-arming the memory to keep it at bay. "I kind of thought he was dead."

"Well, I guess…I guess it's good to hear he's okay," Mom said. She said it like a platitude, without really thinking about it, just to be polite.

I didn't want to be polite. Not about Stan. "He's alive, but he's not okay. He's a horrible person who murdered his own son. I wish he *were* dead."

Trudy gasped.

"I do," I said. "I hate him. And everything he stands for."

They both went quiet.

"Oh, come on," I said. "You can't think the world wouldn't be a better place without him. And it's not like he's having a fun life. He's miserable, filled with hatred and fear and judgment. Who knows, maybe once he's dead he'll get to be with the God he's so obsessed with. Or even better, with a God that's kind and loving instead of vengeful. Maybe he can get started making up for all the pain he's caused with his misguided hatred. Or maybe he'll just disappear into the void, if that's what's waiting for us. That'd still be better than having him walking around here on Earth."

Trudy stared at me, shocked. She was even more shocked when Mom quietly said, "No, you're right."

We were silent after that, which was fine with me. I had a lot on my mind. We all did.

My plan when we got home was to go to my room and close the door, close out the rest of the world and take a break from it all, just for a little while.

When we pulled into the driveway and I got out, for the first time in a long time, I shivered at the sight of Stan's house next door. Lately I'd gotten more accustomed to its silent vacancy, but in the months after Pitman, I'd had to suppress a shudder every time I stepped out of the house and every time I came home.

For my entire life, the house we shared a driveway with had been the home of my best friend, Del Grainger. But after Pitman, it was the home of the man who had driven Del to run away, and who had then killed him. Stan disappeared after Pitman, and I'd slowly gotten used to him being gone, had accepted it, had figured he was probably dead, or at least that he was never coming back. Now I knew he was alive, and once again, I had to deal with the reality that at any moment, he could return to live next door to us.

Stan had scared me ever since I was little, and he scared me still, only now at least part of that fear wasn't about what he might do to me, but what I might do to him.

Mom put a hand on my shoulder and squeezed.

"I know, honey," she said. "Come on. Let's get inside."

I nodded and we climbed the steps onto the back porch and went in through the back door.

Trudy immediately started making coffee. I loved the fact that she felt at home in our house, that she and my mom had grown so close after having been estranged for years. And that she and I had grown so close, too, after I had grown up barely knowing her. As much as I wanted to hang out, though, the plan was still the plan.

I poured myself a glass of water and announced, "I'm going to go lie down."

Trudy looked disappointed, like she pretty much always did whenever I opted out. But my mom said, "Okay, good. I'll wake you before dinner."

On the way to my room I saw that there was a phone message. I pressed the button without bothering to look at the number.

"*Jimi!*" my friend Claudia's voice blared, sounding distressed. "I just heard about the bombing, that you were there." She sounded like she was on the verge of tears. "I hope you're okay. Call me as soon as you get this, alright?"

My bed was calling me, but she sounded upset. I knew I had to get back to her.

I hit the call-back button, and the phone rang once. Then a low voice I didn't recognize said, "Hello?"

It sounded a bit like her dad, but more like it wasn't. "Um, hello?" I said, caught off guard. "Is Claudia there?"

"Is this Jimi?"

"Yes?" I said, sounding more like I was asking a question than answering one.

"This is Claudia's dad." It still didn't sound like him.

"Oh, um, hi, Mr. Bembry. Is Claudia there?"

"I'm afraid not," he said. His voice was oddly flat. I was wondering if he was okay, when he said, "Are you okay?"

"Me? Yes, I'm fine."

"That's good to hear. You gave us all quite a scare yesterday. Claudia was most upset."

"Sorry about that. Well, I'm okay."

"Good. That's good. Well, Claudia is out running some errands with her mother. I'll tell her you called and that you're okay."

"Thanks, Mr.—" But then I realized he was gone. I looked at the phone to double-check, and sure enough, he had hung up on me.

I'd met Claudia's dad a few times and spoken to him on the phone, briefly, many more. He was an odd guy, but he'd never sounded like that before. I wondered if maybe he was high. It wouldn't have been out of the question.

I placed the phone back in its charger, and was stifling a yawn, thinking I really needed to lie down, when my mom appeared at my elbow.

"When is Rex coming?"

I shrugged and yawned again. "I don't know. Before dinner, but probably not for a while." Just as I said it, though, the doorbell rang. "Or maybe he's here right now."

I wasn't disappointed that he was there—I don't think I could ever be disappointed to see him—but I really, really wanted some *alone* time.

Then I opened the door, and Rex wasn't there at all. Instead, there were two blue suits, and behind them, next to a pair of black, government-issue SUVs parked on the street, were two more. Wearing the blue suits were Agent Ralphs, standing on the welcome mat, and next to her, a foot taller, was another agent wearing dark shades the same color as the Wellplant embedded in his forehead.

My head sagged to the side as I let out an exasperated sigh. "Seriously?"

"Come on in, Rex," Mom said, as she and Trudy came up beside me. Then she said, "Oh."

Ralphs dipped her head at my mom. "Ms. Corcoran." Then she did the same to Trudy. "Ms. Corcoran." Then she looked at me and paused, I think trying to greet me in a way that would be consistent but not repetitive. She gave up with a sigh and said, "Ms. Corcoran."

"We've been through a lot these last couple of days," Mom said. "Jimi needs to rest. Can't this wait?"

Ralphs smiled sympathetically but shook her head. "Sorry. This won't take long, but it is urgent."

"Do you have any information about my daughter's abductors?" Mom said, her voice accusing.

"Actually, yes I do," Ralphs replied.

Mom looked conflicted: relieved there was information, but maybe disappointed that she couldn't tell them to go away. She turned to me and I shrugged, then she sighed and said, "Okay."

She opened the door and led everyone into the dining room. Trudy kept going, straight through to the kitchen, to check on the coffee.

Ralphs smiled awkwardly and Agent Wellplant looked around like he was scanning the house. I wondered if he was recording it, maybe even transmitting that recording to headquarters or something, and if that was even legal. Ralphs didn't show it in any specific way, but I got the feeling she was annoyed by him, which made me feel a little more warmly toward her.

Mom gestured for the agents to sit on one side of the table, then motioned me over to sit next to her. "Okay?"

I nodded and she turned and nodded to Ralphs.

"We found the white van," Ralphs said. "The one used to abduct you. It was parked behind a house in Camden, where we found bomb-making equipment consistent with the device used in the Seaport Museum attack. Inside was hair that matches your DNA."

I raised an eyebrow at her. "You have my DNA on file?"

Ralphs smiled, but before she could respond, Agent Wellplant added, "Yes, that's right."

Ralphs gave him a sidelong look, her irritation a little closer to the surface.

My mom and I both started to speak at the same time. "I'm sorry…" we both said, then she trailed off as I continued with, "But who are you?"

Mom smiled at me with something like pride. She had been going to ask the same thing.

"Agent Scanlon," he replied without emotion.

"Agent Scanlon is part of a program partnering up agents with Well-plants and those without," Ralphs explained.

Mom ignored her. "And do you have identification, Agent Scanlon?"

Scanlon sat quietly for a moment, his face blank, but his aggravation somehow obvious anyway. He sighed and held up his badge.

Ralphs seemed to be biting back a smile as Mom and I studied the badge. Then he put it away and said, "We also found a photograph of you in the house."

"A photograph?" I said, creeped out at the idea that a bunch of mad bombers in masks would have my photo. I turned to Ralphs. "What kind of photo?"

"We're hoping you could tell us."

She slid a photo out of her folder and put it on the table. My hair was tied back the way I used to wear it when I was younger. I was wearing a bright red sweater and a big goofy grin.

"That's a school photo," Mom said. "From last year's yearbook."

"The year before, actually," I said. "Freshman year." I looked so young, so different. It looked like a different person, a different lifetime. I glanced at my mom, incredulous that she might think that picture was only one year old.

"Oh, right," she said. "The red sweater. You really did love that sweater."

"Any idea how they got it?" Ralphs asked.

I shrugged. "Anyone at my school would have it, and anyone else could get it from my school. The yearbooks are all in the library. Digitized versions, too. But I don't know why *they* would have it."

"Well, that was my next question. Any thoughts?"

I considered it for a second, hard, not just because she was asking, but because it was starting to really bug me. Apart from killing people and screwing up the world with their misguided violence, these CLAD fanatics were seriously complicating my life. "I guess it would make sense that the

people who grabbed me would need a photo, so they'd know what I looked like. But I still have no idea why they grabbed me in the first place."

Ralphs nodded slowly, leaving that question out there.

Scanlon leaned over and slid the photo back away from us, saying, "We have footage of you and your friends running from the altercation yesterday at the Humans for Humanity convention." His voice was flat, but he was clearly implying something, and as he did, a waft of halitosis rolled across the table, so intense and acrid I'm pretty sure I would have been able to see it if it hadn't made my eyes water.

I turned to him, deliberately keeping my face expressionless. "And?"

"A bit of a coincidence."

My expressionlessness faltered as I rolled my eyes. "How is that a coincidence?"

"Well, you were supposed to be at the meeting, but narrowly missed the bombing. Then you were at the protests, but you narrowly missed the violence. Were you tipped off?"

Maybe I was still off-balance from the revelation of the photo, but for some reason, I found Scanlon's insinuation really annoying. I turned to Ralphs as she took a deep breath. "I thought getting spiked was supposed to make you smarter," I said. "Was he just really dumb to start out with, or do you think he might have one of those faulty ones?"

Ralphs snorted despite herself. Trudy, in the kitchen, let out a short, involuntary yelp of a laugh. I couldn't see my mom's face because I was looking at Scanlon's, which betrayed no expression whatsoever.

The doorbell rang again, and Trudy bustled out of the kitchen, drying her hands on a dish towel. "I'll get it," she said.

"No," I said to Ralphs. "Obviously I was not tipped off."

"Then how did you know to run?" Scanlon asked.

"Because I'm not an idiot," I snapped. "It was obvious things were turning violent. I didn't want to be a part of that. Neither did my friends."

Trudy came into the dining room with Rex. We bobbed eyebrows at each

other. He seemed a little freaked out by the FBI agents, and I totally understood, although at this point, I found them more tedious than anything.

Scanlon looked up at Rex and did a double take, giving us the first glimpse of anything human behind those shades. Ralphs smiled at the reaction, then stared at Rex for a moment before looking away.

"Um, I can come back," Rex said.

Agent Scanlon nodded. "That would be pref—"

"No," I said, interrupting him. "We'll be done soon."

"Back to CLAD," Ralphs said. "You really have no idea why they would have singled you out to save?"

Mom was staring at me as intently as Ralphs was.

I shook my head. "I wish I did. I really do."

Ralphs nodded, then produced an envelope and started sliding out photos, one by one, and placing them on the table. They were pictures of chimeras, two men and two women.

The women both had reptile splices, their faces shimmering with smooth, multicolored scales. One of the guys appeared to have a rhino splice, his skin rough and gray with a substantial horn protruding from his forehead. I couldn't help thinking how much it must have hurt to sweat out *that* change. The other guy was spliced with a raven or something, his face framed by shiny, blue-black feathers that were only slightly darker than his brown-black skin.

I looked closely at the photos, then looked up at Ralphs.

"These are known associates of CLAD," she said. "Do you recognize any of them?"

I shook my head. "No."

Scanlon leaned forward across the table, dipping his head so that his Wellplant was staring at me. "You know it's a crime to lie to the FBI, right?"

Ralphs rolled her eyes.

"It is?" I said, feigning surprise. "Well, in that case, I think we need to talk about that thing in your head. I don't think it's working right."

Rex snorted but swallowed his smile as Ralphs looked up at him. Scanlon stared at me and ground his jaw.

"*Jimi!*" Mom said, scolding.

"It's a crime to lie to them, Mom," I said. Then I turned to Ralphs. "I wasn't going to say anything about it, but I don't want to get into trouble." Then I turned to Scanlon. "I hope that's helpful."

Scanlon started to speak, but Ralphs held up a hand to silence him. "No, it is not," she said. "And this is a serious matter."

"I know it's serious," I snapped, then the snark left me, leaving sadness in its place. "Look, I was kidnapped yesterday. By terrorists. Who for some reason apparently wanted to spare me from the bomb they planted, that killed a bunch of innocent people. I'm trying to help, I am, but frankly, it doesn't seem like Agent Scanlon over there is."

Ralphs took a deep breath, then waved a finger over the photos. "So you're sure you don't recognize any of these people?"

"That's correct."

She nodded as she scooped them up and slid them back into their envelope. "Okay. Well, if you have any ideas or new information about CLAD or why they seem so concerned about you, let me know immediately. I believe you, but not everyone does." She paused, and somehow without moving a muscle, she made it clear that Scanlon was among them. "You're right about CLAD, Jimi. They're seriously bad news. Murder, terrorism, who knows what they have planned next. If I find out you're lying to me, there's going to be hell to pay."

ELEVEN

Ralphs and company left just as Trudy came out of the kitchen with the coffee, nicely arranged on a tray. "Really?" she huffed as the door shut behind them.

"Don't worry," Mom said. "I'd still love a cup."

I raised a hand. "Me too."

Trudy looked at Rex. "Coffee?"

"Uh, sure," he said, distracted. "Thanks."

Trudy put the tray down on the table and handed him a mug as she turned back toward the kitchen. "Well, since they're gone, I'll put out some cookies, as well. Seems like a dessert-before-dinner kind of day."

Mom turned to me with a scowl on her face. "Jimi, you shouldn't antagonize people like that, especially not in the middle of something serious like this."

"Oh, please. He shouldn't antagonize me. I'm helping them as much as I can, and he's treating me like I'm some sort of suspect."

Trudy returned with a plate of cookies and put it on the table. We each grabbed one.

With my free hand I grabbed Rex's. "You okay?" I said.

"What? Um, yeah, sure. Why?"

"You seem distracted."

"Nah," he said, giving my ponytail a tweak. "Hey, you know what? Let's go for a run."

Everybody looked at him.

I laughed. "A run?"

I love to run, and I really love to run with Rex, but I was tired and it was hot out and a lot of stuff had gone down. Plus, he had just gotten there.

He looked me in the eye. "Yeah, a short one.... Get some fresh air."

"It's like, a hundred and ten degrees out there and humid."

"It's barely ninety," he said. Then he smiled. "And it's a dry humidity."

I looked down at his feet, at the heavy work boots he was wearing, totally inappropriate for a run. I shrugged. "Sure. Let's go for a run."

Mom and Trudy stared at us, vaguely perplexed.

"We're going for a run," I declared.

We went through the kitchen and out onto the back porch. The heat seemed to be trying to push us back inside. I paused to give Rex a questioning look. He held up a finger as we descended the steps. I was relieved to know he did have something to tell me, that we weren't going to be exercising in the ninety-degree heat, with his work boots on, simply because he was in the mood.

As we trotted down the driveway, Rex looked over at the house next door.

"Yes," I said quietly, "I am kind of freaked out that Stan Grainger has reappeared."

"Yeah, I'll bet."

Rex knew Stan. He had been there when I'd tried to get Stan's help when Del was horribly sick from a splice gone wrong, when Stan refused and called the cops on us instead. Rex had been there when Stan shot Del, when he *killed* his own son. Rex knew all about Stan.

I almost reminded him that Del had lived at that house, too. But then I remembered, once again, that Rex had known Del as long as I had, that we had all been friends together, back when we were little and Del's mom and my dad were still alive, when Rex was still Leo Byron, and life was, if not happier for all of us, at least less complicated.

Even after all these months, I still sometimes had trouble reconciling the fact that Rex and Leo were one and the same.

When we got to the street, Rex turned left and set off running. He fell into an easy jog, but his heavy boots, attached to his heavy self, thudded hard against the pavement.

"So?" I said, running beside him. The sun was lower in the sky, but it was still hot, and it still bathed the world in a golden haze. Perspiration quickly stood out on my face. Within seconds, I could feel droplets rolling between my shoulder blades. I shook my head, sending sweat flying.

Rex looked around again before speaking. "I recognized one of them."

"What do you mean? One of who?"

"The photos they showed you. I recognized one of them. The guy with the bird splice."

"You *know* him?" I said, my step faltering.

"Shh. Not so loud."

"Why didn't you say anything?"

"Well, for one thing, they didn't ask me, they asked you. And second, I didn't know if maybe you knew him, too, and just weren't saying. But also, I didn't know for sure if we should tell them at all."

"What do you mean? Don't tell me you're starting to agree with CLAD!"

"No, of course not. But for whatever reason, they do seem to be taking a particular interest in you. Seems to me, we might want to find out why that is before the FBI does, in case it's something that could hurt you somehow."

"Agreed." I had been thinking along similar lines, that I needed to find out why CLAD was talking about me and saving my life, keeping pictures of me around. It was more than a little bit disturbing.

We got to the end of the block, and as we turned the corner, both of us slowed to a stop.

"So who is he?" I asked, wiping a finger across my brow and flicking the sweat onto the pavement.

Rex did the same. He had a lot more sweat. "His name is Ogden. I don't know him well. He's a tech guy. He was part of Chimerica, but…he left." He resumed jogging, slowly, and I fell into step beside him. "He actually used to work at Wellplant."

I stopped. "Are you serious?"

He stopped, too. "It was a while back. He's a bit older than us. This was long before he got his splice."

"Do you know him well enough to ask him why his pals are getting me into trouble with the FBI?"

"Yeah, I think so. If I can find him. But before I do, you should probably decide how much you want to know."

"What do you mean?"

We started running again. "I mean, you just told the FBI that you didn't know any of the people in their photos. You were telling the truth and they probably believed you. Agent Ralphs seemed to, anyway. If I'm able to get information from Ogden...well, are you sure you want to put yourself into the position that the next time they ask, you have to lie about it?"

I was nodding even before Rex finished speaking. "Yes. I need to know what's going on," I said. "And like you said, if I can, I should find out before Agent Ralphs does. Or Scanlon."

"So...should I ask around? See if I can get in touch with him?"

"Do you mind?"

"Of course not, no. Whatever you want."

"The only thing I don't want is you putting yourself at risk by asking, getting into trouble or getting hurt."

He laughed. "Well, you don't have to worry about me."

I laughed back. "Are you serious?"

"What?"

"Rex, in the months since you've come back into my life you've been arrested twice, you've been shocked, beaten, almost had your lungs altered, and been imprisoned in a mine. Yes, I *do* have to worry about you."

He glanced at me. "Sounds kind of bad when you put it like that."

"Yeah, well..."

"Wait a second, you've been through all kinds of hell, too. Threatened. Abducted, shocked, mine collapses, and hospital implosions."

"Don't forget about the mudslide," I said helpfully.

"How could I forget about the mudslide?"

Rex had a point. We had both been through a lot, and a lot of it was together.

"So," I said, "I worry about you, and you worry about me, right?"

"I guess so. We worry about each other."

"I guess we do, yeah."

"Well, if we're going to worry about each other, I guess we should stop running before we both drop dead of heat stroke."

I laughed, but he was right. I was dying out there. We stopped, turned around, and walked slowly back to the house.

TWELVE

Mom was disappointed that Rex didn't stay for dinner, confused that he came all the way out there for such a short visit, and suspicious about our jog, as well. With all of it combined, I think she knew something was up. But I didn't let on, and she didn't press it.

The window for taking a nap had closed, and instead I stuck it out, yawning through dinner then going to bed early. I had nightmares about the bombing.

The next day was Saturday, but Mom had to go into work. I woke up at six as she was getting ready and couldn't get back to sleep, so I stayed in bed reading. At eight thirty the phone rang.

Mom had already left for work, so I rolled out of bed and hurried downstairs in case it was Rex.

"Hey," he said when I picked up. "Found him."

"Ogden?"

"Yup. He's staying at a squat in South Jersey."

"That was fast." Not to slight Rex's investigatory skills, but if he had found Ogden that quickly, I wondered how far behind us the FBI would be.

"He can meet with us if you want. This afternoon."

━━ ━━ ━━

The squat was in what was left of a tiny town called Pedricktown, just across the Delaware River. Jerry had kind of given Rex his old truck, a long-term loan. I still didn't have my license, and after being caught driving without it—even though I had very good reasons—I now had to wait another few months before I could get it.

We took the Commodore Barry Bridge into New Jersey. To get to the bridge, you had to take the Smartway around the city, meaning your car had to be in Smartdrive on the way. But the bridge itself had a lane for manual drivers. Some old federal law mandated that interstate crossings couldn't be restricted to Smartdrive, even though all the roads leading up to them were. Rex enjoyed driving manually, so we were in the manual lane doing seventy as the cars in the Smartdrive lanes zipped past us at the legal Smartdrive speed limit of ninety-five.

At the midpoint of the bridge, I looked out at the drones crisscrossing the river. I glanced north, toward the city skyline, the cluster of towers shooting up over the older skyscrapers—Wells Tower the tallest of them. I tried to find the Seaport Museum, but it was too far away.

Twice I thought I noticed vehicles following us, hanging behind us even as we crawled along—a beat-up gray van when we were still in Philadelphia and a newer sedan while crossing into New Jersey.

But before I mentioned either sighting to Rex, they faded into the traffic and disappeared. I told myself I was probably just being paranoid, but I'd been paranoid before, and I'd been followed before, too. I kept an eye on the rearview but didn't see anyone else.

I turned my thoughts to Ogden. I was anxious about meeting someone who might have been involved in the bombing, who might have played a part in killing all those people. Thinking about it, I got so upset that I wondered if I'd even be able to speak to him. As impossible as it seemed, I knew I'd have to put my anger out of my mind, at least while I was there. If I couldn't, it wasn't going to be a very productive conversation.

The bridge let us off in the middle of the zurbs. The zurbs in Jersey tended to be in better shape than the ones outside of Philly. Or rather, the ones still on dry land were. A lot of the others were simply gone, sunk into the swamps or reclaimed by the river to the west or the ocean to the east. But where we were driving, things seemed pretty intact at first.

We made good time up until the last mile or so, which took longer than the rest of the trip. Like a lot of towns in that part of Jersey, much of Pedricktown had been flooded or washed out entirely by the river years earlier, so we had to try several different approaches before we found a road piled high enough with gravel and crushed shells to form a passable causeway. All the false starts and turnarounds left me confident that even if someone had been following us earlier, they weren't any longer.

On either side of us, abandoned houses and businesses were sinking into the muck, but when we finally turned onto the street leading to Ogden's squat, it was high and dry, or at least dry. The land was flat, lined with brown grasses and low, scrubby trees.

At the end of the block, a narrow three-story wooden house overlooked a broad swath of swamp. Several rows of portable solar panels stretched off to the left of it, their wheels sunk several inches into the soil.

Ogden was standing on the porch, chewing on a toothpick. As we got out of the car, he flicked it into the swamp. The sun was hot, and the buzz of insects was loud.

Ogden looked just like his picture, but lankier than I expected. He put his hands in his pockets and came halfway down the steps as we approached. He didn't look like a terrorist.

"Rex," he said, tipping his head in greeting.

"Ogden," Rex replied.

Ogden looked at me and said, "Nonk." It was a bit of a slur, short for "nonchimera," but he said it in the same tone he'd said "Rex," seemingly without malice.

"Really?" Rex said, annoyed and disappointed.

Ogden shrugged without taking his hands out of his pockets.

"My name's Jimi," I said, stepping forward and putting out my hand.

He looked at it for a second, then took two slow steps down and shook it. "Ogden," he said.

"Nice to meet you," I said with exaggerated politeness.

He snorted as he turned and went back up the steps. "Come on in," he said, over his shoulder.

We followed him up onto the porch and into the house. It was dark and faintly musty, but not too bad. That close to the swamp, it could have been a mess.

Ogden led us into the kitchen, which was worn but also bright and clean. At the far end there was a metal table with chipped white enamel paint surrounded by four mismatched metal chairs and windows on three sides looking out over the swamp.

Ogden sat in one of the chairs and gestured toward the others.

"So, what do you want to talk about?" he asked as we sat.

"You're with CLAD now," Rex said.

Ogden was quiet for two seconds, one to stare at Rex and one to stare at me. "I might be," he said. "Why?"

Rex turned to me and I leaned forward in my seat.

Why did you kill all those people? I thought, but that's not what I said. "My full name is Jimi Corcoran."

"I know who you are."

"Right, well, apparently a lot of people in CLAD know who I am. I want to know why."

He shrugged. "You've been on the news, you're active with E4E, et cetera. I'm sure a lot of people know who you are."

"In the last four months, the FBI has been to my house. Twice." He stiffened when I said it, and I felt somehow gratified. "First they wanted to know what I knew about CLAD, saying that CLAD members had been talking about me. More recently, members of CLAD abducted me off the street while I was on my way to that lunch meeting that was bombed."

He tilted his head as he stared at me, a hint of a sneer on his lips. "You were going to the meeting? With all the H4Hers?"

"And E4E, yes." I looked into his eyes, trying to see if they matched any of the eyes that had peered at me through their masks in the van. I was pretty sure he hadn't been there.

"Well, I wasn't part of that," he said, looking down. "But I'm sorry about your friends."

I didn't say anything.

"So, someone intercepted you on your way there?" he continued. "How do you know they were with CLAD?"

"Do you know someone named Cronos?"

His face froze for an instant, then he started laughing.

"What?" I asked.

"You met Cronos?"

"That's what he said his name was."

The smile fell away from his face. He glanced at Rex, then back at me. "You're serious."

"So why would they care about me?" I asked. "The FBI keeps asking, and I want to know before they do."

"I don't know," he said. "Like I said, you're known. A minor celebrity for the cause and all that. Which could be handy. Cronos keeps a pretty low profile, but you've also seen some action, and seen firsthand what we're up against. We need people; maybe he's hoping you'll join us."

"So I can blow up buildings and kill people? Not a chance."

"No, so you can help take down Wells, take down the Wellplant network and with it, H4H. And we're not just 'killing people.' We're taking down the enemies of chimeras. Before they can kill *us*."

"'Enemies of chimeras'? Are you serious? There were people from E4E in that blast. They were *not* all enemies of chimeras."

"Maybe they were collaborators, then. I don't know. Like I said, I wasn't in on that. But don't be so sure you know all about E4E, or Chimerica even."

Rex sat up straighter. "What's that supposed to mean?"

Ogden laughed. "Come on, you know as well as I do that getting them to actually *do* anything is damn near impossible. Why do you think that is?"

"Because they don't blow people up for trying to have a dialogue?" I demanded.

"No," Ogden shot back. "Because they don't *do* anything. Not a damn thing. And you know it yourself. I heard about Omnicare, about how you told people at Chimerica what was going on at that hospital and they refused to help. Why do you think that is?"

He had a point, although I wasn't going to concede it.

"What are you getting at?" Rex asked, his voice tight.

Ogden leaned forward and lowered his voice. "We know Wells and his people are funding some chimera groups, to infiltrate and undermine the fight. We think E4E and Chimerica are among them."

"That's ridiculous!" Rex shot back, losing the fight to keep his voice under control.

"Is it?" Ogden asked. "What are they doing then?" He shot me a look. "Other than having lunch with the enemy?"

Before either of us could say anything, he continued. "Look, Nonk, you've seen some pretty bad stuff that Wells's friends have done to chimeras. That Jasper guy at Pitman you all took down, and the doctor at Omnicare, the one who killed all those people—"

"Charlesford," I whispered.

"Exactly. But that's not all of it. There's more stuff like that going on. And this time Wells's involvement isn't indirect or tangential. It's not just people Wells is connected to. This time it's Wells himself who's responsible."

"What are you talking about?" Rex replied.

"I'm talking about Wells Life Sciences. One of their facilities in Delaware. People are saying chimeras are being imprisoned there, held against their will. Maybe getting hurt and killed."

"How do you know about it?" I asked.

"People talk," he said. "Friends of friends have gone in there and never come out. I told my connections at Chimerica about it earlier this year, and they told me not to do anything. They said they would take care of it. And then *they* did nothing. So I left." He laughed bitterly. "Sometimes I wonder if maybe Chimerica is make-believe after all."

What he was describing sounded chillingly similar to both Pitman and Omnicare. Deep down, I felt scared. People had died in both those places, and in both places, I had almost been one of them. I cleared my throat, making sure my voice was steady. "You said people might be hurt and killed. How?"

Ogden took a deep breath, staring at me, then at Rex. "To be honest, I don't know. But I'm going to find out. And CLAD is going to help. They took my information seriously, and said they'd help me find out more. And if it's as bad as it seems, if it's like Pitman or Omnicare, they'll do what it takes to stop it. That's what CLAD is about." He looked at each of us, then said, "We're going to take a look at the place soon, see what we can see, do a little LIDAR mapping. You know what that is?"

We both nodded. LIDAR was a laser-based radar system that could take quick, superaccurate measurements.

"Why don't you come with us?" he said. "You can see for yourself what's going on, what Chimerica and E4E are allowing to go on, and if you still think they're doing everything they need to be doing, then that's fine. And even if you decide we're wrong, I'll still see if I can find out why CLAD's head honchos are so concerned with Jimi Corcoran. But you might decide you want to help us as we try to put these bastards out of action permanently."

Rex stayed quiet. I knew he probably had a clear idea of what he thought we should or shouldn't do next, but he was leaving it up to me. Probably because I was the one getting visits from the FBI, the one who'd been abducted off the street and almost blown up. I snuck a glance in his direction, but his face was blank. He didn't want to lead me one way or another. I loved how he respected that this was my decision, but frankly, I wouldn't have minded his input on this, even if I ended up disregarding it.

I was struck by what Ogden was saying about Chimerica and E4E. I couldn't imagine they were in cahoots with Wells. Even though I barely remembered her and didn't even know her anymore, I couldn't imagine my aunt Dymphna being a part of that. But while both groups had been serious defenders of chimeras, Ogden wasn't wrong; their refusal to act in the face of clear threats to chimeras had at times been exasperating. And

I was curious about what he wanted to show us. If it was anything like Pitman or Omnicare, it needed to be stopped right away.

I was about to say as much, but then stopped. I'd been asked more than once why I needed to be the one to get in the middle of every fight. Those other fights had been unavoidable, in my mind. I hadn't injected myself into them, I simply hadn't run away. Maybe this one was someone else's fight. Then I pictured Reverend Calkin falling down those steps and I knew I never wanted to be a part of CLAD. However right they might be about anything else, their methods were clearly wrong.

I shook my head. Rex and Ogden both sighed, one in relief, the other frustration.

"No," I said. "The FBI is already breathing down my neck, thinking I'm somehow involved. Plus, I can't condone the bombings, the killings. I can't be a part of that."

Ogden didn't argue, he just silently nodded. When we left, he watched from the porch as we walked to the car. Rex and I didn't speak. We waved as we got in and Ogden waved back.

He watched us drive away, and as the road curved and the house disappeared, I said, "Did I do the right thing?"

"I have no idea," Rex said with a low, rumbling laugh. "For what it's worth, you did what I would have done."

The road sloped gently down in front of us. The puddles of standing water on either side of the road grew wider and deeper as we drove.

"I wonder what we would have found there, at the place in Delaware," I said as we turned back onto the same causeway of gravel and shells that we had driven in on.

Rex didn't reply, concentrating on keeping the truck on the road, which somehow seemed even more narrow and precarious than on the way in. When we reached relatively solid land, Rex let out a deep breath I didn't realize he'd been holding. As we turned onto the road leading back toward the Smartway, I spotted a beat-up gray van partially blocking the road ahead of us.

"Uh-oh," I said, putting my hand on Rex's arm.

"Who is it?" he said, glancing at me then back at the van.

"I don't know, but I think I saw them following us earlier, back in Philly."

"Why didn't you say anything?"

"They disappeared. I thought I was just being paranoid. I thought a car was following us, as well, but it disappeared, too."

Rex slowed and as we drew closer, the driver climbed out. Dark shades partially obscured his face, but I could make out the angle of his jaw, the pointy nose that seemed to separate the rust-colored fur above from the white of his throat and chin.

Rex's foot slipped off the accelerator and we both leaned forward.

"No way," I said, grinning. "Is that Sly?"

THIRTEEN

t was Sly. Rex laughed as he pulled over behind the van.

Rex and Sly had been friends for a long time. They'd shared a squat together in the zurbs with some other chimeras for a few years before Pitman happened, and after that, they'd gotten involved in Chimerica together. Sly was a little more hardcore about it and had worked his way up in the hierarchy. I'd only seen him a handful of times since we met in the fall, but those times had been intense. I considered him a close friend.

As soon as the truck stopped, I jumped out.

"Sly!" I called out as I ran over and wrapped my arms around him.

"Hey, Jimi." He laughed and squeezed me back.

"What are you doing here?" Rex asked as he walked up. He smiled as he said it, and he held out his hand for Sly to shake, but there was an edge to his voice, as well. He wasn't just asking as a pleasantry.

I took a step back away from Sly and screwed up my face at him. "Yeah, were you following us?"

He smiled awkwardly. "Guess I need to work on my tailing skills. Yeah, I was following you."

"What's that about?" Rex asked. All that was left of his previous smile was a slight tug at the side of his mouth. Then that went away, too.

"I was sent to pick you up," he said, turning serious. "Jimi, actually."

"Who sent you?" I asked. "And why?" It's different when you know the person picking you up and they don't put a hood over your head, but I'd kind of had my fill of unanticipated van rides.

"I'm not supposed to say," he replied quietly.

I looked at Rex and rolled my eyes. It was a phrase I'd heard too many times from Rex when he couldn't tell me the details of some involvement with Chimerica. I understood why he couldn't, but I still didn't like it, and I was glad that in recent months it hadn't come up. But here it was again.

"'Not supposed to' isn't the same as can't," Rex said.

Sly snorted. "Come on, man. You know how it is."

"Yes, I do," Rex said, his voice hard. He was still involved in Chimerica, although not like Sly was, but I don't think Sly would have told him even if I hadn't been there.

I poked Sly in the midsection, playfully, hoping a friendlier tactic might work. "Come on, what's it about?"

His face softened. "It's important. I can tell you that much. So will you come?"

"I don't know. I don't have my passport with me, and last time you swooped in like this I ended up whisked out of the country and held against my will." Last time he had swooped in I was also being pursued by bad guys, but I didn't mention that.

"It's not that far," he said. "No one's going to hold you anywhere, and we'll have you home for dinner. I promise."

I glanced at Rex and he shrugged. I could see in his eyes his protectiveness toward me conflicting with his commitment to supporting Chimerica.

"It really is important," Sly said again.

"And I'm just supposed to take your word for that?"

He looked hurt. "You think I'd lie to you?"

"People don't always agree on what's important."

"Well," he said, sounding only slightly mollified. "I guarantee you'll agree that it's important."

I growled in frustration. The truth was, I *did* trust Sly. "So, you want me to trust you, but you don't trust me, or at least not enough to tell me what was so important."

"Jimi, you know it's not like that." Now he looked hurt again, which was starting to bug me, too.

I growled again and threw up my hands. "Fine. Whatever," I said. "Let's go."

Sly turned to Rex. "She'll be fine."

Rex snorted. "Oh, I know," he said. "I'm coming with you."

Sly started to say something, but Rex simply nodded, slowly but insistently.

"Okay," Sly said. "Sure, why not."

Rex and I turned toward the front passenger-side door, and Sly cleared his throat. I stopped and looked at him with one eyebrow raised. "What?"

"You're supposed to get in the back."

The windows in the back were covered with an opaque film. "Sorry," I said. "I'm trusting you; you can trust me." I looked in the window and saw that it was a bench seat. "Besides, there's room up front for all of us."

Sly threw up his hands. "Okay, whatever."

There actually wasn't quite enough room in the front for all three of us, not if one of us was Rex. But by the time that was obvious, we were already packed in—with me in the middle—and Sly was driving us away.

Rex held onto the strap over the window, like he was trying to pull himself tight against the side of the van, so as to not smoosh me.

"Cozy, ain't it?" he said, looking down at me.

"Plenty of room in the back," Sly muttered.

"No, we're fine," I said, squeezing Rex's knee.

Things were vaguely awkward at first. I don't think Rex and Sly were used to being on the opposite sides of any kind of issue, but Rex seemed to want to make it clear that as dedicated as he was to Chimerica, if sides were to be chosen, he'd be choosing mine.

Before long, though, that point had been made, and the fact that we weren't really on opposite sides of anything became clear. Still, it was strange, and we didn't talk a whole lot, because all the things we wanted to talk about, we couldn't. We wanted to ask Sly questions about where we were going and why, and he couldn't answer those questions. And Rex and I wanted to talk about what Ogden had said, but we both knew we couldn't discuss that in front of Sly until we had discussed it more just between the two of us, and until we had a better understanding of the situation.

We were headed east on the Atlantic City Smartway, toward the coast. "Man," I said. "I haven't been to the shore in years."

According to my Mom, when she was a kid, the Jersey Shore was a hugely popular resort. When I was a kid, they were still trying to keep up with the erosion and the sea-level rise, dredging sand from the ocean floor to build up the beaches and the dunes and building sea walls to keep the towns from being inundated. Now, the fight had been abandoned in a lot of places, with some towns partially or fully submerged and others having become stilt towns, with houses up on pilings that were completely surrounded by water half the time. The houses that weren't up on pilings were mostly washed away.

"I remember coming here with your family a couple of times," Rex said, looking off into space as if he were picturing it. "What town was it?"

"Wildwood," I said. "Yeah, that was fun." I smiled at the memory, but I also remembered being disappointed because most of the rides on the boardwalk had been washed out the previous winter. They looked fine from a distance, but they were closed and the lights were off. One night we were walking on the boardwalk and my dad was trying to make me feel better by describing what they used to look like, with all the colored lights, and the rides swinging and spinning and zipping along tracks, and hundreds of families laughing and having fun. I could almost picture it from his description, but all I could see were the skeletal hulking shapes, black against the dark blue night sky, looking strange and sad and out of place. It did not make me feel better.

He told me they'd be up and running by the following summer, and we'd come back, but that winter they got hit even harder, and in the spring, they tore them all down. We missed the Golden Age of Wildwood, New Jersey, by one year.

Sly laughed. "I always forget that you two go way back. It's weird."

I gave Rex a sidelong glance to say *Yes, it is weird.* He shrugged.

We'd been driving for half an hour by then, and I turned to Sly. "Are we going to the beach?"

He kept his eyes front and said, "We'll be there soon."

We turned north onto the Garden State Parkway, away from Wildwood and the other beaches I vaguely knew.

Rex and I exchanged a glance and a shrug. We'd be there soon.

Fifteen miles later, we took the exit for Little Egg Harbor, then zigged and zagged a couple of times before ending up on Dock Road, a narrow causeway that had been built up to stay above the water pressing up against it on either side. It was similar in ways to the road we had taken to get to Ogden's house, but instead of shells and gravel it had been built up with concrete and asphalt, and instead of puddles or swamp on either side, it was the bay.

The road narrowed and in places one side or another was washed out; then we came to a padlocked gate that blocked the road entirely. A sign on it said, UNSAFE ROAD. NO ENTRY.

Sly pulled up to the gate and started to get out.

"Okay, enough. Where the hell are we?" I asked under my breath.

He didn't answer—not that I expected him to. He just unlocked the gate and dragged it open.

"Remember, you're not supposed to be seeing any of this," he said as he got back in.

We drove through the gate and past a few houses, or partial houses, right on the side of the road, but semi-submerged in the water. One was completely washed away except for the front wall, looking like a façade from an old movie set.

A little ways past that, the road itself disappeared under the water, resurfacing again maybe thirty yards away, on a little circle of land with a single large beach house surrounded by a low concrete sea wall. It appeared to be in perfect shape, as if it was still inhabited.

Sly got out again and walked up to a rusty old mailbox on the side of the road. He opened the side of it, revealing a crude metal security panel. He pressed a few buttons on the panel, and immediately the water started to churn between where the road disappeared under it and where it emerged on the island. One by one, a series of metal pontoons rose to the surface, forming a kind of floating bridge.

Sly got back into the van and drove us slowly out across the water. It was unsettling, not being able to see the road from either side of the van.

I gave him a sideways look. "Seriously?"

He shrugged but didn't say anything.

The island looked bigger once we got over there. It was mostly taken up by the house, but there was a driveway leading to a two-door garage and a patio on one side. On the opposite side of the house, outside the seawall, a tiny private beach sloped down to the water.

We drove off the floating bridge, and Sly stopped the car next to a pylon on the side of the road. He flipped up yet another panel and pressed a couple of buttons. With a soft burbling sound, the bridge behind us sank back under the water as we parked next to the garages.

When we got out, the sun was still hot, but the breeze coming over the water brought some relief. Sly smiled at me and said, "She's waiting for you. On the beach, around the other side."

Rex whipped his head around and stared a question at Sly, but Sly ignored him, still focusing his reassuring smile at me. Rex's question was *"Who?"* and I was wondering the same thing. But I got the impression Rex already knew the answer. And somehow, I suspected I did, too.

FOURTEEN

She was standing on the beach, looking out over the water. I didn't know exactly what I had imagined, because that previous image was wiped away and replaced by what was in front of me. She was tall and broad-shouldered, with a single, long, gray braid running down her back.

I stepped over the sea wall and as soon as my foot touched the sand, she turned to look at me. She was obviously spliced, maybe more than once. It was hard to determine with what, exactly. Maybe some sort of wolf. She had a prominent nose and mouth and a strong brow over eyes that were an almost electric blue, blazing with intelligence. The overall impression was striking and strong. She must have been quite beautiful when she was younger, and she still was, but more striking than her beauty was the dignity and wisdom she exuded. Through the years I could almost recognize her, my dim memories reconciling with the person I saw in front of me. And through the splice, I could see the resemblance: to my father, to Aunt Trudy. To me.

"You're Dymphna," I said.

"And you are too," she said, with a smile that brightened the world around us, as if the sun had emerged from behind a cloud. "But I know you go by Jimi. I've been watching you, you know. On the news . . through our friends. The pictures don't do you justice: you're even more beautiful in person."

I was pretty sure I was not all that beautiful, but I got the sense she meant something other than just my outward appearance. I preferred to believe that than to think she was just flattering me. But I was too floored to be meeting her to respond right away.

"How's your mother?" she asked. "How's Kevin?"

"They're . . . good," I replied, thrown by the normalcy of the conversation, considering the circumstances. "Kevin just went off to college, although I suspect you already know that."

"And Trudy? How's—"

"She's fine. Everybody's fine," I said, cutting her off. It didn't seem the time or place to tell her Trudy was probably worried about her, and angry at her for leaving. My mom, too. "They miss you."

"And I've missed them. You and Kevin, too. More than you can imagine."

"So...where have you been all this time?"

She laughed. "Everywhere, it seems. Where haven't I been?"

"You haven't been here," I said quietly.

"No," she said sadly. "I have not been here."

The energy radiating from her dimmed considerably, as if maybe that aura of hers took more effort than it appeared, and for a brief instant she couldn't maintain it. In that moment, she seemed old and tired. I felt bad for causing that reaction, but I had only asked one question, and she had sidestepped it completely. I smiled and raised an eyebrow at her, letting her know I wasn't angry, but I still wanted an answer.

Her energy seemed to return as she smiled back, almost shyly, like she was acknowledging my indulgence and grateful for it. "Truthfully, I've been all over," she said, with a trace of her earlier weariness. "Ireland, for quite some time. Before that India. Thailand. But in between, all over. More places than I can remember."

"Why did you go away? When I was little. Why did you abandon the family? What was that all about?"

She paused for a moment, maybe deciding whether or not she was going to answer. Then she gestured toward a table and two chairs set up on the beach. "It was the toughest decision I've ever made," she said as she walked toward them. I fell into step beside her. "I went away to protect you. All of you. There were...people after me. People who wanted to stop me, to hurt me. I had to disappear, had to cut all ties, or else they might come after my family, too. Which is you."

"Why were they after you? Who?"

She took a deep breath, thinking again. "When I came up with the technology for splicing, I—"

"'Came up with the technology'?" I said, unable to stop myself from interrupting her. "You invented splicing?"

"Well, not just me, no. The technology is based on the work of countless other scientists, pioneers in the field. But the technology that made splicing possible the way you know it today, that started the chimera movement, I developed that, yes."

We both sat, and she continued.

"I used to work with Howard Wells, you see."

"You worked for Wellplant?"

"No, no, this was before all that. And I didn't work for him, I worked *with* him. Our work overlapped."

"But…he's terrible."

Her face filled with sadness. "He is, now. Worse than I could ever have imagined. But he wasn't then, not at first. That part of him, the part that is most of him now, that was just a small bit then. A short fuse, an impatience, an objectivity that sometimes neglected human compassion and focused on solely cold facts. Back then, those were the flaws in an otherwise sweet young man with a very bright future."

She took a deep breath then let it out. "We met in grad school. He was working on his PhD in biomedical engineering. I was working on mine in genomics. He was brilliant. And very charming. A fascinating mind. When we met, we agreed about so much more than we disagreed. One of the things that we agreed on was that it was a very exciting time. After the Cyber Wars, before the flu pandemic, there was a brief moment of optimism. The possibilities seemed endless. We were both consumed with exploring the potential of humans to change themselves, to shape themselves instead of shaping the world to fit our needs. To decide proactively what was next for humanity, and for the Earth. But my work pulled me in one direction, and his work pulled him in another. A darker direction."

"And your work focused on biology," I said.

Dymphna nodded. "I started out trying to isolate specific genes for specific traits from other species. It's a very Western idea, like isolating the 'active' compound from a plant, disregarding the context, ignoring how that plant may have had a multitude of compounds that combined to produce a given effect. It was the same thing with genetic research. The field was obsessed with isolating genes, and so was I, at first. And I identified many, some with great practical applications, but they all seemed ultimately disappointing, the sum of the parts never quite measuring up to the whole. So I began exploring broader splices, including more and more of the adjacent genes. The broader splices seemed more promising, more powerful in their context.

"My graduate advisors disapproved. Everyone disapproved. It seemed that the more promising my research became, the more I was cut off from the resources I needed to pursue it. I leased the patents to many of my discoveries, sold my car, borrowed money from friends, but it wasn't enough to pay for test subjects. So I did tests on myself. Little splices at first, a single gene at time. I altered my ability to process certain proteins in milk. Then I moved on to bigger ones, broader ones, my first animal splices. I found that the broader splices brought intangibles, hidden benefits to be gained, insights."

She stretched out her arms and looked at her hands, admiring them. It reminded me of Del, the first time I saw him after his tiger splice, looking at the muscles in his forearms. Admiring himself.

"When the North American gray wolves went extinct, and I chose them as the source of my broadest splice ever," she went on, "that was one of the first splices along the lines of what today's genies do as a matter of course." She shrugged. "It changed the way I looked at the world, the way I saw life. I felt I experienced universal truths by stepping outside the strictly human experience—does that make sense?"

"Yes," I said quietly, although I didn't know for sure, having never experienced it. "I guess so."

"The splices also brought health benefits, rewriting or overwriting damaged genes in my genome. But the more profound benefit came from moving closer to the natural world, in reintegrating my humanity with the rest of nature. But at the same time I was experimenting on myself with gene splices, Howard Wells was experimenting on himself with increasingly sophisticated computer implants, what would later become his Wellplants. The better he became at integrating them into his brain, the more they changed the way he looked at the world, too. My experiences changed me in many ways. His work changed him, as well. He became judgmental, harshly so, and impatient of others, especially those who were different from him. We grew apart."

"I can't believe you and Howard Wells were friends."

She looked away from me, at the strip of land on the far side of the bay. "We were more than that."

"Wait," I said. "You—you dated Howard Wells?"

She nodded. "I did. He was my first serious boyfriend." She laughed, sadly. "He was my last serious boyfriend, too, for that matter."

I sat back, my head spinning.

"He came to disapprove of my work," she continued, "of me, really. And I disapproved of what his work was doing to him. Soon, the differences outweighed the similarities, until we had almost nothing in common."

"So, you had to run away because you broke up with Howard Wells?"

Dymphna laughed again. "No, it was much more complicated than that. Getting spliced didn't just help me see the world differently, it helped me see how *other* people see the world. It helped me recognize that Howard Wells increasingly regarded the planet as an object to be commodified, to have value wrung from it. He didn't think beyond his own lifetime, which I guess makes sense if you're a sociopath who doesn't care about other people. And that's what his Wellplant was turning him into."

She paused and cleared her throat. I got the feeling she was struggling against a pain that was old but not at all dissipated. "Our worldviews diverged…completely. There was no room in his world for someone with my views." She spread her arms, displaying them once more. "For someone like me."

"Are you saying he tried to kill you?"

"I may have been paranoid at first, but over the years I've seen plenty to convince me those fears were legitimate."

"Are Wells and his people still after you? Is that why all the secrecy, with you and Chimerica? The cloak-and-dagger stuff?"

"That's part of it. Chimerica wasn't meant to be secret. It started out as an informal group committed to helping chimeras and the people who administered splices. In fact, it was mostly comprised of genies at first, and a lot of the early focus was on health and safety, making sure the viral splice medium was safe and effective, that people knew how to store it and use it, setting up informal standards, trying to minimize the chances of a splice going wrong." She shook her head. "Splicing is one-hundred-percent safe and effective when done properly, but some of these genies out there cut corners. People were getting hurt."

"They still are," I said. Del's splice had gone wrong, and I'd seen others, too.

She nodded. "It's infuriating. Totally preventable. But soon we realized those weren't the only chimeras getting hurt out in the world. As more people started getting spliced, more people reacted to them with hatred and fear, and Chimerica became more focused on protecting people from the anti-chimera fanatics. When Howard Wells became a part of the anti-chimera movement, and brought his vast resources to bear, we realized that a certain level of discretion was essential."

"If you were trying to keep a low profile, maybe you shouldn't have named the group after a mythical chimera utopia."

She shook her head. "Chimerica the organization came long before the imaginary…whatever it is people envision. Apparently not everyone kept it one-hundred-percent secret. That's how the legend of Chimerica got started. Anyway, as our mission changed, that secrecy became even more important."

"What is the mission now?"

"That is a bigger question than we have time for right now," she said. "Although I would love to sit down with you sometime soon and talk to you about it in depth. I would love to hear your thoughts, actually. Right now, though, I have some questions for you, if you don't mind."

I sat back in my chair and looked at the bay. Here and there, bits of wreckage from old houses poked through the water, echoes of the world that used to be there. But it was still peaceful and still beautiful. A large seabird flew past us, a heron or something, its shadow sliding across the marsh grasses and the water.

"Okay," I said.

"What is the nature of your connection to CLAD?"

I laughed and shook my head. "You sound like the FBI."

"Sorry, but it's important."

"I have no connection with CLAD that I know of."

She stared at me for a moment, studying, appraising. The sun was behind us now, so her face was in the shade. Her blue eyes glowed as they rested on me. "Weren't you just meeting with a CLAD operative? Isn't that where Sly picked you up?"

"We were there trying to get an answer to that same question." I paused, thinking about how that sounded. "Okay, I guess it would be more accurate to say I don't *know* what my connection is to CLAD. They grabbed me off the street, I think to make sure I didn't get blown up by their latest bomb. The FBI said that members of CLAD had been heard talking about me, and my picture was in the house where the bomb was made. So yes, there is some sort of connection, but I don't know what that is. I am trying to find out."

She nodded slowly, considering my words. "Did you learn anything today?"

I shook my head. "Not really. Ogden, the guy we talked to, he said he didn't know what the connection was."

"Is that it?"

I shrugged. "I think he was trying to enlist me in CLAD, or at least convince me their philosophy was right. He said he'd look into it if we helped him break into this Wells Life Sciences facility in Delaware. He thinks something bad is going on there." I looked her in the eye. "He used to be in Chimerica, you know. He said he had told Chimerica about the facility and nothing happened."

"What kind of thing did he say was going on there?"

"Do you know about what happened in Pitman? And Omnicare?"

She nodded solemnly. "Of course I do. And I'm very proud of you for what you did to stop them."

It felt weird to hear her say she was proud of me. It felt good, but I couldn't help bristling a little. Despite all her reasons, I wasn't entirely over the fact that she had abandoned the family, had disappeared from our lives. She had accomplished so much that she deserved to be proud of, but I wasn't sure she deserved the right to be proud of me. "Well, he said whatever was going on there was worse than Pitman or Omnicare."

"Did he say anything else?"

"He said he went to Chimerica with his concerns and they did nothing," I repeated. "Do you know about that?"

She was still for a moment, then she nodded. "I do. And all I can tell you right now is that this is a very delicate situation. The governing council is taking it very seriously."

"The governing council?"

"Our executive board." She took a deep breath and continued. I got the feeling that this was her making an effort not be so secretive. "There are twelve of us, one from each regional division. We deliberate on all major decisions. I serve at-large, the others all lead their divisions. They oversee the twenty-seven training locations around the world, like the one you visited on Lonely Island. Plus all other Chimerica operations. The Mid-Atlantic region would be responsible for the Wells Life Sciences facility in Delaware."

"So, you think there is something going on there?"

"As I said, we are taking it seriously. Did he say anything else?"

I thought back to what Ogden had said about E4E and Chimerica, about the suspicions that they were somehow being funded or controlled by Howard Wells. It made even more sense knowing that the head of the organization, the founder, was at one time extremely close to Wells. I wanted to trust Dymphna, but before I told her more, I had to be sure.

"He said Chimerica and E4E are being funded by Wells."

She shook her head with a wry smile. "That's preposterous."

I shrugged. "Just telling you what he said."

"I oversee all of Chimerica's finances, and I know and trust every member of the governing council, but apart from that, they wouldn't be able to get anything like that past me or past one another. I can tell you, without the slightest uncertainty, that is not the case." She leaned forward. "In fact, we have reason to believe CLAD itself is receiving funds from Wells."

"Really?" I said, unable to keep my doubts out of my voice. The counteraccusation seemed like a tit for tat.

Dymphna ignored my tone, her face gravely serious. "Think about the damage CLAD has done. Think about the wave of anti-chimera fervor they have provoked, wiping out the sympathy generated by what happened in Pitman and Gellersville."

"It wasn't just pro-chimera types killed in that blast, you know. Senior members of H4H's governing board were there, too."

Her eyes flashed. "Yes, moderate voices who were exploring reconciliation and compromise. Think about it: CLAD managed to generate sympathy for Wells and H4H while at the same time purging the few sane voices that might have challenged Wells's extremism."

What she was saying made more sense than the other way around would. And Ogden used to work at Wellplant. Then again, so did Dymphna, more or less.

"Look," she said, "we don't know it for sure, and if there is a connection, CLAD might not even be aware of it. But it's not just a supposition. We have intelligence to support the idea. And it makes sense."

I nodded, conceding the point.

"Was there anything else?" she said, pressing forward.

"Yes," I said, deciding I needed to trust her. "He said something about a plan to take down the Wellplant network, to hit back at Wells that way."

"Hmm." She thought about that for a moment. "That's ambitious. Did he say how?"

"No. I don't know if they even have a plan. Seemed like bluster."

"Probably so. Wellplants use a distributed network. There's no central node, just the individual implants, all networked together in a single powerful array. That makes it very stable, and very powerful. So, when he asked you to go with them to the facility in Delaware, what did you tell him?"

"I said no. I said I couldn't condone what CLAD had done. And the FBI was already suspicious, so the last thing I wanted to do was prove them right."

She reached across the table and put a hand on mine. It was cool and dry and soft, but somehow emanated such strength that I glanced down at it. A faint haze of gray and black hair coated the back. She squeezed my hand and stared into my eyes. "Do you think you might reconsider?"

"*What?*"

"We need to know more about CLAD and what they're up to. What they know and what they are planning to do next."

"Why?" I asked, shaking my head. "Look, I know you two are philosophically opposed or whatever, but I don't want to get drawn into some kind of competition between groups."

She shook her head. "It's not that at all."

"Then what is it?"

"As I said before, that is a longer conversation that I look forward to having with you, but right now, I have to ask you to trust me. I assure you, it is vitally important."

I sat back and looked away, shaking my head. "I don't know," I said. "I wasn't lying when I told Ogden about the FBI, about how I didn't want to be an accessory to CLAD's murders. I wasn't making that up."

"I know," she said, squeezing my hand again. "And I wouldn't ask if this wasn't important. But we've been unable to get inside and determine what they're really up to. You do that, earn their trust and find out what they're doing, and the benefit could be incalculable."

"Why?"

"Because I have some very sensitive, big-picture plans to undermine Wells that CLAD could be putting into serious jeopardy, whether they know it or not." Her voice was calm, but her eyes betrayed her anxiety. "Will you at least consider it?"

I thought for a moment, then nodded again.

"Excellent. I'll look forward to our next conversation, and to answering more of your questions, but meanwhile, you can report back what you learn through Sly."

"If I agree to help."

"If you agree." Then she sat back and seemed to fully relax. Her eyes twinkled. "So. You and Rex. That's terrific."

"Do you know him?"

"We've met briefly. But everyone speaks exceptionally highly of him."

"He's great."

"How long have you two known each other?"

"We met right before Pitman. But as it turns out, we were friends as kids."

"Really?"

"His name was Leo Byron."

She screwed up her face for a moment, thinking, then her eyes went wide. "Wait a second, do you mean the tiny little boy who used to live on your block?"

I nodded and she whipped her head around, looking toward the front of the house, where Rex was waiting with Sly. Trudy had told me Dymphna had been present in my life when I was very young, but I never expected she might have known Leo.

Dymphna shook her head. "Well, I had no idea." She thought for a moment. "And when did he get his splice?"

"Five or six years ago. Why?"

"Wow, he must have been young. I don't know if I can condone getting spliced at such a young age," she said. *And this from the woman who invented splicing*, I thought.

The sparkle in her eyes faded and suddenly she seemed almost cagey. "Do you have any friends who've gotten spliced more recently?"

"Most of them. My friend Claudia got spliced in the fall. Why?"

She relaxed a bit but waved off my question. "Just curious," she said. Then she added quickly, "How about you, have you ever thought about getting spliced?"

"I've thought about it, but so far it hasn't seemed right for me." I shrugged. "Sorry."

"Not at all," she said, shaking her head. "I was just curious. It's a big decision. And it's not for everyone."

Dymphna walked me around to the front of the house, where Sly and Rex were drinking iced tea and catching up. They both shot to their feet when they saw us—or more accurately, when they saw her.

"Sly," she said, dipping her head at him.

He didn't salute, but he might as well have, his body was so rigidly at attention. "Dymphna," he said, dipping his head back at her.

"And Rex," she said, reaching up to squeeze his shoulder. "It's such a pleasure to see you again."

His face blushed slightly as he glanced in my direction. He hadn't told me they had met before, and I guess he was wondering how this was going over. I cocked an eyebrow at him, leaving him wondering.

"Ma'am," he said.

"And apparently we go back a little further than I realized."

He tilted his head. "Ma'am?"

"When Jimi was a preschooler. Before I went away. I remember her little friends. You were the sweetest child."

The blush on Rex's cheeks deepened to a full-on red face. "I...I don't remember..."

"Of course not, honey. You were too young," she said, smiling at him just like Mom and Trudy did. I was worried what would happen if his face got any redder. Sly looked away, biting back a grin.

Dymphna turned back to me. "Jimi, I can't tell you how much it means to me to see you again." She pulled me in and hugged me tightly, then stepped back, holding my shoulders at arm's length. "I'm sorry to say I have to get back to work. But I intend for us to meet again. In the meantime, please think about what we discussed, keep in mind how important it is, and let Sly know what you decide."

Rex gave me a questioning look, but I ignored him for the moment. We would talk in the car.

"Maybe..." I started to say, but suddenly got choked up. I cleared my throat and fought back the emotion. "Maybe while you're still in the area, you could come and see Trudy and my mom."

She smiled, and suddenly she seemed choked up, too. "Sure," she said quietly. "We'll have to be careful, but that would be very...nice."

We hugged once again, then Sly, Rex, and I got back in the van.

Dymphna stood in the driveway, watching us. Sly pulled us up to the pylon and raised the bridge. Rex and I waved through the window and Dymphna waved back.

We drove across, and when we got to the other side I looked back, but she was gone.

FIFTEEN

We pulled up next to the rusty mailbox and when Sly got out to lower the bridge again, Rex turned in his seat. "So? How did it go?"

I shook my head. "It was very, very strange."

"I'll bet."

"She wants me to change my mind about going with Ogden."

"She wants you to *go*?"

I nodded. "She says Chimerica needs to know what CLAD is up to. She wants me to find out. Or us, if you're in."

"If you're in, I'm in. But…are you in?"

"I'm thinking about it," I said, as Sly got back into the car.

"Thinking about what?" Sly asked.

I looked at Rex and he shrugged. I decided then that if we were trusting each other, we were trusting each other. "We met with a guy from CLAD earlier. He wanted us to help him break into one of Wells's Life Sciences facilities. He said there's something bad going on there. We said no."

Sly grunted but didn't say anything.

"Dymphna wants us to change our minds and tell him we'll go," I continued.

Sly nodded. "And you're thinking about it?"

I nodded back.

Rex leaned forward, looking around me at Sly. "Thoughts?"

Sly shrugged. "Well, I don't know Dymphna well, but everything I've seen tells me she's one of the smartest people out there, and everything she does seems to be focused on doing what's best for chimeras, and for the world, really. I've never been much of a follower, but I guess Chimerica has changed that. If Dymphna asks me, I say yes."

As we drove back along the Atlantic City Smartway, we talked it out.

By the time we were halfway back to Pedricktown, the decision had been made. We were going with Ogden.

I spent the rest of the drive thinking about Dymphna. I tried to remember her from when I was little, before she left, before she was spliced, but couldn't conjure any solid memories.

By the time Sly dropped us off at Jerry's truck, it was late in the afternoon. We both hugged Sly before we got in. He thanked us and said he would tell Dymphna our decision, then he got back in the van and drove back the way we'd come.

Rex and I got into the truck, and we headed back to Ogden's house.

The sun was low when we reached Pedricktown. Fiery light bounced off the standing water that surrounded the roads, mirroring the sky. The house looked ominous rising up in front of us, black against the blazing sky.

Ogden came out onto the porch as we approached the steps. "You're back."

"We changed our minds," I said. "We're coming with you."

"Well, alright," he said, opening the door, welcoming us back inside. "You changed your minds just in time," he said, leading us back into the kitchen. "We're doing this tomorrow. I told my people at CLAD you said no, and they're sending some help, but they said we need to act fast because we don't know how long Wells's people are going to be doing whatever it is they're doing."

Rex and I exchanged a glance and a shrug.

Ogden took out a map of Delaware and spread it out on the table. "Here's the facility," he said, pointing at a spot southeast of Wilmington. "Our mission is just to gather information about it. I've driven around it a few times, but we're going to need to get inside, cut through the outer fence that surrounds the entire property."

"What kind of fence is it?" I asked.

Ogden shrugged. "Don't know. Looks like a regular fence."

"Is it electrified or monitored? Barbed wire?"

"Razor wire at the top. I don't know about the rest."

"How are we going to cut through it?"

"We'll have to play it by ear. If it's a smart system, I can hack it."

"You're sure?"

Ogden nodded. "I used to work at Wellplant. It was my first job. They recruited me when I was still at Stanford."

"Right," I said. "Working for Wellplant. So...what's up with that?"

Ogden shrugged. "If you want to work in computer systems, Wellplant is the best of the best. So am I."

"But..." I grasped for words. "Working for Howard Wells?"

Ogden laughed. "I know. This was a few years ago, but even then, most of my friends were chimeras. But Wells wasn't such a fanatic yet. Or at least he didn't let on."

"This was before you got spliced?"

Ogden laughed. "Oh, yeah. You'd never get hired at Wellplant Corporation if you had a splice. But I'd been thinking of getting one. So when Wells started getting into all this BS with H4H, I quit. That's when I got spliced."

"So what if it's not a smart fence?" Rex said. "What if you can't hack into it?"

He shrugged. "We'll decide how to go when we get there."

I glanced at Rex. He didn't seem happy with Ogden's reply. Neither was I.

"Our friend Claudia is good with security systems," I said, glancing at Rex. He thought for a moment then nodded. "I'd like to invite her along, if she'll come."

"I don't know. This is kind of..." Ogden paused. "Wait, do you mean Claudia Bembry?"

I was shocked. "Do you know her?"

"No. I read about her in the news stories about Omnicare." He grinned. "Some people had her pinned as the one who crashed the Smartpike, right?"

I glanced at Rex and he gave his head a tiny shake. Probably wise not to admit to anyone outside our circle of friends that it was Claudia and I who did that.

"No comment," I said.

Ogden laughed. "'No comment,' huh? I hear you. Well, sounds like she has some skills that could come in handy. If you vouch for her, go ahead and ask her." He turned to Rex. "Are you coming?"

"Yup."

Ogden nodded. "Okay. With whoever CLAD is sending, that'll make five. That's a lot, but I guess it'll be okay."

We talked logistics and agreed to meet up at eight the next night in South Philly, in the Stadium District, one block west of the Levtrain stop.

By the time we left Ogden's house, the sun was almost down. As we drove down the gravel-and-shell causeway, the water on either side that had been ablaze with orange and red an hour earlier now reflected the cool blue sky overhead.

Rex was quiet as he drove. I knew he wasn't sure about any of this. I wasn't, either.

"Do you think Claudia will come?" he asked.

"If she can, she will. It'd be good to have her along."

He nodded as he turned off the gravel-and-shell road and onto firmer land. We stayed quiet as he zigged and zagged his way back to the Smart-route. As we were crossing the bridge back to Philadelphia, I turned to him. "So you met Dymphna before?"

He took a deep breath and let it out, like he had known this question was coming and he'd been dreading it.

"I met her once," Rex said. "Briefly. While I was training with Chimerica." He glanced at me. "Sorry, I would have told you if I could. Technically, I'm probably still not supposed to, but…seems kind of silly now."

"I understand," I said. "Hard to know what's silly these days."

SIXTEEN

Rex wanted to drive me all the way home, but I insisted he drop me off at the Levline station. When I got home, I found a note from my mom on the fridge. She and Trudy had gone to a lecture, but there were leftovers if I wanted them. I opened the fridge and found a container of lentil stew. Not my favorite. Peeling up the lid, I spotted a dozen pieces of cooked celery, and that was just on the surface. Who knows how many were hiding underneath?

No thank you.

I grabbed a box of mac and cheese from the cupboard and was reading the directions—as if I didn't know them by heart—when the phone rang.

I picked it up and said, "Hello?"

"*Jimi!*" Claudia's voice said brightly on the other end. I smiled at the sound of it.

"Hey!" I said.

"I'm so glad you're okay!"

"I'm fine, totally. It's been a crazy couple of days, though. How are you doing? I feel like we haven't talked in weeks."

"I'm fine." Something about her voice seemed strange.

"You sure?" I asked.

"Yeah, why?"

"I don't know. You sound a little off."

She took a breath, then sighed. "Hold on a second."

I could hear the muffled, hollow plastic *doink* of the phone being jostled or juggled, banging on something, then footsteps followed by a door opening and then clicking shut.

"Sorry," she said. "Such a big house, you wouldn't think it was so hard to get a little privacy."

"What's going on?"

"I'm fine. Really. But…I'm not so sure about my dad."

I thought back to how weird he'd sounded on the phone when I called. "What's wrong?"

"Remember a few months ago, I told you he was thinking of getting spiked?"

"Tell me he didn't!"

"He did. Last week."

"What the hell was he thinking?" Apart from Wellplants being intrinsically tied to Howard Wells, getting spiked was a big deal, and it wasn't something you could easily change your mind about. Wellplant Corporation didn't like to talk about it, but the fine-print warnings clearly stated that removing a Wellplant could be much riskier and more dangerous than putting one in. And the longer it was implanted, the more time the brain had to integrate it, and the more problematic removal could be.

"He was thinking he needed access to the most powerful tech out there, that he didn't want to get left behind. More and more of his competitors are getting them, and he wanted to literally be connected to the data he needs to run his business, to global intel and secure communications and advanced medical diagnostics and all the rest of it." She paused and took a deep breath. When she resumed, her voice was thick with tears. "But apparently he *wasn't* thinking about how he was buying into a company that profits off murder and oppression, that hopes to define his own daughter as a nonperson."

She paused again, but I sensed she wasn't done, so I stayed quiet. When she spoke again, her voice was back under control. "And he wasn't thinking about how much it might change him."

"So…he seems different, huh?"

"Yeah," she said quietly. "He does. It was a big production, you know? Not just the implantation, but they do all this immune-system prep beforehand, suppressing it, then boosting it. The whole process was intense. But he's over that part now, and still he's…different. A lot more different than I even feared he'd be."

"I spoke to him yesterday, when I called. He did sound…not himself."

"He insists he's fine. Just getting used to it. But I wonder if there's something wrong with it. Or with him."

"What does your mom think?"

"She keeps telling me it's fine. *'If Dad says he's okay, then he's okay.'* But I know she's freaked out, too."

"Eesh." I didn't know what else to say. I wanted to reassure her, but I also didn't want to dismiss her concerns. And it creeped me out *big-time* that her dad had gotten spiked. "Well, maybe he does just need to get used to it. I mean, it's got to be incredibly distracting having all that…stuff, whatever,…all going on inside your head."

"I know. But what if that's just how it is? I mean, he's very distractible. What if he's just always distracted like that from now on?"

"Then that would suck."

"Yeah." Claudia sighed. "Anyway, I need to get out of the house. Have you eaten?"

"No, I just got home."

"How about I take you out to dinner?"

"Sure, that would be great. Actually, I need to ask you about something. Are you busy tomorrow night?"

"Tomorrow? No, I don't think so. Why?"

"I'll tell you in person."

"Okay, cool. I'll pick you up in twenty minutes."

— — —

Claudia was loaded. And I was not. I usually paid my own way when we went out together, but sometimes she insisted on paying—especially if she insisted on going somewhere expensive—and sometimes I let her.

I put the mac and cheese back in the cupboard and ran upstairs to get ready, then left a note on the fridge: WENT OUT WITH CLAUDIA. I drew a heart for good measure.

Twenty minutes later, Claudia's Jaguar pulled up in front of my house. As I ran down the front steps and got in, I couldn't help wondering if my mom, wherever she was, had at that moment paused and looked off into space, knowing that her daughter was in some way disappointing her and failing to meet her expectations.

"Hey!" Claudia said as I got into the car.

"Hey," I said, hurrying to get my seatbelt on before the car reached its cruising speed.

As soon as we had pulled away from the curb and were in our lane of traffic, she flipped the switch to activate Smartdrive and wrapped me in a big hug. "It's really good to see you, Jimi," she said. "I was so worried when I heard about the bombing."

"I'm fine," I said, as we pulled apart. "But it was really messed up."

She put her hand on the wheel but didn't take the car out of Smartdrive. "Okay," she said. "Tell me all of it."

I did not. But I told her a lot. I told her about being abducted by CLAD, and then arriving at the museum just before the bombing. I told her about spending the night at Rex's—and about telling my mom that I was spending the night at Rex's.

That earned a look that made me simultaneously proud and ashamed.

"What?" I demanded in response. "She knows. She's known for months. It wasn't that big a deal."

Claudia was struggling so hard not to laugh, I was worried we were going to crash, even with the car in Smartdrive. "And if I asked your mom if it was a big deal, she'd say the same thing?"

She lost her struggle after that, and so did I, the two of us laughing like hyenas as the car took us unerringly to our destination. I love Claudia.

The conversation got pretty serious after the laughter at my mom's expense. We talked about things with Rex, which were all good, then we talked more about her dad, which was not good at all.

The conversation trailed off after that, a somber quiet that lingered until we got to our destination.

"The Mayfair Diner!" I laughed, as we pulled into the parking lot. "Oh, man, I remember coming here when I was a little kid." The Mayfair Diner was this amazing classic diner a few miles away in Northeast Philly.

"Right?" Claudia said, laughing, as well. "My dad used to take me here all the time." Her eyes fell a bit when she mentioned him again, the worry in them obvious.

"He'll be okay," I said, hopefully with just enough conviction that she'd take some comfort from it, but not so much that she'd never again take seriously anything else I said.

She nodded as we got out of the car. "I hope so."

"So, when you first told me he was thinking of getting spiked, you said he wanted you to get a Wellplant, too—if he did it."

She nodded. "Yeah, and my mom, too. So we could stay connected." The car locked with a beep behind us. "I'll admit, I thought about it for a minute. I mean, it would be cool to be connected all the time, to have access to all that information and resources and stuff, but I couldn't get used to the idea of having a spike in my head, especially not one manufactured by Howard Wells, not after seeing what they're willing to do to get what they need to make them. I tried to talk him out of it, too, you know? But…I guess I couldn't convince him. Maybe everything'll be great in a few days, but from what I've seen so far, I doubt it."

The diner was mostly empty. We took a booth in the front and Claudia grabbed the menus from behind the napkin dispenser and tossed one to me.

"It's good to be out of the house," she said.

She glanced at her menu, then nodded and tossed it aside, staring at me over the table. "You said you had something you needed to talk about. What's up?"

The menu was stupid long—like a good diner menu should be—and I'd barely had time to look at the front page. "You already know what you're getting?"

"Psh." She snapped her fingers. "Tuna melt. That's *actually* why we're here."

The server arrived and Claudia said, "Tuna melt and an iced tea, please," then looked at me expectantly with innocent eyes and a smirk that was just this side of evil.

"I…" I started to say I needed more time. Then I saw BREAKFAST ALL DAY plastered across the top of the menu. "Two eggs over, rye toast, veggie scrapple, and home fries." I started to hand over my menu, then I added, "And orange juice, please."

Claudia grinned. "You've always been good under pressure, Jimi." As the server took our menus and disappeared, her face turned serious. "Okay. What did you want to ask?"

First, I resumed the chronology of recent events, picking up with the brawl after Wells announced his presidential campaign, then the second visit from the FBI and their questions about me and CLAD. Claudia was duly creeped out that the FBI had found a photo of me at the CLAD house they raided. I told her how Rex and I had decided I needed to find out what that connection was before the FBI did.

"So, here's where it gets really weird," I told her softly, looking around to make sure no one was close enough to listen in.

I quietly told her about Rex recognizing Ogden's picture, and about us meeting with him.

She gasped. "You went there? How did that go? What did you find out?"

"Not much, actually. He didn't know why CLAD might be interested in me, but he told us about this Wells Life Sciences facility, where he thinks something bad is going on. He wanted us to help him break in and check the place out."

"Are you serious?" she said, her voice getting louder before she quieted it down again. "He wants you to join CLAD?" she whispered.

"No, not exactly. I think he wants to sway me to their point of view."

"I hope you told him no with great certainty."

"Well, yeah, I did....At first."

"At first!? Jimi—"

I held up a hand to stop her. "There's more," I told her.

She folded her arms and closed her mouth, waiting impatiently for me to finish so she could continue getting on my case.

I had already decided that if I was going to ask her to help us, I needed to tell her everything that was going on—and there was already some information that I'd kept from her. Technically, I was not a member of Chimerica, even though it was starting to feel like the family business. I hadn't signed anything or been sworn in or had an induction ceremony or anything like that. And I hadn't been sworn to secrecy, or even asked to keep secrets. It had been explained to me—often, if inadequately—how important secrecy was to Chimerica, but no one had asked me to keep secret what I had learned in the last few days.

"Okay," I said, leaning forward and inducing her to do the same. "Remember a few months ago, how much it was bothering me that Rex was being cagey about where he was disappearing to and what he was doing?"

"I remember you mentioning it once or twice. Daily."

"Yeah, well, eventually he shared a few things with me, secrets that I then had to keep, and that I did."

"Go on."

"Remember how I found out I had an aunt who was also named Dymphna?"

She nodded.

"Well, it turns out, she's in charge of Chimerica."

"What do you mean? Like, the executive director or something?"

"I don't know about her job title, but yes. She started it. She's the head honcho."

She sat back and laughed. "Man, Jimi, whenever I get upset that my family is messed up, you do help put it in perspective."

"My family's not messed up."

She laughed even louder at that.

"Okay, whatever," I went on, trying to keep my voice low and talk over her laughter at the same time. "So hold that thought about Dymphna. After we told the CLAD guy no, we left. As we're leaving his neighborhood, who shows up to intercept us, but Sly."

"Sly! Wow, haven't seen him in a while. How's he doing?"

"He's fine. Anyway, he takes us to this, like, secret safe house or whatever, down the shore. He says it's important but won't tell us what's going on. But we get there, and Dymphna's there."

"Your *aunt*?"

"Yes. The head of Chimerica."

"Whoa. So how was that?"

"It was really, really weird. She's amazing, but the whole situation was bizarre."

"What did she say?"

"We talked for a while. We talked about family stuff. She told me some of what she'd been up to, back then and more recently. Get this: apparently, she used to go out with Howard Wells."

Claudia clapped a hand over her mouth. "Are you serious?"

I nodded. "Years ago."

"No, you're family's not messed up at all."

"Shut up. Anyway, here's the thing. She asked me to tell Ogden, the CLAD guy, that we'd help him break into the Wells facility. She's concerned about what CLAD is up to, and she wants us to try to get closer to them, so we can find out."

"What did you tell her?"

"Well, I told her that the FBI was already harassing me because they think I'm involved in CLAD and the last thing I wanted was to give them any evidence to support that idea or to do anything that would make it true, but…Well, she's pretty persuasive." I shrugged. "I said I'd do it."

"That's crazy."

I steepled my fingers in front of my face, choosing my next words carefully. "So we went back and told Ogden we'd do it. But when he told me about some of the challenges involved in getting onto the property, past the security system or whatever, I realized that we could really use some technical support."

"Technical support?"

I nodded, slowly folding all my fingers except my index fingers, which now pointed at Claudia.

She sat back. "Me?"

I nodded again. "We need to get through a fence, and I don't know how hi-tech it is or whatever, but I was wondering who could possibly help us with that…"

She started shaking her head. "Jimi, I don't think—"

"Who would be badass enough, game enough, to help out with something like that…"

"Jimi—"

"And who would be fun to have along? I mean, it would be just like old times, right?" By "old times" I was referring to the events in Gellersville a few months earlier.

She tilted her head to one side and rolled her eyes. "I don't think so, Jimi. I've actually been trying to cut back on the 'breaking-and-entering-and-risking-life-limb-and-jail-time' stuff. Especially while all this stuff is going on with my dad."

"Okay," I said. "I get it. And besides, this guy Ogden says he can hack into the system if it's a smart fence. I imagine if it's just like, electrified or alarmed or video-monitored, or whatever, he can deal with that, too."

"Jimi, those are totally different challenges. Totally different skill sets."

"Right, I know, but hacking a computer system has got to be more involved than bypassing simple electronics."

"It's not a matter of simpler or more involved, they're just different," she said, getting herself oddly worked up about it. "It's not just about snipping a wire or two, for Pete's sake."

"Okay, okay," I said. "Point taken. But whatever the case, I'm sure we'll be fine without you. I just thought it would be good to have you there, that's all. But I totally understand—"

"I know what you're trying to do, and it's not going to work."

"What do you mean?"

"Reverse psychology or whatever it is you're doing."

"I'm not!" I said, laughing a little. "Look, I totally understand. You don't want to go. I totally respect that."

She looked over at the server, headed our way with our orders.

"When are you going?"

"Tomorrow night."

She growled as she shook out her napkin and laid it across her lap. "Okay, well it sounds like I better come along so this Ogden guy doesn't get you all fried to a crisp."

SEVENTEEN

The next night, I was eating dinner with my mom when Claudia arrived to pick me up. Mom insisted on serving her a plate, pasta primavera with basil, and made her sit with us while we finished. My mom likes Claudia, but I think she's confused by her, so she always welcomes the chance to pepper her with questions about her life.

I looked down, smiling at my dinner through the worst of it, thinking maybe it'll teach Claudia not to show up fifteen minutes early. When Mom and I finished eating, and Claudia finished pushing around the food on her plate because she had already had dinner, I announced that I was running upstairs to get ready and I'd be down in a minute. Claudia announced that she was coming with me, I think having had enough of my mom's questions.

"Ugh, she's worse than the FBI," Claudia said, closing my bedroom door and slumping against it.

I laughed. "Sorry about that. She means well."

"Hey, when we're done with this tonight, you want to come back and crash at my house?"

"What, like a sleepover?"

She laughed. "Sure, why not? We can make popcorn and paint each other's toenails."

"Weirdo."

"No, come on, it'll be fun."

She laughed again as she said it, but there was a pleading quality, as well.

"Sure," I said. "Why not?"

I grabbed a few things to spend the night, and on our way out I told my mom where I was staying.

After a minor grilling about whether I had any obligations in the morning—I didn't—and an admonishment not to stay up all night, she said, "Okay, have fun."

We picked up Rex a bit before eight and got to South Philly twenty minutes later. The roads were packed and so were the sidewalks, everybody walking in the same direction. We drove around for ten minutes before we found a parking spot.

"What the hell is this all about?" Rex asked as we got out of the car.

Claudia looked around, bewildered, as she pulled a backpack out of the trunk. "I have no idea. The Phillies are on the road...maybe it's a concert?"

"*Mixie trash!*" someone yelled.

We couldn't see who had said it, but Claudia held up her hand, clenched into a fist except for a lone finger that stood out among the others.

"Disgusting," said a woman with shellacked gray hair, shaking her head. I couldn't tell if she was referring to Claudia's gesture, or the fact that she and Rex were chimeras.

"Great," Rex mumbled as we fell into step with the rest of the crowd. His eyes scanned the people around us, as if he was assessing the threat each of them posed, trying to determine who he had to be most wary of.

We turned the corner, onto the block where we were supposed to be meeting Ogden. Up ahead, the massive Holotron in front of the arena lit up the sky with, PHILADELPHIA WELCOMES HUMANS FOR HUMANITY! ENJOY YOUR JAMBOREE!

It was unsettling to think that the H4H jamboree was too big even for the massive Convention Center, and they had to hold it in the basketball arena, instead. And I knew the welcome probably came with the venue rental, but it bugged me that a city that was supposed to be all about "brotherly love" would be welcoming a group that was so decidedly not.

"Ugh," Claudia muttered. "Well, that explains a lot. Whose idea was it to meet here?"

"Ogden," Rex said.

Claudia rolled her eyes at me. "Well then, I guess it *is* a good thing I'm here. And what the hell is a jamboree, anyway?"

"It's like a party," Rex said. "Apparently a big party."

"Huh. And I didn't even get an invitation."

The upside of everyone walking in the same direction we were was that at least we didn't have to deal with people coming toward us the opposite way. The downside was that we got stuck walking alongside the same people.

One guy muttered, "Mixie scum," and then we were stuck walking next to him for the next block and a half.

Ahead of us, a white van flashed its headlights. As we got closer, I could see Ogden behind the wheel. It looked very much like the van I had been abducted into just a few days earlier. If I hadn't known that van was being held by the FBI, I would have wondered if it was same one.

As we got closer, Ogden lowered his window and said, "Y'all should probably get in the back, so it looks like I'm riding alone. Just in case anybody ends up looking for us later."

We nodded and walked around to the passenger side.

Having seen what could happen when a bunch of overly exuberant H4Hers got together, I was relieved no violence had broken out so far. I was looking forward to getting off the street, but when the door slid open, all three of us paused. I may have even taken a step back. I was at a total loss for words. So was Claudia.

Rex didn't do a whole lot better. All he could manage to say was, "*Roberta?!*"

Claudia and I had met Roberta that winter at a Chimerica training outpost called Lonely Island. It had been a strange situation. One minute, Claudia and I were being chased across Pennsylvania by Howard Wells's thugs, then next minute we were being whisked to safety by Chimerica operatives—Sly and Roberta—who took us to this tiny, snow-covered Canadian island in Lake Huron. I was grateful at first, until the Chimerica people informed me I had to stay there. Which I had no intention of doing. It was an incredibly awkward few hours, but the worst part by far was Roberta, who was an antagonistic, belligerent bully, especially toward me, because I wasn't spliced.

Rex hadn't been there with me at the time, but I knew he'd been to the island before, and apparently he knew Roberta from his previous visits.

Except now, apparently, she was with CLAD, and not Chimerica.

"Hey, Rex," Roberta replied, as he climbed past her. There were two bench seats in the back. She sat in the one closest to the front. She looked the same as the last time we had seen her: big and strong, with coarse fur from a black-bear splice that brought out both the paleness of the skin underlying it and the unpleasantness of her personality. She was even wearing the same tactical black as the last time we had seen her.

She curled her lip at Claudia, then turned to me and said, "Hey, Nonk."

Rex caught my eye with a questioning look.

"Oh, great," said a stranger on the sidewalk behind us. "Now there's a whole van full of them."

"You folks know each other?" Ogden called out to us from the driver's seat. "That's great, but you can catch up on the way. We need to get out of here."

"I'm not getting in there with her," Claudia said.

I felt the same way, but this was too important to get hung up on the fact that Roberta was an absolute jerk and I despised her.

I let out a sigh and climbed in.

"Jimi, seriously?" Claudia called after me.

"In or out, kitty cat," Roberta said. "Out's fine with me, but either way, I'm closing the door."

Claudia growled and climbed in, squeezing into the rear seat with Rex and me rather than sitting with Roberta.

"You didn't tell me this part," Claudia said in a loud whisper.

"I didn't know!" I replied.

"How do you know each other?" Rex asked.

"Lonely Island," I told him.

"Oh. Right."

Roberta looked at Rex. "So you finally came to your senses and left Chimerica, huh?" she said. "Better late than never, I guess."

He shook his head. "I'm still with Chimerica."

"I guess they kicked you out?" I said to her. "Because of your bad attitude and being an asshole and everything?"

Claudia snorted. "Or was it for sleeping on the job?"

Roberta's face turned a deep red. The last time we had seen her, she was sleeping off the effects of a dart gun.

"No," she snapped. "I left Chimerica because it's a useless organization filled with nonk-loving apologists who don't know how to fight for people with splices." She glanced at Rex and shook her head.

Claudia turned to me and said, "They totally kicked her out."

"By 'fight for' chimeras, you mean, like, blowing them up?" I said.

She glared at me, then looked away.

I was surprised to see Roberta, but I wasn't shocked she'd been kicked out of Chimerica, or that she had ended up with CLAD. Frankly, it reinforced some of my worst suspicions about CLAD.

Rex stared a question at me, I guess wondering what the animosity was about. I shook my head. I didn't want to explain it in front of Roberta. If he knew her at all, surely, he knew she was a jerk.

Ogden looked back at us, like he was trying to understand the dynamic, as well, but he turned back around when Roberta barked at him, "Just drive."

EIGHTEEN

We took the I-95 Smart-route south into Delaware and exited just past Wilmington, turning onto a series of progressively smaller roads. We drove by a row of tall vertical farms, converted from old office towers, glowing green from the low sunlight shining horizontally through the racks of crops growing inside them. We also passed an energy farm with turbines and solar panels, then the small town that it was powering, little more than a commercial intersection surrounded by a few square blocks of houses, all tied together by a network of old, first-generation super-efficient transmission lines. In Philadelphia and most other places, the Super-E lines were underground, but some of the early adopters had simply installed them where their old lines had been, on utility poles up in the air. The town didn't look like it had ever been particularly scenic, but with the bulky transmission infrastructure, black against the setting sun, it was downright ugly.

Before long, we turned onto a windy and pitted country road, past another small town that at one point had probably looked almost identical to the earlier one, but without the Super-E lines or energy farm. The main drag had a bar, a small grocery store, and a self-serve diagnostic clinic, each with a cluster of solar panels on the roof.

The residential streets leading away from them were gap-toothed where the houses had been torn down. The ones that remained were sagging and slouching in on themselves, clearly abandoned and left to fall apart. A haze of smoke hung in the air from a wildfire somewhere not too far away. Mom told me that when she was a kid, wildfires were unheard of in our region, but now they were a part of summer. The smoke and the fading light combined to make the town even more depressing.

Just past it, we entered an agricultural zone, with rolling farm fields on all sides. A couple of miles later, as the sun finally set, we came to a property surrounded by a tall metal fence.

"This is it," Ogden said, easing off the accelerator.

We had agreed we would circle the property once to get the lay of the land before we tried to enter. According to Ogden's information, there was an outer fence surrounding the entire property, then an inner fence around the facility itself.

We drove for what seemed like miles, up and down over the rolling landscape, the fence extending on and on beside us, rising and falling with the road. When the fence veered left, we did, too, following it for another long stretch before we saw a crossroad up ahead, bathed in dim artificial light.

A pair of large gates, an entrance and an exit, flanked a guard booth set in the median between them. To the right was a large sign that said WELLFOOD PROTEIN SERVICES–POULTRY DIVISION. Underneath it said SECURE FACILITY: NO UNAUTHORIZED ENTRY.

We didn't slow as we passed it, but we all craned our necks, studying it as it slipped by then receded behind us.

"Poultry division?" I asked when we were past it. "Howard Wells is doing *food* now?"

Ogden nodded and looked at me in the rearview mirror. "It's supposed to be some kind of chicken processing plant."

"You mean real live chickens or VGP?" Almost all the chicken in grocery stores was Vat-Grown Poultry. Only rich people ate real chicken anymore.

"Real chickens," he said.

I guess if you can afford a Wellplant, you can afford real chicken.

The fence turned to the left again, and we turned along with it, our headlights shining off the undulating ribbon of metal mesh as it stretched into the growing darkness.

Within the fence, there was an expanse of solar panels mounted above waterlogged fields, the glass squares and the standing water reflecting different parts of the sky, different shades of dark blue that both looked strikingly out of place against the darkened ground. The effect was surreal and disorienting, as if the distinction between up and down had become confused, and the sky was both above and below.

An access road ran down the middle of the field of panels, and nestled alongside it in the darkness was an old barn. On the right-hand side of the road, outside the fence, an old farmhouse was collapsing in on itself, surrounded by fields strangled by vines. An overgrown driveway led up from the road and curved around and behind the house.

"We'll park behind that farmhouse," Ogden said.

We turned left again and found ourselves back at the spot where we first came upon the fence.

"Big place," Rex rumbled under his breath.

"Seriously big," Claudia said.

Roberta shrugged, like she wasn't going to concede that. She seemed the kind of person who didn't ever want to concede anything. We doubled back, and Ogden barely slowed down as he jerked the wheel to turn up the driveway and behind the farmhouse.

The sun had completely set. There was still residual light in the sky, but on the ground, it was nighttime. Roberta and Ogden got out. He was a big guy, but Roberta towered over him, a solid column of muscle. Rex and Claudia and I got out, too, and I was hit with a stench so bad it stopped me in my tracks. By reflex, I almost retreated back into the van.

"Ew," Claudia said, pulling her shirt up over her nose. "What's that smell?"

"That would be the chickens," Ogden said, visibly trying not to react to the odor.

Claudia shot me an evil look. "You didn't tell me about that part, either."

I held up my hands, defensively. "I didn't know!" The air was thick with humidity, as well, and the faint whiff of smoke from a brush fire somewhere. Combined, they seemed to make the smell even worse.

Ogden opened the back of the van and pulled out a backpack.

"Can't believe we didn't bring any weapons," Roberta said.

"It's not that kind of operation," Ogden said, sounding like this wasn't the first time they'd had this conversation. "We're just here for reconnaissance. Have a look around and LIDAR-map the exterior, in case another operation is warranted."

He rummaged around in the backpack and pulled out a small container of mentholated ointment. He scooped out a small dollop and rubbed it under his nose. "It helps," he said, offering it around.

Roberta took a dab first and smeared it under her nose, then handed the jar to Rex, who did the same and passed it to Claudia, who passed it to me.

The smell was almost strong enough to block out the stench.

"Are we good?" Ogden asked. We all nodded, but without much enthusiasm. "Okay. The fence looks electrified, but it doesn't look like a smart fence, so we just need to block the charge and get over it. I've got a rubberized mat we can throw over the top and help each other climb over."

"What if it causes a fault?" Claudia asked.

He shook his head. "What do you mean?"

Claudia glanced at me with a barely perceptible head-shake/eye-roll combination. "When one of us climbs over the fence, our bodies will press the wires together. So they're going to touch. Just because it's not a smart fence doesn't mean it's not going to register somewhere that there's a short. That's going to raise suspicions."

Ogden sighed. "Okay, what do you propose we do instead?"

"I brought some gear," Claudia said, holding up a small toolkit. "We can bypass the current along the bottom of the fence and cut a hole."

"You want to cut a hole in the fence?" he said, alarmed. "You don't think that's going to draw some attention?"

Claudia smiled and shook her head. "Not if you do it right. You have to bypass each wire before you cut it."

Ogden looked at me, but I had no idea if she was right or not. I shrugged and said, "If that's what she says."

He let out a sigh. "Okay, what's the plan?"

The plan was for the rest of us to wait behind the house while Claudia discreetly bypassed the current running through the lower levels of the fence and cut a hole big enough for us to slip through. Once inside, we'd make our way to the inner fence and try to get a look at the inner compound, where the chimeras were supposedly being detained. Then we'd assess what was next.

"And then we bust everybody out, right?" Roberta said, her face scrunched up.

Claudia nodded, then seemed to realize she was agreeing with Roberta and stopped.

"*No,*" Ogden said, slicing the air with his hand for emphasis. "Like I said before, we're not here to bust anybody out. Not this time. We're here to map and to confirm they're being held, and that something shady is happening here. Then we'll report it and come back with reinforcements."

Roberta snorted and shook her head. "Sounds like a Chimerica plan to me."

Rex glared at her. "Because it makes sense?"

"Because it's chickenshit," she snapped back.

Claudia laughed. "What better place for a chickenshit plan?"

"Stop it," Ogden said, his voice quiet but sharp. "You all want to bicker, save it for the ride back to Philly." I found Rex's hand in the darkness and gave it a squeeze.

Ogden turned to Roberta. "Are we good?"

Everyone nodded but Roberta, who instead looked off to the side.

Claudia crept down the driveway, looked around to make sure no one was coming, then darted across the road and up to the fence. She knelt down and took off her backpack, and then we saw a faint blue spark, right at the ground. A minute later we saw another, a few inches higher, then another a few inches higher than that.

In minutes, she had cut a flap into the bottom of the fence and rolled it up and secured it, leaving a hole. She brushed herself off and ran back to where we were.

"How did it go?" I asked.

"Good and bad. I got the hole done, but the fence is reinforced with alloy steel that I can't cut through."

"What does that mean?" Ogden asked.

"The hole is barely a foot wide. I don't think Rex and Roberta are going to fit."

"Okay," Ogden said, turning to Rex and Roberta. "I guess you two will have to wait here."

Rex nodded reluctantly but Roberta scoffed. "Just make the hole bigger," she said.

Claudia took a breath and turned to her. "As I just said, I can't. It's alloy steel."

"Well…" Roberta fumed, looking around in the darkness, as if searching for something to say. "If you all can fit, I can fit."

With that she turned and strode down the driveway.

NINETEEN

Roberta!" Ogden called out, part shout and part whisper. *"Get back here!"* She ignored him.

With a growl, he hurried after her, then we all did, staying low and looking around cautiously while Roberta seemed to be making a point of holding her head up high.

We caught up with her just as she reached the fence. The wires had been cut to create a rectangular hole roughly a foot by a foot and a half, and the severed section was rolled up and taped up out of the way. The hole was bordered on all sides by the thick alloy steel cable that reinforced the fence. Each of the snipped electrical wires had been spliced with a generous length of insulated wiring, bypassing the hole.

Rex shook his head. "Not a chance," he said.

"See?" Claudia said.

The hole in the fence was so tiny I had my doubts about whether *I* would even fit through it. Roberta was twice my size, and thickly muscled. But instead of backing down like Rex, she just glared at us, then dropped down onto her stomach and started wriggling through. She got her head in—I didn't think even that was going to happen—but then her shoulders touched the steel cable, eliciting a bright spark, a brief *tzzzk*, and a faint whiff of ozone. She shuddered and pulled back out, glaring up at Claudia.

"Roberta, come on," Ogden said, but she was already trying it again, this time feetfirst.

She got as far as the middle of her thigh before the fence sparked again and she shot back out, cursing under her breath.

"This is ridiculous," Claudia said. "If she keeps sparking it, someone's going to come looking to see what the problem is."

"Roberta, we don't have time…" Ogden began wearily, shaking his head as she flipped onto her stomach and tried to scoot in that way. She moved carefully and made it past her thighs, but I knew there was no way she was going to get much farther than that.

Claudia stamped her foot. "Enough," she said to Ogden. "She's never going to fit. The only thing she's going to accomplish is getting us all caught."

Roberta pushed herself another inch farther, so that the steel cable was digging into her flesh, even as the shocks continued. Finally, with a growl, she clawed her way back out and scrambled to her feet, rubbing her behind and muttering curses.

She put her face right in Ogden's. "They didn't send me along to hide in the shadows," she said, scowling as Claudia dropped to the ground and gracefully slipped through the hole. "They wanted me to go with you in case there's trouble."

Claudia got to her feet on the other side of the fence and said, "Maybe there won't be trouble if you'd just wait back across the road instead of calling attention to us."

"Screw you!" Roberta snapped, stepping up close to the fence to glare at Claudia, who didn't step back.

"Stop it!" Ogden snapped at her through gritted teeth. "This is not the time or the place." He turned to Roberta. "And you're supposed to be here to help me, not cause problems. I'll tell you when I need you. Meanwhile, go back across the street and wait for us there." He looked at Rex. "Both of you." He dropped to the ground and slipped through the fence in a single fluid motion. "Now."

As Roberta stalked off across the street, Rex turned to watch her. Then he turned back and looked down at me.

"You be safe," he said.

I nodded. "I will. Sorry to leave you with Ms. Congeniality over there."

He smiled and nodded as I dropped to the ground and tried to slip through the fence the way Claudia and Ogden had done. Halfway through,

I got zapped on my butt—not as bad as a shock baton, but enough to propel me through the fence.

Luckily, Roberta hadn't seen it, but I heard a snicker anyway and whipped my head around to see Claudia covering her mouth.

"Sorry," she said, as I got up rubbing my stinging behind.

━━ ━━ ━━

Claudia unfurled the rolled-up section of fence, so it hung down more or less in place. Up close, it was obvious it had been cut, but in the darkness, the cuts were invisible from just a few feet away.

Ogden seemed frazzled by the confrontation with Roberta. He took the lead and Claudia and I fell into step behind him.

The terrain was hilly enough that you couldn't see far. We stayed low, walking around the hills instead of over them. Then Ogden whispered, "Wait here."

He climbed one of the hills and dropped into a crouch. He scanned the surrounding area with night-vision binoculars, then backed down the hill and gathered us into a huddle.

"The second fence is about thirty yards ahead," he said quietly. "Beyond it, there's a couple of long, low buildings to the right. Those are the coops, where they keep the chickens. Then there's three other buildings: two basic brick squares that could be anything, and a taller building with corrugated metal walls and lots of smoke stacks and ductwork. I imagine that's some kind of processing facility. And I bet that's where there are chimeras being held prisoner and forced to work. They're probably being housed in one of the brick buildings."

"So what's the plan?" I whispered.

"We just get a little closer, set up the LIDAR, get some good scans from each angle, see if we can get a look at what's going on in there, then we leave."

The LIDAR-mapping camera was about the size and shape of a thick fantasy novel, with an egg-sized dome on the top, and a lightweight tripod on the bottom. Ogden ran back up the hill, raised the tripod into the air for a second, then lowered it and ran back down.

We followed him to the next rise, about forty yards away, and waited while he repeated the maneuver, getting a scan from a slightly different angle that included a small shed with a smokestack. After that, we followed him another forty yards or so, where he did it again, then again forty yards after that.

Halfway around, we crossed a long, illuminated driveway that ran from the gate in the outer fence to a gate in the inner fence. Claudia and I hung way back while Ogden took his time capturing that view with the LIDAR, then we darted across a dark stretch of the driveway and continued on.

As we returned to the spot where we had started, completing the circle, I moved next to Ogden and whispered, "We haven't seen a single person, chimera or otherwise, or any evidence of anyone being held against their will or anything like that."

"I know, it's weird," he said, apparently oblivious to the not-so-subtle accusatory tone in my voice.

"Do you think it's bogus?" Claudia asked. "Bad information?"

Ogden shrugged. "Or maybe we need to dig in a little deeper." He glanced at Claudia. "Maybe get through the next fence and poke around inside."

She shrugged a half-hearted yes, but was clearly unconvinced.

"Okay," I said. "Where?"

"We passed that shack a little ways back, just inside the fence. That should give us some cover. We can cut through there and have a look inside."

I was increasingly concerned about the possible fallout if this was bogus, and getting caught breaking into a facility owned by Howard Wells with a pair of CLAD members. The FBI would be sure I was part of CLAD, and there would be nothing I could do to convince them otherwise. I gave him a dubious look, but I nodded. "Okay."

We doubled back the way we'd come, and after a minute, Ogden crept up one of the hills, then came back down. "Okay, the shed is right there."

We hurried up over the hill and down the other side, right up to the fence, keeping the shed between us and the rest of the compound. We crouched in the shadows at the base of the fence.

"Can you tell what kind it is?" I asked Claudia.

"It doesn't look electrified," she replied. "But I can't tell if it is a smart fence or not. It might be something new." She turned to Ogden. "What do you think?"

He shook his head. "Doesn't look like any smart fence I've seen. I think it's just an old-fashioned chain-link." He reached into his backpack and pulled out a pair of heavy-duty wire cutters.

As he moved to place them over one of the fence wires, Claudia put her hand on his, stopping him. "Whoa, whoa, whoa," she said. "Are you sure? If that's a smart fence and you snip it, they'll be all over us in minutes."

He grinned. "If it was a decent smart fence, they'd be here already from the heat and motion sensors."

Then another voice said, "Hey, who are you?"

We jumped at the sound and looked up to see a slight, shadowy outline, a young guy who looked like he had a bird splice. His eyes were large and far apart, like an owl, and he seemed to move easily through the darkness. He was carrying two bulging trash bags.

"We're here to save you," Ogden said without hesitating.

"To save me?" the guy laughed. "Awesome! Save me from what?"

"From this place," Ogden said, standing and stepping closer to the fence. "We're going to get reinforcements and break you out. You and the others." He peered over the kid's shoulder. "How many others are there?"

The kid put down the bags and looked behind him. "There's about twenty, twenty-five of us, I guess. But what do you mean 'break us out'? I mean, I'd love to get the hell out of here, but would we still get paid?"

"Paid?" I said, stepping up to the fence, as well. "You're getting paid?"

He studied me in the darkness. "Wait a second, are you from corporate?"

I realized he was suspicious because I wasn't a chimera. "No," I said. "We're not from corporate."

"Okay." Then he laughed. "And of course we get paid. Jeez, you think I'd be lugging these around for fun?"

I looked at Ogden, but he ignored me. "We were told chimeras were being held here," he said. "Against their will. Like prisoners."

He shrugged. "Well, kind of, I guess. You sign an eight-week contract, you're not allowed to leave until it's done, but you know how it is these days. Just glad to have a job. Even at a crazy place like this."

"Crazy how?" Ogden asked.

He stepped closer to the fence. "All sorts of crazy," he said, lowering his voice. "I mean, I don't know what they're up to, but this place is *weird*."

Ogden glanced at me as if he felt vindicated. Maybe there was something here after all. "In what way?" he asked.

The kid looked behind him, then looked back. He raised the trash bags. "Look, I need to dispose of these and get back or I'm going to get in trouble." He nodded at me. "You're sure she's not from corporate, right? This isn't some kind of trick?"

"Are you kidding?" I laughed. "I'm seventeen years old."

"We're just here to make sure you're all okay," said Ogden. "To help."

The kid nodded. "Okay, well look, I'm about to get off, and then I'll be at The Dive, if you want to talk."

"The Dive?" I said. "Where's that?"

He smiled. "That's just what we call it. There's a power farm on the eastern side of the property, two fields of panels."

Ogden nodded. "We saw it."

"Between the two fields, kind of underneath the panels, there's an old barn. We sneak through the inner fence and hang out there sometimes." He opened a door in the shed. "I can meet you there in twenty minutes."

As he turned away from us, Claudia asked, "What's in the bag?"

"Dead chickens," he said, shaking his head. "We go through a lot of dead chickens."

TWENTY

The Dive wasn't far from where we were, or where we had come in, but between the darkness and the rolling terrain, it took fifteen minutes to get there. The sky was now dark except for the stars. Walking between the puddles reflecting the sky, seeing the stars below our feet, I felt a mild sense of vertigo that was only slightly eased as each step sent ripples across the nearby water.

I was just getting used to the sensation when we entered the power farm itself, row after row of solar panels. The barn soon appeared ahead of us—a low, slouching lump of shadow on a dirt road that had been invisible until we stepped onto it. To our left, the road led to the outer fence, and to our right it slanted across the solar farm into the distance.

We had to circle the barn once to find the door. When we opened it, Claudia turned on her flashlight and swept the interior, revealing a couple of crates around a makeshift table made from planks and cinderblocks.

"I know it's not much to look at but, well, it's not much to look at," said a voice behind us. We turned to see the kid from before, smiling and flanked by two others. They also had bird splices. "I'm Earl," he said. "This is Melanie and Hitchcock."

Ogden introduced himself, then so did Claudia and I.

Earl nodded for a moment, then edged past us through the open door of the barn and said, "Come on in."

He pulled a string inside the door, illuminating the interior of the barn with a dull orange glow. I saw that Melanie was carrying a sack, similar to the ones Earl had been carrying before, but not as full.

"So, you told Earl you're here to help us," Melanie said. "Who are you?"

"And how did you get in?" Hitchcock added.

"We cut through the fence," Ogden said. "We're from CLAD."

"CLAD? So, what, are you going to blow the place up?" Earl said, prompting the other two to laugh.

Hitchcock cackled. "Please! Not until after I get paid!"

"*Some* of us are from CLAD," I said. "But we're all concerned with what's going on here." I looked at each of them. "So…what *is* going on here?"

Melanie put the bag on the floor and opened it to reveal a chicken carcass. "Chickens," she said. "Sick chickens. And lots of them."

Claudia wrinkled up her face in disgust. I might have done the same.

"Chickens?" Ogden said, cocking his head as if to ask if there was more to that story.

"Yeah. Lots of them," Earl said. "They have us in there feeding them, watering them, cleaning up. They pay us okay, or they will, but it's not pleasant work."

"It's depressing as hell," said Hitchcock.

"Because of the conditions?" I asked.

"And because the birds be dying all the time," he replied. "It's sad."

Melanie nodded in agreement. "It is. And it's weird because we take pretty good care of them, and we monitor their health closely."

Earl laughed. "But not as closely as the bosses monitor us." The other two laughed, as well.

"What does that mean?" I asked.

Earl waved his hand dismissively. "It's nothing. Inside joke."

"Our employers just seem weirdly concerned about our wellbeing, is all," said Hitchcock. "They give us, like, a two-minute physical a couple times a day: pulse, blood pressure, temperature. And in the morning, they take height and weight, too."

"Well, it's not *just* us," Melanie said. "They do it to the nonk staff, too."

"But not the senior staff," Earl added.

Melanie shrugged. "They probably do it to them where we don't see. In the offices or something. Plus, all the senior staff are Plants. I heard the new-version

Wellplants run constant diagnostics. So I bet they don't have to take their temperature or whatever, because it's already being uploaded automatically."

"That makes sense," Earl said. "Maybe that's what's going on when they zone out."

"Zone out?" Claudia asked, her eyes intent on Earl.

Hitchcock glanced at Earl, then said, "The last week or so, all the senior staff, they'll come into the coops to take readings or whatever, or even if they're just out and about, sometimes they just seem to stop all of a sudden, stare off into space. I mean, they're probably like, reading their mail or whatever, but the shit is creepy."

"It *is* creepy," Melanie said. "Sometimes they're like, in the middle of a sentence or something, then they're just…gone. Somewhere else."

"At least they seem happier now," Hitchcock said.

"You mean your bosses?" I asked.

"Yeah, the folks running the place," Melanie said. "When we first started working here, what's it been, a month or so? All of them seemed really stressed out."

"I think they were overworked," Earl said.

"Are you kidding me?" Hitchcock shot back with a laugh. "They hardly do anything, as far as I can tell. How could they be overworked?"

"Yeah, I know," Earl said. "But as soon as they brought in the extra help, the bosses started to finally relax a little."

"Which makes no sense, because the newbies hardly do anything, either," Melanie said. "They're so damn sick all the time."

"I know, how about that, right?" Hitchcock laughed. "We're doing all the work and they're the ones getting sick. And right away, too. I would have thought they was faking it if they didn't look so terrible."

"Sick how?" I asked.

Melanie shrugged. "Just sick. You know, coughing and sneezing, aches and pains, upset stomach, fever. But even the ones who aren't sick hardly do anything."

Earl shook his head. "Right? And the bosses don't even ask them to." He turned to us. "Like I said. It's a weird place."

"And you're not allowed to leave?" Ogden said. "Isn't that what you said? What's up with that?"

Earl and Hitchcock looked at each other and shrugged. Melanie looked away.

"That's just the deal," Earl said.

Hitchcock nodded. "That's the deal going in. They said they need us to commit for eight weeks, no leaving the facility. But the pay is alright. They gave us five hundred up front, and the rest when we're done. Plus, it ain't like I got anywhere else I got to be, so…"

"But you're working for Howard Wells, the biggest chimera-hater in the world," Ogden said. "Doesn't that bother you?"

"Hey, screw you," Hitchcock said, bristling. "Just 'cause I got spliced don't mean I don't gotta eat. You do what you gotta do."

"But it's not just the H4H stuff, right?" Claudia said. "Did you hear about what happened at Omnicare? At Pitman? How do you know something like that isn't going down here?"

Hitchcock shook his head, dismissively. "Yeah, I heard about that. Not sure I believe it all. But this isn't like that. My cousin did a gig here. Eight weeks, got his five hundred up front, cash, and the rest at the end. He said it sucked, but when he was done, he went on his way with money in the bank. So that's what I'm going to do. Besides, it's just chickens."

"But they are up to something, though," Melanie said without looking at anybody.

"What do you mean?" I asked.

"I mean they're raising all these chickens, and the bosses don't seem to be doing anything with them. They're just keeping them. The chickens hardly lay eggs, and they don't seem to be selling them for the meat. They don't even seem to be experimenting on them. They just… keep them."

Hitchcock looked like he was struggling not to roll his eyes. "She thinks they're working on some kind of secret plan."

"Wellfood is owned by Wells Life Sciences," she said. "They're not keeping these chickens as pets."

"What do *you* think they're up to?" I asked.

She shook her head. "I have no idea. But I don't think the change in the bosses' mood has anything to do with their workload."

"What do you mean?" I asked.

"Well, like I said, this isn't a chicken farm. There's too much money involved, too many Plants in white coats monitoring everything, so they're up to something else. And they really did seem frustrated before, like whatever they're trying to accomplish just wasn't working, you know? And since they started bringing in those nonks onto the custodial staff, I mean, it's no joke, those guys are actually sick *all* the time, so they're basically paid to do nothing, as far as I can tell."

"Well, for as long as they're here," Earl said. "Lately they only seem to stick around for a day or two."

"Exactly," she said. "Apparently, they don't have to make the same time commitment as the chimeras. But even so, it seemed like once they came on board, the bosses got happy. Like they'd figured out whatever the problem was and fixed it."

Earl nodded. "Yeah, I got that sense, too."

"Any idea what the problem was?" I asked.

They all shook their heads.

"At first I thought maybe it was about the chickens getting sick and dying all the time," Melanie said. "But they're still getting sick."

The barn went quiet for a few moments, then Earl said, "We should get back to the bunk house before they come looking for us. And you folks should get out before anyone realizes you're here. I don't know how you got through the fence undetected, but they're serious about security. If they find you, they're going to come down pretty hard."

Ogden nodded. "What about you, though? What happens after your eight weeks are up?"

Hitchcock shrugged. "I told you. They pay us what they owe us."

"They said they might offer us another eight weeks, or they might not," Earl added. "They'll let us know when we were done."

"Would you take another eight weeks?" Claudia asked, not quite hiding the judgy tone in her voice.

Melanie hefted the sack with the chicken carcass. "Look," she said. "I'm only here because I really need the money. I hate working for Howard Freaking Wells, and I don't know what they're up to here, but...something's not right." She held out the sack. "If you're looking into it, maybe a sample might be helpful."

Ogden reached out to take it, but my hand got there first.

"Thanks," I said. "It might."

We filed out of the barn and Earl made sure we knew where we were, where we were going. We turned to go our separate ways, but then I stopped and turned back, suddenly struck by a curious question.

"Hey, can I ask you all something?" I called out.

They stopped and turned back, and Claudia and Ogden paused, waiting for me.

"You all have bird splices. Do all the chimeras here have bird splices?"

They were quiet for a moment, then Melanie said, "Yeah, actually. Never thought of it, but I suppose they do. Why?"

I shrugged. "Chickens are birds, too. Does it bother you, especially, seeing them cooped up, so many of them dying?"

Hitchcock laughed. "Hawks eat chickens. Owls do, too." He shrugged. "Frankly, chickens are pretty dumb. But they are tasty."

Earl snickered at that. Melanie looked away, vaguely disgusted.

We thanked them for the information, and they thanked us, laughing, for trying to save them. Then, they turned and headed back to their hole in the inner fence and we made our way back to the hole Claudia had made in the outer fence.

With the hilly terrain, I couldn't see where we were going, but just as I was figuring we had to be getting close, I saw a pulse of red and orange lights reflected in the sky.

"Hold on," I said.

Ogden said, "What the hell is that?"

"That's what I was afraid of," Claudia said. "Thanks a lot, Roberta."

TWENTY-ONE

Peeking over the next rise, we saw a pair of private security vehicles approaching slowly along the inside of the fence to our left, sweeping it with mounted spotlights and heading toward our escape hole.

"Dammit," Claudia muttered. "Roberta drew them here. They're going to find that hole, and then we're screwed."

The hole was practically invisible in the darkness, but those spotlights were bright. If one of them even got close to it, security would see it for sure.

"What are we going to do?" I asked.

"We need to cause some kind of diversion," Claudia said.

Ogden opened his mouth to speak, but his face didn't show much confidence in whatever he was about to propose. Before he could say anything, though, a sharp but distinct *zzzzap* rose to our right.

Both spotlights jerked toward the sound, slashing into the night. We turned to see what they were aiming at, but my attention was snagged, just for an instant, by the rough edges and slack wires as the light swept past our hole. Then another light appeared way down on the fence line, an angry orange ball of fire, bright enough to cast shadows even where we were.

Instinctively, we flattened ourselves to the ground.

"Well, there's your diversion," I whispered, as the security vehicles sped right past our hole and toward the fire.

We watched as they dwindled in the distance, then Ogden said, "Let's go."

I reached the fence first and slipped through the hole. Apparently I'd learned my lesson on the way in, because I managed to get through without a spark. I held the cut section out of the way as Claudia and Ogden slithered through.

Down the fence line, the fireball had subsided and was now just fire, a large, flaming tree branch lying across the fence. I smiled, knowing that Rex was almost surely responsible.

We dashed across the road and up the driveway next to the old farm-house. But when we reached the van parked in the back, there was no sign of Rex or Roberta.

"Where the hell are they?" Ogden asked in a hoarse, exasperated whisper, his head jerking around as he looked for them.

I was about to point out that they had probably just caused the diversion that allowed us to escape, when I heard a distant crashing, thrashing sound, quickly drawing nearer.

"Start the van," I said. "Turn it around."

Ogden nodded and hit the start button, but kept the lights off. Claudia and I got out of the way as he pulled it around in a tight three-point turn. Rex and Roberta burst through a curtain of vines, both of them running flat out.

Claudia and I scrambled into the back of the van just before Rex and Roberta did.

"Go! Go! Go!" Rex shouted as soon as he was inside.

Ogden hit the accelerator, spraying dirt and gravel high enough that I could hear it raining down onto the vines behind us. We lurched when we hit the bottom of the driveway, then he cut the wheel hard. The tires screeched as they grabbed the road surface.

From down by the fire, about a quarter mile down the road, the two spotlights swung toward us, momentarily painting the van's windows with overlapping shadows of the fence pattern. The security vehicles took off after us, their headlights flickering through the fence as they sped along it.

"They're coming after us," Rex announced.

"Inside the fence or outside?" Ogden called back.

"Inside, for now," I said. "The entrance is on the far side of the property. We should be okay."

"Unless they radioed ahead and they have people waiting for us," Claudia said. "Like the cops."

The headlights were getting brighter and closer.

"They're catching up," I said.

I knew from firsthand experience that fences could be driven through.

The security vehicles were relatively small, little more than armored golf carts, but with enough speed, they might be able to punch through the alloy steel. They could also start shooting—which would be an extreme reaction, especially since they had no idea who we were or what we were up to, but they worked for Wells, so it was possible.

Another pair of headlights appeared up ahead, coming toward us.

"Crap," Ogden muttered.

The security carts had drawn almost even with us and the vehicle ahead was fast approaching, but so was the edge of the property, the corner, where the fence made a ninety-degree turn away from us. Our pursuers would have to stop or try to punch through the fence.

"Hold on," Ogden said, but everyone already was.

As we flew through the intersection, past the edge of the Wells property, the car coming at us passed by without incident. It was just a regular civilian car. One of the security carts swerved away at the last second as the other skidded to a halt. Both remained inside the fence.

Through the back window, I could see the red taillights of the other car receding behind us and the spotlights from the security carts stabbing the night sky at skewed angles.

Claudia let out a deep breath. "That was close."

I leaned toward Rex. "Thanks for the distraction."

He nodded toward Roberta. "It was Roberta's idea."

She turned to look at me, her usual sneer turned down to nine or even eight, but still definitely there. Of course, if she hadn't been such a bonehead, insisting on trying to fit through the hole when it was obviously too small, the security types probably wouldn't have come looking to see what was the matter in the first place. But I was trying to take the high road.

"Thanks," I said, in a tone that I fully intended to be free of sarcasm.

Roberta's sneer notched back up to its usual ten. "Psh," she said dismissively. "Whatever."

TWENTY-TWO

On the ride back to Philadelphia, Claudia and I filled Rex and Roberta in on what had happened, with Ogden chiming in now and again to fill in bits we'd left out. Ogden seemed ambivalent about what we had found. Yes, there was weirdness, but the chimeras were there voluntarily and they were getting paid—a far cry from the kind of stuff that had gone down at Pitman or Omnicare.

I think we all knew we needed to discuss what we'd learned down there, but I wanted to talk it out with Rex and Claudia before sharing any thoughts with Roberta and Ogden, and I imagine they wanted to talk in private first, too.

By the time we got back to the city, we'd pretty much said everything we felt comfortable saying, including making plans to meet in the next day or two to discuss next steps. Claudia directed Ogden to her car. I was relieved to see that the sidewalks in South Philadelphia were now pretty much empty.

"There it is," Claudia said, pointing as we approached her car. A massive RV was parked in front of it, almost touching the front bumper.

"A Jaguar?" Roberta said, snorting. "Looks like someone's got rich parents."

Claudia glared at her but didn't respond.

As we got out, I grabbed the bag Melanie had given me.

We mumbled our goodbyes, Rex specifically addressing Ogden and Roberta while Claudia and I just said, "See you later." It was directed at Ogden, but vague enough that Roberta could feel included, if she cared. She didn't respond to us, or to Rex for that matter.

As Rex, Claudia, and I walked over to Claudia's car, a group of people came around the corner toward us, from the direction of the arena. There were six of them, and even in the dim streetlights I could see where their pale skin had been singed red by the summer sun, like they'd been standing outside all day protesting. I wondered for a second whose side they were on, but as they drew closer, I got my answer.

Three of them had Wellplants: a woman with her hair pinned up in an elaborate mass of braids, and two men, one bald and the other extremely tall and thin, with bright red glasses and a thick tuft of silvery white hair. The three without Wellplants were almost identical: stocky and muscular, each wearing an H4H T-shirt.

Rex sighed at the sight of them, and Claudia caught my eye, but before any of us could say anything, Ogden's voice called out behind us, "Hey, hold up!"

We turned to see him coming around the front of the van, pointing at the bag in my hand. "I need that," he said.

"I was going to see if I could get it tested," I said. "For pathogens or poisons or whatever."

He held out his hand. "I can do that. My people are going to want it."

I didn't want to be difficult, but I also thought Dymphna and Chimerica would probably have better resources to run whatever tests could be run by *his people*. And I worried that if Wells really was funding CLAD, the sample might disappear. Of course, Ogden had made similar accusations about Chimerica, so he was probably afraid of the same thing. I wanted to ask Rex and Claudia what they thought, but during the time I was thinking all this, the group of H4Hers had closed the distance between us.

Ogden called out, *"Hey!"* just as one of them snuck up and yanked the bag out of my hand.

We spun to see the six of them standing right behind us. It turned out the T-shirt triplets weren't quite identical, but the stupid belligerent looks on their faces were. They reminded me of the rioters back in the fall. One of them, with a buzz cut and a neck tattoo, was loosening the bag he'd just grabbed from me.

The three Plants looked on, smug and disdainful.

"Give it back," I said.

"A little early for trick-or-treating," said the guy, reaching into the bag.

"Man, they're even more hideous than they are on TV," said one of the others. He had a patchy beard and close-set eyes.

"That's right, you three have never seen one in person, have you?" said the woman with the braids.

Suddenly, Buzzcut snatched his hand out of the bag. "What the hell?"

I tried to grab it back from him, but he pulled it away and tossed it to the guy with the patchy beard, who reached in to check it out, as well. "What is it? What's in there?" he said. Then he pulled out the chicken carcass and screwed up his face. "Ugh, you people are sick!"

He dropped the carcass back into the bag and made a show of wiping his hand off on the T-shirt of the third guy, who swatted his hand away.

"Give it back," I repeated evenly.

The trio of Plants stepped up closer, and the triplets spread out, until they were surrounding us.

"No," said the Plant with the silvery hair. The other two Plants smiled, all at the same time, all with the same smile. It was creepy. Then they stepped toward us, again all at the same time.

"Don't do this," Rex said.

"Or what?" said the guy holding the bag. His back was toward the van. I had left the door open when we got out, assuming Roberta was going to want to ride up front with Ogden.

The van swayed slightly, as if someone was moving inside. Then the sack disappeared from the moron's grip as Roberta's left hand appeared in the air over his head. She brought it down with a vicious chop, right where his neck met his shoulder.

He collapsed onto the sidewalk, like a marionette whose strings had been cut.

"Anybody else want to try to take this?" Roberta said, holding the bag in her right hand, grinning as she stepped over the fallen moron.

"We don't want any trouble," Rex said.

"Maybe *you* don't," Roberta said with a snort. "I'm just getting started."

One of the remaining T-shirt morons flicked open a collapsible baton, but in unison the three Plants said, *"Enough!"*

The two guys in the T-shirts froze.

"Pick him up and let's get out of here," said the woman.

The guy with the baton put it away, then he and his pal went over to their fallen friend, keeping their eyes on Roberta the entire time as they bent to pick him up.

She didn't step back, holding her ground and standing over them as they hoisted the guy off the ground and carried him over to the RV parked behind Claudia's car.

It had North Dakota license plates.

The Plants turned as one and followed them.

The rest of us stood in place as they got into the RV, and then watched as it swung out into the road. As they sped off, one of the yahoos leaned out an open window in the back and shouted, "Mixie trash!"

"Assholes," Roberta muttered. She tossed the bag to Ogden, who one-handed it.

I looked at Rex, who shrugged, and then I turned back to Ogden. "So, you're going to get it tested?"

"That's the plan," he replied.

"For what?"

He shrugged. "I don't know. I guess microbes, toxins. Like you said. Whatever else they can think of."

Roberta closed the sliding door and got in the front passenger seat.

"And you'll let us know what they find?" I said.

He nodded.

"And you're also going to find out why CLAD has photos of me and why they're talking about me and abducting me off the street?"

"I'll see what I can find out about that, too."

I glanced at Rex and Claudia, then I said, "Okay. We'll talk tomorrow."

"Or the next day."

I nodded. "Okay."

Rex and I gave him our phone numbers.

Roberta lowered her window and banged her palm against the door. "Let's go!"

Ogden's face soured and he shook his head, just a little. "Talk soon," he said as he walked around to the driver's side and got in.

They drove off, and as we walked up to the car, Claudia said, "What the hell?"

I went over to look and saw that someone had scraped the words MIXIE FREAKS into the paint on the driver's side door.

I let out a growl. "Jerks!"

Claudia shook her head and got in. I got in the passenger side and Rex got in the back.

As we drove off, Rex leaned forward and said, "Hey, I know Roberta isn't the easiest person to deal with—"

"She's the worst!" Claudia said, turning in her seat and abandoning any pretense that she was driving.

"She *is* the worst, Rex," I said. "The whole time I was back at that Chimerica camp on Lonely Island, she kept calling me names and trying to start fights. I'm totally not surprised she's with CLAD. Hell, she could be the one trying to frame me or set me up or whatever, with the pictures and all that, and the FBI coming to my door. Honestly, apart from Ogden, who I only just met, she's the only person I know in CLAD. For all I know, she could have been the one who planted that bomb."

He nodded, hearing me out. "I'm sorry, Jimi. I didn't know about any of that," he said when I was done. "But you also don't know all the stuff she's been through."

"Okay, what's she been through?" I asked.

Rex looked slightly sheepish. "I don't know the details. I probably never will. But I do know she's had a rough time. I know she's been harassed a lot by the chimera-haters."

Claudia snorted. "I've been harassed, too. But I don't take it out on people who had nothing to do with it."

Rex sat back. "I'm just saying."

"I hear you," I said. And I did. I could imagine that *being* Roberta was even less fun than being *around* her. Surely, she wasn't consciously deciding to be the kind of person she was. Who would choose that?

Claudia snorted again and rolled her eye in disgust. "But who cares what made her the way she is? I mean, not really, but if she had a hard life or whatever and that made her a jerk, well that's a shame, but she's still a jerk!"

After a moment of awkward silence, Claudia restarted the conversation. "While we're on the subject, how about the smell of that place?"

We talked about that, then, after we caught Rex up on everything he'd missed inside the fence, we recapped the rest of the evening, including the behavior of those three Plants at the end, and the bizarre way they moved and spoke all together.

Rex theorized that maybe it was like a flock behavior, that the Plants all arrived at the same conclusions or decisions because the same inputs were being processed with the same computing power.

When we got to Rex's place, he got out and paused, like he was expecting me to get out with him.

"Oh," I said. "Sorry. I'm going to crash at Claudia's place tonight."

Claudia leaned forward to look at him with a fake innocent grin, like she had somehow gotten one over on him.

"Oh," he said, clearly disappointed. "Okay."

At that moment, I was disappointed, too. "I'll see you tomorrow?" I said.

"Yeah, definitely," he said, but the smile that he forced totally undermined his sad eyes.

"You okay?" I said, leaning through the window.

"Yeah, of course," he said. "It's just, you know..." He smiled and blushed. "I'll miss you."

I might have blushed, as well, especially knowing that Claudia was witnessing all this. "I'll miss you, too."

I stuck my head out the window, and he crouched down to give me a nice long kiss.

"Okay, see ya, Rex," Claudia said, her voice loud and bright.

He looked over my shoulder. "Good night, Claudia."

As the car pulled away, Claudia turned to me, shaking her head. "You two are adorable together and all, but I think a few hours apart might be good for both of you."

TWENTY-THREE

'd been to Claudia's house before, but not enough times that I was used to it. It was nice. *Really* nice.

It was perched on a hill overlooking the incredibly scenic Wissahickon Gorge, which followed the Wissahickon Creek through northwest Philadelphia, part of the city's extensive park system. My dad used to take Kevin and me there when we were little, hiking or wading in the creek. Del and Leo, too. Occasionally, I'd glimpse one of the fancy houses right on the edge, and wonder who lived there. Now I knew.

These days, the creek alternated between drying up and flooding, brush fires were a constant worry, and the trees were losing the battle with the vines that were growing over everything, but it was still a really cool place to live. From the front, the house looked fantastic and modern, all angles and windows—big, but not ridiculous. But it was built into the hillside, so while it was two stories in the front, it was four in the back.

I could see the lights on through the trees, even before we turned down the driveway. Claudia parked on the circular part of the driveway, in front of the main entrance. The windows cast geometric designs across the ground in golden light.

As we stepped out of the car, I was hit by the heat and humidity, and the faint smell of smoke. I hadn't realized how comfortable I'd been in the car. The night was still, but it wasn't quiet: the woods around the house were alive with the buzzing and chirping and droning of a bazillion insects.

"Are you sure your folks are going to be cool with this?" I asked as we walked up the front steps.

"Absolutely," Claudia replied. "My folks love you, but in all likelihood they're both going to be distracted, doing their own things."

"What are they working on these days?" Claudia's parents worked harder than practically anyone I knew, except maybe my mom.

She started opening the front door but stopped. "The usual, mostly—business stuff for my dad and school stuff for my mom. She's prepping for fall semester and working on a few journal articles." She pushed the door closed for a second and screwed up her face. "But my dad's still preoccupied with getting used to his Wellplant," she said quietly, "and my mom is preoccupied with trying not to freak out about it."

Before I could respond, she pulled the door open again and walked into the house. "I'm home," she called out.

The climate control was luxurious. We walked through the front hall, past the great room and the wide stairs leading up to the second floor.

Her dad was in the cavernous family room. A single light in the corner dimly illuminated the high ceiling and far-flung corners. He was sitting in a rocking chair staring out the darkened windows.

In the daytime, I knew, there would be an impressive view of the surrounding woods and, when the trees were bare, the gorge below. Right now, it was just blackness and reflections of the room.

"Hey, Dad," Claudia said.

He turned his head to look at us in the reflection of the window. It could have been my imagination, but the movement seemed odd, almost robotic. I didn't know him well, but I could tell this was very different from his usual slouchy style. He was generally warm, easygoing, and friendly to the point of being a little goofy. Now he seemed distant and distracted.

"Hello, pumpkin," he said. He turned his head so he was looking directly at us over his shoulder. "Oh, hello, Jimi," he said.

"Hi, Mr. Bembry."

He nodded once and smiled. "Chris, remember?"

"Right," I said. "Hi, Chris."

"Is Mom home?" Claudia asked.

"In the kitchen, I believe." Then he turned to look out the window again.

Claudia stared at him another second, looking worried. Then she turned to me. "Come on," she said quietly.

I followed her through to the kitchen, which was almost as big as the family room, but done up in whites and grays and silvers.

Her mom was sitting on a stool at the island, reading something on a tablet with a large glass of white wine at her elbow.

Claudia stopped at the entrance to the room and leaned against the wall. "Hey, Mom."

Her mom looked up and smiled. She looked like she had aged five years in the month or so since the last time I'd seen her. "Hi there, Claud," she said, holding out an arm, beckoning Claudia to come closer.

As Claudia went over to her for a hug, her mom said, "Hello, Jimi. What a nice surprise."

"Hi, Bonnie," I said.

Claudia kissed her on the cheek.

"What have you two been up to?"

"Just hanging out," Claudia said quickly, as if maybe she was concerned that I was going offer something a little too close to the truth. "Is it okay if Jimi stays over?"

"Of course."

"How's it going?" Claudia asked, tipping her head in the direction of the family room, where Chris was sitting.

Bonnie closed her eyes and took a deep breath. For an instant the façade she'd been wearing fell away, revealing a much deeper level of worry and weariness. "Okay, I guess," she said. "Same as it's been."

They stood there for a moment, looking into each other's eyes. I don't know what passed between them, but they seemed to be communicating on a level that would rival anything provided by Wellplants.

We got some lemonade and hummus and chips and went upstairs to Claudia's room.

She flicked on the holovid, and a movie that I was pretty sure was still in theaters came on—obviously courtesy of some super-premium holo-channel. Neither of us watched it, though.

"See what I mean?" she said, gesturing to the floor below us.

"Has he been like that the whole time?"

"Pretty much. I mean, he was totally out of it at first, right after he got spiked. But since then, yeah. And my mom is totally freaked out, too, which means I've pretty much lost both of them for the time being. And he won't even talk about it. Refuses to acknowledge there's anything weird going on."

"And that's the 10.0, right?" I asked. The Wellplant 10.0 was the newest and most ambitious model yet. There had been a lot of criticism of it, rumors of bad reactions and speculation that maybe they had rushed it to market and there'd been difficulties meeting demand due to problems with raw materials—problems aggravated by what happened at Omnicare.

My understanding was that all of the 10.0 inventory was being prioritized for existing Wellplant users who wanted to upgrade. Chris must have paid someone off or used his business connections to jump the line.

"He insisted he didn't want to start with the 9.3 and then have to upgrade." She shrugged. "My mom didn't know he was getting a 10. I don't know if she would have let him if she'd known."

"She didn't want him to get it, either?"

"She wasn't crazy about the idea. She was afraid of malfunctions or infections or other complications, but she knew he really wanted one and that there were all sorts of advantages."

Claudia suddenly leaned forward, looking closer at the holovid. "Hey, that's Sarah Chao," she said, getting off the bed to look even closer. Sarah Chao was one of my favorite actors and had starred in three of the biggest movies in the last two years. "It's true. She really did get a Wellplant." Just before she said it, the image pulled in for a tight close-up, and there above her eye was a little gray glass disk. Claudia sat back on the bed, shaking her head. "Man, they are *everywhere* these days."

"Seriously," I said, staring at Sarah Chao. It seemed like just a year ago, only the superrich were getting spiked, but since then it seemed like all sorts of people were getting them. With Wells's programs to give them to government officials and cops and whomever else, you couldn't get away from them. *Invasive Plants,* I thought.

For the next half hour or so, we talked about Claudia's dad and mom, then we got down to business, talking more about Ogden and CLAD and Earl and Melanie and Hitchcock. We both felt there was something to be concerned about, and we came up with some crazy theories, but none of them ultimately made sense.

By the time the movie was over, it was getting late and we were a bit talked out. When the next movie started, we went quiet, and we both fell asleep before the end and woke up to the credits. Claudia staggered sleepily to her feet and stretched, and for a moment her head was in the middle of the credits, words like BEST BOY and KEY GRIP appearing to slice through her skull. Then the holoplayer recalibrated and the hologram display moved back away from her.

She waved it off and climbed into bed. I climbed in next to her. By the time I was under the covers, she was already asleep. I heard her snore once, then I was asleep, too.

I woke up around two a.m., my throat parched, and I went downstairs to get a glass of water. As I walked past the family room, I saw that Chris was right where he had been earlier, in the exact same spot, the exact same position. The only difference was that I could see in the reflection of the window that his eyes were closed and his mouth slightly open.

That's why I jumped when, without opening his eyes or turning to look at me, he said, "Hello, Jimi. Couldn't sleep?"

"Just getting a glass of water."

His eyes opened, looking right at me in the reflection in the window. "I see." He stared at me for a long moment, like he was studying me, analyzing me. Then he said, "Well, don't let me stop you."

His eyes closed again, and he went back to whatever he had been doing.

Thoroughly creeped out, I went into the kitchen and filled a glass from the dispenser in the refrigerator. Then I stood there for a few seconds drinking it, putting off going back. When I finally did, he was gone.

I knew he was the same guy as always, and that there was nothing to be afraid of, but making my way back upstairs to Claudia's room, through that big, unfamiliar, darkened house, I was scared like a little kid, afraid I was going to bump into him in the darkened hallway or see him staring at me from the shadows.

When I got back to Claudia's room, she was curled up on her side of the bed, breathing softly. I closed the door behind me, making sure it clicked, then I climbed under the covers and lay there staring at it. I fell asleep wondering what was going on inside Chris Bembry's head.

TWENTY-FOUR

When I awoke the next morning, Claudia was already up. I went downstairs and found the Bembrys all drinking coffee in the family room, in front of the holovid. They seemed comfortable at first: Chris in the armchair, Bonnie on the sofa, Claudia next to her with her feet on her mom's lap, all of them drinking coffee and watching a Sunday morning news show on Tru-News, the cheesiest but most-watched of the holovid news networks.

The scene was incredibly homey at first. But as I looked on, I noticed the worry on Bonnie's face, only slightly less pronounced on Claudia's, and Chris had that strange flatness and rigidity about him. I got the sense that all three of them were acting out a scene from their normal lives. They weren't really relaxed, they were pretending to be.

Chris looked over at me first. "Good morning, Jimi." He smiled after he said it. In the morning light, his face looked pale and gray, except for a ring of pink surrounding his Wellplant.

Bonnie and Claudia looked over, and Bonnie said, "Good morning, Jimi. Can I get you a coffee?"

"That's okay, thanks," I said. "I'll get it."

"Cups are in the cabinet over the coffee maker," Claudia said, but then she got up to come into the kitchen with me anyway.

"*Day One* is doing a story about CLAD and H4H and Howard Wells and everything," she said as she poured me a cup. *Day One* was Tru-News's flagship show. She smiled as she handed me the coffee, whispering, "Otherwise, we wouldn't be watching such garbage."

"I don't know if I can watch any more Howard Wells," I said, as I sipped my coffee—which was incredibly good. "It seems like every time I turn on anything, there he is."

"I hear you," she said. "And now that he's running for president, it's just going to get worse."

She paused and looked over her shoulder, back toward the living room, then lowered her voice. "Since he got his Wellplant, my dad's fascination with Howard Wells has reached a new level."

"He doesn't support him, does he?" I whispered.

"He says he doesn't, but sometimes it seems like it. And I get it—as a tech entrepreneur, Wells is pretty compelling. It's a revolutionary technology, he just shipped his ten millionth unit, and that doesn't include the free or discounted ones he's given to cops and the military or sold to politicians. But he's also the worst, and it bugs the hell out of me when my dad insists on pointing out that he has good qualities, as well.... Anyway, I'd probably watch it, just to keep up, but the way he 'fanboys' out over him, I don't like it."

"Hey, kids!" he called out from the living room. "It's about to start."

She rolled her eyes and shook her head. "We don't have to watch if you don't want."

"No, that's okay," I said. "I'm curious to see how his announcement is going over."

Bonnie smiled at us as we walked in with our coffees. Chris watched her, then smiled, as well.

Bonnie stared at him for an instant, then patted the seats next to her on the sofa for us to sit down.

The title sequence started, with all sorts of flashy shapes and colors holographically flying through the air in front of us as the announcer intoned about how *Day One* was the most-watched Sunday news show, now hosted by Alenka Bogdan.

"Oh, I like her," I said.

Bonnie looked at me and nodded appreciatively. "Yes, Bogdan is a serious journalist. I never thought she'd leave *60 Minutes*."

"I know, right?" Since it was Tru-News Network, I had been expecting a bunch of questions about what holovid shows Wells liked or his favorite chili recipe, that kind of fluff. But I'd seen Bogdan interview Wells before, and she asked him some tough questions. Now that he was running for president, I expected her to be even tougher.

Claudia screwed up her face at me. "You watch *60 Minutes*?"

"Sometimes," I said. "I watched it when she interviewed Wells in January."

Bonnie said, "Yes, she did a great job. Apparently, Tru-News paid her a tremendous amount of money to switch networks. Maybe they're trying to become a legitimate news organization after all...."

Her voice trailed off as Bogdan's face came on the screen. She looked much as she had when she interviewed Wells before: the signature spiky gray hair, with eyes the same color. But her gaze didn't seem quite as intense, and above her right eye, there was a little gray-black glass disk, half an inch across.

Claudia and Bonnie looked at each other, stricken.

"Hey, look at that," Chris said, smiling. "Alenka Bogdan got a Wellplant, too."

"Whoa," I said. "Wasn't expecting that."

"I'm telling you," Chris said, looking at Bonnie and Claudia. "Everyone who's anyone has one. Every company, every government, all the people in charge have Wellplants. I know Wellplant Corporation has been involved in one way or another with some shady things, and obviously I disagree with Wells's views on chimeras." He gave Claudia a lingering smile. "But the truth is, the world has grown too complex to operate at a high level without a Wellplant. If you want to compete, you're at a disadvantage without one."

At this, Bonnie got up and left the room. Claudia looked at me, the worry even more obvious on her face. Then she got up and followed her mom.

The holovid cut to commercials, and Chris seemed to be watching them intently at first. By the third one—toilet paper—I realized he wasn't watching them at all: he was lost in his Wellplant world, doing stuff inside his head.

Without looking at me, he said, "I know they're worried about me. But they shouldn't be. I feel better than ever. Faster, smarter, better informed. And maybe it seems weird, and maybe Howard Wells isn't perfect, but this"—he turned to me and pointed at the glass disk embedded in his forehead—"this is powerful technology, and overwhelmingly beneficial. It's only a matter of time before everybody has one, and humanity can reach its true potential."

As the commercial break ended, Claudia returned, alone. Her eyes were red and her cheeks pink.

Chris looked over at her, then looked back at the holo without saying anything.

Alenka Bogdan appeared after the commercials, with an oddly serene smile on her face.

"Welcome to *Day One*, the best way to start your week. This morning, we'll be talking with Howard Wells, founder, president, and CEO of Wellplant Corporation and Wells Life Sciences; inventor of the Wellplant; president of Humans for Humanity; and, as of his announcement the day before yesterday, an independent candidate for President of the United States. Howard Wells, thank you for joining us."

Bogdan shrank as the display zoomed out to reveal her sitting across from Wells. The Bembrys had a really nice holovid console, so the illusion that Wells and Bogdan were in the room with us was convincing and unsettling.

Bonnie returned and sat on the sofa. Chris didn't look at her.

"Thank you, Alenka," Wells said. "Always a pleasure to speak with you."

"And you, of course," she said. "Before we talk about your candidacy, I'd like to ask your thoughts on last week's tragic bombing at the Seaport Museum."

They both looked somber as Wells shook his head. "Terrible," he said.

"Just terrible. I lost some dear friends in that senseless act, including Reverend Bill Calkin, some true heroes in the fight to preserve humanity." The camera cut to a close-up as he took a deep breath and dabbed at one eye with a knuckle—although if any tears were there, even the Bembrys' super-hi-res holovid wasn't quite good enough to pick it up.

"They weren't friends," I said, and the Bembrys all turned to look at me. "Reverend Calkin told me so himself. He specifically said he and Howard Wells weren't friends."

"...But I'm not surprised by what happened," Wells continued, and they all looked back at the holovid.

"You're not?" Bogdan asked.

"Sadly, no. I urged Reverend Calkin not to go, not to even hold the luncheon in the first place."

"Don't you think dialogue is important?"

"You can't have dialogue with the mixies."

The camera cut to Bogdan, looking on placidly. In their previous interview, she had called him on it when he said "mixies." This time she let it go.

"They're animals," Wells continued. "They've *chosen* to be animals. It should come as no surprise when they behave like animals. People don't like to talk about it, because they want to be nice, but mixies bring joblessness and crime. They bring disease."

"This is bullshit," I said under my breath. Chris and Bonnie both turned to look at me. "Sorry," I said.

"No, you're right," Bonnie said.

Bogdan seemed like a different interviewer from before, fawning instead of challenging, tossing one softball after another: "How has your experience as a successful entrepreneur prepared you to be president?... What about your experience leading Humans for Humanity?...What made you decide to give back as a public servant?"

In her previous interview, on *60 Minutes*, she had asked about the inequity of this technology and how it widened the gap between rich and poor. This time, the closest she got was to ask about Wellplant Corporation's program to make Wellplants available to those who can't afford them, especially those in public service. She described the program in such glowing terms that even Wells seemed taken aback.

"Well, yes," he said, awkwardly, stumbling as if he was having trouble finding something positive to say about the program that she hadn't already said. "It is an excellent program, and we are delighted to be in a position to give something back to those who do so much for all of us."

She asked him about the growing trend of political and business leaders getting Wellplants.

"Of course, it makes perfect sense," Wells said. "These people are the best and the brightest—even brighter now—and they want to do what is best for their constituents, for their employees and clients and customers and shareholders. It is a simple fact that however good you are at your job, a Wellplant will make you better."

She asked him about his policy proposals, but didn't press him in any way when he sidestepped or deflected or answered with a platitude or with the answer to the question he wanted to answer instead of the question she had asked.

She brought up Wellplant's production problems, but didn't mention the events in Gellersville, with Omnicare, and how that had exacerbated the production shortages. She didn't even call him on it when he suggested that high demand was the only reason they were having trouble filling orders. And when he pointed out that supply couldn't be too bad since *she* was able to get one herself, Bogdan practically giggled.

"Yes," she said, "and I love it. Don't know how I got by without it, actually."

For a moment, they beamed at each other, as if having some kind of silent conversation.

"As I recall, you had your doubts about Wellplant, isn't that right?" Wells asked her.

"Yes, it's true," she said, with a sheepish laugh. "But not anymore. No doubts whatsoever."

"I'm so pleased to hear that," he said, looking very, very pleased, indeed.

"This is pathetic," I said, finally.

"I know, right?" Claudia said. "I thought Wellplants were supposed to make you smarter. Alenka Bogdan's seems to have turned her into an idiot." Then she added, "No offense, Dad."

Chris shrugged. "Well, perhaps it's made her smart enough to realize that maybe Wells isn't entirely bad after all."

Claudia snorted. "Really, Dad? Next you'll be saying it makes people smart enough to realize that chimeras really are nonpersons."

Chris laughed, as though it was entirely a joke. "Don't be silly, pumpkin."

Bonnie got up and left the room again. I was thinking of following her, and I think Claudia was, too, but then the holovid cut to a view of the Convention Center concourse, packed with thousands of people, all looking up at a massive two-dimensional video screen showing the *Day One* interview. There was a slight lag, with the screen showing Wells and Bogdan sitting across from each other. Then it shifted to the image of the crowd itself, and a thunderous cheer rose up.

Those closest to the camera turned to look at it. One of them was very tall and thin, with red glasses and a shock of silver-white hair on top of his head.

"Claudia, look," I said, pointing at him. "It's that jerk from last night." The woman with the braids was standing next to him.

Claudia got up, too, and we both moved closer to the holodisplay.

"Last night?" Chris asked. "Where were you kids?"

"That *is* him," Claudia said, ignoring him. "The woman, too."

The people next to him turned toward the camera, as well, and it was the same group that had been with him last night.

The three guys who had been wearing the H4H T-shirts looked terrible, with sunken eyes and blotchy, sweaty faces. They looked sick. One of them hunched over to cough, a deep wracking cough. A woman standing in front of him wiped the back of her neck, then glared at him in disgust.

Right away, I knew that was important, although I didn't quite understand why. I looked at Claudia and she looked back, her eyes full of meaning I couldn't decipher. Then the holovid cut to a view from a vantage point on the other side of the room, closer to the screen.

"Do you know those people?" Chris asked.

"No, Dad," Claudia said, exasperated. "We saw them on the street. That's all. They're a bunch of H4Hers." She glanced at me and picked up her coffee. "I'm going upstairs."

"Okay," Chris said. "Breakfast'll be soon."

I'd had enough of Wells and the new Alenka Bogdan, and the segment was over anyway. I grabbed my coffee and headed after Claudia.

She was waiting for me in the hallway, but she turned without a word and headed up the stairs. I followed close behind.

TWENTY-FIVE

Well, that was disturbing as hell," Claudia said as we entered her bedroom. She closed the door behind me. "I swear, Alenka Bogdan is acting weirder than my dad."

"Did you see the other people from last night?" I asked. "The ones with the tall guy?"

"Yeah, they looked terrible," she said with a half grin. "Serves them right."

I grabbed her arm and pulled her down with me as I sat on the bed. I could feel her looking at me, questioning, but I had my eyes closed and my forehead creased in concentration.

"I think that's important, somehow," I said. "But I don't know how. Not exactly."

"What, the fact that they got sick?"

I nodded. "Right after touching that carcass."

"Huh.... Earl did say a lot of the employees got sick at the farm."

"And Wells keeps talking about chimeras spreading disease. He said it again just now, in that interview. And he said it when he announced his candidacy, even though he knows it's not true."

"But we didn't get sick."

"That's true. I hope Rex is okay."

"So, what are you thinking?"

"I don't know," I told her. "There's a few things that I can't help thinking are related, but I don't know how."

"What else?"

"Okay, so Wells keeps talking about chimeras and disease, right? Saying that chimeras make it possible for pathogens to jump species, and that they're responsible for the flu pandemic."

"Yeah, but lots of the haters say that. It's one of their favorite bullshit talking points."

"And those jerks from last night seem to have gotten sick after having come into contact with that chicken carcass. And like you just said, Earl said people at the farm were getting sick, too."

We were quiet for a moment after that, both of us thinking. Then I said, "Last night, Melanie said all the chimeras working the chicken facility had bird splices."

Claudia furrowed her brow. "Yeah? What does that mean?"

"I don't know for sure, but Wells is constantly going on about chimeras being the source of the flu pandemic—the *bird* flu pandemic—and even the scientists who have disproven that acknowledge the logic behind the theory that chimeras could act as a bridge between species. Now Wells has a bunch of chimeras with bird splices working with chickens who are obviously sick, with something that may or may not have infected those yahoos from H4H."

Claudia screwed up her face. "So, what, do you think he's trying to get the bird flu to jump species from the chickens to the bird chimeras to everyone else?"

I shook my head. "I don't know. I don't know what to think. I mean, why would he want that? That's stupid."

"No, it doesn't make sense. I mean, his followers would be hit as hard as everyone else."

"Well, not all of them."

"What?"

"The yahoos from last night. They didn't all look sick. Just the ones without Wellplants."

"Right…" she said. "But still, why would anybody do something like that? It doesn't make sense."

"I don't know. You're right, it doesn't. Maybe he just wants to make his lies seem more plausible." The flu pandemic had killed my father. The idea that someone would risk a new one was incomprehensible. Then again, so was using a horrific tragedy that had killed hundreds of millions as the basis for twisted lies manufactured to promote hatred and fear. Howard Wells was way past that at this point.

Claudia looked dubious, and she was right to be. But there was too much for this all to be nothing. "So what should we do?" she asked.

"I guess we'll see what results CLAD's testing comes up with. But in the meantime, I need to call Rex."

Claudia had a phone in her room, because of course she did. She grabbed it off her desk and handed it to me, then waited for me to make the call while I waited for her to give me a little privacy without having to ask for it.

After a few awkward seconds, it dawned on her. "Oh," she said. "Right. How about I get us some more coffee?"

"That'd be great," I said, handing her my mug. "Thanks."

I punched in Rex's phone number as she slipped out the door and closed it behind her.

He answered on the first ring. "Hello?"

"Hey. It's me. How are you feeling?"

"Feeling? Um…fine, I guess," he said. "Why? How are you feeling?"

"I'm okay. Did you watch the Wells interview on *Day One*?"

He let out a sad laugh. "Yeah. And I'm wondering if Alenka Bogdan is angling for a position on the Wells campaign staff."

"Seriously, right? But in the video of the crowd, did you see those H4Hers from last night?"

"Yeah, I did. They didn't look too good, did they?"

"Not all of them," I said. I recounted the conversation I had just had with Claudia.

"Whoa," he said when I was done. "That's…troubling. What do you propose we do about it?"

"We need to talk to Ogden. To find out if they tested that carcass and see if they discovered anything."

"Okay." He paused. "I don't think we should tell them our suspicions. Not yet."

"No, me neither. But we need to get word to Chimerica."

TWENTY-SIX

As Rex tried to get in touch with Sly, I told Claudia about our conversation. She agreed with our plan of action, but she was worried about her parents, especially her dad. She was going to stay behind this time, but she drove me to New Ground to meet Rex. He met us out front, leaning against Jerry's truck holding two iced chai lattes.

She pulled up next to him and I quickly repeated the main points I'd been making on the drive: her folks were going to be okay, I'd call her when we got back, and I'd be around if she needed me for anything. I gave her a quick hug, then I got out.

"Hey, Rex!" she called out before I closed the car door.

"Hey, Claudia," he replied. He looked vaguely embarrassed, like he knew he had probably come up in conversation once or twice during our sleepover. I made a show for Claudia of standing on my tiptoes to kiss Rex on the cheek, then flashed her a big grin.

She laughed and drove off, shaking her head.

I turned to Rex again, my face serious now, as I looked up into his eyes. "Hey," I said softly.

"Hey," he replied, his voice slightly croaky.

"I missed you," I said, and I could feel my face light up, hotter than I could blame on the heat.

"I missed you, too." He laughed and shook his head. "Kind of pathetic, isn't it?" He looked at his watch. "Twelve hours."

I laughed, too, kissed him again, then grabbed the chai he was holding for me.

"I figured you'd probably already had your coffee by now," he said.

"Good figuring," I said. "Thanks."

We both sipped our drinks.

"Did you talk to Sly?" I asked.

He shook his head. "Left him a message to call me here if he didn't reach me at home."

"What do you think we should do?"

He shook his head again. "I don't know. It's only been an hour or so."

"Dymphna definitely thought whatever we learned could be important, and that was before we saw that those idiots had gotten sick."

He nodded. "Sly usually gets back to me pretty quick."

I thought for a moment. "I think we should just go straight to Dymphna."

He raised an eyebrow. "Do you think?"

I shrugged, unsure.

"Do you remember how to get there?" he asked.

"I think so. If we can Smartdrive it to the Little Egg Harbor exit, I think I'll remember the way from there."

"What about the submerged bridge?" he said. "Any idea how Sly got that to come to the surface?"

I winked at him. "I'll guess we'll have to"—long, dramatic sip of chai—"cross that bridge when we come to it."

He shook his head and groaned, sliding around me as he headed for the driver's side door of the truck.

"Come on," I said, getting in the passenger side. "That was a good one."

▬ ▬ ▬

Rex drove manually through Silver Garden until we got to Broad Street, then he directed the truck to the Little Egg Harbor exit of the Garden State Smartway. He turned to me as we drove. "So. Alenka Bogdan, huh?"

"Ugh, I know, right? I used to think she was a badass. A serious journalist."

"Apparently, she was just in it for the money."

"You think that's what changed her?"

"Probably. You don't think so?"

"I don't know. It wasn't just her questions, it was her attitude, her demeanor. She was like a different person. And she has a Wellplant now."

Rex grunted. "You think that's the reason?"

I nodded. "Claudia's dad got spiked, too."

"Seriously?" he said, his head swinging around so fast and hard that if he had been manually driving, I think we would have veered off the road.

"Yeah," I said, realizing then just how distracted I'd been in the past couple of days. Normally, important news like that wouldn't have slipped my mind. "She's freaking out about it. Her mom, too. He's acting different. Acting strange."

"That's creepy. And you think it's the Wellplant that's causing it?"

"I don't know him that well, but I don't see what else it could be. There's no doubt in Claudia's mind."

"Weird," he said. "I've known people who got Wellplants before. Not close friends, but people I knew. They didn't change all that much, they were just insufferable gearheads becoming even less sufferable."

"Well, that was before the 10.0," I said. "I think this one's different."

He was quiet for a second, then he whistled.

"What?" I asked.

"Just thinking about all these politicians and celebrities and CEOs getting Wellplants. The idea of all these people in power being somehow changed by their Wellplants."

"That is scary."

We were silent for a while after that. A wall of clouds rose up behind us, to the west, as if it was following us from Philly. As we passed the first sign for the Little Egg Harbor exit, the clouds overtook us, and a salvo of fat raindrops pelted the windshield. It paused for a minute, then resumed as a steadier drizzle.

Rex leaned forward and looked up at the sky. "There's a brush-fire warning today. Hopefully, some rain will help with that."

As we approached the exit, we talked more about CLAD, and about

Wells and his candidacy. Between the rain and the topic, by the time we took the exit and Rex switched off Smartdrive, we were both feeling somewhat subdued.

"A left?" I said at the bottom of the ramp.

Rex nodded and turned. We both scanned our surroundings, looking for landmarks. The rain started coming down harder, but we made our way without too much trouble, mostly agreeing on where to turn and when.

Before long, we found Dock Road, the narrow road that cut across the bay to the gate that led to the house. The water seemed higher than before, and I wondered if it was high tide, or if it just seemed higher because we didn't know exactly what the hell we were doing.

We slowly drove around the spots where the asphalt had washed out, squeezing perilously close to the opposite edge of the road. As the road narrowed, the wind picked up, sending wavelets splashing across the asphalt, and making me nervous that the tide might rise even farther and wash us away or strand us there.

We reached the gate with the sign on it that said UNSAFE ROAD. NO ENTRY.

"I don't think it's locked," I said, squinting through the rain.

"How can you tell?" Rex asked, squinting as well. The rain was coming down hard now, and even with the wipers on, it was impossible to see.

"Wait here," I said.

"Jimi, wait!" he said, but I had already released my seat belt and slipped out the door.

I was drenched by the time I'd taken three steps, but it was still hot, and even the rain was warm. It felt kind of nice. With the briny smell of the bay, I almost felt like I was swimming in the ocean. The chain was there, wrapped around the frame on one side of the gate, the padlock dangling from one end.

I pulled one side of the gate open, then the other, and waved Rex through.

He drove past me and stopped just inside the gate, waiting.

I thought about leaving the gate open, in case we needed to beat a hasty retreat, but we were guests here, even if uninvited, and I thought that would be rude. I closed the gate and got back in the truck.

"You're soaked," Rex said. "I would have done that."

"Then you'd be soaked," I said. "It's fine. Just a little water."

But I did take it personally when the rain all but stopped moments later.

We drove past a few hundred yards of abandoned and collapsing houses, right up to where the road disappeared under the water.

Rex turned to me. "What now?"

"I don't know." I got out and shook my hair to get rid of the excess moisture as I walked over to the rusty mailbox on the side of the road. I ran my hands over all the surfaces but couldn't find the seams for the panel that Sly had opened before. I don't know what I did to activate it, but with a slight hiss and a groan of metal, the panel where the mail pickup times were once posted opened up, revealing a row of numbered buttons and a touch screen.

I put my palm against the screen, but nothing happened. Then I pressed the 1 button. The screen came to life, with the words ENTER PASSWORD over a green rectangle with a single asterisk in it.

I turned and called over to Rex. "Numeric password. Any ideas?"

He shook his head, then got out and came over. "None," he said as he came up next to me. "Four digits?"

"Looks like," I said, judging from the size of the box and the size of the asterisk.

"Did you try one-two-three-four?"

I snorted. "No, but if that works, I say we turn around and go join CLAD because I don't think I want be associated with an organization that has that kind of security."

I keyed in the 2, 3, and 4, then we both looked over at the water, hoping it was about to start bubbling as the bridge rose to the surface, but definitely also hoping it wasn't.

It didn't.

"Score one for Chimerica," I said under my breath. Then I looked up at Rex. "One-one-one-one?"

He shrugged. "I don't know if that would be all that much better."

"Whatever the password is, if we guess it, someone needs to be fired," I said as I keyed in the digits.

We looked over again, but again nothing happened.

"What now?" Rex asked.

"I don't know. There's a good chance it'll lock us out if we get it wrong a third time." I was still soaking wet, but I didn't relish the idea of swimming across to the other side.

"Right. So having come to it, maybe we won't be crossing this bridge after all."

I screwed up my face at him, then kneeled down and studied the keys up close. "The three is smudged," I said.

"Meaning what?"

"Meaning it's been pressed a lot. Meaning it's probably part of the password."

He knelt down beside me. "Good thinking. Any of the others?"

Several of the others had smudges on them, but none were as pronounced as the 3. "I don't know," I said. "Could be. Not as much though."

"Maybe it's three-three-three-three."

"Could be. Should we try it?"

He shrugged and looked around. "What else are we going to do?"

I pressed the 3 once, twice, three times, and as I was about to press it again, a voice came across the water: "*Stop!*"

We turned and saw Sly standing where the road emerged from the water on the other side. "See?" he yelled. "This is what I get for not making you two ride in the back." He went over to the pylon next to the road and pressed a few buttons. "What the hell are you doing here, anyway?"

The bay started to bubble, and over the sound of gurgling water, I shouted back, "We need to talk."

TWENTY-SEVEN

W here's Dymphna?" I asked as we got out of the truck.

"She's gone," Sly said as he entered the code and the bridge sank once more under the water.

"Gone?" I said.

"Let's go inside." He motioned for us to precede him up the steps. As we approached the house, I saw a large box truck parked on the far side. I hated the thought of driving something so big and top-heavy down that narrow road. "She's gone because she's a genius and she knew that since I hadn't insisted that you two ride in the back of the van, there was a chance you would come back. And a chance you'd be followed. We couldn't risk her being here if that happened."

The inside of the house was clean and seemed mold free. The windows were intact, and there were lots of them: north and south looking out onto the bay; west looking back at the salt marsh; and east, across the bay toward the barrier island that separated it from the ocean.

It was unfurnished, apart from a bedroll in the corner and a trio of folding chairs in front of a bank of windows.

Sly turned one around so it was facing the others and sat in it, gesturing for Rex and me to sit, as well.

I sat, and the chair creaked ominously under me.

Rex laughed. "Seems like a nice little chair. I think I'll spare us both the embarrassment of flattening it." He leaned against the wall and slid to a seated position on the floor.

Sly leaned forward and looked at him with his eyebrows raised. Rex turned to me and said, "You tell him."

It took me ten minutes to explain what had happened the night before, what we had observed that morning, how we had put all those things together, and what we thought about it. Sly interrupted me once: when I first said, "Roberta," he said, "Roberta? *Ugh*. What the hell was *she* doing there?" I found that extremely gratifying.

Other than that, he just listened, taking it all in. When I finished, he sat back in his chair, nodding slowly. "Huh," he said. "So, what do you think we should do about it?"

"I think we need to find out what it means, for sure. I thought Chimerica would be interested in looking into it."

He nodded again. "Yeah…okay. It sounds weird, but it's probably nothing."

"Probably nothing?" I said, annoyed at being dismissed so readily. "If that chicken carcass made those people sick, they could be out in the world making *other* people sick right now."

Sly seemed to be making a point of not looking at me. "Well, it sure would help if we could get hold of that carcass you think made those people sick. So we could see what it's infected with."

"I tried to get it, but Ogden took it and said CLAD would test it. I assumed Chimerica would be better able to do that, right?"

"Are you kidding? Absolutely. That's Dymphna's specialty. Or one of them." He shrugged. "Well, I guess let's see what CLAD comes back with and then we'll have a better idea of what we should do next."

"If that thing is infectious, if it did make those H4Hers sick, it could be spreading as we speak," I said. "We need to tell someone, whether or we have the bird or not, right?"

"Um…sure," he said.

I glanced at Rex and then back at Sly. "You don't sound very sure."

"No, no, it's not that."

"Then what?"

"No, you're right," he said. "I'll tell my superiors."

"By your superiors, do you mean Dymphna?"

"No." He laughed. "I'm just kind of her local point person, while she's in the area. I've worked my way up a little, but there's a few levels between me and the governing council."

Rex nodded, like he understood the hierarchy. I didn't—and I didn't laugh, either. "Right," I said, "but maybe we could tell her about it *anyway*."

"Yeah, okay," Sly said. "I'll see what I can do. And you'll let me know what you hear from this Ogden guy. When are you going to talk to him?"

I looked at Rex. "I guess we'll head over there now."

He nodded again, then turned to Sly. "Are you going to be here later?"

"Nah. I'm headed back to the city, to New Ground. I need to talk to Jerry."

As Sly walked us back out to the truck, he said, "You mentioned to Dymphna that Ogden said CLAD has some kind of plan to bring down the Wellplant network?"

"Yeah," I said. "But I think he was just blowing smoke, trying to make himself and CLAD seem important."

Sly shrugged. "Maybe. But if you can find out anything more about that, Dymphna wants to know."

"Okay."

He went over to the keypad and started keying in numbers. "Three-three-one-three, by the way," he said.

"So now you trust us?" I said, as the bridge once again rose to the surface.

He shook his head. "Of course I trust you, but it's not about that. Other people trust me to be discrete. It's about security, and now I'm out here breaking this place down and getting everything out of here, including the pontoons, because I violated security protocols before when I brought you out here. Like I said, Dymphna decided it wasn't safe to be here any longer, because she figured you'd come back at some point and there was no way to be sure you wouldn't be followed. After today, none of us will ever come back here again. And don't think I didn't get an earful about it."

As we got in the truck, I felt like a little kid who'd just been chastised, but Sly didn't seem angry. He gave us a cheerful wave as we drove back across the bridge.

As soon as we were on dry land, the bridge sank back under the water.

— — —

Ogden was sitting on the front steps drinking coffee when we pulled up in front of his house. As we got out of the car, he stood, looking wary. "What are you doing here?"

"How are you feeling?" I asked.

He tilted his head at me. "I'm feeling fine. Why? How are *you* feeling?"

"We're okay," I replied. "Is Roberta here?"

"Roberta?" He seemed confused by the question.

"Yeah, aren't you two partners?"

He scowled. "Hell no. That chimera's trouble. I mean, don't get me wrong, she can be helpful in a pinch. But otherwise, not worth the BS."

I couldn't help glancing at Rex, but he didn't look over.

"They sent her to help, and she did that," Ogden continued. "Now she's back wherever she goes."

"When did she leave?"

"This morning."

"And she was okay?"

"Grumpy and rude, so yeah, perfectly normal."

"Have your CLAD buddies tested that carcass yet?" Rex said.

Ogden snorted and shook his head. "Since last night? No, not yet. Why?"

Rex and I looked at each other.

"It's kind of urgent," Rex said. "Don't you think?"

Ogden looked away. "I hear you."

"Did you watch Howard Wells this morning?" I asked.

He shook his head. "I've seen too much of that asshole as it is. Why?"

"It's probably nothing," I said quickly. I wasn't ready to trust him yet with details of our earlier conversation. "But after what Melanie and Earl said about people getting sick at the facility, we were worried the chicken might be diseased."

He laughed again. "It was definitely diseased. That's why it's dead, I imagine. But that's not surprising in one of those big poultry facilities."

"Right. But we need to know what it was sick *with*. That's what you're supposed to be testing for, right? Pathogens and stuff? Like we talked about?"

He took a deep breath and let it out. "Come on inside."

We followed him into the house, and as soon as we were inside, he turned to face us. "Okay, Jimi. Full story? It looks like CLAD doesn't have the resources to do testing like that after all." He shook his head then gave Rex a sidelong glance. "I guess maybe Chimerica isn't the only one half-assing it a bit."

"Chimerica has the resources," Rex said. "We can do it."

"They told me to throw the chicken out."

"You threw it out?" I said. "Where?" I pictured a public trash can, and a municipal worker emptying it, getting the flu, spreading it around.

Ogden rolled his eyes. "I didn't say I threw it out. I said they *told* me to throw it out."

"So do you still have it?"

He looked at me, then at Rex. "Yeah, I got it."

"Let us get it tested," Rex said. "We'll share the results with you, with CLAD, let you know what comes back."

He looked at us both again, studying us, thinking, then he went into the dining room and opened the closet door, emerging a few seconds later with a bundle wrapped in a trash bag and duct tape. "Okay, so you're going to tell me what you find, right?"

We both nodded and he handed it over. "Made me nervous having it in the house, to be honest," he said.

"Okay," Rex said. "We'll let you know the moment we hear. What's the best way to reach you?"

He laughed, spreading his arms. "I'm right here. Come and visit, I guess."

Rex nodded. "Okay, so maybe not the exact moment." Then he turned to go.

I paused before I followed him. "Ogden, earlier, you said CLAD was planning on taking down the whole Wellplant network. What's that about? How are you planning on doing that?"

Ogden smiled and shook his head. "Just a little something I came up with. But I shouldn't have said anything about that. You join up, become part of CLAD, maybe I can tell you more. Otherwise, I got no comment."

TWENTY-EIGHT

We caught up with Sly outside New Ground and gave him the package. I didn't want to bring it into the coffee shop, in case it was as contagious as we feared. I also didn't like the idea of leaving it in the truck, or anywhere really, especially in the heat. It wasn't stinking yet, but it was sure to start soon. I was a little bit worried that if things dragged on any longer, they might not be able to do whatever tests they had in mind.

Sly was more concerned about CLAD's plan to bring down the Well-plant network. He was unhappy that I wasn't able to get any more information about it. When I told him Ogden had said he could tell me more if I became a part of CLAD, he looked at me expectantly, like he thought I should go ahead and join up in order to get that info.

"*No*," I said. "I'm tired of having the FBI showing up at my front door. The last thing I want is to give them a legitimate reason to think I'm involved with CLAD."

He was clearly disappointed but said he'd let us know as soon as he heard anything, and that he'd be home for the next few days if we needed to reach him. He had a tiny apartment at the southwest tip of the city, in a flooded-out part of Eastwick.

After Sly left, Rex wiped down the inside of Jerry's truck with disinfectant, just in case. I went into the bathroom and gave my hands a good scrubbing, then Rex did the same.

I was relieved to be rid of that package, but felt a bit of a letdown, now that all we could do was wait.

As we sat there, Jerry came out from the back and asked Rex to take care of a few things for him at one of his buildings.

"I won't be long," Rex said to me. "Want to hang out after I'm done?"

"Nah, I shouldn't," I said. Then, I smiled. "I feel like I haven't been home enough lately."

Rex understood, and after an extra-long hug and kiss goodbye, he left and Jerry returned to his office.

I looked around the coffee shop and realized I didn't know anybody else there. It was weird. Over that past nine months I'd been coming so regularly, I almost always knew someone—at least Ruth or Pell.

I used the pay phone in the back to call my mom, just to check in.

"Hey Mom," I said when she answered. "It's me."

"Who?" she said, sounding confused.

"Your daughter," I said. "Jimi."

I realized as soon as I said it that she was messing with me. "Jimi… Jimi…" she said, as if searching her memory. "That's right, I *did* have a daughter named Jimi." She laughed—loud, long, and breezy. "You know, I forgot all about her. Thought she'd run away to join the circus or something." This was not the first time we'd played this game.

"More like 'run away *from* the circus,' I'd say."

"Ha, ha, ha. Very funny. So, where've you been?"

"You know where I've been. I spent the night at Claudia's. I'm at the coffee shop now, but I'm about to head home. I'm just checking in to see what you're up to and how you're doing. Like a good daughter."

"*Kind of* like a good daughter."

"Mom!"

"Kidding! I'm just kidding."

"You better be!"

"So you're coming home?"

"Yup. What's for dinner? Need me to pick anything up?"

"Thanks, but I think we're all set. I was thinking tacos, and maybe going to a movie later. There's a new holarium in East Falls that's supposed to be nice. How about it?"

That sounded good to me. On a hot summer day, there was something very special about sitting in a big, dark, over-air-conditioned holarium, and losing yourself in the movie playing out over your head.

"What do you want to see?"

"I don't know. Let's see what's playing and decide when you get home."

"Perfect."

— — —

On the spectrum of holomovies I'd seen with my mom, this one wasn't so bad. A romantic action comedy with a couple of actors I liked and one I didn't (but whom my mom *loved*), it had something for each of us.

On the way home, we stopped for soft ice cream at a little place on top of a steep hill in Roxborough, on Ridge Avenue, which was the ridge between the Schuylkill River gorge and the Wissahickon gorge. We used to go there when I was little, when my dad was still alive. He would pack the whole family, and half the kids in the neighborhood, into the minivan.

There were only a couple of people in line when we arrived, but by the time we got our ice cream, at least a dozen were waiting behind us.

The evening had cooled off and there was a nice breeze. Mom got a double—perhaps the first time I'd seen her get anything bigger than a single, or her usual kiddie cone—so I did, too. It seemed to be that kind of night.

We sat on the bench, trying to keep up with our cones while looking out at the sky over the Schuylkill River. Lightning flickered in the distance, illuminating a large thunderhead towering over the hills to the south. Early summer had become the dry season. We'd had a fair amount of lightning at night, but no significant rain, not in a while. Tonight, though, I almost didn't notice the smell of smoke in the air from the brush fires.

We sat there talking, mostly about nothing at first, and it was nice, until she innocently asked me what was new. She'd meant it to be a softball question, but it made me freeze for a second. There was so *much* going on; a lot of it she knew about, but a lot of it she didn't. I had a moment of confusion about which was which. But without a doubt, chief among the big things that were new, that she didn't know about, and that I couldn't tell her about, was that Dymphna was around, that I had met with her.

I had known for some time that Dymphna was the head of Chimerica. Rex had told me months earlier, and I had been holding that secret ever since. But now—having seen her, having her back in my life—the secret felt bigger, more immediate. More like a lie.

I buried it yet again and instead we discussed Wells running for president and chatted about some of the people we both knew at E4E, especially those who were close to Davey and Myra, who had died in the bombing. She grilled me about Rex but didn't push any of the questions I sidestepped. I knew she had come to like Rex a lot, which of course made sense, because pretty much everyone did.

Then she asked how I was holding up.

"Fine," I said, automatically, then, "You mean because of the bombing?"

She suppressed a shudder, and it struck me again how hard a lot of this must have been for her, being a mom and asking your kid how she was faring after an act of terrorism.

"Yes…but not just that," she said, gently placing a hand on my knee. "Jimi, sweetie, you've been through so much this past year. First Pitman and what happened to Del, then Gellersville, now this. You've seen some terrible things, had some horrific experiences. That's all going to take some…processing."

I took a deep breath and steeled myself. This was a conversation we'd had before, and I knew she was just concerned for my well-being, so I was determined not to be difficult about it.

"Are you sure you don't want to talk to someone about it?" she said softly. "A professional?"

I was also sure she was probably right to bring it up, but that didn't make me any less sure that no, I absolutely did not want to see a shrink about any of this. Not yet, anyway.

"Yes. It has been a really intense year," I said with a reassuring smile. "But I'm okay, Mom. Really. If I wasn't, I would say so."

She opened her mouth, like she was going to argue the point, but thankfully she decided not to. A second later she said, "Well, how's it going with Marcella?"

Whenever she said Marcella, it always took me a moment before I realized she meant DeWitt.

"It's good," I said. "I mean, it's only been a few weeks, and the actual work I'm doing is boring, but I'm learning a lot just being around her."

"That's great," she said, her eyes twinkling with something like pride. "It's a great opportunity for you, a high-powered internship like that while you're still in high school."

"Yeah, I know," I said. "And she does important work."

"Your dad would be so proud," Mom said, her voice suddenly thick. She looked away and dabbed her eye with her napkin. "Of Kevin, too. He'd be so proud of both of you."

I didn't know what to say to that. I knew she was right, not because of anything Kevin or I had done, but because of who my dad was. And I knew she was proud of us, too.

"I know, Mom," I said. I put my arm around her shoulders, and she leaned into me for a moment, a brief moment when, for the first time in my life, I felt like I was giving her strength instead of the other way around. And it wasn't about any weakness on her part, it was about honesty, about sharing her vulnerability with me, letting me see it. Treating me like an adult. "If Dad was around, he'd be proud of you, too."

Mom leaned away from me and cleared her throat, as if vaguely embarrassed. She looked at her ice cream and said, "I think I'm done."

My ice cream was dripping over my fingers, my eating having been slowed by the hug, and the massive lump in my throat. "Yeah," I said. "Me, too."

Without a word, we both got up and had one last lick as we walked over to the trash can to dump our cones. As we headed back toward the car, she handed me another napkin, and just like that, we were back in our regular mother/daughter roles. It was nice.

TWENTY-NINE

t was barely nine o'clock when we got home, but Mom went to bed as soon as we got inside. I settled into the armchair—*her* armchair, really—with an old crime novel I was reading. By nine thirty, my eyelids were heavy, and I was thinking maybe I needed to go to bed, too.

That's when the phone rang. It was Claudia.

"Hey," she said when I answered. Her voice sounded thick, like she'd been crying.

"Hey, are you okay?"

She sniffed. "I'm scared."

"What's going on?"

"My mom and dad had a fight, then he started acting funny, and now he's just...*sitting* there. He won't talk or move."

"Did you call a doctor?"

"Yeah, my mom did, but they said it sounds like it's something to do with his Wellplant, and that we need to call Wellplant about it."

"And did you?"

"Yes! My mom did and they said they'd send someone out, but it's been over an hour. Can...Can you come over? Just to...to be here?"

"Um, yeah, of course," I said. "It might take me a little while, but I'm on my way." Truthfully, I didn't know how I was going to get there. It was too far to walk, and I really didn't want to ask my mom to take me out again. Of course, I still didn't have my license, so even though the car's Smartdrive could take me there, legally I needed a licensed driver with me. I didn't relish the thought of taking the Levline into the city and then back out to Chestnut Hill, and then walking from there. But that's what I would have to do.

"Thanks," she said, sniffling. "I'll send a pod, if that's okay?"

"A pod?" A self-driving pod or taxicab was an option I hadn't considered, because it was an option I couldn't afford. But again, Claudia was loaded. "Um, yeah, if you're sure, that'd be great. I'll see you soon."

My mom's bedroom light as still on, and when I rapped lightly on the door, she responded with a sleepy, "Come on in, Jimi."

Her eyes were nearly closed and her book was lying shut on her lap.

"That was Claudia," I said, sitting on the edge of her bed.

Her eyes opened slightly wider. "Is everything okay?"

"I don't know, really. Her dad got spiked."

"He got a Wellplant? You're not serious!"

"Afraid so." I told her about all the weirdness that had followed, culminating in what Claudia had told me about what had happened that evening. Mom's face grew increasingly dismayed as I spoke—sad, concerned, and definitely creeped out.

"Ugh, poor Claudia," she said, shaking her head. "What was he thinking getting one of those things put into his head?"

"I don't know," I said. "He's a really smart guy. And successful. I think he feels it's like, for people competing at the highest levels of anything—business, politics, whatever—there's a lot of pressure not to concede any advantage. His competitors all got spiked, so he felt like he needed to, as well."

"His wife must be beside herself."

"Yeah, I think she is. So's Claudia. Anyway, she asked me to come over, just to keep her company, so I said yes."

"Of course," she said, reaching out and squeezing my hand. "Although, you know, one of these days, you're going to have to spend a night at home."

She smiled to let me know she was razzing me.

"I know, Mom," I said. "I was actually looking forward to an early night at home tonight."

Outside, a tinny horn beeped twice, announcing the arrival of the pod. "That's my ride," I said.

She raised an eyebrow. "You're taking a pod?"

I put up my hands, defensively. "I didn't order it. Claudia sent it to get me."

"Well, that was nice of her."

I kissed her on the forehead then ran downstairs, and out to the waiting pod.

When I approached, the scanner on the roof scanned my face, then a robotic voice asked for confirmation: "Good evening. Are you Jimi Corcoran?"

When I answered yes, it recited Claudia's address and asked if that was the proper destination. When I again answered, "Yes," the door opened and I got in.

It was one of the newer ones, a tiny single passenger car that didn't even have a place for a driver. It was basically a nice, comfortable seat in a light metal shell with windows and a video screen—high-end but two-dimensional, since there wasn't really room for a holovid display—and an overhead light if you'd rather read or whatever.

When I got to Claudia's house, she and her mom were both standing at the front door, looking through the glass. As I got out of the pod and they saw it was me, Bonnie walked away, and Claudia opened the door.

Her eyes were damp and red. She looked scared, which was something I hadn't seen in her in a long time. I'd known her nearly a year and gotten used to her as someone who was brash and outspoken, brave and competent, and ready to do whatever needed to be done. But when we first met, right after her splice, just as the riots were erupting after the Genetic Heritage Act was signed into law, she had been desperate and frightened and insecure. It was a side of her I hadn't seen since then. But I sure saw it now. And I expected that with everything going on with her dad, it was a side of her I'd be seeing a lot more of.

I wondered about how it would be, if my dad was still alive, if something like this happened to him. I shuddered just thinking about it. Claudia was a badass, but she wasn't invincible. I needed to be sure I was available for her, to do whatever I could to help her get through this.

"Hey," I said as I walked up to the door. "You doing okay?"

She shrugged, hugging herself. "My mom was hoping you were the Wellplant doctor."

"How's your dad doing?"

"Exactly the same. Staring into space, barely blinking."

I followed her past the great room and the stairs to the entrance to the family room. Chris was sitting in his armchair, same as before, but his head was tilted back. Instead of looking out the window, he was staring at a spot where the wall met the ceiling. Even from where we were standing, I got the strong impression that his eyes were unfocused.

"Has he seemed distressed at all?" I asked quietly.

She shook her head. "No. No sign of that. Just...this. Like he's in a coma or something." As soon as she said "coma," a tear rolled down her cheek, as if she had just said out loud the thing she was most afraid of.

I put my arm around her shoulder and gave her a squeeze.

"Come on," she said.

As I followed her into the kitchen, I saw Bonnie leaning against the counter, holding a goblet the size of a small fish bowl, sloshing with pink wine. Her face looked like the stress was becoming a permanent part of it.

"Hi, Jimi," she said, patting my shoulder then letting her hand slide off as she walked past. "I'm going to lie down," she said to Claudia. "Let me know if the Wellplant people show up."

"Okay, Mom," Claudia said, feigning calm until her mom left the room.

We sat at the island where her mom had been sitting the night before. An open pizza box sat on the marble—vedgeroni and mushroom, with two pieces missing.

Claudia gestured at it. "Hungry?"

"No, thanks," I said as we sat. "So what's the plan?"

She shook her head. "I don't know. The Wellplant people specifically said not to move him or do anything until their doctor got here, but they also said the doctor would be here soon. And that was hours ago."

"So what should we do?"

She shrugged and looked over her shoulder toward the family room. "I guess we keep waiting."

She let out a deep sigh, then reached out and grabbed a piece of pizza, biting off the tip and chewing joylessly.

I did the same. I still wasn't hungry, but with vedgeroni pizza that doesn't always matter. We ate our pieces in silence. When we were done, she said, "Let's go to my room."

We slid off our stools and I followed her upstairs.

When we got to her bedroom, she turned on the holovid and flicked through the channels with the sound off while I told her about my evening with Mom, and what had happened with Sly and with Ogden earlier.

"Hey, look, it's your uncle Howard," she said with a feeble effort at a mischievous grin.

One of the news channels was showing Howard Wells, looking distinguished and handsome and rich while speaking at a banquet of some sort, smiling and working the crowd, getting them to laugh and applaud.

It took me a moment to get her dig—a reference to Dymphna and Wells's long-ago romance. "Don't even joke about that!" I said, although I was relieved to see a little levity from her. That levity faded as she turned up the volume and the crawl underneath the holo image said, NO COMMENT FROM WELLS CAMPAIGN AFTER HEALTH SCARE.

In the video, Wells paused in mid-sentence, his eyes looking unfocused as they drifted up, looking into space. It appeared at first as though he was trying to think of a word, but then it was clear that his face was absolutely blank. Just like Claudia's dad.

"Hey, Mom!" Claudia called out. "Mom, you should see this!"

A moment later Bonnie appeared in the doorway.

On the holo, there was a moment of nervous laughter from some in Wells's audience, as if they thought he was making a joke of some sort. Then the murmurs rose to a buzz and several members of Wells's entourage rushed to his side, whispering into his ear and looking increasingly frantic as he failed to respond. They eased him backward, sitting him down in his chair. Then he disappeared from view as the entire entourage swarmed around him.

The voiceover said, "Wells was rushed to the hospital, and his campaign released a preliminary statement saying that he was suffering from exhaustion, but they have made no comment since."

Claudia turned to her mom. "Do you think he's got what Dad's got?"

"I have no idea," she said. "But it's interesting that they sent Wells to the hospital while telling us to keep your father here."

The newscaster continued. "There have been reports of other Wellplant users, or 'Plants,' as they've come to be called, experiencing similar episodes, but so far none of those reports have been confirmed."

Bonnie picked up the phone from Claudia's bedside table and retreated into the hallway, punching in a number as she did.

"In related news," the newscaster droned on, "the week-long Humans for Humanity national convention has seen a number of attendees come down with some sort of viral infection. A spokesperson for the organizers confirms that eleven members of the group have come down with symptoms of the unidentified illness, including body aches, coughing and sneezing, upset stomach, and a high fever. The illness appears to be unconnected to Mr. Wells's health scare."

Claudia and I looked at each other as the newscaster moved on to a story about how the latest International Conference on Climate Change had ended with no new agreements on carbon limits, or climate remediation measures, despite increasingly dire projections about worsening weather patterns and accelerated sea-level rise. Things were getting better and better.

"Do you think it's from those idiots?" I whispered. "The ones who grabbed the chicken carcass?"

"Could be," she said. "And Ogden showed no signs of being sick?"

I shook my head. "And he said Roberta hadn't either, or at least not by the time she'd left the next morning."

Bonnie came back into the room and put the phone back in its cradle. "Straight to Wellplant's damn messaging service." She shook her head, then looked at me. "Jimi, there's pizza if you're hungry."

"We had some," Claudia said.

"Thanks," I said.

Bonnie nodded and forced a smile. "Are you spending the night? You're more than welcome."

Claudia looked at me intently. "Can you?"

"Um....Yeah, okay. I mean, if you're sure I won't be in the way."

"No," Claudia said, "that would be great."

As Claudia got ready for bed, I called Rex and told him what was going on with Claudia's dad.

"Wow," he said, sounding concerned. "It sounds just like what's going on with Howard Wells."

"Yeah, I saw that on the news. And unconfirmed reports of similar problems with other people who have Wellplants."

"Did you see that a bunch of other H4Hers at the convention got sick, too?"

"I sure did," I said. "Do you think it's from those guys...that bag... from us?"

"I can't help thinking it might be."

"There's eleven of them now. If that's what it is, it's spreading. It's contagious."

"You still feel okay, though, right?"

"Yeah, I'm fine. Claudia, too. You're okay?"

"Okay except for pangs of longing because my girlfriend abandoned me saying she needed to spend some time at home and then went out to her friend's house."

I laughed. *"Rex!"*

He laughed too, with his low rumbly chuckle. I could feel it in my sternum, even over the phone.

"Have you heard anything from Sly?" I asked, turning serious again.

"Just that he brought the...bag...to our friends. He hopes to hear back from them tomorrow morning and that maybe we could meet up at New Ground to talk about it in the afternoon."

"Good. That would be great. Okay, I'll call you in the morning."

"Tell Claudia I'm thinking of her. Tell her everything's going to be okay."

"Will do."

THIRTY

Claudia and I were both exhausted, and we fell asleep pretty early. The next morning, we were awake at seven. The sun was up, filling her room with light. I caught a faint whiff of wood smoke, like a fire in a fireplace, or more likely a candle that's supposed to evoke that smell.

As we went downstairs to make coffee and breakfast, and to check on Chris, I could sense Claudia's anxiety, her worry about him. She hurried ahead of me, so I was a few steps behind her when she got to the family room and froze. When I stepped up next to her, I saw Bonnie, asleep on the sofa, and Chris, wide awake, smiling beatifically at her.

He turned to look at us, and his smile widened. "Hey kids," he said. Then he turned back to look at Bonnie. "Isn't she beautiful?"

"How do you feel, Dad?" Claudia asked, her tone so flat that I wondered if she might be in shock.

"Never better," he said, with that same smile. "Why?"

"Because you were in like, a coma or something last night," she said, sounding exasperated and annoyed. A little more like herself.

"Oh, that." He laughed, condescendingly, it sounded to me. "That was just a system upgrade." He reached up and touched his Wellplant. "A powerful one, too."

Claudia said, "Mom!" raising her voice enough to awaken her mother.

Bonnie jerked and her eyes half opened, looking at us, then at Chris. At the sight of him, wide-awake and smiling, she shot upright. For a long moment she just stared at him. Then she said, "You're back."

"I was never gone."

"Bullshit," she replied, her voice sharp with anger and fear and relief and hurt. "I don't know where you were last night, but it sure wasn't here."

"Baby—" he said, but Bonnie cut him off.

"Girls," she said, turning to us, "can you give us a minute?"

"Sure, Mom," Claudia said. She lingered another moment, studying her dad as if making sure it was really him. Then she turned back toward the stairs. I glanced longingly at the kitchen, my system primed for coffee, then I turned and followed Claudia back upstairs. I guess the kitchen wasn't far enough away.

When we were halfway up the stairs we heard Bonnie snap, "So what the hell was that?"

"Just a system upgrade. A big one. Making my Wellplant even better than before."

"A system upgrade? With no warning? No scheduling? Sounds more like a system failure. You had us worried sick, Chris. I called the doctor, but they said only the Wellplant's med team could help you, and when I called *them,* they said they'd come out here to have a look at you but they never did. What if it had been serious? What if you were hurt, or dying?"

"Well, I wasn't, honey," he replied. "I've never been better. I can see things clearly for the first time. I can understand complex problems at a level that would have been impossible as a mere human."

"A 'mere human'?" Bonnie cut in with a laugh that was absolutely devoid of any kind of mirth. "Do you even hear yourself?"

We were just at the door to Claudia's room when her mom said, "I want you to get rid of that thing."

Claudia glanced at me, then we went inside and she closed the door behind us. I couldn't tell if she was just being respectful of their privacy or if it was too upsetting to hear them arguing. I think I would have listened in.

We sat on the bed, and she turned the holovid on and raised the volume.

"Smells like a lot of smoke today," I said as she flicked through the channels.

She nodded. "I know. A lot of brush fires this year. The fire-drones will take care of it." Then she nodded toward the holo image and said, "Hey, look at this."

The title graphic under the image said WIDESPREAD OUTAGE ROCKS WELL-PLANT CORPORATION. A trio of talking heads—none of them spiked—were discussing the ramifications of the outage as the graphic changed to MILLIONS INCAPACITATED WORLDWIDE.

"Holy crap," I whispered.

"There are long-term, existential issues raised by this outage," said one of the experts, a woman with close-cropped blonde hair. The graphic said, SYLVIA BASCONE, MD. "Wellplant Corporation has been hit by numerous crises this year, and during this, the company's most serious, acute, and widespread outage, the entire leadership was incapacitated by whatever it was that knocked out everyone else." As she spoke, the image cut to a montage of clips from around the world, important people with Wellplants suddenly rendered unresponsive: heads of state, CEOs, celebrities of all sorts. "Going forward, they are going to have to acknowledge that this is a vulnerability and come up with a strategy that will address this critical flaw."

"Millions incapacitated," Claudia whispered, reading the graphic.

The panel of experts shrunk and moved to the side as the host's face took up the bulk of the holofeed. He had a shaved head, and a thick beard and mustache. He hadn't been spiked, either. "And on that note, Wellplant Corporation just released a statement explaining that the outage was a 'simple software update' that should have taken place when the clients were asleep."

He put his finger over his ear as if listening to something on his earbud then said, "I'm told we have a comment from Senator Hiddleton, who many expect to be joining the presidential race any day."

The image cut to a paunchy man in his sixties with prominent jowls, penetrating eyes, shockingly bad hair, and no Wellplant. He was surrounded by a circle of reporters, all pointing microphones at him.

"The fact of the matter is," he said in a broad Midwestern accent, "we have a man running for president who could be rendered comatose at any moment due to the technical flaws of his own technology."

A reporter said, "Wellplant Corporation says it was a routine system update that should have been staggered to take place overnight in each time zone, while the wearers were asleep."

Hiddleton laughed and shook his head. "Routine? So we're supposed to feel better that this happens all the time? I don't think so. And so what if it *is* supposed to happen overnight? When it's three a.m. here, it's mid-afternoon in Southeast Asia and mid-morning in the Middle East. International crises don't always happen during business hours. If there's a crisis in the middle of the night, we can't have a president who is out of commission because of a, a *system* upgrade."

The holofeed cut back to the host, who said, "Up next, we discuss with our panelists what impact this outage may have on Howard Wells's presidential ambitions. But first, we have statements from some of the most prominent individuals impacted by the outage. While our expert panel and many others have expressed grave concerns about the ramifications, official statements from those directly affected seem crafted to minimize the issue and support Wellplant Corporation."

The feed cut to the prime minister of Japan, who wore a Wellplant, addressing the Japanese parliament with a voiceover translation. "I would like to reassure the Japanese people that this temporary interruption was minor and short-lived and did not at any time impact my ability to lead. I would also like to take this opportunity to thank Wellplant Corporation and Howard Wells for my Wellplant and for yesterday's system upgrade, which have enabled me to provide Japan with a higher caliber of leadership than ever before possible. For this, I and the people of Japan are grateful."

The anchor read aloud while the feed showed excerpts from similar statements released by the prime minister of England; the secretary-general of the United Nations; the CEOs of America's two largest, rival software companies; and even several pop stars. He went on to read the names of other celebrities and leaders, while images of their statements piled up, forming a collage of sorts, all of them voicing support for Wellplant Corporation and Howard Wells.

"So what do you think of that?" the host asked with a nervous laugh. "Have you ever witnessed a technology suffering such a widespread and cataclysmic failure, and then had so many of its users—the people impacted by the outage—all come out in support of the company?"

The panelists all answered at once: "Never." "Nope." "This is unprecedented. And frankly a little creepy."

"Creepy is an understatement," Claudia said, muting the holovid.

I was thinking the same thing but didn't want to say it out loud because her dad was part of the whole mess. I felt like I should say something, but with the holovid sound off, we could once again hear her parents downstairs.

"For the last time, no, I'm not going to get rid of it," Chris was saying, his voice emphatic but even. "My Wellplant has made me a better person, in every sense of the word. It is without a doubt, the best thing that ever happened to me."

"Really?!" Bonnie shot back, her voice raw and shaking. "Better than me? Better than your own daughter? Your brilliant, *chimera* daughter?"

"That's not what I meant and you know it," he replied. "And if you would just trust me and get one, as well, like I asked, you would see the same benefits."

The last thing I wanted to do was to go downstairs into the middle of that argument, but I knew I shouldn't be there at all. I turned to Claudia and said, "I should probably go."

She nodded. "Yeah, I guess so. I'd give you a ride, but I should stay. Okay if I get you another pod?"

"Thanks. That would be great."

THIRTY-ONE

The pod arrived fifteen minutes later. Claudia and I hugged at the front door and she thanked me for coming over.

"Tell your folks I said bye," I said softly. "I'm really glad he seems better now."

"Me too," she said. "I hope he really *is* better."

"I'll check in later, okay?"

"Thanks."

She opened the door and I stepped outside, where the air was still thick with the smell of brush-fire smoke. The pod was waiting at the bottom of the steps, and once it had confirmed my identity, the door opened. As I was getting inside, another vehicle drove up, this one a heavy-looking SUV, black with dark tinted windows. I paused as it pulled up behind the pod and two men got out wearing shades and dark suits. They had Wellplants.

They both looked at me then looked away without saying a word as they climbed the steps to the front door.

Bonnie answered the door, and one of the men said, "We're here from Wellplant."

Bonnie said, "Well, it's about bloody time."

She let them in and closed the door.

I got into the pod and as soon as it pulled away, the newsfeed came to life, more on the Wellplant Blackout, as they were calling it now. As we made our way through the woods, the smoke grew denser. To our left, the landscape looked otherworldly, blackened and smoldering but frosted in places with bright pink fire retardant. In the distance, a small swarm of drones was dropping more of the stuff on other areas that were smoking, half a dozen tiny plumes of pink falling from the sky.

By the time we were past it, the newsfeed had moved on to the other big story of the day: forty-three people had now been sickened by the mysterious bug making the rounds at the Humans for Humanity convention. H4H had issued statements downplaying the seriousness of the situation, but several hundred convention-goers had gone home early.

After a recap of the weather forecast—hot and dry with dangerous brush-fire conditions, go figure—the topic returned to Howard Wells and a very repetitive conversation about how the blackout might impact the presidential race. I watched it anyway, my mind wandering the entire way home. As the pod pulled up in front of my house, the newscaster announced that Wells would be holding a rally in front of Philadelphia's City Hall at noon.

When I got inside, I flopped on the sofa. I felt tired and out of sorts, and I decided maybe a soak in the tub would make me feel better. Before I could go upstairs to fill the tub, however, the phone rang. It was Rex.

"Hey!" I said.

"Hey! I called Claudia and she told me you'd already left."

"Yeah, I just got home. How are you feeling?"

"I'm fine. Tired, but not sick. How about you?"

"Same. They're saying forty-three H4Hers are sick now. Whatever it is, it's spreading fast."

"I know," he said. "Hopefully when we talk to Sly later today we'll get a better idea of what's going on, and what to do about it."

"Yeah…."

"How are things at Claudia's house? How's her dad?"

I told him Chris had regained consciousness, and how things were when I left.

"That sounds really tense. How's she holding up?"

I sighed. "I don't know. She's tough, but she is definitely freaked out."

"I'm sure she is." Rex sighed before switching gears. "Hey, did you get the call from E4E?"

"I don't know. I just got in. What's up?"

"They're organizing a protest for Wells's big speech in front of City Hall today. They want a show of strength, so there's an 'all hands on deck' call, to get as many of us there as possible."

"Oh?" My heart sank a little. After everything that had happened at the last rally, I felt a tiny, creeping doubt, wondering exactly how much good these protests were doing. Even so, I knew there was no doubt I would be there at this one, too. "What time?"

"Noon. We can head over to meet Sly after."

I looked at the clock. It was only ten. I probably still had just enough time for a bath, even if not a long one. "Okay," I said, with as much enthusiasm as I could muster.

We agreed to meet at the southern-most part of the protest area. When I got off the phone, I poured myself some orange juice and drank it down, then ran up the stairs to get the tub started. The water had just warmed up when the doorbell rang. Cursing under my breath, I turned the faucet off and went to the door.

I could see through the peep hole that it was Ralphs and Agent Scanlon. I cursed once more before opening the door.

Agent Scanlon was holding up his badge. "Agents Scanlon and Ralphs."

"Yeah, hi to you, too," I said. "Look, I'm busy, my mom's not here, and I really don't have time for this. Don't you people ever call first?"

Ralphs opened her mouth, but Scanlon spoke first. "Dymphna Corcoran, we're here from the FBI and we need to question you."

I stared at him for an instant, then turned to Ralphs, who rolled her eyes and shook her head. "Sorry," she said. "It won't take a minute."

I knew my mom would be angry. She didn't like the idea of me talking to law enforcement without her present. But I also knew that if I didn't talk to them now, I'd have to talk to them later, and it would probably be a much bigger deal. "Sorry," I started to say, but Scanlon cut me off.

"We do not have a subpoena, but we can get one if necessary," he said. "Then a few minutes would become many long hours."

"It's just a couple of quick questions," Ralphs interjected.

Scanlon's head swiveled to look at her. "Depending on the answers."

Ralphs rolled her eyes. "Can we come in?"

"How about we just do it right here?" I said.

Ralphs looked around, then shrugged. "Okay, sure. When was the last time you saw your Aunt Dymphna?"

The question took me by surprise, and Scanlon seemed to pick up on that fact, his brow furrowing behind his dark shades.

"Dymphna?" I paused. Part of me just wanted to blurt it out, to tell Ralphs about the chickens and the mystery disease and everything. And I might have, if not for Scanlon. Maybe it was the Wellplant, or the attitude, but I didn't like him, and I didn't trust him. "Not since I was little. Why?"

"We're asking the questions here, Ms. Corcoran," Scanlon said.

Almost at the same time, Ralphs said, "We have reason to believe she's in the area, for the first time in a long time. You're sure she hasn't reached out to you or your family?"

"Well, I can't speak for my mom, and as I said, she's not here. But I imagine if my Aunt Dymphna had gotten in touch, Mom would have mentioned it."

"Any idea why she might be in town?"

"Hopefully not for the H4H convention," I said, with a laugh that no one else shared. "No, I don't." I shook my head. "Why are you looking for her?"

"She has some old warrants," Ralphs said. "Nothing serious, but we want to talk to her about some other matters. It's very important."

Scanlon glared at her, then he turned to me. "You do know that lying to the FBI is a serious crime, don't you, Ms. Corcoran?"

"Yeah," I said. "You pointed that out last time we spoke."

Scanlon stared at me for several seconds, his head tilted forward, as if his Wellplant was studying my face. I glanced at Ralphs, who was looking back and forth between me and Agent Scanlon. She looked confused and slightly concerned by his behavior.

"Is that it?" I asked her, determined not to show how unsettled I was by Scanlon's scrutiny.

"Yes, that's all for now," she said. "You have our contact info. Let us know if your aunt Dymphna gets in touch."

"Or if you have any new dealings with CLAD," Agent Scanlon added without moving his face. "Any dealings at all."

I smiled. "Okeydokey."

THIRTY-TWO

From the Levtrain, the sky seemed smudged with a haze of gray smoke. It was densest to the northwest, the general direction of Claudia's neighborhood, but there was so much of it, and it was so widespread, there were obviously fires burning elsewhere, as well. As I watched, a pink plume of fire retardant appeared in the sky, gently falling to the earth. I couldn't see the drone that had released it or the fire it was intended to smother, just the stuff itself, drifting down through the hazy sky.

I had thought about calling Claudia to tell her about the protest, but she had enough going on. She had already said she felt she should be at home with her family as they worked their way through the immediate crisis. I didn't want to put her in a position of having to choose between obligations and feeling guilty either way.

My stomach tightened into a knot as I worried about the Bembry family, the arguing and the tension, the fear and uncertainty. I knew a lot of kids whose parents had gotten divorced, and that in the end, it could be a positive thing. But whenever I had seen them together, Bonnie and Chris had always seemed very much in love; it was heartbreaking to see them arguing like that.

But Bonnie and Claudia were right: Chris *was* different. His Wellplant had changed him. And as much as Bonnie might want him to get rid of it, even if she could convince him to, it wasn't really an option, not a simple one.

When I got off the train, the Lev station was more packed than I'd ever seen it. I squeezed my way through the crowd, feeling claustrophobic as we all ascended the escalator, with people pressing from all sides. I desperately wanted to get out onto the street, but it was even worse up there.

The cordons had been set up to keep the pro-chimera groups separate from the H4Hers, much like the previous protest. But the H4H area was much bigger than before, and there was less of a buffer between the two groups. There were a lot more cops than before, too, and more of them seemed to have Wellplants—or maybe I hadn't noticed it before.

A stage was set up next to the H4H area, with lots of American flags, a huge picture of Howard Wells, and a massive H4H logo. In front of the stage, there was an impressive bank of video and holovid cameras.

I slipped into the pro-chimera area and made my way toward the southernmost part. It was already crowded, probably more chimeras than not. More and more protestors were cramming in, pushing the rest of us up against the partition. The H4Hers behind their partition were barely ten feet away, looking at us with disgust. A surprising number of them had Wellplants, too.

I was worried I wouldn't be able to find Rex, but I spotted him easily, looming over the crowd, six inches taller than pretty much everyone else. He was casting about, looking this was and that, and I smiled, because I knew he was looking for me.

I jumped and waved, but he couldn't see me until I was almost upon him. His face lit up when he saw me.

"Hey!"

"Hey!" I said back.

I put my arms around him and kissed him, then we had a hard time parting because so many people were pushed up against us.

I didn't mind the excuse to stay close.

For the next twenty minutes, more and more people crowded into both enclosures. Rex and I talked quietly about the brush fires and the drought and the climate conference, about the Bembrys and Chris's Wellplant, the broader Wellplant Blackout, and about Howard Wells and his candidacy.

We did not talk about the mystery illness spreading through the H4Hers, or about Sly or CLAD or Chimerica or any of that, but I knew he was thinking about it as much as I was.

I caught a glimpse of Ruth and Pell and Jerry, but by the time they showed up, the crowd was so dense they just waved and stayed where they were.

As a bunch of guys in suits climbed onto the big stage in the H4H area, Donna Bresca from E4E stepped up onto a plastic crate and led a few chants, but they were drowned out by the deafening cheers as Howard Wells ascended the H4H stage. He walked from one end to the other, waving, clasping his hands over his head, pointing to people he knew in the crowd, or pretending to. After a few minutes of milking the crowd for applause, he waved to them to quiet down, as if he hadn't just gotten them all worked up.

"Thank you, thank you all," he said, as the crowd quieted. When they were silent, he waited a few more moments, letting the anticipation build.

Pell shouted out, "Howard Wells, you suck!" earning laughs and applause on our side of things. But at the same time, a woman in the other enclosure shouted out, "We love you, Howard!" Everyone around her erupted in cheers.

Wells put a hand over his heart and pointed at the woman who had shouted, and the crowd cheered again, forcing him to calm them down again. This time he didn't wait for absolute quiet, leaning toward the mic and saying, in a singsong voice, "I'm ba-ack!"

As the crowd cheered, he thundered over them, "And I'm better than ever!"

When the cheers subsided, he continued. "Some of you might have heard that I was down for a minute. That I closed my eyes and took a nap." He put his hands together and held them up to his head, closing his eyes and resting his head against his hands, pretending he was asleep. The crowd laughed.

"And it was a heck of a nap I assure, you," he said, in a conspiratorial aside. "I woke up feeling ten times better, smarter and more powerful. If you ever get a chance to take a nap like I just did, I urge you to do so, because I feel *great*!"

Cheers.

"I know some of our brothers and sisters here at the convention are still under the weather, with this bug going around. And I want to wish them to get well soon, so they can enjoy the rest of this convention and resume the important work of Humans for Humanity."

More cheers.

"Now, speaking of illness, some people out there are trying to make a big deal out of the fact that I took a sick day, to try to score political points. As if I am the first person ever, the only person ever, to be indisposed for a few minutes. As if no one else ever slept or, or sought a few minutes of solitude in the bathroom, am I right?"

Laughs.

"The only difference is that after this nap, after this momentary interruption, I woke up with a fully upgraded operating system," he said, tapping his Wellplant. "Faster, smarter, better informed." Tap, tap, tap. They were the exact same words Chris Bembry had used to describe his upgrade. Maybe the phrase was from an ad or a brochure.

He smiled, then laughed at his own private joke. "There are people out there. Over there." He waved his fingers at us and raised his voice in a mimicky whine. *How could you ever be president with an implant in your head?*

The crowd laughed and cheered and turned to look at us, making it clear, if it wasn't already, that he was talking about E4E. He shook his head and said, "Simpletons." Then he looked over again, and just for a moment, he seemed to be looking right at me. I knew it was ridiculous. He was too far away, and I was hidden in a crowd, but for that second, he seemed to be staring me right in the eye. Then he looked away.

"These are complicated times," he continued. "We face challenges of a complexity our forefathers could never have imagined. So…if you ask me, the better question is: How could you *not*? How could you vote for someone to hold the highest office in the world, to perform the most demanding job in the history of mankind, *without* the aid of the most powerful tool humanity has ever known? Across the world, government officials and captains of industry, leaders of every type, have invested in the future by investing in Wellplant. Because it makes them smarter. It makes them faster. It makes them better."

The crowd clapped, or half of them did, but they didn't cheer. As I watched them, it seemed like the only ones clapping were the Plants. The others seemed restless. I guess waiting for him to get on with the chimera bashing.

"H4H!" someone yelled out, prompting broader cheers from the H4H side and loud boos from the pro-chimera side.

"Yes, yes," he said, pacing the stage again and nodding his head. "H4H. Enough about me and my Wellplants—although I will tell you, they're a lifesaver!"

A smattering of laughs drifted across the crowd, mostly from the Plants, as far as I could tell. A few of them close to the edge of the H4H rally area peered over at me; a handful of blank faces with Wellplants turning and looking me in the eye, much like Wells himself had done. I was about to elbow Rex and tell him, but then I thought I recognized one of them: a pale, pinched face, under a short buzz cut. Then he smiled, and I elbowed Rex hard, pointing.

"Ow!" Rex said, grabbing his ribs.

"That's Stan," I said. "Stan Grainger. Right there!"

"Where?" he said, trying to follow my finger. But by the time he looked, Stan had turned around and disappeared into the rival crowd.

"This has been an incredible week," Wells started up again. "The first annual Humans for Humanity National Convention. You…have made it amazing. The speakers, the panels, getting to meet so many of you. Probably the best week of my life. Truly. But it was also a terrible week." He nodded sadly. "I would like to take a moment to right now, to remember the friends we lost this week in the tragic bombing at the Seaport Museum."

He bowed his head as a hush fell over the entire street, both sides falling silent. After a few seconds, he looked up. "I would also like to take a moment to remember who was responsible for that cowardly attack." Once again, his eyes found me.

"That responsibility lies, not just with the terrorists who planted the bomb, who detonated it," he said, still staring at me, "but also with those who sympathize with them, who give them comfort or shelter or support."

Maybe he isn't really looking at me, I thought. Maybe there was a camera behind me, or a teleprompter somewhere in front of me. Maybe that's where he was really looking. But then, seemingly all at once, all of the heads with Wellplants in them turned around, and all of them stared directly at me. This time, there was no doubt. And even under the hot, noonday sun, goose bumps rose on my arms.

Rex looked around, then down at me. "What the hell is going on?"

I shook my head and whispered, "I don't know."

"These people are every bit as guilty, every bit as responsible," Wells said, his voice rising to a thunderous crescendo. "They must be stopped. They *will* be stopped, and they will suffer the consequences of their actions!"

Some of the other H4Hers seemed to notice that Howard Wells and his fellow Plants were looking at something. They turned, too, trying to figure out what it was.

Then, from the corner of my eye, I saw something arc up into the sky from the H4H crowd, a ball of foil from a hot dog or something. As it descended, I realized it was coming right for me, but there was no room to move out of the way. I put up my arms to fend it off, but at the last second, Rex reached up and caught it in midair, earning cheers from the pro-chimera folks around us.

Then another ball of trash rose up into the air, from the other end of the H4H enclosure. Once again, it arced through the air, right at me. I caught this one, but there were no cheers this time. I think the people around us knew something strange was happening.

I locked eyes with a guy wearing a Wellplant standing in the H4H enclosure, maybe fifty feet away. He smiled as he threw an apple core, which missed me only because I ducked.

Rex put his head next to mine and said, "Let's get out of here."

I nodded. "Yeah."

As we turned and started pushing through the crowd, I saw another trash missile sailing through the air. Then two more, from different directions. All three of them headed directly at me. The accuracy was astonishing.

Before they landed, several more rose up, then several more after that. With Rex pushing ahead of me, and trash raining down, people got out of our way. As we moved across the enclosure, the debris being thrown followed our every step, matching our movements, finding us even as we zigzagged through the crowd.

The remains of a sandwich hit the back of my head, and something similar bounced off my shoulder. A plastic bottle hit my arm.

I couldn't see the people doing the throwing, and there was no way they could see me in the middle of the crowd. But somehow, they knew where I was, could tell where I was headed, and were able to throw with pinpoint accuracy.

We finally made it out of the enclosure, Rex pulling me by the arm. Trash was still raining down as we hurried past two cops, both wearing Wellplants. They smiled as they watched us, neither of them doing anything to help.

We ducked into the street entrance to the underground Lev Hub. Rex pulled me in after him, then turned me around, checking me for injuries. "Are you okay?" he said, his eyes wide and scared. "Are you hurt?"

"No, I'm okay," I said, running my hands up and down his arms to soothe him. "I'm fine. What about you, did you get hit?"

He shook his head and picked a bit of mustard-covered bun off my shirt and flung it aside, then pulled me to him and held me tight. I hugged him back, reassured by the contact, safe in his arms.

When I pulled back from him, he glanced back out on the street. "What the hell was that?"

Wells was still speaking, and the two crowds were taking turns cheering and booing.

"I don't know," I said. "Wells was looking at me. Then everyone else was, everyone with a Wellplant."

"When?"

"Right before the throwing started."

"And what was up with that? Why were they throwing stuff at *you*? And how were they able to hit you like that? Most of them couldn't even see you."

"I don't know," I said, shaking my head and fighting off another shiver as I considered the implications. I thought back to the three Plants from that RV, how their actions had been synchronized, and I could feel my guts squirm inside me. "I guess it's some kind of...Wellplant thing."

THIRTY-THREE

We went back to my house and I showered, letting the warm water rinse the food out of my hair and ease the tension out of my shoulders. I was shaken by what had happened at the protest, but probably more shaken by the look in Rex's eyes, the fear, as we were fleeing.

While I was sorting myself out, Rex made tea, and after I'd changed into clean clothes, we sipped it quietly while sitting on the sofa, close enough that we were touching, comforting each other with our presence. By the time we were finished, it was time to meet Sly.

When we got to the coffee shop, Ruth and Pell were standing with him in the corner. The three of them hurried over to us as when we walked in, all asking if we were okay.

"We're fine," I told them. "We're both fine."

"Ruth and Pell were just telling me what went down out there," Sly said, shaking his head. "That sounds crazy intense."

"It was," Rex said. "Crazy *and* intense."

"And creepy, too," Pell added. "They were definitely targeting Jimi? And targeting accurately."

"Right?" I said, rubbing the back of my head at the memory of it. "That was the creepiest part: most of the people throwing stuff, I couldn't see them, and they couldn't see me, but their aim was incredible."

"And how about Wells, too?" Ruth said. "I swear, at one point he was looking right at you. Singling you out."

I nodded. "I thought it was my imagination at first, but then all of them turned to look at me. All of the ones with Wellplants. That was even creepier."

Ruth reached out and squeezed my hand. "I'm really glad you're okay."

I squeezed back. "Thanks." Then I turned to Sly. "So? What have you got for us?"

He nodded in a way that gave me pause, as if he was going to deliver bad news. "Um, let's go in the back. Jerry said we could use his office." He turned to Ruth and Pell. "Excuse us."

Then he turned and walked toward the back.

Pell feigned indignation. "Well, excuse *us*."

"Sorry," I whispered to Ruth and Pell as Rex and I followed him.

We entered Jerry's office, and Sly leaned against the desk while Rex and I sat in the two chairs facing it.

"So?" Rex said. If he shared my suspicions, he wasn't showing them. "Did you find anything?"

Sly nodded again, like he was putting off saying what he was about to say. "So…Chimerica's scientists tested the carcass, but unfortunately, they decided they can't share the results."

"What? We told CLAD we'd pass along whatever Chimerica found. They're going to be furious if we don't," Rex said. "Why, what did they find?"

Sly took a deep breath and let it out. "I mean with anybody." He looked at Rex and then at me. "Including you and me."

I let out a short, sharp laugh. "You're joking, right? *We* got the sample. *We're* the ones who gave it to *you*."

"I know, and they appreciate that," he said. "They really do. But this is very sensitive, and we have to be very careful."

"Meaning they don't trust us," Rex said quietly.

Sly shook his head. "Rex, man, you know it's not like that."

"No, obviously it is," he said. "Damn, Sly, after all the stuff I've done? All the secrets I've already kept?"

"I know," Sly said. "I know. They won't tell me, either, and it's not about trust. Apparently, this is incredibly sensitive."

"It's bullshit is what it is," I said. "There's people getting sick out there. More and more of them. And maybe it's H4Hers for now, but so what? They're people, too. And the way it's spreading through them now, it won't be long before it's spreading through us, too."

"I know," Sly said quietly.

"If it's related to this chicken thing, that means we're partly to blame," Rex said. "*We* were the ones who brought the carcass into the public. And it also means Wells is somehow behind it, because the chicken came from his plant, or whatever the hell it is. We need to know what you know."

Sly laughed sadly and shook his head. "Not what *I* know. They won't tell me, either, remember?"

"And you're okay with that?" I demanded.

"I have to be. I trust them. I trust Dymphna. She knows what she's doing."

I was fighting the rage building inside me, trying not to tremble or curse or throw things around. I wasn't sure any longer that *I* trusted Dymphna. Yes, we were related, but so what? It wasn't like I really *knew* her, not in any meaningful way. "Well, I'm not so sure *I* do. All the secrecy, all the bullshit. You know I don't agree with CLAD, killing people and blowing stuff up, but I'm starting to think they might be right about Chimerica."

Sly pushed himself away from the desk, standing upright. "What the hell is that supposed to mean?"

I stood up, too. "It means you don't *do* anything."

Rex stood up and put himself between us. "Hey, let's calm down here."

"No, I'm serious," I said, Ogden's complaints echoing in my head. "What the hell does Chimerica do? Rex, when you were stuck in jail, they wouldn't do a thing to get you out. Nothing. All those people down in that mine at Omnicare, and Claudia and I had to steal a damn quadcopter to go get you out."

"And I helped with that," Sly said.

"Yeah, but you had to violate orders to do it, right?"

"I also seem to remember saving you and Claudia from Wells's people when they were after you," Sly said.

"Right," I shot back. "But then we had to escape because Chimerica was holding me against my will when I was trying to get Rex out of danger."

"Jimi, you've got to understand that sometimes things are bigger than you know," Sly said. "That maybe you don't know the whole picture."

"Could you *be* any more condescending?" I was so furious that I didn't even wait for him to respond. "If I'm so in the dark, then *tell* me, Sly! Enlighten me about the big picture, I'm begging you. Because the only picture I see is Chimerica sitting back, playing army, and keeping its precious secrets while the world is going to *hell*!"

Sly's face turned cold. "Really? That's all you see?"

"Unless you show me more, then yes, that's all I see!"

"Sly, Jimi, come on," Rex said.

I turned to Rex. "No. Ogden needs to know what's going on. The world needs to know what's going on. If it seems like this bug or whatever it is came from Wells Life Sciences, we need to tell people."

"You can't," Sly said, folding his arms with great finality.

Rex ignored him. "How?" he asked me.

"I don't know. Maybe we can go to the press. Or the police even."

Sly ground his jaw and shook his head. "Chimerica can't let you do that."

I laughed again, bitterly. "They can't *let* us?"

Sly wasn't laughing. Not at all. "No."

"Sly," Rex said, finally getting annoyed, as well. "It's not up to Chimerica to *let* us do anything."

"This isn't some little thing," I said. "We need to warn people about this, before more people get sick. Before people start to die."

"Sorry, Jimi," Sly said. "I feel you, I do, but all I can tell you is what Dymphna told me: 'This is bigger than that.'"

I turned to Rex. "This is useless. I'm out of here." Then I turned back to Sly. "As long as you're ready to *let* me leave, that is."

I glared at him for a moment, half expecting him to actually try to stop me. But he didn't, and I stormed out of the office.

Ruth and Pell were at the counter as I rushed through the front of the coffee shop. They both stared at me with the kind of wide-eyed look that made it clear they had overheard the tone of the conversation, if not the actual words.

Rex came out after me. "Jimi!" he called out, in such a rush that he bumped into me from behind when I stopped to look at the holovid behind the counter.

I recognized the face it was showing. Rex followed my gaze, and I think he recognized it, too.

"That's the guy who grabbed the carcass from us," I whispered.

Rex nodded without speaking.

The image was a two-dimensional photo. Under it, the caption read:

NORTH DAKOTA MAN SUCCUMBS TO MYSTERY FLU

87 NOW HOSPITALIZED WITH SYMPTOMS

"They're calling it flu, now," Rex said.

"They said it doesn't seem too bad," Ruth called out. "They had a doctor on, saying the man who died must have had some other condition that made it worse."

Rex and I looked at each other. "You still feel okay?" he asked.

I nodded. "You?"

He nodded, and I kept going, through the door and out onto the sidewalk.

"We need to do something," I said as Rex fell into step beside me. "I don't know what Wells is up to, but between the sick chickens and now the sick people, it definitely seems he's got something going on. Something big and terrible. And I don't know what Chimerica's deal is, but we can't just sit back and do nothing about it."

The last flu pandemic had ended when I was a little kid. I couldn't remember much about it, on a global scale. I was too young to be watching the news and understanding what was going on. But I understood when my dad died—to the extent that a little kid can understand that type of thing. Or a teenager or adult, for that matter.

But in the back of my mind, I couldn't help thinking, *What if someone had been able to stop that pandemic before it got started? What if all those lives could have been saved? What if my father was still alive?*

I was already worked up from arguing with Sly. Thoughts of my dad hit me with such clarity and such emotion, I suddenly felt hot tears running down my cheeks. I wiped them away, annoyed at myself for crying.

"Hey," Rex said softly, still rushing to keep up with me. "Are you okay?"

"Yes," I said, wearily, slowing a step. "I'm fine. But this is wrong. We need to do something."

"You mean go to CLAD, like you said back there?"

I turned to look back at the coffee shop. Sly was out on the sidewalk, looking after us, assessing us, maybe wondering what we were going to do next. I was wondering that myself. I picked up my pace again.

"I don't know," I said. "I guess so. Or maybe we really *could* go to one of the news stations and tell them our suspicions. We don't have proof, but it's a pretty sensational accusation. They'd probably at least broadcast it."

"Yeah, maybe," he said dubiously, "…if it comes from the girl from Pitman."

"Or we could go to the police," I said. "But I don't know if I would trust them with something like this. It's too big. And Wells is too powerful."

"And a lot of them have Wellplants now."

"Yeah, more and more of them. If we couldn't trust them before, I definitely don't want to trust them now. And the same thing is true with the press, actually. More and more Wellplants. I mean, Alenka Bogdan used to be such a badass, and now she's like Howard Wells's lapdog." I shook my head. "They're not going to be any help."

"So what do you want to do?"

I thought about it for another second and then made up my mind. "Ralphs said that when CLAD released their statement claiming responsibility for the bombing, they sent it to all the media outlets, locally and nationally. Maybe *they* can get word out about this. We do need to go to Ogden. We need to talk to CLAD."

THIRTY-FOUR

J erry's truck was parked near Rex's apartment, a little ways from the coffee shop. We discussed next moves as we walked. Rex was reluctant to go to CLAD at first, but he was as alarmed as I was about the mystery flu and the possibility that it had originated at Wells Life Sciences. And he was almost as dismayed as I was at Chimerica's—and Sly's—refusal to do anything about it, or even tell us what they had found.

This was not a decision I took lightly. As I had told anyone who would listen, I had massive concerns about CLAD and their goals and their tactics, and my resolve faltered as I considered how this meant I would be officially allying myself with the same people who had killed Reverend Calkin and Myra Diaz and Davey Litchkoff and so many others—so many of them allies in the fight to protect chimeras. But there was nowhere else to go, nowhere we could think of. And we had to tell someone. We had to *do* something.

By the time we got to the truck, Rex was on board. As we drove through the city and across the bridge into New Jersey, we talked a lot—about Wells's presidential bid, CLAD's bombings, the mystery flu, the sick chickens, the strange Wellplant outage, Stan Grainger's reappearance, meeting Dymphna, Chimerica's inaction—the conversation going in circles as we tried to make it all fit together.

We were still trying by the time we left the Smartway and were zigging and zagging through the flooded areas around Pedricktown. We were almost at Ogden's, driving down one of the narrow roads flanked by stagnant water when Rex looked in the rearview mirror and grunted.

I turned to look back and saw a black van behind us, approaching fast.

"That better not be Sly," I growled.

Rex shook his head. "It's a different van. Bigger tires and higher suspension."

It was built for driving through the zurbs, where the roads were all chunked up.

"Coming up fast," I said. There was a faint yellow line down the middle of it, but the road was barely one lane wide. "Do they have room to pass us?"

"It'll be tight if they try it here."

The van pulled to within a few car lengths, close enough that I could see the windows had a reflective coating to conceal whoever was inside. Then it slowed down and gave us more space.

"It's easing back," I said.

Even as I said it, a hatch opened in the roof of the van and a pair of drones rose up from it and came toward us.

Rex hit the accelerator, but the van behind us kept pace as the drones flew straight toward us and disappeared overhead. A loud *clunk* came from the roof, and almost immediately, our truck skidded to a halt, and so did the van behind us, dust from both vehicles' tires drifting out over the muddy water alongside the road.

"What the hell?" he muttered.

"What is it?" I said. "What's happening?"

"Something's commandeered the Smartdrive."

A thick, gray cloud of mist or powder descended over us, quickly settling on the windows, all of them. In seconds the glass was covered, and the interior of the truck was dark except for the light from the dashboard.

Rex hit the windshield wipers, and we could hear them come on, but they did nothing to remove whatever was coating the windows.

I tried my door, but it was locked. I pulled the latch to unlock it, but it didn't make any difference. "It's overriding the door locks, too."

Rex tried his door but got the same result.

"What do we do now?" he asked.

I shook my head. "Who do you think it is? Wells?"

"I have no idea."

Panic rose inside me as I thought about all the horrible things Wells and his accomplices had done, and for an instant I pictured all those things being done to Rex and me. Then the truck began to move, which was totally disconcerting with no way of seeing outside and no idea who was controlling it.

Rex tried to pull some fuses from under the dashboard to see if he could make the truck stop, but apart from messing with the lights and the radio, it had no effect. After ten minutes of freaking out, the anxiety and fear of driving blind and at the mercy of some unknown entity gave way to a quieter feeling of surrender.

At fifteen minutes, we were both sitting back with our arms folded and our eyes closed. Rex said, "Jerry's going to be pissed if we can't get this stuff off the windows."

A few minutes later, the truck lurched up onto some kind of ramp and kept going, a curved ramp judging from the centrifugal force that pushed us both to the right. When we finally came to a stop, Rex and I looked at each other in the darkness. Then the door locks clicked into the unlocked position.

"I guess we're there," Rex said.

"I guess so."

We opened our doors and stepped out into a wide, open space with a concrete floor and ceiling, cement columns, and green walls with thin blue strips. Two sides, presumably south and west, were backlit by the sun, bright enough that we had to blink and shield our eyes after the darkness inside the truck. The other two walls were darker. Looking closer, I saw that the green was from leafy plants, lettuce or spinach or kale, taking up the walls. The blue strips were tubes of liquid, probably some kind of nutrient water.

It was a vertical farm, apparently converted from an old parking garage.

The van that had intercepted us was parked behind us. Leaning against it was a tall, striking woman with a bird splice.

Rex and I both said, *"Dara!?"*

We knew her from our previous experiences with Chimerica. I had met her on Lonely Island. She and Sly had helped Claudia and me escape and had been instrumental in helping take down Omnicare, and rescuing Rex. I hadn't seen her since then.

"What are you doing here?" I asked.

Her mouth tugged into a half smile. "Bringing you here."

I could feel my face darken. "That was you?"

Rex turned and looked at the truck and the charcoal-gray coating on all the windows.

"It comes off with dish soap," she said. "A quick wash and it'll be good as new. Or good as it was. Sorry about the cloak-and-dagger stuff. They didn't want to risk having to find another safe house, like they did after you apparently insisted on riding up front with Sly. The costs add up, you know?"

"Who's 'they'?" Rex asked.

"Me," said a voice behind us.

We turned and saw Dymphna emerging from the shadows. "I get it, you know," she said, waving a hand. "I understand wanting to know where you are going, wanting to know what's going on. But Chimerica's imperatives are more important than any one person's preferences, especially now."

"And what are those imperatives, exactly?" I demanded. "What is all this about? Because all I see is a lot of Chimerica not doing anything."

"Well, that's why you're here," she said, with a smile. "So I can tell you what it's all about. And so we can plan what to do next."

THIRTY-FIVE

Dymphna led us to a table and chairs off to the side, close to one of the green walls. The furniture looked like the same as what had been at the shore house. The leaves in the section of green wall next to them fluttered as a breeze pushed through. Somewhere behind it, a window was open. She groaned slightly as she sat in one of the chairs and directed us to sit in the others.

"Coffee?" she asked as she took a sip from a mug on the table.

Rex and I both declined, and she nodded at Dara, who turned and left us, walking down the ramp we'd driven up.

I had a lot of questions, and more than a few comments, as well. But Dymphna had such a presence, such a gravity about her. You knew she was in charge, you could feel it. And you knew that she *should* be, too. She radiated intelligence and authority, but humility, as well. Out of respect, as angry as I was, I still let her go first.

"I'm not, by nature, a secretive person," she said, smiling at me and then at Rex. "It's a behavior I've had to learn over the years, as circumstances have warranted it. As events have shown me the importance of it. I'm sorry if you find such precautions onerous. But I've learned my lessons well, and these precautions have saved lives. Including my own. So..." She sat back. "I know you have questions, and I'll do my best to answer them, but first I wanted to give you some background, so you understand what's at stake, and so you know how we got to this point, how *I* got to this point. Is that okay?"

Rex and I looked at each other, then nodded.

Dymphna nodded back. "Good. Your suspicions about the Wells Life Sciences facility are correct. Our tests on that chicken carcass have confirmed it. We've known for some time that Howard Wells has been working on perfecting a new avian flu. And he's been trying to use chimeras with bird splices as the vector, an intermediate step by which the virus can jump from birds to chimeras to non-chimeric humans."

"He's trying to start a new pandemic?" I felt short of breath as the reality of that sank in. "That's insane," I said, my voice barely a whisper; then, louder, "Why would he do that?"

"Because he *is* insane. Maybe he would have been anyway, but that Wellplant, he's had it so long, I believe it has permanently altered his brain, warped his mind." She looked at the floor for a moment, thinking. "When I still knew him, many years ago, Howard was deeply concerned about the future of the planet, the future of humanity. We used to talk at length about how we could possibly save it, to prevent disaster."

She smiled sadly. "He saw overpopulation as the primary problem, that there were simply too many people and that was the root of all the planet's ills. I had to concede the point, to some extent, but I argued that it wasn't the billions of poor people that were the problem, but the few, the super-rich who were using up the bulk of the planet's resources. The rest could live sustainably, if not for them. But he only saw a species that was, in his words, 'growing in number instead of in strength, vitality, or intellect.' As he began to experiment with the early Wellplants, his views became more extreme. He saw his implants as a way for those who had already proven their superiority—defined using the capitalist metric of wealth, and ignoring how such wealth is so often amassed by corruption or luck or inheritance— to pull further away from the rest of us, as a way for them to become, in essence, a superior species, one more worthy of Earth's limited resources."

She took a deep breath and let it out slowly. "The last flu pandemic, the one that took Danny, resulted in a substantial decline in carbon emissions and consumption of resources."

For an instant, I didn't know who she meant by Danny, then I realized it was my father, her brother. I felt that familiar stab of pain at the thought of his death, but it also hit me in a way it hadn't before. He wasn't just my dad who had died, he was also Dymphna and Trudy's brother, my mom's husband. I had known all this of course, but hadn't *felt* it, not like this.

Dymphna continued. "Some experts think that without that dip in emissions, the planet might have already surpassed a tipping point by now, a climate collapse that could have rendered the Earth uninhabitable. Howard saw the pandemic as a tragic but ultimately beneficial step in the right direction. Since then, apparently, as the population has started to rebound, as consumption and emissions have crept back up, and as the climate has continued to degrade, his views have become more extreme."

Rex laughed harshly. "More extreme than that?"

"We've managed to get a few people close to him," she continued, "nonchimera allies, and we've intercepted enough communications that we've more or less determined his current goal: in order to save the planet for those who matter—those whose intelligence and capabilities have been augmented with Wellplants—he sees the need for rapid, and drastic, depopulation."

Rex had gone pale. "He's—he's going to kill billions," he said.

Dymphna nodded. "That's his plan. We've strongly suspected it for some time. But the tests on the chicken carcass you secured for us essentially confirm it."

"He's running for president...." Rex said, musing out loud.

Dymphna waved a hand. "We believe that's been a ruse from the beginning. Part megalomaniacal whim, part diversionary tactic."

"How is he planning to spread this flu?" I asked.

She shook her head. "That we don't know. In order to achieve the critical mass necessary for the kind of pandemic we think he is aiming for, he'll need to release it broadly, globally. And we haven't been able to determine how he plans to do that."

"We need to do something," I said. "We need to find out and stop him."

"We *are* doing something," she said softly. "We *have been* doing something. But we need more time."

"Doing what?!" I said "And more time? We don't *have* more time. Wells's super-flu is out there *now*," I said, my voice rising. "We need to let the world know, so people can set up quarantines, start work on vaccines. And we need to tell them that Wells is behind it all, so he can be stopped from doing anything else to make matters worse."

"Wait a second," Rex said. "Won't Wells's *customers* be sickened by it, as well? Won't the Plants be killed, too?"

"No," Dymphna said. "They won't."

"Why not?"

"There's always been an immunological component to the Wellplant procedure, to prevent rejection. But two years ago, we discovered that Wells had added another step to that process, exposing the subjects to a virus, a highly effective live vaccine that conferred broad immunity to the avian flu."

"So, Plants are immune, but everyone without a Wellplant will get sick and die?" Rex shook his head in disgust. His eyes looked frantic. "Jimi's right, we need to tell people about this now."

"No," she said, very deliberately. "Not yet."

"Why not!?" I said, increasingly exasperated.

She took a deep breath and sat back. "Several years before the great pandemic, there was a smaller epidemic of flu. People forget about that now, because it was overshadowed by the pandemic that followed. But at the time it was unprecedented. Devastating. Over a million people died in that smaller wave. It's not uncommon, you know, for pandemics to be preceded by precursors of a sort. Anyway, that earlier epidemic prompted me to begin working on a new sort of live-virus flu vaccine, one that would be more stable and more effective against a rapidly mutating virus. It would train the immune system to attack the stem of the virus, which is relatively immutable, instead of the outer part, the head, which most vaccines target, but which is much more prone to mutations that can make a vaccine ineffective.

"I had just met Howard, and while this wasn't right in his area of expertise, his brilliance was obvious. I enlisted his help. That was how we first got to know each other, really. The immunity virus never panned out, not then at least, but the virus we developed had some unique properties that made it a perfect vector to deliver gene therapy, and for splicing. The epidemic resolved and we both moved on to other projects. I continued to work on the splicing medium and Howard returned to his work on implantable computers. And we became close. As different as we were in some ways, we were very similar in others, including flouting some of the norms of science and academia.

Later that year, I had a breakthrough, and I tried the new procedure out on myself, just a tiny little splice, a smattering of leopard spots across my back. Intellectually, I just wanted to see if it could be done, but on a deeper level, this was also something I'd wanted since I was young. I wanted to be a chimera, more a part of the natural world, not separate from it. I thought that showing that allegiance was especially important as we tried to save what was left of the world from the ravages of corporate industrialism and consumerism. Howard was furious, he called it unnatural and sacrilegious"—she shook her head and snorted—"even while he was working on putting a machine into his head. We actually broke up over it, briefly, before getting back together. Not long after, though, Howard finished his first Wellplant, and had it implanted into his brain. I was devastated but determined not to be a hypocrite about it. Soon enough, though, he began to change deep down. And I guess I did, too."

"But you stayed together," Rex said.

"For a time. Over the next few months we both became more and more absorbed in our work. Howard was fixated on the question of overpopulation and continued refining and upgrading his Wellplants. I assembled a team of grad assistants, and some of them got spliced, too. Many of them became close friends and allies. Some still are.

"That fall, flu season started early, and it was quickly clear it would be a bad one. Later, we would look back and realize it was the first year of the great pandemic. Anyway, with so many people getting sick, I returned to work on the immunity virus, hoping to make headway, but I never managed to crack it. Howard declined to help, saying he was too busy with his other work." Her face twisted at the memory. "He said it was a dead end. And even with the death toll rising, quickly skyrocketing, even when it became clear we were looking at a full-blown pandemic, Howard spoke about letting nature take its course. He said the flu was nature self-correcting, trying to reestablish some sort of sustainable equilibrium. Theoretically, it was an interesting argument, but this wasn't theoretical. Millions of lives were at stake."

"Including my dad," I said quietly.

She nodded gravely. "Yes, including your dad...my brother....Anyway, we argued about that. A lot. Even so, I continued working on both tracks—a flu vaccine and the splicing technology—both using the same virus. I made much more progress with the latter, and soon I was ready for the next round of tests, a broader and more ambitious sort of splice."

"I bet Wells was thrilled about that," I said.

"I didn't tell him. Not yet. But as we were preparing for the next round of tests, the North American gray wolf was declared officially extinct. I was devastated. I acquired a small sample of the wolf's DNA and used that as the basis for the next test, the broader splice, which once again I administered to myself. A broader splice meant broader changes. The transition took twenty-four very unpleasant hours. When Howard saw me after I'd sweated out the procedure, he was enraged. He called me a freak, an abomination."

"Sounds familiar," Rex said.

"It does now." Her eyes were pained and unfocused, recalling the painful memory. "But back then, it was an escalation. Things had grown increasingly tense between us, but this was the first time he actually scared me. Later that night, a fire broke out in my lab, a suspicious one. I lost all of my work on the immunity virus *and* on the splice medium, everything that wasn't in my head. But more tragic, one of the university's security staff died in the fire. When the police came to question me, it was clear they thought I had set the blaze."

"Why?"

"There was overwhelming evidence to suggest as much. Charges on my credit card, my ID card being used to swipe in before the blaze. They thought I was trying to hide a lack of progress in my research. I realized I was being set up, clumsily, but convincingly. I also discovered that someone had broken into my apartment. I feared for my safety."

"What did you do?" I asked.

"I fled. I had a little bit of money from a few patents I'd licensed. I packed up and I disappeared."

I thought back to what Trudy had told me about that time, about how upset Grandma and Grandad had been about how Dymphna left. I wondered how much of it was because she'd spliced herself, and how much was because of the police's suspicions. I made a note to ask her later.

Dymphna dabbed at her eyes. "I tried to continue my work, but it took several years before I learned enough about life on the run, and staying hidden, that I could resume it. In all likelihood, I wouldn't have solved the immunity virus anyway, but when…when your father got sick, Jimi, when he died, I couldn't help but feel responsible. If I hadn't failed, Danny would still be alive."

I put my hand on her wrist. "It's not your fault," I said. "You tried. Maybe it just wasn't possible."

She put her hand over mine. "But it was, you see."

THIRTY-SIX

ymphna sat back, letting her words sink in. "How do you know?" I finally asked.

"I kept in touch with friends who were still working with Howard," Dymphna said, "friends personally closer to me, even though their work was more adjacent to his. They kept an eye on him for me over the years, even as he left academia and started building his empire. His scientific work continued to break new ground, but they were all concerned about his increasingly extreme personal views, and his obsession with me. Two years ago, they told me about this new stage to the Wellplant implantation procedure: infecting the subject with some sort of virus that would bolster the patient's immunity. They got hold of a sample, and some of Wells's data on it."

"Your immunity virus?" Rex asked. "He finally perfected it?"

She looked at him grimly and nodded. "It was an almost perfect genetic match to my virus, with one simple but brilliant tweak, one I might never have thought of. Maybe Howard wouldn't have, either, if not for his Wellplant. But it was definitely a version of the same virus. He had indeed perfected it. I don't think he realized his virus had any connection to the splice medium—he might not have wanted it had he known, he's such a bigot. But here's the thing: from his notes we learned that he'd actually perfected the immunity virus quite some time ago. A decade, in fact. The second year of the great pandemic. But he never released his findings."

"Why?" Rex asked.

She ignored him at first, turning to me with eyes welling as she waited for me to do the math. It took me a second.

"But"—my own tears came on fast—"that means he had perfected it before my dad died. Before so many other people died."

She nodded. "I'm afraid it does," she said softly. "He was serious about letting nature take its course. When it suits his purposes, at least."

I had no words. I was breathless, drowning in an ocean of fury and sorrow.

"I'm sorry, Jimi," she said. "I was devastated, too, when I realized that implication. But there were other terrible implications, as well."

Rex stepped closer and put his arm around my shoulders. "Like what?" he asked, his voice grim.

"Like, why would he start administering the immunity virus to his Wellplant customers now?"

"And…why would he?" Rex asked her.

But I spoke first, as the answer clicked into place in my head. "Because he was also perfecting his super-flu. And he was planning on releasing it. To finish the job the first pandemic started."

"Precisely," Dymphna said. "They call it a slate-wiper in epidemiological circles, an extinction-level event that would reset the planet. Wells was immunizing his subjects against the avian flu because he was entering the operational phase of his genocidal master plan. And he didn't want his chosen few to perish with everyone else."

She paused for a moment, maybe to give us a chance to respond or ask questions. But we were both speechless.

"I called an emergency meeting of Chimerica's governing council," she continued. "And we came up with a plan. We were pretty sure chimeras were already immune to whatever Wells would unleash, because I had used our original attempt at an immunity virus as a medium."

"But you couldn't be positive?" Rex asked.

She shook her head. "Not without a sample of his super-flu. To be sure, though, we changed up the splicing medium. We started using an altered version of Wells's own improved immunity virus as a vector, and we pushed it out through the genie distribution network."

I turned to Rex. "That's why the chimeras working at that facility never got sick. When they got spliced, they got immunity from avian flu."

He nodded thoughtfully. "So that's fine for the chimeras who've gotten spliced since the changeup. But what about the ones from before?"

"And everyone else?" I added.

She smiled, weary but smug. "Wells built on my work, and I built on his. Before introducing it to the splicing medium, I tweaked his immunity virus to be highly contagious. It still confers immunity, but it comes with a very slight cough. Mild enough that you probably wouldn't even know you were sick, but enough to get the droplets into the air, so it can spread immunity through the general population."

"But it's still a form of the flu," Rex said. "Aren't you worried someone could get sick from the vaccine?"

"No," she said. "Just the minor cough, like I said. I admit, we were uneasy inoculating so many people without their consent, without their knowledge. But the threat was too serious. By the time we explained ourselves, it would have been too late. For the sake of humanity we had to try to vaccinate as many people as possible before Wells could release his plague."

"And when will that be?" I asked quietly.

Dymphna shook her head. "When he's ready. We've been trying desperately to make sure he doesn't know about our operation, so he doesn't accelerate his plans to release his super-flu before the immunity virus has penetrated the population at large. The fact that his flu has already escaped from that chicken and is spreading, that might cause him to release it, as well. It certainly seems to be in fine working order, but we don't know if *he's* satisfied that it's ready."

I felt a momentary wave of guilt so intense my insides felt like they'd turned to liquid: *we* had caused that escape, when we broke into the facility and left with the carcass. But I reminded myself that it was Dymphna who persuaded me to go.

"The people we spoke to at the chicken facility," I said, "they told us the supervisors were constantly checking the workers' vital signs, temperature and stuff, and that the supervisors had seemed frustrated by the fact that the chimeras were all healthy," I said. "Then they brought in nonchimeras as laborers, and they all got sick."

Dymphna grunted softly in response. "How sick?"

"Pretty sick, it sounded like. But I think once they got sick, they never came back."

"So, possibly fatal."

"Maybe," I said.

Now, Dymphna looked grim. "So Wells may already know that his super-flu is highly effective, and that the chimeras are somehow immune. We're simply going to have to hope time is on our side as immunity spreads through the population."

"So, people with splices are spreading immunity," Rex repeated, shaking his head. "And any nonchimeras they spread it to can also pass it along?"

"That is my hope and expectation, and our research suggests it is working."

"How *is* it transmitted?" I asked. "The immunity virus?"

Dymphna shrugged. "It depends, really. At its most contagious, with a new infection, all it would take would be breathing in the same room for a few minutes. When it's less infectious, it might take a day or two of proximity, or kissing or hugging, physical contact like shaking hands. But even at its least infectious, mere proximity would be enough, if it is over the course of more than a day or two."

"So what about the people who got sick?" Rex asked. "The ones who were hassling us, and came into contact with the chicken carcass. What about them?"

She leaned farther forward and pointed at him. "That's the crux of the situation. It takes a while for a bug like mine to penetrate a population, and since the initial vector is through chimeras, the last people to gain immunity are going to be those with the least direct contact with people who have been spliced. The people out there who do not have Wellplants and have not interacted with chimeras, they will be the last to be inoculated."

Rex snorted. "Was that intentional? Leaving the chimera-phobes out there unprotected?"

Dymphna turned solemn. "I would never intentionally try to harm them, or allow them to be harmed." Then she softened. "But the irony is not lost on me."

"So, is that why we can't tell anyone?" I asked. "Because the immunity hasn't spread enough?"

"Precisely. The last thing we want is to tip our hand so that Wells accelerates his time frame and releases his virus before ours has completely spread. Unfortunately, if Wells Life Sciences has figured out that chimeras are immune, and that the super-flu is lethal and highly contagious to everyone else, that's exactly what he might do. Especially if he realizes it's already out there."

I nodded slowly, considering what she'd just told us, trying to reconcile it and the reality of having met her, with all the mystery surrounding her on one hand, and the deep-down, intimate family connection I had with her on the other. She held a special place in my mind, in my heart, really, but now there was something even more. I knew she was a brilliant scientist, but I didn't realize she was a brilliant tactician, too. As the head of Chimerica, she was playing a long game, and the stakes were millions of lives and the future of the planet, of humanity. I felt my face turn hot with shame. Dymphna was doing her best to save the world, and I was being a pain-in-the-ass teenager, getting in the way, condemning all the secrecy and demanding to know why, instead of trusting her, instead of helping her.

Rex snorted. "I'd love to see the look on Howard Wells's face when he finds out he's just killed everybody but the mixies and mixie-lovers."

Dymphna frowned. "We've seen the type of use he deems suitable for chimeras. I imagine he'll come up with something horrific."

The was a sobering thought, as if the preceding conversation hadn't been sober enough.

My mind turned back to the idea of trust. I had perfectly good reasons for not simply trusting Dymphna at first: I didn't know her, really. I had no idea what she was up to. And when I'd needed help in the past, when dozens of lives were at stake, Chimerica had let me down. Still, knowing what I did, I wanted to tell her I was sorry for having caused so much trouble, for not trusting her when so much was at stake. But now was not the time. Instead, I added it to the list of things we'd talk about later, and I asked, "How long will it take for his super-flu to spread?"

Dymphna furrowed her brow at me for a moment, maybe wondering why my face was so red. "Assuming he has some method to release it broadly, simultaneously around the world, I'm guessing it shouldn't take more than a week or two for it to spread everywhere."

"And you said you have no idea how he's going to release it?"

She rubbed her eyes. "That's the one thing we can't figure out. I'm sure he has something in mind, something global and synchronized, so big and in so many places that it would be impossible to defend against, but I can't figure out what that might be. We've identified thousands of ways he could be planning to do it: through the water, through the air, through food, clothing, pharmaceuticals. I've modeled many different methods that he may have access to, but none are broad enough for what he seems to have in mind. But he must have a vector in mind, something that will spread his virus more effectively than a simple contagion being distributed through the splice medium."

"And do you have any idea how well your immunity virus is spreading?"

"We have sophisticated computer models and we've been doing a lot of monitoring, on every continent. There are twenty-seven Chimerica camps around the world, like the one on Lonely Island, and close to three thousand individual operatives who have completed training. They're prepared for actual fighting, should it ever come to that, and they have, on occasion, intervened to help or defend chimeras in danger. But we've had to be extremely judicious in how we allow ourselves to get drawn out, because virus monitoring has been our primary task of late, using devices like air sniffers and sticky pads, tens of thousands of them, all around the world, and hundreds of operatives who go around and collect them, send in the samples."

"Wait a second..." Rex said suddenly. He looked at Dymphna questioningly.

She smiled at him. "Yes, Rex. When you were out West, you were part of that effort."

I looked at Rex. "So *that's* what you've been doing? That's what you couldn't tell me about?"

"Apparently, yeah," he replied. "I thought I was doing climate testing."

I turned to Dymphna. "So, you didn't even tell your own operatives what they were doing?"

"I know it seems excessive, Jimi, but as much as I want to trust everyone, the stakes were simply too high. If Wells caught on to our plan because one of our operatives was overheard talking shop with a friend or something, if he somehow found out that with each passing day, more and more people would be immune to his super-flu, he undoubtedly would move up its release. Absolute secrecy was an absolute imperative."

"Okay....And now? Where do we stand with that?"

"The immunity virus is spreading rapidly now, and we're approaching a tipping point, half of the population exposed and half immune. But it's possible the spread will slow as fewer and fewer people are left unimmunized. It may take a few more weeks before we get the level of penetration to achieve herd immunity, when there are too few people susceptible to Wells's super-flu for it to spread."

"We really screwed up," I said, feeling guilty again. "By taking that chicken carcass, giving the virus an opportunity to spread prematurely."

Dymphna leaned over and patted my knee. "CLAD would have gone in with or without you, and it was important for us to know how much they knew about Wells's plan, and how close to completion Wells thought he was....Besides, I asked you to go."

"I understand your taking precautions, Aunt Dymphna. I really do. But if we'd been told before," I said quietly, "if Chimerica hadn't been so obsessed with secrecy across the board, we might have suspected what we were dealing with and been more careful with the chicken carcass."

"Maybe," she said. "Or, maybe word would have gotten out earlier and Wells would already be releasing the virus globally."

"So what now?" Rex asked.

"Again, we must do our best not to tip our hand, avoid doing anything that would prompt Wells to move up the release. And meanwhile, we keep an eye on him and his people, and see if we can figure out how he is planning on releasing the virus, so that when he makes his move, maybe we can stop him. If he releases that virus, even if it's not an extinction-scale event or a slate wiper, it will still kill millions and be massively disruptive. Breakdowns in food production and medical care could take as many lives as the virus itself."

"But won't the Plants be impacted by that, too?" I asked.

"To some extent," Dymphna said. "Many won't, because they have much more in the way of resources, but plenty of others will be killed in the chaos and carnage. It is a plan born of insanity."

We were quiet for a minute after that as Rex and I absorbed the magnitude of Wells's plot, and Dymphna allowed us the space to do it.

After a minute, Dymphna cleared her throat. "I'm sorry," she said. "I know this is a lot to lay on you young people. But now I have some questions for you," she said.

Rex was still in a daze.

I nodded. "Go ahead."

"You mentioned that CLAD had a plan to take down the Wellplant network. Have you managed to learn anything else about that?"

I shook my head. "No. But I don't see what that has to do with a flu outbreak."

"It's important for the same reason Chimerica hasn't done anything overtly to head off Wells's plans for the super-flu. If he realizes people know what he's up to, he's going to release the virus as soon as possible. Taking down the Wellplant network might make it harder for him to do that, but it will be back up before long, and he will pull the trigger on his plan as soon as it is. The bottom line is, if CLAD attacks him or the Wellplant network, he's going to release that virus. And we're simply not ready."

"Are you doing this alone?" I asked. "I mean, is Chimerica? Are any governments or other organizations helping you?"

She let out a sad sigh. "We are alone. We considered enlisting help from kindred organizations, but I'm glad we didn't. With Wellplant's public service program, giving free stripped-down versions to law enforcement and first responders, and deeply discounted, fully loaded models to political leaders, CEOs, and heads of nonprofits, Wellplants have become ubiquitous, particularly among the ruling class. Once an organization has been…infiltrated…we can't fully trust them."

"Why is that?" I asked, although I suspected I knew the answer.

"They're networked," she said. "We don't know exactly what that means, whether every person with a Wellplant is privy to everything every other Plant knows or sees, but we do know they are connected in ways we can't completely understand."

"What about CLAD?" I said. "They're not networked."

She smiled condescendingly. "CLAD is hopelessly misguided. As I've said, they may even be secretly funded by Wells himself, a tool to further divide chimeras and our nonchimera supporters from the rest of humanity. So yes, I'd like to reach out to them and see if we can delay any action on their part, but I cannot trust them, so I cannot tell them what I've just told you, because I can't be sure it won't get back to Howard Wells."

Just then we heard a noise, the soft scuff of a shoe against grit and concrete. All three of us turned and saw Dara walking toward us, her hands raised, her mouth duct-taped, and her eyes blazing.

Behind her was Cronos, wearing the same mask and shades as before and holding a sleek black machine gun that looked like death itself.

THIRTY-SEVEN

Cronos was flanked by two other CLAD members. They were wearing hoods identical to the ones worn by the people who had abducted me before the bombing, but I got the sense these two were not my abductors. Behind them, unhooded, was Ogden. He looked nervous.

Rex and I moved closer together, between Dymphna and Cronos, protecting her, protecting each other.

Cronos ignored Rex and Dymphna, at first. He seemed to be looking only at me. "Are you okay, Jimi Corcoran?"

I looked at Rex, then at Dymphna, confused. "Of course," I said, turning back to Cronos.

"We saw this one hijack your vehicle," he said, giving Dara a slight shove that turned up the temperature in her eyes.

"What do you mean you saw it? Were you following me? Spying on me?" Between CLAD, Chimerica, and Wells and his goons, I was sick of being followed and spied on and abducted and hijacked.

"We picked you up as you approached our Pedricktown site. That's how we saw your vehicle intercepted. Like it or not, you are important, Jimi Corcoran, both to those who want to protect you, and those who wish you harm."

Dymphna stepped around Rex and me. "You must be Cronos," she said.

"And you must be Dymphna," he said back. He gave Dara a gentle push, away from him, and said, "You can take that off now, if you like."

She glared at him as she peeled off the duct tape, leaving a pink rectangle of irritated skin around her mouth.

"It is about time we met," Dymphna said. "We have much to discuss."

"And much to do," Cronos countered. The two masked figures behind him spread out. He turned toward me again and took off his shades, revealing dark, gray-brown irises surrounded by yellow and streaked with red, eyes that seemed ravaged by disease or trauma. But even as I took a step back, involuntarily, recoiling or retreating, I also sensed something familiar about them. "You and I need to talk, as well."

"About what?" I asked, stepping forward again to reclaim the space I had abandoned.

Cronos looked at Ogden and held out his hand as if to say, *Go ahead*.

"First, whatever it was you were coming to tell me," Ogden said. "Before you were taken."

I looked at Rex, who shrugged, and at Dymphna, who nodded.

"Well," I said, "I was going to tell you that Chimerica has tested the chicken carcass from Wells Life Sciences and they refused to share the results of the testing. But since then they've confirmed that it's infected with some sort of flu. The mystery bug spreading among the H4Hers started with the people who harassed us that night back in Philadelphia, who handled the chicken. The guy who reached into the bag is already dead."

"Our testing indicated that the chicken was infected with a particularly virulent engineered variant of the H7N7 virus," Dymphna said. "A version of a virus that Howard Wells has been working on for quite some time."

"For what purpose?"

"He wants to start a new pandemic," I said. "Worse than the last one. He wants to kill people on a massive scale, to relieve the pressures on the planet, the climate."

Cronos turned his gun toward Dymphna. "You knew this, and you concealed it?"

She took a deep breath and let it out slowly. "Chimeras are immune to Wells's bug. That's because the virus that makes the splicing medium work is a variant of the same virus as Wells's."

"And you developed the splice medium?" he said.

"Yes, that's right. Both the original and this one. Two years ago, when we first became aware of Wells's plan, we—Chimerica, that is—released a new version of this immunity virus through the splice medium that we distribute to the genies in our network. Just like the previous variant, this one confers immunity, but it's contagious, so it is spreading immunity to everyone who come into contact with chimeras, and to those who come into contact with those people, and so on."

Cronos was silent for a moment after she finished, then he shook his head. "But while you're waiting, Wells is still preparing." He laughed bitterly. "There's nothing Chimerica likes more than putting off action. The longer you wait, the more prepared Wells will be."

Dymphna's eyes hardened. "The longer we wait, the more people will be immune. The less impact the virus will have."

"If Wells was ready to release his super-flu, he would have done it already. You said the virus was transmitted through the splice medium. And that chimeras are all immune, right?"

"Probably so, yes."

"Then we need to act. Now. We need to tell people what Wells is doing, try to stop it. And if that forces his hand and prompts him to act before he is ready to reveal himself, so much the better."

Dymphna took another deep breath. "I'm told you have a plan to take down the Wellplant network."

Cronos shot Ogden an acid glare. Then he turned back to Dymphna. "That's right. And the recent outage proves it will work."

"How?"

Cronos laughed, a bitter raspy cackle. "I'd love to have you join us. But if you're not part of us, you're against us."

"Is that how you see it? We're either collaborators or enemies?"

"If you're not with us, I can't tell you anything at all."

"And you expect me to sign on to a plan I don't know?" She shook her head. "I'm afraid that's not how it works."

He paused, studying Dymphna. "Fine. You've been candid with me, so, seeing as how someone has apparently already been talking about it"—he shot another glare at Ogden before continuing—"I guess I can share some of the details. We plan on releasing an operating system patch into the Wellplant network. Malware, they used to call it, back in the Internet days. It will crash the network and incapacitate anyone with a Wellplant for forty-eight hours. It will demonstrate to the world the vulnerability of Wells's technology, the vulnerability of every brain that is connected to it. It will destroy Wells's empire."

Dymphna raised an eyebrow. "You're going to incapacitate all of them?" She tilted her head. "There are pilots with Wellplants. People running factories, power plants, heavy machinery. If you incapacitate them all, people could get hurt."

Cronos chuckled under his mask. "That's a chance I'm willing to take," he said. "We are going to stop the people who are trying to hurt us."

"Not everyone who has a Wellplant is trying to hurt chimeras, for heaven's sake," Dymphna said. "Many are working hard to make the world a better place, working for nonprofits or in the public sector, even running businesses, keeping people employed. We are fighting against the hatred and fear that defines our opponents. Fighting it with hatred and fear simply begets more hatred and fear. It plays right into their hands, into the lies they've been saying about us. It takes love to combat hatred and fear, compassion, figuratively and in this case literally, as well. Togetherness will save lives, while at the same time giving those who fear us a chance to see that there is nothing to be afraid of at all."

Cronos laughed, but it sounded forced. "Your heavy-handed fairy tales are what's going to get us killed. Telling us to love those who want to hurt us." Once again he sounded vaguely familiar, and I wondered if it was because he still seemed to be doing his best to sound like some kind of super villain.

"Okay, what of those who have been made a part of the network as part of their jobs?" she demanded. "The police, the first responders? What of the world leaders who have implants? Taking them down will lead to massive disruptions across the planet. You'll make even *more* people hate and fear us."

"They *should* fear us! And they hate us already. Even those who didn't before they got spiked. Once they got their Wellplants, they became the enemy. Or part of the enemy."

"'Part of the enemy'?"

Cronos turned to Ogden and nodded.

Ogden stepped forward and cleared his throat. "I've been monitoring communications traffic over the Wellplant Network, and I've detected certain...phenomena...among the Plants."

"Monitoring them how?" Dymphna asked.

Ogden looked at Cronos, who laughed and shook his head. "Sorry. Can't give away all our secrets."

"Anyway," Ogden continued, "we've detected these behavioral and cognitive similarities among those who have had a Wellplant 10.0 for more than a few days, and levels of communication and coordination far exceeding what we've seen in the past."

A chill went up my spine, and a buzzing, rushing noise filled my ears as I thought back to how all the Plants at Wells's speech had turned to look at me.

The buzz grew louder as Dymphna tilted her head back and looked down her nose at him.

"What kind of coordination are you talking about?"

The buzz no longer seemed to be coming from inside my head, and as I looked around, trying to find the source of it, a shadow passed across one of the green walls that surrounded us.

"It's a drone," I said, almost to myself, but as everyone turned to look at me, I shouted, "*Get down!*"

THIRTY-EIGHT

S o many things happened at once that even in the perceptual slow motion of sudden, spectacular violence, it was impossible to keep track of it all. A volley of bullets burst through one wall of greenery, followed a microsecond later by a cloud of spinning daggers of razor-sharp glass from the windows they had just torn through. The air was suddenly saturated with the incongruous smells of gun smoke and chlorophyll and the roar of violence and destruction.

Dymphna dove to the floor as her mug exploded into shards on the table, then the table itself exploded. Rex pulled me behind a cement column as another hail of bullets erupted from the green wall to our left. A bullet impacted just above our heads, spraying us both with hot chips of concrete.

I peeked around the edge of the column as the rack holding the plants collapsed, spilling green plants and blue water onto the cement floor. The windows behind it fell away completely, revealing a police drone hovering in the open air, firing from a pair of massive guns—more like canons—each shot accompanied by a *boom* so loud I could feel it in my skull and in my chest.

Two men in tactical garb swung in on ropes through the hole where the window used to be, one on either side of the drone, both firing handguns, both wearing Wellplants. I recognized them immediately—one with gray eyes in a ruddy face and the other thin and blond. The creeper and the car salesman is how I had thought of them before, when they had come after Claudia and me back in Gellersville, when we were trying to save Rex from Omnicare. They worked for Howard Wells.

At the same moment, three other figures in similar gear came running up the ramp, all with Wellplants. I recognized one of them, too. It was Stan Grainger.

Cronos and his people turned to face the men coming up the ramp. Cronos froze, but the pair with him tore their hoods off in order to fight. One of them was a chimera I didn't know, a heavyset guy with shaggy hair and a zebra splice. The other one was Roberta. Cronos remained motionless as his comrades started firing.

Stan and his fellow Plants simultaneously dove and rolled, in different directions but precisely synchronized, like some sort of dance troop or even more like a computer animation.

Stan was strong, but he had never been graceful. This was something new.

All three of them came out of their rolls at the same instant, and all disappeared behind cover and started shooting.

Cronos took a bullet in his bicep, but still he didn't move.

Dara dove into her van and came out with a gun, firing back at the creeper and the salesman. The drone swiveled in the air—the word POLICE clearly visible on its side—and started firing at her, pinning her back into the van, shattering the windshield.

I darted out from behind the column, grabbed one of the chairs, and hurled it through the space where the windows used to be. It hit the drone just hard enough to give it a good wobble and screw up its aim. As the chair tumbled away into the air, the drone swiveled in my direction, and directed its guns at me—*boom, boom, boom*—as I ran back to the column.

Rex pulled me to safety as bullets slammed into the other side of the column we were hiding behind. Chunks of concrete tumbled onto the floor. I wondered how long the column could withstand such an assault, and which would get us first: the bullets or the ceiling coming down on top of us.

The headlights of Jerry's truck came on and the tires squealed as it surged toward the gaping hole. With the windows still coated, I didn't know who was in it, or what they were planning, but I was grateful that the drone focused its fire on the truck instead of us.

The truck picked up speed, driving straight toward the drone. Inside the van, Dara sat upright, watching the truck with a look of determination and intense concentration.

I smiled as I realized what was happening. There was still a drone stuck to the roof of the truck—Dara was controlling it remotely.

As the truck sailed through the hole and out into the open space, the drone banked away, but too late. The truck slammed into it and they both fell out of the air. Hopefully, if anyone was down there, the chair I had thrown earlier had chased them out of harm's way.

There was a momentary lull in the shooting as everyone stared at the empty space where the drone had been, and the thought crossed my mind that if we survived this, I didn't want to be the one to tell Jerry what had happened to his truck. As the column we were hiding behind cracked and buckled and the ceiling above it sagged, raining chunks of concrete, I heard footsteps behind me.

I turned to see Stan Grainger, just a few feet away, his gun pointed at me. He smiled, as if he recognized me and he relished the thought of pulling the trigger. It could have been coincidence, or my imagination, but it seemed as though at that same moment, simultaneously, all the other Plants turned toward me, as well.

I didn't have time to think about that. Stan was closing in fast. I shoved Rex out of the way in one direction, then I threw myself in the opposite direction and scrambled behind the next column.

Stan came after me as his two paramilitary friends went after Rex. Stan's smile broadened as he aimed his gun at my head. Behind him, the van shot forward with Dara at the wheel, headed toward the two men stalking Rex. The van glanced off the broken column and smacked into one of the paramilitaries, flinging him against another column with a horrible thud.

Stan paused, as if savoring the moment, and that's when Dymphna appeared out of nowhere, swinging a piece of the table. Just before she connected, Stan turned to look at her, and she hit him right in the forehead, squarely against his Wellplant.

The glass disk cracked, and he screamed, clutching at it as blood squirted out around the sides.

With a murderous glare, he swung his gun toward Dymphna.

And he pulled the trigger.

Even amid the cacophony of gunfire around us, this single shot seemed a million times louder, its reverberations drowning out my screams. Everyone stopped and turned to look, as if they all knew something terrible had happened.

Dymphna stepped back, looking down in disbelief at the blood soaking her chest. She took another step backward and collapsed against one of the intact plant racks.

"*No!*" I screamed running to her side. Her eyes were already glassy, the vivid blue dimming. But her lips were trembling. She was still alive.

Behind me, the creeper hissed, "You weren't supposed to do that." When I glanced back, he was staring at Stan with eyes filled with equal parts fury and fear. Stan looked back at him, confused and scared, maybe not quite comprehending what had just happened.

"We're going to get you help," I told Dymphna.

She shook her head unsteadily. "Too late," she said. Blood appeared on her lips. "Just remember what I said, okay? Love and compassion."

I nodded. "Of course."

She touched my cheek and smiled. "So glad I got to know you...even just a little....Your father would be so proud."

Her blood was everywhere, tricking down the racks and onto the floor. Some had made its way into the tubes of water and nutrients feeding the plants, a pink blush darkening to red as it flowed through the tubes.

Her head sagged and her eyes lost focus as she let out a long raspy sigh, her final breath.

My eyes clouded with tears as a rage built inside me.

Screaming, I lunged at Stan, one fist connecting with his nose while the other hand raked his eyes. He swung the butt of his gun at my head. I ducked and avoided the worst of it, but he still connected and I crumpled to the floor, dazed.

Stan walked up to where I lay, his gun once again extended in my direction. The creeper followed close behind.

From the corner of my eye, I saw Dara helping Rex to his feet, blood streaming down the side of his head. They looked over and saw Stan and the creeper standing over me. Dara raised a gun, pointing it at my attackers as Rex launched himself toward me, but the building shook with a sound like thunder as the cracked column finally collapsed, bringing with it a large section of ceiling, the rubble walling off Rex and Dara and whoever else was over there.

Stan and the creeper turned back to me as the massive cloud of dust from the ceiling collapse rolled over them. It stung my eyes and clogged my nose and mouth. For a moment I couldn't even see them standing over me. Then it cleared, just enough that I could see Stan. The creeper had vanished, replaced by another figure who now loomed over Stan. I couldn't make out the face, but as the dust continued to settle, I realized it was because the person was wearing a mask. It was Cronos.

With a strangled roar, he grabbed Stan by the wrist of the hand holding the gun and lifted him off his feet. The gun tumbled to the floor and Stan tried to pry Cronos's fingers loose. But they wouldn't budge. Stan kicked his feet and his eyes bulged. I heard a loud, dry snap, then another, and Stan screamed as the arm Cronos was holding bent between joints. With another roar, Cronos threw Stan violently to the side, sending him tumbling across the floor.

I could hear sirens approaching outside as I ran toward the rubble that separated me from Rex. I knew the sirens weren't cause for hope. The police had been in on this from the beginning, they were part of it.

Cronos stalked after Stan, but he stopped, listening, and pivoted toward me. He clamped a hand on my shoulder. "We need to get you out of here," he said, his ravaged eyes softened by something like worry or compassion.

"I need to make sure Rex is okay," I said. "And Dara."

Cronos shook his head. "There's no time."

I pulled away from him and continued on, but he grabbed me around the waist and slung me over his shoulder like a sack of potatoes, apparently unfazed by the bullet wound in his upper arm.

"No!" I yelled, wriggling and pushing and punching his back, horrified at the thought of leaving Rex behind, and humiliated at being carried like that. Cronos was trying to save me, but I was as sick of being moved around against my will as I was of being followed. "Put me down!"

He ignored me, breaking into a trot as he carried me toward the ramp. Through the thick dust, I saw the creeper lying on the floor, dead or unconscious. As we headed down the ramp, Roberta fell into step behind us.

We picked up speed as we descended, around and around, both Cronos and Roberta running flat out, and impressively fast, although I imagine the downward slope helped with that. Each step shook me to my core, jostling my brain and my guts. By the time we reached the bottom I was nauseous and disoriented.

Cronos kept me over his shoulder as he opened the sliding door to a green van not unlike the one he had abducted me in the day of the bombing. He heaved me into the back, and just before he shut the door, there was a moment when he looked me in the eye and I got that feeling again, like there was something familiar about him. Then he slid the door closed. As he and Roberta got into the front, I threw myself at the door to open it, but it was locked.

Cronos started the motor and the tires screamed as he accelerated away toward the exit. I checked the rear door, but it was locked, too.

As we shot out the exit, I saw the wreckage of the drone and the truck, a tangled heap of twisted metal, spitting sparks and releasing tendrils of black smoke. On the other side of the building, almost overhead, the Ben Franklin Bridge arced across the Delaware River and into Philadelphia.

As we skidded into a left turn and sped away, a copter took off from the roof of the farm and shot across the sky, over the river, while at the same time another police drone showed up, lights flashing as it hovered over the wreckage of the first one. As we turned again, rounding the building, the drone disappeared behind it.

The road curved around the building on three sides before heading away, and as we rounded the next corner, Roberta said, "Look, there's Zak!"

The guy with the zebra splice emerged from a stairwell, limping. Cronos swerved and skidded to a halt right in front of him.

I heard a distinct *click* of the power locks and braced my back against the inside of the van, muscles tensed. When the door slid open, I launched myself through it, planting my shoulder into Zak's chest. He was easily twice my size, but I caught him off-balance enough that I was able to knock him back and run away, back toward the farm.

"Stop her!" Roberta cried.

Cronos got out and yelled after me, "Jimi! No! Come back!"

Two more police drones were circling the building. One peeled away, zipping by right over my head to inspect the van.

Without slowing down, I looked back and saw Cronos bracing his legs, with both hands wrapped around a handgun. He fired, and the bullet dinged off the drone, causing it to wobble and spin before its automatic stabilizer righted it.

Panels on either side opened up and two guns came out. They fired once, raising a divot of asphalt in the road next to the van. Then Cronos fired again, and a plume of sparks erupted from the drone. It spun again, but this time the stabilizers didn't correct it. Instead, it just hovered in place, continuing its slow, lazy spin.

When I reached the stairwell Zak had emerged from, I looked back and locked eyes with Cronos. Then he got back in the van and sped off, and I entered the stairwell and ran up the steps.

THIRTY-NINE

The first four floors were wide-open concrete spaces, flanked on all sides by orderly rows of plants and tubes of pale blue nutrient water, identical to the floor we had been on. Or identical to what it had been like up until a half hour ago.

The fifth floor was littered with blood and rubble and bodies and dust. The stairwell let me out on the same side of the rubble pile that Rex and Dara had been on, but the only sign of them was a trail of blood spatter that ended abruptly in the middle of the floor. Dara's van was gone, as well.

The blood filled me with worry about them, but the fact that they and the van were gone was a good sign.

I hurried around the pile of rubble and stopped in my tracks.

Visible through the dusty air was Dymphna's body, splayed out, tangled in the bent and bloody plant racks. Blood pooled on the floor below her. The irrigation tubes were now thoroughly mixed with it, bright red against the green plants.

For a moment, I was overcome with sorrow and anger. I didn't want to just leave her there, but I knew I didn't have a choice—and I didn't have time, either. There was no sign of Stan, or the creeper.

"Rex?" I called out, my voice unsteady. Then I took a deep breath, and called out more forcefully, "Dara?"

I heard the low thrum of a heavy drone fast approaching, and I ducked back behind the rubble as a police drone entered the building through the missing windows. Its rotors stirred up more dust, thickening the air with it. A powerful spotlight came on, and I ducked farther back when I saw that its canons were out.

The drone spun in a slow circle, pausing several times as it took in the scene, then it zipped back out the window.

I needed to get out of there before the police showed up for real.

I took one last look at Dymphna, then I turned and ran back down the stairs. At the bottom, I paused long enough to count the drones circling the building—there were three now. I waited until none were in sight. Then I started running.

———

The vertical farm had the river on one side and was surrounded on the other three by blocks of flood-plain housing, up on stilts. But it was separated from all of that by a wide buffer of open space. I felt small and exposed and vulnerable as I ran across it, between the bridge looming in the sky ahead of me and the police drones angrily buzzing circles around the farm behind me. I ran full out. Imagining those drones coming after me with their big guns helped me go a little faster.

I eased up half a step when I reached the first block of stilt houses, and another half a step after I had zigged and zagged a few blocks into the tightly packed maze of streets. A few people peered out their windows at me, looking scared and suspicious, but the streets and sidewalks were deserted.

By the time I reached the bridge, I was running for distance and no longer for speed. I climbed the ancient steps up to the pedestrian walkway, overlooking the roadway, which was a blur of speeding cars below.

There was a decent breeze up there, and I fell into what I hoped seemed like a casual jog. I ran with my head down, not even looking up as other joggers and walkers passed me going the other way.

When I got to the middle of the bridge, I stopped to catch my breath and to look back at the vertical farm. I spotted it immediately, a glass enclosed building with a greenish tinge from the plants behind the glass. Dust still drifted out of the gaping hole where the windows were missing, mixing with the black smoke rising from the wreckage of the drone and Jerry's truck. I counted ten drones buzzing around the building: some were frenetic police drones with flashing lights, and the others, I suspected, were media drones hovering to capture 3D holo-footage. There were also full-sized crew copters, both in the air and on the ground. In the distance, a few gray smudges drifted up into the sky, smoke from brush fires most likely. A few more rose up on the Philadelphia side of the river, beyond the city. There seemed to be a lot more copter traffic than usual, including a swarm over by the Convention Center and buzzing around Wells Tower.

Off to my left, the clouds parted over South Philadelphia, letting down a shaft a bright sunlight that swept across the row homes, lighting up the brick walls and silver roofs. The sunbeam slipped across a smaller glass tower and caught an angle, flaring bright for a moment before moving along, then disappearing altogether, as the clouds closed up.

My breathing slowed, then sped up again, as the adrenaline ebbing from my body was replaced by a rise of emotion. My eyes streamed with tears. I had barely known Dymphna, but she was family. I had wanted to open my heart to her, to connect, to make up for lost time, on some level maybe even to recapture a piece of my father. Maybe to apologize for being so demanding when I didn't have the full picture. Maybe to give her a chance to apologize to Mom and Trudy for how she had hurt the family, or at least to explain.

And now she was dead, and my father, in ways, had died a little bit all over again.

I forced myself to get it together, afraid that standing on the middle of a bridge, bawling my eyes out, someone might try to come help me. With a sigh, I wiped the tears from my eyes, and the sweat that quickly replaced them. Then I put my head down and started running again.

FORTY

I needed to find Rex. If he was okay, he'd probably go to either his apartment or the coffee shop, both in Silver Garden. From there he'd call my house. I thought about finding a phone to try to contact *him*, but I was desperate to *find* him, and I didn't want to run any farther out of my way to locate a phone.

At the end of the bridge, there was a cluster of police vehicles, lights flashing, more than the usual one or two that were always there. I ran past them without glancing over, and as I exited the walkway, I felt a moment of relief. The whole time I'd been up on the bridge, I'd been worried in the back of my mind that the drones or the cops or Wells's hench-assholes might still find me. Now I was pretty sure they wouldn't. At least, not immediately.

That relief was fleeting as I picked up a distressing vibe on the street.

I ran up Vine Street to Ridge Avenue, one of the old diagonals that cut across the city all the way out past the ice cream place. This portion of the road was densely built up with apartment hives, tiny affordable housing units, mostly for people working service jobs in the towers or tourist spots.

One of the hives was surrounded by caution tape and police cars and other official vehicles with flashing lights on their tops. As I jogged past, I saw that some of them were from the Pennsylvania Department of Public Health.

My skin prickled as I wondered what that was about. I could feel trouble gathering in the air. It reminded me of the feeling on the street when the Genetic Heritage Act was passed in the fall, right before the riots.

A trio of police cars zipped past me, accompanying an ambulance. A few blocks up, I passed another hive, another scene eerily similar to the last one.

The hives in this neighborhood were virtually identical, built at the same time by the same developer based on the same design. This block had the same caution tape, the same circle of vehicles and flashing lights. But as I ran past this one, the front door opened and a small knot of figures in biohazard-type suits emerged carrying a stretcher holding a body bag.

A feeling of intense dread stopped me in my tracks, and I stood there for a brief moment, watching. Then I took off at a sprint.

Rex's apartment was closer than the coffee shop, so that's where I headed first. The nearer I got, the more frantically I ran.

He had given me a key to his apartment, and my hands shook as I fumbled with the lock on the front door. When I finally got it open, I charged up the steps—two at a time—to the third floor. I fumbled with the keys once again, but before I could unlock his apartment door, it swung open, and there he was.

"Jimi!" he said, and I saw in his eyes the same deep, intense relief that I felt. "Thank God you're okay," he said as I put my arms around him, and he wrapped me up in his.

For several long moments, I couldn't speak, I just squeezed him tight, holding on like I was never going to let go, anchoring myself to him. Only at that moment did I realize how much my lungs and legs were burning from the run, and how filthy I was from the dust and grit of what had just happened at the farm. I sobbed once, and he did, too.

"I was so worried about you," I finally whispered, the side of my face pressed against his chest. I could feel his heart thumping in his chest.

"Me too," he said softly, the rumble in his chest louder than the words leaving his mouth. "I thought Cronos had abducted you again."

"He did," I said. "Well, abducted or rescued, depending how you look at it. I got away from him and went back for you, but you were already gone." I pulled back to look at him, gently turning his head to look at the jagged cut at his temple, along the hairline. "Are you okay?"

"Cuts and bruises. You're okay?"

I nodded.

He took a breath. "I'm so sorry about Dymphna," he said, without letting it out.

His face became a blur as my eyes filled with tears again. He pulled me to him once more, smoothing my hair as he drew me inside and closed the door behind us. The holovid was on in the background, playing breathless local news coverage.

"What about Dara?" I asked.

"She's okay. She went to find Sly. They're setting up a meeting at the coffee shop tomorrow morning, to get together some of the Chimerica bigwigs in the region, tell them what happened to Dymphna and figure out what to do next."

I could see from Rex's face that he had something else to say. And I could tell it wasn't good.

"What is it?" I asked.

He nodded toward the holovid. "Things have been deteriorating, even since this morning."

He caught me up while he made us tea. "The super-flu is spreading *really* fast," he said. "Over a hundred cases now, twelve dead, forty in critical condition."

"All in a matter of hours?" I said softly. "I know Dymphna told us to go with CLAD, Rex, but…this is still all our fault."

Rex held me by the shoulders and slowly shook his head. "No, it's not. Wells created the virus. Those idiots took it on themselves to start trouble and grab that bag." He pointed at the mayhem on the holovid. "That's not on us."

I knew on some level he was right, but on some level, I was, too. "So what's next?" I asked quietly.

He shook his head. "I don't know. The governor is talking about declaring a health emergency in the city, but he's getting a lot of pushback from some of his cabinet and the head of the legislature. They're even talking about impeaching the governor, or recalling him." He gestured at the holovid. "There they are now."

The crawl at the bottom of the image said STATE LEADERS OPPOSE

GOVERNOR'S PLANNED EMERGENCY DECLARATION. Above it was a panel of politicians from across Pennsylvania. It was a diverse-looking group—different ages and genders and ethnicities and political parties—and it included the secretary of Health and Human Services.

But they did have one thing in common.

I turned to Rex. "They all have Wellplants."

He nodded, his eyes filled with worry. "I noticed that. Not exactly sure what it means."

I wasn't sure, either.

"How connected do you think they are?" I asked, watching the holovid as the health secretary spoke and the others stared at him with identical expressions.

"What do you mean?" Rex asked. He tensed as he said it, as if he knew what I might say, maybe even as if he wanted someone else to say it out loud before he did.

"Well, you know how right before the H4Hers started throwing stuff at me, Howard Wells looked right at me, and then all the other Plants did, too—they all turned and looked at me at the same time, with the same expression."

He leaned against the kitchen counter, slowly nodding.

"And then back at the vertical farm, Stan and the other two with him, they moved like machines, like *one* machine. They were totally synchronized."

"Yeah," he said quietly. "I noticed that, too."

"And Ogden said he'd been picking up strange, synchronized communications," I stared at the holo image again, and he followed my gaze.

"They *are* networked, right?" he said. "I mean, we knew that. Dymphna said so. And Wellplant advertises the communication part of it."

"Yeah, but what if it's…more than that?"

He nodded, rubbing his chin, as if he had considered that and he was considering it some more. Then something seemed to catch his eye, and he said, "Oh no."

I turned to follow his gaze, and saw a BREAKING NEWS graphic, over a crawl of text that said ANONYMOUS ACCUSER: HOWARD WELLS BEHIND RECENT FLU OUTBREAK.

"Oh, crap," I said. "Do you think that's CLAD? Do you think they went ahead, even after everything Dymphna said?"

"They wouldn't have, would they?"

We both sat on the sofa, across from the holovid, as the view cut to the news anchor, a young guy whose ruddy cheeks were flushed with nervous excitement.

"Joining me now is Ainsley Sinclair, who has been following this breaking story for us. Ainsley, what can you tell us?"

The feed cut to Ainsley Sinclair, looking equally amped and more than happy to tell quite a lot.

"Well, Dorian, the accusations were widely distributed less than an hour ago in the form of a letter faxed to news organizations and government health and law enforcement agencies around the world, and they have caused *quite* a stir. While the document provides no actual proof, the level of specificity has been described as compelling by experts familiar with Wells's companies and those on the front lines of the flu outbreak that has been spreading through attendees of the recent Humans for Humanity convention. The letter alleges that the flu virus is a particularly virulent new strain of the H7N7 virus, intentionally altered to make it more lethal, that it was created at a Wells Life Sciences-owned poultry facility in Northern Delaware, and that the initial cluster of cases involved people who came into contact with an infected chicken from that facility."

"That's like, word for word what Dymphna told Cronos," I said. "And what *we* told him, too."

Rex nodded as the reporter continued.

"No motive is given for the development of the virus or its release," she said, "but the letter makes a point to specify that those who have gotten

Wellplants were also immunized against the flu. A spokesperson for Howard Wells has vehemently and categorically denied the allegations."

The image cut to a gray-haired man in a suit, standing at a bank of microphones in front of Wellplant Corporation headquarters. The text at the bottom of the image said DONALD WESTEN, CHIEF COMMUNICATIONS OFFICER, WELLPLANT CORPORATION.

"These ridiculous allegations are absurd, entirely baseless," Westen said. "They are nothing but lies, and frankly I am outraged that so many media outlets are reporting them, and, not to put too fine a point on it, exposing themselves to legal action. Maybe it's because so many mixies have worked their way into positions of power or celebrity that people are afraid to bring it up, but I also find it striking that no one is looking into the most likely source of this flu—that once again, by making themselves part animal, the mixies have put us all at risk, inviting deadly viruses to jump from pigs and birds and whatnot, to the mixies or chimeras or whatever you want to call these semi-human creatures, and from there to the good, God-fearing people out here just trying to live their lives. And it's not the first time this has happened, either."

Westen was greeted with a barrage of questions from the unseen reporters. At least one of them added something to the effect of, "If you're implying a connection between splicing and the Great Pandemic, that connection has been completely disproven."

Westen rolled his eyes. "Well, we'll just have to agree to disagree."

The feed cut back to Ainsley Sinclair. "But certain portions of the letter have been, if not confirmed, then at least supported."

An older woman appeared on the feed, a square head with pale blotchy skin under thinning gray hair. Her eyes were pink and wet. The graphic said DOROTHY CULLEN: MOTHER OF FIRST FLU VICTIM. "All I know is, my Billy was part of our county delegation to that convention, and everybody got sick except the ones with them things in their heads." She broke down into sobs. "And now my poor Billy's dead."

My eyes met Rex's. It was just like Dymphna had said. None of the chimeras or their friends had gotten sick, and none of the Plants, either.

Sinclair's voice returned over a 2D feed of another reporter, apparently trailed by her camera operator, being turned away at the security gate at the Wellfood chicken facility in Delaware. "Requests for comment from the Wells Life Sciences facility mentioned in the letter have been denied," she said. As the guard at the gate was turning the reporter away, the exit gate opened in the background and the camera swung over to show half a dozen small delivery vans leaving the facility, followed by a huge 18-wheeler, all of them the same pale blue with the Wells Life Sciences logo on the side.

I looked at Rex, feeling suddenly old—not mature or grown up or anything like that, but tired and worn out, like I didn't have enough life in me to comprehend something this big, much less do anything about it. But I also knew that now more than ever, doing nothing was not an option.

"What are you thinking?" Rex asked.

"I'm thinking we need to be there tomorrow. At that Chimerica meeting that Sly and Dara are setting up."

He smiled. "I don't think we're invited." I could tell from his tone that he wasn't pushing back. He was just pointing out a fact.

I smiled back at him. "I don't think I care."

He nodded, still smiling. "You make a good point."

"But first," I said, my smile falling away as I let out a sigh, "I need to go home. I need to tell Mom and Trudy about Dymphna."

FORTY-ONE

Rex had insisted on coming with me and I hadn't protested even a tiny little bit. It was going to be a rough evening, and even if him being there in the middle of this family thing might be awkward, I wanted him there, for sure.

As we walked up the hill from the Lev station toward my house, Rex and I talked about everything that had happened at the vertical farm.

We talked about Roberta, and we talked about Stan, who had now killed two people close to me: first Del and now Dymphna. We also talked about Cronos, about his obstinance and callousness, his attitude.

"There's something else about him," Rex said. "I can't put my finger on it, but there's something about the way he talks."

"*Yes!*" I said, whipping my head around. "I was thinking the same thing. He's familiar, but I can't think of how. Like I've seen him on the holo or something."

Rex laughed. "Maybe he just seems familiar because he has this super-villain thing going on, with the mask and voice and everything."

I laughed with him. "That's what I thought, too! Like, 'You are vanquished! It is useless to resist.'"

My laughter faded, though, as we turned the corner onto my street and I spotted a black SUV parked in our driveway. My body instantly tensed. I may have even stopped walking. The first thought to cross my mind was that it was Stan. But then I spotted the blue federal government license plate, and I realized it most likely wasn't Stan at all. It was the FBI.

"Are you okay?" Rex asked.

"I'm fine," I said. "There's a car in the driveway. I thought it might be Stan, but I'm pretty sure it's the FBI."

"Is that better?" he asked with a half smile.

"Anything is better than Stan," I said, although I wasn't entirely sure. We went in the front door, into the living room.

Ralphs and Scanlon were standing there—Ralphs looking concerned, her eyes pained and her forehead creased. Scanlon was inscrutable as always, his expression unreadable apart from the way his features constantly proclaimed, *I am a jerkface.*

Mom and Trudy were sitting on the sofa, both looking up at me with tear-filled eyes.

I ignored Ralphs and Scanlon and ran to them. "Mom, Trudy, what is it?" I said, perching on the arm of the chair.

"Oh, Jimi," Mom said, grabbing my arm and hugging it. "It's your aunt Dymphna. She's—she's been murdered."

Trudy burst into sobs that broke my heart. She had lost her parents, then her brother, and now her sister was gone, too. Apart from Mom and Kevin and me, she was alone in the world.

But even as this new level of sorrow hit me, I glanced at Scanlon, staring intently at me, as if gauging my reaction, and I wondered what he knew, what his Wellplant was telling him about Dymphna's death. It had been witnessed by a handful of people with Wellplants, so it was entirely possible that he had watched it go down in real time, that he had seen Rex and me there, in the middle of it. There was already a big part of me that wanted to come clean right there, to tell everyone that I had been there when it happened, seen it with my own eyes when Stan Grainger had killed her. Knowing that Scanlon could well already know made me want to even more. But I couldn't.

As far as I knew, that thing in Scanlon's head could transmit straight to Howard Wells. Admitting I'd been at the vertical farm would open up a whole slew of questions I didn't want to answer, and could let Wells know that we were onto him and prompt him to release his virus. It would also confirm the FBI's suspicions that I'd been conspiring with CLAD all along. And if they determined I was committing a crime of some sort when the murder took place, they could charge me as an accessory. I knew I had to react to my mother's news with as much shock and innocence as possible.

"*What?!*" I exclaimed. "How? When?" Tears welled up in my eyes, and I let them. They were real, coming from the horrors I'd just witnessed, but I still felt kind of icky, using them as part of my act. Even so, I turned to Ralphs and Scanlon, making sure they could see the tears on my cheeks. "Are you sure?"

Ralphs nodded, somber and respectful.

Scanlon tilted his head, as if trying to make sense of my reaction. "I thought you didn't know her," he said. The way he said it made me realize, with some relief, that he didn't know we'd been at the scene of the crime. Maybe the cheapo public-servant Wellplants weren't networked like the others.

Ralphs scowled at him. I ignored him.

"What happened?" I asked my mom. I made an effort not to look at Rex, in case he was having a harder time being deceitful that I was.

She shook her head. "She was such a remarkable person. I'm...I'm so sorry I didn't try harder to make her part of your life."

Trudy sat forward, patting Mom on the back. "It wasn't your fault, Christine. Dymphna left *us*, not the other way around."

"It's true, Mom," I said. "It's not your fault." The tears I was crying were still heartfelt, but I was relieved that my mom bolstered my story.

Rex moved closer. "I'm so sorry," he said. His sadness and sympathy were genuine, as well.

I gave him a brave smile, and Mom and Trudy both glanced up at him, then looked down again. "Thanks," Mom said, barely audibly.

Trudy nodded, weeping quietly into a tissue.

Ralphs and Scanlon both turned their attention to Rex. Ralphs gave him a small, reassuring smile.

Scanlon said, "What happened to you?" With his finger, he pointed to a spot on his own temple corresponding to where Rex had that scrape.

"Some H4Her threw a rock," he said, without a pause.

"Did you get it looked at?" Ralphs asked.

"It's fine," Rex said.

Scanlon stared at him for another moment, his head tilted forward so his Wellplant was his most prominent feature. Then he turned and took a step closer to me. "We were wondering if you knew anything about your aunt's death."

I fought back a minor swell of panic as I looked at his Wellplant and now wondered if it gave him some kind of lie-detection capability.

"Only what I just learned," I said, standing, resisting the urge to look at Rex for support or consultation. "As I've told you before, unfortunately, I never actually met her. Or at least, not since I was a kid."

"You're sure?" he said, taking another step closer.

I tried not to freeze with fear as I reconsidered the possibility that maybe he had seen what happened after all, and maybe he even had proof that I was there when she was killed. "Of course I'm sure," I said, shaking my head at Ralphs, like, *What is with this moron and why did you bring him here?*

She shrugged, almost imperceptibly.

"Where did it happen?" I asked, trying to keep my eyes round and innocent, without overdoing it. "The murder, I mean."

Ralphs looked at Scanlon, who gave her a slight nod.

"Camden," she said. "Just across the river."

"Dymphna was *here?!*" I said, trying to sell but not oversell my fake surprise. "She was practically home!" I turned to my mom and Trudy. "Did you know this? Was she coming here? What's that about?"

Mom shook her head. "I have no idea." She waved a finger toward Ralphs and Scanlon. "According to them, she was a leader of some secret chimera group."

"Was it CLAD?" I said, feigning alarm. "Is that why they kept me away from the bombing?"

"No," Ralphs replied. "Chimerica."

"Wow," I said, slumping back down onto the arm of the chair, pretending to be stunned. "I guess it's real after all."

After a moment, Ralphs cleared her throat and turned to Trudy. "Well, as I said, we'll be in touch with you as next of kin when we're able to release your sister's remains."

Trudy nodded, silently weeping.

Ralphs turned to Mom. "You still have my contact info, right? Just... please let us know if you hear of anything that might help our investigation."

Scanlon looked at her blankly, then he whipped out a business card and handed it to my mom. "Actually, I am in charge of this investigation, now," he said. "If any of you have any information pertinent to this case, you are legally mandated to share it with us immediately."

Mom glanced at Ralphs, who nodded without expression. Mom took Scanlon's card and placed it on a side table. "Well," she said, "if that's everything, I think we'd like some private time to process this family tragedy."

Ralphs nodded, like she understood, then turned to Scanlon with a raised eyebrow, as if checking with him first. Apparently, he really was leading the investigation.

"I guess that's it, then," he said. He looked at me, then at my mom and Trudy, then quickly glanced at Rex. "Remember what I said. You are legally required to tell us anything you know about this. Immediately."

"Yes, we know," I said, huffing like a stereotypical teenager. "Anything else we need to remember?" I hoped my tone adequately conveyed the implied but unspoken final word: *Anything else we need to remember, dumbass?*

He stared at me for another awkward second, as if he didn't quite know what to make of me. Then he turned and left.

Ralphs watched him go, slowly shaking her head. She took a breath and let it out. "Sorry for your loss," she said. "And for"—she glanced at the door, where Scanlon had just exited—"well, just sorry."

Then she left, as well.

Rex gave me a tight-lipped smile and I replied with one of my own. I knew it must have been awkward for him, but I was glad he was there. As soon as Ralphs was out the door, I knelt in front of my mom and Trudy and wrapped them in a hug.

They both cried quietly as I held them, then. After a few minutes, Mom got herself together. She patted Trudy's back a few times and then pulled away. After a few seconds Trudy pulled away, too.

"Sorry," she said.

"Don't be sorry about that," I said.

We sat quietly for a while, Mom, Trudy, Rex, and me, talking softly and occasionally about Dymphna and the pro-chimera group she led. At several points, my mom's eyes lingered on me, as if she was still trying to decipher the whole truth from me, as well.

I had been prepared to tell her the truth, or at least the part about Dymphna's death, but the FBI had forced me into a lie, and now I couldn't undo that. If I told her now, even a little bit, she'd know I had lied to the FBI, and I was pretty sure she'd be more inclined than I was to take Scanlon's warning seriously.

I felt a wave of intense guilt, once again keeping secrets from my mom, and from the investigators, for pretending I didn't know anything about it when I had been right there. I had seen it, I knew who had done it, but I couldn't reveal it, not right now. Ralphs and Scanlon would freak out for sure, maybe even lock me up. And it would hurt my mom, I knew. Eventually, she would believe me that I had every intention of telling her before the FBI got involved, and eventually she would understand why I couldn't tell her once I had lied to the FBI, but before that understanding there would absolutely be a long period of judgment, of her feeling injured and deceived, and that would have practical ramifications, perhaps up to and including the end of the world as we knew it.

Of course, the way things were going, there was a good chance the end of the world was coming anyway, in which case I wouldn't have to tell my mom at all. Since we were so friendly with so many chimeras at this point, we would likely survive, but most likely we'd be so busy hunting rats and harvesting bark in order to stay alive that it would put a little deceit into perspective.

After an hour or so, Trudy announced she was going home, and Mom insisted on driving her. As we said goodbye, I felt the tears coming back again, and I guess Trudy did, too, because she left in a hurry. Mom gave Rex and me a kiss on the cheek and hurried after her.

After they left, Rex and I were sitting on the sofa. He put his arm around me. "That was kind of bad," he whispered. "With the FBI I mean."

I took his hand and squeezed it between mine. "Sorry."

"No, I meant for you, too."

I nodded. "I'm glad you were here."

He nodded back.

"I should call Claudia," I said. "Let her know what's been going on and see how she's doing, how her dad is doing. How the whole family is doing."

I took the phone from its cradle and selected Claudia's number. As I thought about what I was going to tell her, the emotions rose up in me again. I was worried that when she answered I wouldn't be able to talk. I almost hung up so I could collect myself and call back, but before I could, I got an error tone and a message saying that number was unreachable due to problems with the transmission lines.

"Weird," I said to myself.

"What's that?" Rex called from the living room.

"It says Claudia's phone is out of order. Problems with the transmission lines."

"Huh. She's kind of out in the woods, right? Maybe it's because of the brush fires."

"Yeah, maybe...."

"It's weird, though, you're right," he said. Then, he sighed. "I guess these are weird times."

"Yeah," I said as I hung up the phone. "Weird and terrible."

FORTY-TWO

After I took a quick shower, Rex and I heated up a frozen pizza. It wasn't very good. I'd had real pizza twice that week, and this was not that. It was probably left over from before Kevin had left for college.

As we ate, we talked about the ramifications of my lies about Dymphna, and not telling the FBI—or my mom—that Stan Grainger had killed her, or even that I had seen him in the area again, this time for sure. Rex reassured me that I had done the right thing, that I had no other choice, really. I tried to call Claudia a few more times, but I got the same message. I decided I would go out there the next day.

Mom came home as we were eating our second pieces. She grimaced at the pizza, but she grabbed a piece and started eating it, too. She seemed to share my opinion of it.

"How's Trudy?" I asked.

Mom shook her head, her eyes welling up. "She's devastated. I think she always thought one day Dymphna would resurface, and they could be like sisters again. But…" She shrugged and wiped her eyes. I squeezed her shoulder and she put a hand over mine. We ate in silence for a few minutes before she got up, put her plate in the sink, and turned on the news.

The big story was the flu outbreak. A counter on the side of the feed tallied reported cases, and deaths, attributed to it. When the anchor reported on the anonymous allegations that Wells was behind the outbreak, Mom turned and stared at me. I ignored her, keeping my eyes front.

"Pretty wild that they're saying that Wells is behind this mystery flu, huh?" she said.

I could feel her eyes scouring me for signs that I knew about it. I could feel Rex stiffen up beside me.

"Yeah, it is," I said, keeping my eyes front. "I wouldn't put it past him though. Not after all the other stuff he's been involved in."

We watched as the talking heads argued whether the allegations should be taken seriously or whether it was a hoax to be disregarded. The debate apparently had gone all the way to the White House, where the president—who was running for reelection and was now Howard Wells's political rival—vowed an investigation. All of his cabinet members, on the other hand, continued to insist the allegations were baseless. A panel of so-called experts argued both sides. It consisted of public health officials, politicians, and pundits, one of whom was Alenka Bogdan, who ridiculed the allegations and what she called the "hysteria" over the flu outbreak. All those dismissing the allegations and the threat of the mystery virus had Wellplants, and those voicing alarm and urging action did not.

The next story was about Wellplant Corporation, and how it had come to light that the recent network outage or system update or whatever had been far more disruptive than they had admitted. And with so many users in positions of authority in major corporations and governments around the world, the security ramifications of that outage were still rippling through-out the global economy. Once again, those with Wellplants were dismissing the concerns, while those without Wellplants were calling for investigations into the stability and security of the Wellplant network.

Wellplant's stock prices were fluctuating wildly around the world, plunging with each new revelation or allegation, then soaring back due to a surge in Wellplant orders, apparently from people afraid this might be their last chance to get one. I wondered if Cronos's plans to crash the network would cause a similarly mixed reaction. Would it bring down Wells's empire, or would people simply get over it, like they seemed to be doing now?

The tension remained high as the next few stories chronicled a string of strange events around the world, including several countries massing forces at their borders, seemingly without provocation. Along with the usual litany of global weather disasters, local brush-fire reports, and dire warnings about a climate tipping point, they contributed to the ominous sense that things were somehow coming to a head.

Then a story came on about a mysterious shoot-out at a vertical farm in Camden.

"Camden?" Mom said, pausing. I froze as the holovid cut to a 3D image of the vertical farm where Dymphna was killed. It showed the window panel missing and the wreckage of the drone and Jerry's truck smoking on the ground. As the image slowly rotated, the Ben Franklin Bridge came into view. I wondered if I was up there on it, looking down at the drones and everything. Or if I was still running through Camden trying to get to the bridge.

The newscaster talked about the massive destruction at the scene and the fact that only one body was found, an unidentified woman in her fifties.

"Oh my God," Mom said. "Do you think that could have been Dymphna?"

I faked a gasp, hating myself for it. "Oh wow. I don't know."

Mom stared at me again, and it took a tremendous force of will to keep my eyes directed at the holovid.

"Looks like it was a pretty intense scene there," I said, watching the feed.

Eventually, Mom shook her head. "I can't watch anymore."

As she went into the kitchen, Rex and I risked a quick, mortified glance.

Mom game back with a glass of water but stopped at the stairs. "I'm going to bed," she said. "I'm exhausted, and I have a meeting first thing tomorrow. When are you working for Marcella next?"

"Wednesday or Thursday. She's out of town."

"Okay, well don't stay up too late, okay? With this flu going around, you need to be good to your immune systems."

Rex said, "Yeah. I should get going."

"You're leaving?" I said.

"It's late."

My mom gave him a smile, but couldn't hold it, like it had used up the last speck of energy she had. "You're welcome to stay the night, Rex. Jimi can set you up in Kevin's room."

"Oh, thanks," he said, looking to me. I nodded and he said, "That would be great."

Mom said, "Of course. Good night, kids." Then she put her hand on my head and kissed my cheek before heading upstairs.

— — —

Kevin had tidied his room before he went away to college, but it still had a faint but distinct reek, as if the walls and floor were permeated with years of sweaty socks and gym clothes. Rex seemed oblivious to it, so I didn't bring it up, but I remade the bed with fresh sheets and set the vent to HIGH and EXHAUST.

"Okay, there you go," I said when I was done. "I'll be next door if you need anything."

"I'll keep that in mind," he said, flashing me a borderline lewd grin that was totally undermined by the yawn that interrupted it.

We laughed and kissed good night. I brushed my teeth and washed up in the bathroom, then put a new toothbrush out for Rex.

As tired as I was, I had a hard time getting to sleep, and when I finally did I was haunted by dreams of death. Dymphna and Del and Reverend Calkin, memories real and constructed surrounded me as I ran toward a dark, ominous horizon.

The next morning, I woke at seven thirty feeling unsettled and unrested. Rex emerged from Kevin's room a few minutes later. He had already remade the bed.

My mom was already gone, which made the morning a little less awkward, but it still felt strange, Rex and I sitting there at the kitchen table, drinking coffee. When we were at his place, it felt natural and normal and comfortable. Here, it felt like we were pretending at something. Playing house.

As soon as we left, I felt more at ease. When we got to the Levstation, the people waiting for the train were oddly spread out. Usually, people clustered where the doors would be when the train stopped, but apart from a couple of pairs of people talking to each other in hushed tones, everyone seemed to be standing as far from one another as possible. Several people had on breathing masks, to filter out any pathogens. A few people looked over as we came up the steps, their faces filled with fear and suspicion, but I got the sense that it had less to do with anti-chimera bias than fear of the flu.

On the train, everyone looked out the windows, as if trying to get a sense of where things stood. From the train, you could always see drones and copters in the sky above and occasional emergency vehicles with flashing lights on the streets below, but there seemed to be a lot more of both than usual.

When we got to the coffeehouse, the front door was locked and a handwritten sign said CLOSED UNTIL 11 A.M.

We walked around to the back and Rex knocked on the door. A girl I'd never met before appeared in the window. She had a panda splice and looked mildly exasperated, as if maybe we weren't the first to come knocking despite the sign.

"We're closed!" she said, loudly, to be heard through the glass.

"We need to talk to Jerry," Rex said.

"He's busy," she said. "Come back at eleven." Then she turned away from us.

I understood that she was just doing her job, and it wasn't her fault that she didn't know who we were, but I was getting a little impatient myself. Before I could say anything, Rex put his hand on my arm as he knocked again.

"It's important," he said. Then, when she came back, "Tell Jerry it's Rex and Jimi."

She rolled her eyes and muttered, "Hold on." She disappeared for a few seconds, then returned and opened the door.

"Thanks," I said, smiling sweetly. "I'm Jimi. Who are you?"

"Sorry," she said. "Been a crazy morning. I'm Stacy."

Rex said, "Rex," and they shook hands.

"They're all in the office," Stacy said, stepping aside to let us pass. "It's—"

"We know where it is," I said. I knew it was petty, but I wanted Stacy to know that we knew the place well.

The office was small enough that the handful of people already in there pretty much filled it. Jerry was behind his desk. His expression seemed even more sour than usual, but Rex said he'd taken the news about his truck pretty well, so I assumed his demeanor was about Dymphna's death and the way the world seemed to be spinning apart. Sitting around the desk were Sly and Dara, whom I knew, Martin, whom I'd met in Canada, and two others, a tall woman with olive skin and a giraffe splice and a heavyset Asian guy with pebbly, reptilian skin. It was weird seeing Martin. He and I had butted heads on Lonely Island—he was in charge there—but now I understood he was acting on Dymphna's orders. And in the end, he'd been the one to let Dara help us in Gellersville, which saved a lot of lives.

"This is Rex and Jimi," Dara said. "They were there, too. In Camden."

A chorus of disembodied voices erupted with different versions of "Hello, Jimi" and "Hey, Rex," coming from the speakerphone on Jerry's desk.

Rex and I said hi, and the woman with the giraffe splice pointed at me and said, "Jimi from Pitman?"

I nodded, resisting the urge to correct her on where I was actually *from*.

She nodded back at me. "I'm Audrey." She turned to the guy next to her. "This is Gary."

Gary moved his eyebrows in acknowledgment, if not quite greeting.

"Dymphna was Jimi's aunt," Dara added.

Gary's attitude thawed slightly amid a soft murmur of grunts from the Holocon.

"Oh, wow," Audrey said. "So Jimi from Pitman is Dymphna's niece. That's perfect. You knew her pretty well, then, huh?"

"Not really," I said. "I'm named after her, but she's mostly been out of my life, until just recently." My eyes clouded for a moment, but I willed myself not to cry.

"Okay, if you're coming in, come in," Jerry said. "And close the door behind you."

We pushed far enough into the room that we could close the door behind us, then stood with our backs against it.

"Anyway," Gary said, "like I was saying, it's going to take at least a week to get the council together, and I'm just saying that we, as the ones who are here, on the ground, need to decide what is to be done with the body. We can't wait for the whole group to chime in."

"The body will to be released to the family, obviously," said Audrey. "*We* can't have anything to do with that; it'll expose us. Maybe a private memorial within the organization is the safest bet."

"Well, I was actually thinking more about what is going to happen with the body, literally," Martin said. "I can't imagine Dymphna wouldn't have had clear ideas on her body's disposition."

Audrey tipped his head in my direction. "Maybe the family knows."

Everyone looked at me, expectantly. I took a half step backward, my shoulders pressing harder against the door behind me. "I…I don't know. I could ask my mother, my aunt. They might know."

Audrey smiled gently and nodded.

"But there's a more pressing issue," I said, stepping forward again. Jerry raised his hands like he was going to shush me or tell me I was not on the agenda, but if I was going to get their attention, now was the time. "Dymphna told me about Howard Wells's super-flu virus, and about the immunity virus she released through the splice medium, how it's spreading through the population. We need to get word out about that, to tell the world that people can get immunity through contact with chimeras."

"We can't do that," Martin said, shaking his head wearily.

"Wells's virus is already out there," I said. "Spreading."

Martin continued to slowly shake his head while I spoke.

"But we also need to figure out how Wells is planning on releasing his virus on a large scale," I said. "And we need to stop him."

"Dymphna's orders were very clear," Gary said. "She was emphatic that we don't tip our hand and reveal to Wells that we know what he's up to, that once he knew we were onto him, he would accelerate his plan, and release his flu before the immunity virus has adequately spread."

"Yes," I said, "but that was before that fax went out to all those news agencies and governments. The allegations are out there. The virus is, too, and—"

"She's got a point," interrupted a voice on the Holocon. Two other disembodied voices weighed in, one agreeing with me and one disagreeing.

"The allegations are out there because CLAD sent them out," Gary said, sneering. "They're probably to blame for her death."

"No," I said. "That was Howard Wells's people."

He snorted. "And are you sure they're not one and the same?"

"Look, I know Dymphna suspected they might be getting funded by Wells, but I can assure you, if they were, they didn't know it. Cronos, the leader of CLAD, he seems to hate Wells more than anyone."

"We're not about hate," Audrey said quietly.

"And you know this Cronos pretty well, then, do you?" Gary said.

I rolled my eyes. "Since I only seem to have conversations with him when he's trying to kidnap me, no, I wouldn't say I know him especially well."

Rex gave me a small smile.

"Look," I continued, "none of that is important right now. Wells is probably already accelerating his plans. If this is for real, if Dypmhna was right, it's probably happening right now, or about to. We need to stop him, and we need to try to head him off, to minimize the damage if we can't stop him, and that means telling people they can get immunity from chimeras, that chimeras can save their lives, and their friends and family." I looked them each in the eye, hoping they'd see reason.

Audrey looked semi-convinced, but Martin said, "No," still shaking his head. "There is a lot we need to figure out in the wake of losing Dymphna, but this is clear. She was certain that this was essential, it was a priority she maintained right up until the day she died."

"But the situation has *changed* since she died," I shot back. "Drastically."

"Jimi's right," Audrey said. "We need to bring it up with the full council. It should be our first priority when we meet next week."

"*No!*" I said. "That's too late. From what Dymphna said, a week from now could be too late."

"Well, we can't vote on anything without a quorum," Audrey said, "And we can't get the rest of the council together before then."

"Then we need to act now, right now."

"She's right," Rex said. "This can't wait."

Martin had just about stopped shaking his head, and now he started up again with renewed vigor. "It's going to have to. Even when Dymphna was alive, this was a democratically run organization. We can't abandon that now, so soon after her death and with so much at stake."

"'So much at stake'?" I said throwing it back at him. "*Exactly!* Now isn't the time to be sitting here doing nothing. *Everything* is at stake."

"Let's vote," said Audrey.

"We can't vote," Gary said. "We don't have a quorum and there's no motion."

Audrey took a breath and gathered her patience. "Okay, then, in light of the special circumstances, I propose a motion that this partial meeting of the council should consider next steps, even without a quorum."

"Second," said a voice on the Holocon.

Gary looked at Martin and raised his hand. "I say we wait."

Martin nodded, as if that was the only way he could stop shaking his head. "Me too," he said, raising his hand, as well.

"Everyone else?" Audrey said, and three voices chimed in over the Holocon, two opposed and one in favor.

Audrey turned to me with a sad, resigned shrug. "I agree with Jimi, here. But I guess it's four to two opposed."

I looked at the rest of the faces—Sly and Dara and Jerry and Rex—apparently, they didn't get a vote. They weren't on the council.

"Sorry, kid," Jerry said. "But they're probably right."

"So that's it?" I said. "We're going to let the end of the world happen, so once it's too late, the full council can vote on what they should have done before it was too late? This is insane! Billions of lives are on the line."

I looked at Sly, then Dara, but they were both looking at their feet, avoiding my gaze. The rest of them looked at Rex and me with the same condescending smile, like I couldn't possibly grasp the complexities of what they were dealing with. And maybe they were right—lord knows Dymphna had held plenty of information back from me in the past. I was assuming she had told me everything, or everything relevant, but maybe there were more big secrets, secrets that, if I knew, would make all the difference and convince me of the wisdom of their inaction. But everything I knew told me they were wrong, that we needed to act quickly and decisively, and that if we waited, it would be too late.

Rex put his hand back on my shoulder. "Jimi, come on." He held my gaze and said quietly, "We're wasting our time here." It seemed like he was trying to convey something with his stare, but I couldn't decipher what.

"Okay," I said, throwing my hands up in the air. Then I turned to the others. "Well, if there's anyone other than Howard Wells left to write the history books when this is all over, there's going to be a chapter about how Chimerica might have prevented the biggest mass murder in the history of the world, but instead they decided to wait a week."

I felt hot tears threatening, tears of anger more than anything else, and I knew I needed to get out of there before they came. I wanted to storm out of that room, but it was so crowded the best I could do was to mutter a disgusted "Excuse me" and squeeze past Audrey and Martin so I could open the door and slip out. Rex came out after me a moment later, grabbing my hand and pulling me through the back door.

FORTY-THREE

S o now what?" I asked as we walked toward the Lev station.

Rex turned to me and shrugged. "Now, I guess we talk to CLAD."

I shook my head and growled, but out of frustration, not disagreement. As hard as I was trying to keep CLAD at a distance, circumstances kept leading us back to them. When I was done shaking my head, I sighed and nodded. "Yeah, you're right. We're going to need a car to get to Ogden's house. After what happened last time, and after just now, I doubt we can ask Jerry."

Rex laughed wearily and shook his head. "Yeah, I don't think that's an option. Not just yet."

Luckily, I knew someone else with a car, and I needed to get in touch with her anyway to make sure she was okay. When we got to the Lev station, I called Claudia from a pay phone, but the lines were still down.

"Her phone's still out," I told Rex as I hung up the pay phone.

He looked concerned. "I don't like this."

"I know. It's probably from the brush fires, but still."

He took out his wallet and flicked through it. "I've got twenty-three bucks. You think that's enough for a pod out there?"

Claudia's house was in the exact opposite direction from the Ben Franklin Bridge and Ogden's house. It seemed ridiculous to take a pod out there only to turn around and double back, but I couldn't think of a better plan. "Yeah, I think so. Good idea."

To save money, we took the Lev train to Chestnut Hill, figuring we could take a pod from the station. The sky was even thicker with drones and copters than it had been in the morning. As the train took us past the water department's reservoir on Henry Avenue, a familiar-looking pale blue delivery van was pulling up in front of it. I nudged Rex and pointed.

"Wells Life Sciences," he said, reading the side of it.

"Looks just like the vans on the news, leaving the chicken plant."

As we watched, the van turned toward the entrance to the reservoir. The gate rose up and the van drove in.

"What do you think that's about?" Rex said, as the reservoir disappeared behind us.

"Do you think it's flu related? Like, that's how they're going to spread the virus?"

He shrugged. "I don't know. I mean, yeah, they could spread it in the water, and probably sicken a lot of people, but it can't be enough for what Dymphna described. And who knows, maybe they're just delivering water purification chemicals or something."

"Maybe."

When we got off the train in Chestnut Hill five minutes later, the air was thick with smoke. Most of the people getting off with us wore breathing masks, and I wondered if here, the masks had more to do with the air quality than the fear of contagions.

We ordered the pod from the pay phone, and by the time it arrived two minutes later our throats were already feeling scratchy. It was a four-person pod, but it was still a tight squeeze for Rex to get in. We told it Claudia's address, which it repeated back, then Rex fed in a twenty and it took off.

As we drove, the smoke grew thicker. The pod seemed to be taking a roundabout route, and I wondered if maybe some of the nearby streets were closed off due to brush fires.

We passed one area that was actively burning, the dense smoke all but obscuring the orange flames on the ground and the blinking yellow lights of the drones dropping pink flame retardant. I was taken by surprise a few minutes later when we pulled into the Bembrys' driveway. The smoke was so thick, I had totally lost my bearings.

I was relieved to see the house undamaged, and to see Chris's car parked out front, meaning someone was home. The car was a sleek, dark blue Audi, more classy than sporty but still looking like it could go plenty fast. We pulled up next to it and the pod spat out Rex's change. As soon as we got out, it spun on its center wheel and sped back down the driveway, disappearing into a swirl of smoke.

Rex looked at the house and whistled. "Nice place."

"Yeah," I said, stifling a cough. "A little close to the brushfire-action, though."

As we walked up to the front door, it opened and Chris came out, carrying a briefcase and several cardboard tubes, like the kind used to hold posters or blueprints.

His eyes looked pained, but he was smiling. The smile widened when he saw us, but somehow didn't become any more convincing.

"Hi Jimi," he said. "Hi, Rex."

"Hi, um…Chris," I said.

Rex seemed even more confused. He just said, "Hi."

Chris sniffed and wiped his eye.

"Are you okay?" I asked.

He nodded and boosted his smile some more. "Never better." Maybe it was the smoke. "Claudia's inside," he said as he got in his car.

We walked up to the doorway and rang the bell as he drove off.

"I didn't know you'd met Claudia's dad before," I said as we waited.

Rex shook his head. "I'm pretty sure I haven't."

Before I could respond, Claudia opened the door, looking exhausted.

"Hey," I said. "Are you okay?"

She shook her head with a weary laugh. "I don't even know any more." She scrunched up her face waved her hand as if she could dissipate the smoke. "Come on inside, where we can breathe."

"How are you holding up?" I asked, once she closed the door behind us.

"I'm about the same," she said. "Except now I don't know what's worse, having him zoned out and unresponsive, or blathering on about his stupid upgrade like a paid Wellplant spokesperson."

"I'm really sorry, Claudia," Rex said. "I wish there was something we could do."

She nodded. "Thanks. So what are you two doing here?"

"We tried to call," I told her. "But the phones are out."

"Yeah, the brush fires took down the lines." She shook her head and rolled her eyes. "I love being out here in the woods like this, but the brush fires have been getting really bad." She let out a short bark of a laugh. "Of course, my dad is making a lot of money on the firefighting drones. Turning lemons into lemonade, as he likes to say."

"He makes firefighting drones now?" Rex asked. Claudia had told us that her father had his hands in a lot of different enterprises, but firefighting drones was a new one.

She shook her head. "No, just the chemicals. One of his companies makes the pink stuff the drones drop on the fires. He's not a drone manufacturer...yet." She coughed, then said, "What's been going on with you?"

"A lot, actually," I said. "We were worried about you and wanted to make sure you're okay. But also, we need your help. I can tell you more on the way, but...could you give us a ride to Jersey?"

She winced. "Sorry. I'd love to help, and I'd *really* love to get out of the house, but my car's in the shop getting that H4H love letter buffed out and painted over, and my mom's down in Washington for a seminar. I'm sure my dad would let me borrow his car, but he got called in to work. The place that makes the fire retardant, actually. He just left."

"Crap," I said.

"Why?" she asked. "What's up?"

We sat in the living room and told her what had happened at the vertical farm, about Dymphna, and Stan and Cronos, and what we suspected was going on with Wells's super-flu, and how Chimerica's governing council had refused to act.

"Dymphna's dead?" she said, stunned.

I nodded, swallowing hard against the lump in my throat.

She put an arm around my neck and hugged me tight. "Jimi, I'm so sorry."

"Thanks," I said.

We were silent for a minute. Then Claudia said quietly, "I've been so caught up in the craziness at home, I haven't even been watching the news or anything. This is so messed up. So you think Wells is really going to release this flu? How?"

"We don't know how," Rex said. "That's part of the problem. But we need to get the word out that people can get immunity from chimeras."

"And since Chimerica won't do anything about it, we figured we needed to talk to CLAD, and see if *they* will, the same way they got out word about Wells's link to the super-flu." I said. "They might be crazy, but at least they seem ready to act. And apparently, they know how to get the word out."

Claudia sat there for a moment, processing it. "Could we take a pod there? I can pay for it."

Rex shook his head. "The pods don't go outside the city, much less across the river into New Jersey."

"Okay...how about we take a pod to my dad's factory and borrow his car? It's not that far."

Rex and I looked at each other. "Sure, that would be great," I said.

"You're sure he'll let you borrow the car?" Rex asked.

She nodded. "He actually asked me if I needed it today. Said I could drive him to the plant and then take it, but I..." She shook her head. "I needed a break from him, to be honest, from pretending he's normal and everything's fine." She abruptly picked up the phone and ordered the pod.

When she was done, I put my hand on her shoulder. "Speaking of your dad," I said. "There's more."

"What is it?" she said, tensing up, as if preparing for yet more bad news.

"CLAD is planning on crashing the Wellplant network."

"Really?" She screwed up her face, thinking. "Why?"

I shrugged and looked at Rex.

"They're bomb throwers," he said. "They want to topple Wells's empire. I guess they see Wells and Wellplant and H4H as one big enemy front."

"They might be right about that," she said.

"But the people with Wellplants would be incapacitated for forty-eight hours, or that's what Cronos said. Their Wellplants would stop working."

She looked down, thinking about it for a moment. "You know what? I'm okay with that." She looked back up at us. "I mean, I'll be worried about my dad, but I'm worried about him now. And it's not like he wasn't just incapacitated by that system upgrade or whatever it is. Maybe if he gets back to his old self for a couple of minutes, he'll see what a mistake he's made."

The pod pulled up out front and tooted its horn. Claudia shot to her feet. "Let's go," she said, and Rex and I followed her out the door.

Chris's factory was less than ten minutes away, and on the drive there, Claudia peppered us with questions about Wells and the flu, about Chimerica's reluctance to get involved, and what we hoped CLAD would do.

"Ideally, CLAD will use their resources to get the word out about the immunity virus, that people can protect themselves just by shaking hands with a chimera, or whatever," I told her.

"Didn't they just send out a fax?" she said. "I mean, there are fax machines at the library. My dad has them in every office. Could we just send it out that way?"

"Well, theoretically," I said. "But we'd have to figure out where to send them all. And it wouldn't just mean looking up the fax numbers—we don't even know the names of the people or companies or agencies or whatever we'd want to send them *to*. Especially not in other countries. By the time we finished researching and were ready to start sending faxes, half the world could already be dead from Well's super-flu."

She grimaced at me. "Well, when you put it like that…"

"CLAD has already proven they have a system to get information out widely. But also, we want CLAD's help trying to figure out how Wells is planning on releasing the virus."

"There must be all sorts of ways to do that," she said.

"There are," I said. "But none of them seems to be enough to achieve the critical mass that Dymphna suspects he has in mind. It's all little bits and pieces."

"On our way here, we saw one of those Wells Life Sciences vans at the Water Department's reservoir," Rex said. "The same kind we saw on the news, leaving Wells's place in Delaware." He turned to me. "We thought maybe they're using the water department to spread the flu. You could infect a lot of people that way, maybe even millions, but not enough for what Dymphna suspects."

Claudia nodded, thinking about that. Then she looked up and said, "We're here."

The pod pulled over in front of a tall fence surrounding a nondescript brick building. A metal sign on the fence said BEMBRY SUPPRESSION CHEMICALS.

The gate was closed and unattended, but Claudia walked up to the security panel attached to the fence next to it. She pressed a button and held her face in front of the plastic bubble housing the camera.

A scratchy voice came through the speaker: "Bembry Chemicals, how can I help you?"

"Hi, Cheryl," Claudia asked. "It's Claudia. I'm here to see my dad."

"Oh, hi, sweetie. Um…this is Nancy. Cheryl's out sick. I'll tell Mr. Bembry you're here."

Claudia turned to us looking slightly troubled. "Usually they just buzz me in."

We waited silently, maybe not trusting that the microphone in the security panel wasn't listening in. After a few minutes, the front door opened and Chris stepped out.

He smiled when he saw Claudia. She stiffened at the sight of him.

"Hey, kids. Hi, pumpkin," he said. He seemed like he was hiding distress, the smile on his mouth totally not matching the deep ache in his eyes. He walked up to the fence but didn't open the gate.

"Hi, Dad," she said, her voice quiet and guarded. "Can we come in?"

"Well, um, sorry, but actually today's not the best day. We've got a lot going on and it's kind of a mess, so best not to. What's up?"

"Um," she started, her voice breaking before she got it under control. "Can I borrow your car?"

"Now?" He laughed an odd, awkward laugh. "Wouldn't it have been easier if you'd just dropped me off this morning? But sure, yeah, of course. I said you could. It's parked around the corner. Do you have your key?"

She held up a key ring and jingled it. "Got it."

They stared at each other for a second longer, then he nodded and said, "Okay, great. And don't worry about bringing it back here. I'll grab a pod home."

"Okay." She paused, like she wanted to say something else, then quickly said, "Thanks, Dad."

"Sure thing, pumpkin," he replied. "Be safe, okay?"

"You too," she said, then turned on her heel and walked away.

Chris nodded and walked back toward the building. Claudia wiped her eyes and hurried away from us. My eyes found Rex's and we paused before following her. She seemed like she wanted a tiny bit of privacy, so we let her get a few steps ahead.

We followed her along the fence, past a large double gate, then around the corner. Ahead of us was Chris's dark blue Audi. Claudia pressed a button on the key fob, and the running lights came on.

We caught up with her as she got in the car. "Sorry," she mumbled, wiping her eyes again.

"Don't be sorry," I said quietly as I buckled myself into the front passenger seat.

In the back seat, Rex said, "Look at that."

"What?" Claudia asked. "What is it?"

I pointed out the window at a pale blue van driving slowly past. "Wells Life Sciences again," I said. "Same as the vans from the chicken plant. And the one at the reservoir."

She glanced at me, her face suddenly hard and determined. "What's it doing *here*?" Before either of us could answer, she put the car in forward and let it roll toward the corner, lightly pressing the brakes to come to a stop.

The van had stopped in front of the double gate, which Chris was now opening.

"What the hell?" Claudia said under her breath as the van drove through the gate and onto the factory grounds. Chris looked around as he closed the gates and locked them. He didn't seem to have noticed us watching.

"What do you think that's about?" Rex said from the back seat.

I looked back at him, pretty certain he was wondering the same thing I was: Does this have anything to do with Wells's super-flu?

I turned to Claudia. "Should we ask your dad?"

She thought about it for a second, then shook her head and hit the accelerator hard. "I don't think I'd believe whatever he told us."

FORTY-FOUR

Driving through the city, we had to take several detours around areas that were closed off due to quarantines or smoke from brush fires. The traffic was dense, and even though Smartdrive kept the cars moving in an orderly manner, it was slow going. When we finally reached the bridge into New Jersey, we could see a pall of bluish smoke hanging in the air over both sides of the river, with darker smudges here and there where fresh smoke was rising into the air. On the ground, both Philapelphia and Camden sparkled with flashing lights. It looked surreal, beautiful in a way, but also like a world on the brink of collapse. Suddenly, the threat of Wells's insanity seemed very, very present.

"Shit's for real," Rex said, his forehead pressed up against the window.

"I know," Claudia said. "Even just the brush fires, apart from anything else. Worse and worse each year." Then quietly, like she was talking to herself, she said, "Makes you wonder how long it will be before the whole world catches fire."

Once we got off the bridge and the highway, Rex and I directed Claudia through the maze of smaller streets.

When we pulled up in front of Ogden's house and got out of the car, he came out onto the porch, hands in his pockets. "Hey," he said, but his head was shaking slightly from side to side, so subtle I couldn't be sure I saw it.

"Hey," I said. He seemed to be still shaking his head as I said, "We need to talk."

He sighed and his shoulders slumped. "Okay," he said, "come on."

Rex stepped closer and said, "Is something wrong?"

Then the door behind Ogden opened wider and Roberta stepped out, carrying a shotgun. "Everything's just fine," she said. "Come on in."

"Yay!" Claudia said. "Roberta's here."

I sensed movement behind me and turned to see Zak, Roberta's zebra-spliced friend from the vertical farm, stepping out from behind the house, also holding a shotgun.

Rex growled in frustration, I think annoyed at himself for having let them get the jump on us like this. I was annoyed at myself, too, but I put my hand on his arm and said, "It's okay. We came to talk to CLAD, we'll talk to CLAD."

Ogden stared at us as we walked up the steps, looking us each in the eye as if trying to convey some kind of meaning. Maybe if I'd known him better I would have understood, but all I could glean was that he had something to say. When we got up onto the porch, he turned and preceded us inside.

Roberta waited for us to go in first. Rex led the way. As I followed him, Roberta and I exchanged a cold stare. As Claudia moved past her behind me, she said, "Lovely to see you, too."

The house was darker than before. The light was gray, and it was coming in at different angles. The place seemed smaller with the six of us in there.

Roberta pointed her shotgun at Rex and then at Claudia. "You two wait down here with Zak." She nodded at Ogden, who went into the kitchen and brought back two chairs.

"Sit," Roberta said, and Rex and Claudia both looked at me, waiting for my response, as if they were waiting to follow my lead.

I felt an intense love for them both right then. We'd been through a lot together, and were about to go through some more, and I realized at that inopportune moment how deeply grateful I was to have them both in my life.

Less than a year earlier, I had been essentially alone in the world, apart from Del. The pain of losing him had dulled into a constant ache that underlay everything else. But the loneliness that could have overwhelmed me was no match for the affection I felt from Rex and Claudia and my other new friends, Ruth and Pell and Sly. Even cranky Jerry. So much craziness had happened over the last few months, I didn't often stop to appreciate how lucky I was. Of course, I also realized now probably wasn't the best time to do it, either.

Maybe, in the back of my mind, I realized time could be running out to do so.

"It's okay," I told them, my voice betraying enough of the emotion roiling inside me that Roberta snorted and rolled her eyes.

I turned to her and shook my head. "Do you have to be such a jerk at all times?"

She curled her lip at me. "Maybe you bring it out in me." She motioned with the rifle toward the steps. "Now come on upstairs."

I gave Rex and Claudia a shrug, trying to convey a nonchalance I didn't feel. As I headed up the stairs with Roberta behind me, Zak handed Ogden a sheaf of plastic zip ties and stepped back to cover Rex and Claudia with his shotgun while Ogden secured their wrists and ankles to the chairs.

"You know, we came here voluntarily," Rex said. "This isn't really necessary."

Ogden ignored him as he tightened the zip ties.

The second floor consisted of a short hallway with five doors leading off of it, all of them closed except for the bathroom at one end and a bedroom at the other end, unfurnished except for another kitchen chair, identical to the ones Rex and Claudia were sitting in.

Roberta and her shotgun herded me into the bedroom.

I struggled not to show any fear, but there was plenty, and it was growing. I didn't know what she had in store for me, but as she zip-tied me to the chair and stalked out of the room, I was pretty sure it wouldn't be pleasant. As I faced up to my fears about my immediate fate, I had to acknowledge how scared I was about the fate of the world around me, as well.

It was a fear I'd known all my life, to some extent. Between the ever-worsening climate and the possibility of another flu pandemic like the one that had taken my father, ever since I was little, I'd been trying to keep those fears at bay, to live my life as if there wasn't a chance the environment could completely collapse, or that at any moment some tiny, invisible microbe could take away everyone I loved, destroy the world as I knew it, and kill me, too.

And now, with each passing moment, that distinct-but-remote possibility was becoming more and more real, more and more likely. Maybe it wouldn't kill me or my family or my friends, and maybe it actually *would* save the world from irrevocable climate collapse, but the world that would be left was going to be brutal and hard.

I was sitting with my back to the door, facing the window and thinking on all of this when I heard heavy footsteps coming closer and stopping in the doorway behind me. I assumed it was Roberta, but I didn't want to give her the satisfaction of seeing me struggle to turn around. Instead, with my hands tied behind me, I managed to raise a middle finger.

In response, I heard a subdued laugh, raspy and thick and definitely not Roberta.

I whipped my head around and saw Cronos enter the room. He came around and stood in front of me.

"I thought I was going to have to track you down," he said, leaning against the windowsill. "Or show up at your house, which I really, really didn't want to do." He laughed again, as if that was funny. "Thank you for saving me the trip. So, I understand you want to talk."

The sun broke through the cloud cover and light poured in around him, making him somehow even more intimidating.

"That's right," I said, trying to make my voice strong. "We need your help."

"I'm sorry about your aunt.... I didn't get a chance to tell you that before, but I am sorry."

"Thank you."

"She was a great person, if somewhat misguided. All chimeras owe her a debt of gratitude. You nonks, too, even though you might not appreciate that fact." He took a deep breath and let it out slowly. "I met her once before, you know. Many, many years ago. She was very kind."

I was surprised to hear that, but I didn't know how it might have changed anything.

"I barely knew her myself," I said, for some reason. "She'd been gone from my life for so long."

He nodded and his eyes crinkled, as if he was smiling underneath his mask. "So, what is it you want to talk about, Jimi Corcoran?"

Something about the way he said my name resonated in my mind. Once again there was that sense of the familiar. I tried not to let it distract me. I needed to focus on convincing him to help us.

"We need your help to stop Wells. And to tell the world about Dymphna's immunity virus, that people can save themselves by contact with chimeras."

He laughed again, this time full throated and booming, and without a trace of sadness. "We informed the *world* about Wells and his super-flu, and nobody's done a thing to stop him. We've done what we can on that front."

"You can do more. However you got that other letter out, telling people about the super-flu, you can tell people how they can save themselves."

He sighed and folded his arms. "No, I don't think so."

"What? But you wanted to before. You criticized Chimerica for not doing anything. You have to! Millions of people will get sick. Maybe billions. Wells is going to destroy the world."

"A few billion is not destroying the world," he said, waving a hand. "That's just creating a little more breathing room."

"What? But, you said before—"

"And I've changed my mind. That was before your aunt Dymphna told me the chimeras were already immune."

"Yes, but we need to get the word out that everyone else, people like me, *without* splices or Wellplants, can protect themselves by interacting with chimeras, a hug or a handshake, whatever, that's all it takes, and Dymphna's immunity virus will protect them."

"No."

"But…but…" I sputtered, unable to process the fact that he was willing to sit back and let all those people die. "But we need to stop him."

"Plans are underway to do just that."

I tried not to let my exasperation show. "Yes, I know, you're going to crash the Wellplant network. But how long do you think that will stop them? He long before they get the network back up and resume their plans?"

He looked past me, toward the door, and bellowed, "Ogden! Come up here."

I heard footsteps running up the stairs. Ogden appeared in the doorway. "Yes, sir?"

"Explain to Ms. Corcoran your plan for taking down the Wellplant network. The whole plan."

Ogden looked from Cronos to me and then down at the floor. "So, like I said, we have this Wellplant, the one we've been using to monitor the network. It's not implanted into anyone, so it's not fully functional, just connected to an external power supply. But we, um…we created a computer program, two programs, really, like the old-fashioned malware, from the Internet days. And we're going to use our Wellplant to upload the malware into the network. The first package was designed to disrupt the wearers' motor functions, and paralyze them for forty-eight hours."

"Yes, but tell her about the second one," Cronos prodded.

Ogden looked at the floor and spoke quietly. "The second part disrupts their vital functions."

"Speak up!" Cronos said, his voice jovial but scolding. "You should be proud of what you've accomplished."

"Wait," I said. "You're going to…to kill them?"

Ogden nodded, still without looking up.

I gasped in horror. "You can't be serious! Ten million people out there have Wellplants. You can't seriously intend to kill them all!"

Cronos shrugged. "This is a war. That's what people do in war. They kill. And they die. We'll be destroying a handful of people compared to the numbers Wells and his people are planning on killing. We are simply killing the millions who would kill the billions. As an added benefit, they are the same millions who are most guilty of draining Earth's resources even when they know it is killing the planet; who bought bigger and better Wellplants, knowing they were manufactured with the blood and sweat of innocent chimeras, even after they saw how twisted it made Wells himself. They are the millions who are doing Wells's bidding."

I looked at Ogden, but he had retreated into a corner, shrinking, drawing into himself.

"They're not all like that," I said. "You're also talking about innocent people."

"Jimi, Jimi, Jimi," Cronos said, shaking his head condescendingly. "How many times do I have to tell you: There are no innocent people out there. No one is innocent. Except maybe you."

That's when it hit me.

If I hadn't been sitting, I would have collapsed. If I hadn't been tied to my chair, I would have fallen out of it. Squinting through the sunlight streaming around his silhouette, I could barely see him, but I knew there were no visual clues anyway. His eyes were unrecognizable. Everything else was hidden. But the tone of his voice, the countless familiar micro-gestures and tiny clues that had been nagging at the back of my mind. And now those words that had haunted me since Pitman. They all came together in a single impossible truth.

"Oh my God," I whispered. "Is that you?"

His entire body suddenly went rigid. Ogden looked up, confused but riveted.

"Is that you?" I said louder, my voice rising unsteadily. "Is it?"

He pushed himself away from the windowsill and I turned my head to follow him as he strode past me. "Do not run away from me again!" I shouted. As he reached the doorway, I froze him again with a single word: "Del!"

FORTY-FIVE

Cronos stood in the doorway for several seconds, absolutely motionless, before he turned and came back into the room. Ogden watched him in silence.

"It is you, isn't it?" I asked breathlessly. My heart beat erratically, like it was going crazy, like everything was going crazy.

Cronos came slowly around in front of me.

"I'm not Del," he said. "Not anymore."

"How?" I said, my voice catching on the emotions rising within me, shock and hope and fury threatening to spill over. "How could you let me believe you were dead?"

"Del *is* dead. And so is Tamil." Tamil was the name he'd adopted as a chimera, briefly. Before he'd died.

He reached up and pulled off his hood, revealing a face that was more scar tissue than anything else, the skin shiny and tight over lumps and striations. "Those parts of me are gone. I am Cronos now."

"But…how?" I asked again. "I saw you die."

He smiled, and it was both ghastly and sweet.

"No, Jimi, you saw what should have killed me. You saw me shot and burned, by both chemicals and fire. I saw on the news that they said they hadn't recovered my body because the chemicals in that pit had dissolved it. Well, not entirely." He took off his gloves and looked down at his red, raw hands. "It seems my salamander splice kept me alive, regenerating just enough of me after I crawled out of that chemical pit and away from that terrible place. It regrew me as best it could." He laughed under his breath, raspy and bitter, but sounding more and more like Del. "Turns out the best was still not very good. I should have died, but I didn't. For better or for worse."

Then he looked up at me, his eyes burning behind his seared skin. "At first, for me, it was definitely for worse. But I realized it was for a reason. I had to suffer through the nonks' hatred, see the depths of it, so I could serve as a living reminder—or a half-living one—of what they were capable of, what they wanted to do to us all. I've seen it, up close. My experiences gave me the determination to do something about it, to bring together others who felt the same way, who wanted to be a part of the solution. There aren't a lot of us, a few dozen—not like the thousands in Chimerica—but we are acting, doing, not just talking and keeping secrets. We are making a difference, changing the world. And who better to make sure no other chimera suffers like this at the hands of the nonks? Who better to prevent more atrocities from happening, and to avenge those that have already occurred?"

"I'm so sorry," I said. "Sorry for what happened to you and—and sorry I wasn't able to do more to prevent it, or to help you afterward. But it doesn't make it right, Del, what you're planning to do. What you're planning to let happen. Even if we can't stop Wells and his insanity, we can still tell people about the immunity virus. You released the details about the super-flu, you can get word out about the cure, too, the same way."

He paused for a long moment, then he stood. "No. Once Wells has released his bio-pathogen, we'll release our cyber-pathogen. Let him kill the nonks, then we'll kill the Plants. Most of the nonks hate us anyway. Those who are already close to chimeras, friends and allies like you, who don't fear us or hate us or seek to take away our rights, they'll be spared." He smiled as he pulled his hood back over his head. "And those who avoid us like the plague, well…they'll get the plague."

"You can't mean that, Del," I said, as he moved toward the door.

He stopped and put a hand on my shoulder. "I told you: Del is gone. You saw him die. I am Cronos. And I must go. Next time we talk, this will all be over, and you'll see that the world is a better place for it."

Ogden was still in the corner, watching and listening, his eyes wide with horror.

Cronos strode through the door, and from the hallway he called back, "Let's go, Ogden. We have work to do."

Ogden stared at me for another moment, his eyes unreadable, then he dashed through the door after Cronos.

Cronos's revelations had left me reeling. My brain felt like it was split in two, each hemisphere careening in a different direction: one side trying desperately to make sense of a world where my best friend was not only still alive, but the head of CLAD—and the other, trying to get a grip on his and Wells's plans. Two madmen with two different approaches to killing vast numbers of people.

They had to be stopped, both of them. But I had no idea how. CLAD had put out the word about Wells and his virus, but Cronos was right: too many of the people who should be stopping it had Wellplants, and apparently, in some way, they were complicit.

It was hard to imagine all of them going along with it. But maybe they would.

I thought of Chris Bembry, robotically opening his gate for that van from Wells Life Sciences, and I wondered if he was in on it. Conceivably, the drones spraying fire retardant could be used to spread a flu virus, although that would hardly be enough to come close to the kind of impact Dymphna had described. And I didn't know Claudia's dad well, but from what she'd told me about him, participating in such a scheme would be against everything Chris Bembry believed in.

But maybe that didn't matter anymore. Maybe it wasn't Chris Bembry doing it, but the Wellplant. Everyone said the new version was much more powerful than before. Could they be more powerful than a human brain? I felt sick at the thought that maybe the new Wellplants were overpowering the brains they were implanted in. And did that mean Howard Wells was controlling them all?

I had no idea, but even if I knew, there wasn't much I could do tied to a chair.

With enough time, maybe I could shuffle out into the hallway and tip myself down the steps, hope that the chair broke up more completely than I did. More likely, I would just snap my neck.

I could still hear people walking around on the first floor, speaking in hushed tones, so I knew they hadn't left yet. I resolved that once they did, if no other idea presented itself, I would try to get to the stairs.

The front door opened and closed, and it was quiet for a few seconds, then it opened and closed again, and I heard footsteps running up the stairs, and then creeping down the hallway. Ogden appeared in the doorway with his finger against his lips.

"How could you do this?" I hissed in a loud whisper as he hurried closer. "This is genocide."

"*Shh!*" he said, crouching next to me and sawing at the zip tie around my right wrist with a tiny pen knife. "I created that second malware program to be used on one person, Howard Wells, not everyone wearing a Wellplant. This is another one of Cronos's surprise plans. It's like with the bombing at the convention. From what I heard, no one was supposed to get hurt, but he changed the plan at the last minute. He said if I don't go through with this, he'll kill me, and my family." The zip tie fell away and he put the knife in my hand, along with Claudia's car keys. "We're set up at the old RCA building in Camden, up in the tower. That's where we're going now. The Wellplant we've been using can receive, but it can't transmit until we fully activate it. But once we activate it and upload the malware, the network will figure out pretty quickly that it's not implanted and doesn't have authorization, and it will shut us down. I'll do what I can to stop this, but it's a simple process—just click ENTER, and the malware will launch, first one, then the other. Cronos doesn't need me at this point, so…he might just kill me and do it himself anyway. If you want to stop him, you need to get over there quick."

"Ogden—"

"There's a couple of dart guns in the dishwasher. Use them to get in, then destroy the Wellplant. Or even just disconnect it. I'll do what I can to help, but I can't do this alone."

He turned and ran out into the hallway, stopping to flush the toilet in the bathroom—presumably that was his excuse for coming back up here. He ran downstairs, and a moment later, I heard the front door creak open and slam shut. A moment after that, I heard a couple of vehicles start up behind the house then drive away.

I cut through the zip tie on my other wrist, then freed my legs, as well. I crept slowly downstairs, tiny knife at the ready, in case someone stayed behind to guard us. But the only ones down there were Rex and Claudia, bound to their chairs, mouths covered with duct tape. They both turned to look at me, Rex's eyes looking concerned and relieved, Claudia's indignant and angry.

I gestured toward the back of the house and raised my eyebrows, asking if anybody else was there. They both shook their heads. I hurried over and peeled the tape from Claudia's mouth.

"Son of a…" she said, her eyes wide as she gasped in pain. She moved her mouth around, as if trying to work it back into its normal shape.

I removed Rex's tape, as well, eliciting a grunt of pain. "Thanks," he said, in a tone that suggested he only half meant it.

"What the hell is going on here?" Claudia demanded as I cut through the zip tie on Rex's wrist.

"I'll tell you on the way."

"On the way where?" Rex asked as I cut through the zip tie.

"Camden," I said. "They're set up in the old RCA building."

I handed him the knife and ducked into the kitchen, returning a moment later with the two dart guns Ogden had stashed in the dishwasher. As Rex flicked the blade through the zip tie on his other wrist, then his ankles, I turned to Claudia. "They're not just going to immobilize the Plants. They're going to shut down their vital functions."

Rex was bending over Claudia about to free her, as well. He paused and said. "They're going to kill them? All of them?"

I nodded. "Ogden said there's a second malware program. He came up with it as a way to kill Howard Wells, but Cronos wants to use it to wipe out everyone with a Wellplant."

They both took half a second to absorb the implications. Then Claudia said, "Get these damn things off me. We need to stop them."

FORTY-SIX

Claudia floored the accelerator as she turned the car around, raising a cloud of dust and spraying rocks and pebbles out over the swampy water behind the house.

"Where are we going again?" she asked, still rubbing adhesive off of her face and spitting it from her lips as we careened down the dirt road.

"Camden," I repeated. "The old RCA building."

"The Nipper Building?" Rex said, leaning forward in the back seat.

"Exactly."

"Nipper?" Claudia said, as she typed into the navigator.

"The dog," he said. "It was the old RCA logo, the dog listening to a record player, a Victrola. Goes back to the Victor Talking Machine Company."

He took a breath, like he was about to say something else. Before he could, I turned in my seat. "Rex, I have to tell you something. Del's still alive."

"*What?!*" Rex said, shocked.

"*He* is Cronos."

"Holy…"

Claudia turned to stare at me. "Del? Your old friend who died in Pitman?"

I nodded.

"That would explain why he seemed so familiar," Rex said, still looking stunned. "Are you sure?"

"I figured it out when we were upstairs. Something he said up there, combined with just…I don't know. Everything. Gestures, mannerisms. And maybe because he was trying so hard to hide it, with his evil-genius routine, but when I confronted him, he admitted it."

"Did you see his face?" Claudia asked quietly as the car came to a stop at the entrance to the Smart-route. She turned on the Smartdrive, and the car rolled forward, seamlessly merging into traffic.

I nodded. "He was almost unrecognizable. Horribly scarred." I wiped my eyes, thinking of all he'd been through. "Poor Del."

Rex put a hand on my shoulder.

"He said Del's dead. He's only Cronos now." I put my hand over his, squeezing it, holding it in place. I could feel my emotions roiling my insides again—all the pain and sorrow and anger and regret and everything else, some that had been swirling under the surface since Del's death.

"And all this time, he didn't tell you he was alive," Claudia said, shaking her head. "That is messed up."

"Yes," I said. "It is." Del had decided to run away and get spliced without telling me, then he decided to seek sanctuary and disappear forever without telling me. He knew everyone—including me—thought he'd been killed in Pitman, and he never told me otherwise. I had long since realized that our friendship hadn't been what I thought it was. Apparently, I needed to revise it downward once again.

"You okay?" Rex said, quietly.

I nodded. "Yeah, I'm okay."

Ahead of us, a bank of carbon scrubbers rose up, huge facilities that absorbed carbon dioxide from the atmosphere and belched out towering clouds of decarbonized air and water vapor from tall stacks. They were part of the too-little-too-late effort to stave off the worst of the climate change that was ravaging the planet.

"According to the map, we're about fifteen minutes away from this place," Claudia said. "What are we planning to do once we get there?" She turned to look at each of us, then she said, "Oh, crap."

As she tapped the brakes, I turned to see that we were just pulling alongside another Wells Life Sciences van.

"Man, they're everywhere," Rex said.

"They've got to have something to do with all this, right?" I said.

As Claudia slowed, trying not to pull even with it, the van slowed even more.

"Do you think they saw us?" Claudia said, checking the rearview to make sure we weren't about to get rear-ended. Rex reached down to the floor, placing his hand on the dart guns we had taken from Ogden's house.

I leaned forward to see in the driver's side window. "No. I don't think there's even a driver."

The van veered away from us, taking the exit ramp toward the scrubbers. All three of us looked up at the clouds billowing from the top.

"Do you think that's part of how Wells is planning to release the virus?" I asked. "Through those scrubber stacks?"

"Maybe," Claudia said. Then she shook her head. "But that's hardly going to be enough to spread the virus the way you made it sound. I mean, I guess it could spread, for sure, but it seems too localized."

"No, you're right," Rex said, from the back. "When we saw that Wells Life Sciences van at the fire-retardant factory, the first thing I thought was that they could use his firefighting drones to spray the virus into the air. Same thing with the van at the reservoir, spreading virus through the water. But Dymphna described a global pandemic. I can't see how any of those methods could be close to enough to spread the virus widely enough."

"My dad would never be a part of that," Claudia said with a scowl. But in her eyes I could see that maybe the same thought had crossed her mind. It had crossed mine.

"Maybe it's not any one of those things," I said slowly. "The drones or the water supply or the scrubbers back there."

"Then what is it?" Claudia asked.

"Maybe—maybe it's all of them."

Rex sat forward again. "What do you mean?"

"I'm just thinking," I said, and the more I thought, the more chilled I felt. "All these world leaders and CEOs who've gotten Wellplants, plus all those civil servants, a lot of them are in positions where they could spread the virus broadly. Maybe none of them individually could spread it widely enough, simultaneously, to reach the critical mass to create a pandemic, but what if all of them just focus on whatever it is they do? The water *and* the drones *and* the scrubbers, and a million other little things that are systemized to disperse things through air or water or food or medicine—all at the same time, all around the world....I bet that would be enough."

"Whoa," Claudia said breathlessly. "And with Wells's global distribution network delivering it to each of them, they may already have it in hand, waiting for the word to release it."

I pictured the Wells Life Sciences tractor trailer, the one that left the chicken plant at the same time as all those delivery vans, filled with vials of Wells's avian flu, unloading at the cargo terminal of Philadelphia International Airport. That was almost twenty-four hours ago. Its payload could already be distributed around the world.

"That's...terrifying." Rex slowly sank back, then sat forward again. "But that would require all of the Plants to be on board. Not just to go along with it, but to not tell anyone else about the plan. I can't imagine all those people being a part of this, without a single one trying to stop it."

"Exactly," Claudia said, shaking her head. "Like I said, my dad, for one, would never be a part of something like this. Never."

"Not willingly," I said softly.

"What was that?" she demanded, defensive and belligerent.

"I said, 'Not willingly.' Maybe he's being forced to do it. He went on and on about how powerful that new Wellplant upgrade was. Maybe all those people aren't doing whatever they're doing with the help of their Wellplants. Maybe their Wellplants have taken the upper hand, or taken over completely. Maybe these people are being controlled by their Wellplants, and being forced to go along with the plan."

Claudia stared at me, her eyes round. I could practically see her brain sifting through all the interactions she'd had with her dad since he'd gotten spiked.

"Do you think Howard Wells is controlling them all?" Rex asked.

"I don't know," I said. "Dymphna said there is no central node or anything. So it would be hard to control it from a central location. The power of the Wellplant network is all the individual networks."

"So the bigger the network and the more powerful each part of it, the stronger and more powerful the network itself," he said.

"Like a distributed network," Claudia said under her breath.

"Exactly!" I said. "That's exactly what Dymphna called it."

"Holy crap," she said.

"What?" Rex and I both asked at the same time.

"If it truly is a distributed network, and each node has been getting more and more powerful with each upgrade, while at the same time the network has been adding more and more nodes, it's possible that it has reached a critical mass. That the network itself, collectively, is driving things."

"So, it's what?…Sentient? Self-aware?"

"Alive?" Rex asked.

Claudia put up her hands. "I—I don't know. But…maybe, yeah."

"And controlling all those people," I added.

"Whoa," Rex said. "That would change things." His expression turned sad as he glanced out the window.

I followed his gaze, and a cold ache filled me as I saw a green-hued, glass-enclosed building to our left.

"What's that?" Claudia asked.

"That's where Dymphna died," I told her. Thinking back on the violence and death, I felt a physical bolt of fear that maybe we were headed into a similar situation, and a similar fate.

Rex turned to watch the vertical farm go by, but I kept my eyes front. We were quiet for a few moments, driving down a broad empty street of old warehouses or factories that seemed to have been abandoned. Then Rex said, "If Jimi's right, if millions of politicians and CEOs and, I don't know, factory managers or utility technicians or whatever, if a million different people are going to release the virus in a million different ways, how could we possibly stop them all?"

"By not stopping Cronos," Claudia said softly. "Maybe we need to let Cronos's plan go forward." A tear rolled down her cheek. She was talking about letting Cronos kill her father.

"Wait," I said. "I might have another idea."

Claudia looked at me, her eyes now filled with tears, and maybe a tiny spark of hope.

"Good," Rex said, pointing through the windshield as an old-fashioned brick tower came into view up ahead. "Because we're there."

FORTY-SEVEN

The tower itself was actually kind of cute—mostly brick, ten or eleven stories tall, with stained-glass windows at the top featuring an adorable little dog listening to an old-fashioned record player. Claudia—whose face was still wet from her suggestion just a few minutes earlier that we might have to sacrifice her father's life in order to avert a global catastrophe—actually said, "Aww."

As we got closer, we could see that the six-story building that flanked the tower was crumbling on one side and collapsed into rubble on the other. The tower itself leaned slightly toward the rubble, semi-stabilized by a metal scaffold. It was surrounded by a couple of acres of what had probably once been advertised as ample parking, and the whole property was encircled by a thoroughly rusted chain-link fence.

A gate on the far side was partially open, and as we got closer, I spotted a white van, parked next to a squarish hole roughly cut into the brick. I didn't see any sign of anyone up in the tower, but I couldn't help wondering if Cronos was up there watching us.

"Keep driving," I said. "They're here. They might be watching."

Claudia nodded. "Good thinking. Of course, if they're looking, they've probably already seen us."

"Do you see anyone with the van?" Rex asked.

Claudia and I both said no as we kept going, past the tower, toward a block of apartment hives not far from where I'd run to escape Cronos only days earlier.

We parked far enough down the block that we couldn't be seen from the tower. Rex handed the dart guns to Claudia and me, because we had the most experience using them, and he was most able to do some damage with his bare hands, if it came to it.

The original plan was to get inside and find the Wellplant setup, then Claudia and I would cover Rex while he destroyed the Wellplant. The revised plan was a little trickier, a little fuzzier, and a whole lot riskier. It involved finding the Wellplant setup and then launching the first piece of malware, to immobilize the Plants and prevent the release of the super-flu, then destroying the Wellplant before the second part could launch, the one that would kill all the Plants.

The windows were set in the middle of each side of the tower, so to minimize the chance of being seen we approached on foot from the diagonal, climbing rusted-out fences and navigating huge chunks of concrete and asphalt in order to keep our angle.

The massive pile of rubble between us and the tower looked dangerous, an unstable heap of bricks and concrete punctuated by jagged glass and twisted rebar. When we got to the bottom of it, we huddled up.

"I think the entrance is right around the corner," Claudia whispered.

"And probably guarded," Rex added.

I nodded and looked up at the top of the rubble pile. There was a gaping window right above it. I pointed at it. "Maybe we can get in there."

They followed my finger. The rubble pile was three stories tall, half as tall as the structure it had once been. Above it, we could see the exposed brick where the wing used to abut the tower. The window was actually on the side of the tower that faced onto a little courtyard that looked like it used to be surrounded by the rest of the building. It appeared to be an easy reach from the top of the pile.

Rex squinted up at it. "Do you think it's safe?"

Claudia and I looked at each other and both started snickering despite ourselves, and despite the dire situation. It was *totally* not safe.

Rex rolled his eyes. "Come on. You know what I mean. Alright, whatever, just be careful."

"And quiet," Claudia added, elbowing me with a look of mock disapproval.

I nodded and we started up, picking our way around the most dangerous of the debris. We went in order of weight—Claudia, then me, then Rex—to minimize surprises from the rubble shifting.

As we were approaching the top, Claudia looked down onto the other side and held up a hand. Rex and I stopped, and Claudia turned and held up one finger, then pointed down at the side of the rubble pile, at the entrance next to the van. She mouthed the words *One guy*.

I nodded and crept up next to her and peered over the top of the pile. Zak was down there, leaning against the wall next to a gaping double doorway. All of his attention seemed to be focused on a hangnail, but he also had a rifle at the ready.

The open window was just a few feet away from us, but climbing through it would completely expose us. I looked at Claudia and held up my dart gun. We were well within range. She smiled and held hers up, as well.

We lay down as low as we could on the rubble and rested our guns on the rocks.

"On three," I whispered, and she nodded. I counted off. "One…two… *three*."

The guns spat out an almost simultaneous *thwip thwip*. For a moment, nothing happened. Then Zak leaned against the wall and slid awkwardly to the ground.

I gave Rex a thumbs-up, then we climbed to the top of the pile and in through the window.

I'd been in lots of places that had been abandoned for years or even decades, but this place felt like centuries had gone by since it had been used or occupied—or since the pigeon crap had been cleaned out.

The wood floor was unfinished, or maybe more accurately *de*-finished, worn away by time and weather. It was soft and spongy, and felt like it could give way at any moment. The tower was wide open, maybe forty or fifty feet across, with exposed brick walls and banks of windows on each side.

There was a door to a stairway to our right, and what looked like another one on the far side of the tower.

As we stood there, getting out bearings, we heard footsteps approaching—two sets, sounding like they were coming down a set of stairs.

Rex poked his head through the doorway leading to the stairway closest to us. He looked back at us and shook his head, then cocked it toward the doorway, seemingly suggesting that it might be a good place to hide.

Claudia and I nodded and followed him in. As we ducked against the wall, the footsteps grew louder and were accompanied by voices—Roberta and Cronos.

"You vouched for him," Cronos was saying, "so if he has abandoned his post, I'm going to hold you responsible."

"Yes sir," Roberta replied, as the footsteps began to recede. "But Zak is solid. I'm sure it's just a problem with his radio."

I waited another moment to let them get farther away, then I leaned close to Rex and Claudia. "If they're going to check on Zak, they're going to figure out he's been darted, and they'll be back up here in a minute, looking for us."

"We need to hurry," Claudia said.

We ascended the steps—seven flights—trying to be both quiet and fast, so we wouldn't end up caught by Cronos and Roberta before we had a chance to do what we came to do.

Luckily, when we peeked through the doorway onto the top floor, the only person up there was Ogden, standing next to a bank of electronic equipment at the center of a large, open room. It was similar to the one we had entered from the window, except that the ceiling was at least forty feet high, and each of the four walls was largely taken up by an identical huge, round stained-glass window showing Nipper the dog, listening to his master's voice on an old Victrola. Ogden was looking right at us, as if he had heard us coming from a mile away.

He waved us in, frantic, and whispered loudly, "Hurry up. They'll be back in a minute. They've gone to check on Zak."

I held up my dart gun and whispered back, "We darted him."

As we approached, he said, "Well get in here even quicker, then. This is our Wellplant." He pointed at a tiny cylindrical gadget held in the air by four spidery metal arms. I'd never seen one outside of a person's head before. It really did look like a spike, about the size and shape of a tube of lipstick, with a small, gray glass disk at one end, a vicious-looking point at the other, and a huge mass of wires snaking out from various places to the different devices stacked on the racks surrounding it, including a tablet computer and an array of batteries.

Ogden eyed the whole setup with an odd combination of fear, respect, and affection. "Say what you will about Wells, but the Wellplant is one incredibly impressive piece of technology: bio-powered, quantum computing, globally networked. I've only scratched the surface of its capabilities."

"You can tell us all about it later," Claudia said. "Right now we need to get a move on."

Ogden nodded. "You're right, we do. The reason I've barely scratched the surface of that thing's capabilities is because it's really made to be implanted, but I did pick up a high-priority, system-wide alert on the network. 'Operation Wellspring' has been moved up to four p.m. Eastern Time. I assume that's the release."

Rex looked at his watch. "That's barely an hour."

"Exactly," Ogden said, "And we still don't know how they're planning on releasing it."

Rex and Claudia and I shared a guilty look at that. I shook my head— there didn't seem to be a good reason to tell Ogden our suspicions about how Wells was planning on releasing the virus.

"What?" Ogden asked, apparently having sensed the unspoken exchange.

"Nothing," I said. "That's not much time."

"Tell me about it," he said. "So, I'm thinking, we smash the Wellplant, here, and make sure Cronos sees you leave. As long as he thinks it was you, not me, he should leave my family alone."

"There's been a change of plan," I told him.

His eyes flashed with fear. "What are you talking about?"

"You said the first program immobilizes all the Plants, and the second one kills them, right?"

He thought for a second, then shook his head. "Not really. It doesn't work like that. It's not two separate programs, exactly, more like a two-part program. The first part breaches the network and immobilizes them, but it also destabilizes the entire network. The second part, the part that was meant to kill Wells, but now will kill all of them, that also closes the breach and stabilizes the network again."

"So what does that mean?" Claudia asked.

"It means if the second part isn't uploaded within thirty seconds of the first one, instead of immobilizing the Plants for forty-eight hours, the entire system will shut down and reboot into a diagnostic mode."

"And what does *that* mean?"

He shrugged. "I don't know. Meaning it will take a long time to get it started back up again. A lot more than forty-eight hours. It might kill some of them anyway, especially the people who have had Wellplants for a long time. People can get pretty dependent over the years. We don't really know what impact shutting it down will have on them. They could be immobilized until the network is back up and running."

"How long will that take?"

"The upload and execute should only take a few minutes. Then it has to propagate through the network. That could take a little longer, but not much I wouldn't think."

"No, I meant the reboot."

"I don't know. Days. . . . Weeks. And each Wellplant will have to be reactivated individually. That could take months. What's the new plan?"

"We want to run the first program, then disconnect this thing or destroy it before the second program loads. Do you think it'll work?"

He thought for a second. "Yeah, I guess. But like I said, I don't know what the long-term impact will be on the Plants who survive."

Rex and I both looked at Claudia. The fate of the world was on the table, but so was the fate of her father. She thought for a moment, then nodded.

"Okay," I said, "let's do it."

Ogden pulled a stool up to the computer tablet. As he started typing, the screen came to life, then we all jumped as a voice behind us boomed, "Very impressive!"

FORTY-EIGHT

Cronos and Roberta were standing by the doorway to the other stairs, both holding handguns. Roberta wore her usual smirk.

"I can't imagine how you could have possibly found us," Cronos continued. "Unless of course, someone told you where we were." He laughed. "I was wondering if I should have left someone to make sure you didn't cause any more trouble."

Ogden pushed himself away from the keyboard, looking guilty and terrified. "I…I was just…"

Cronos stared at him. "Someone I could trust, that is." He raised his gun in Ogden's direction.

I stepped between them. "Cronos!" I said. "There's no need for this."

Roberta's smirk suddenly looked more intentional as she moved to the side, getting another angle on Ogden. Rex moved with her, blocking her shot.

"We have a better idea," I said. "We can just use the first part of Ogden's malware, to immobilize all the Plants and shut down the network. It will stop Wells and all the Plants. It will shut down Wellplant Corporation and stop Wells from starting the pandemic. His plan will be exposed. He'll be ruined."

Cronos shook his head. "A temporary fix at best."

"No! Each Wellplant will have to be individually reactivated. Once people find out how the network has run amok, they'll never agree to it again. It'll be over. There's no need to kill them."

Roberta's eyes went wide, like she'd swallowed her gum. "Kill them?" Then her smirk returned, and she shook her head. "We're not going to kill all the Plants, stupid. Just Howard Wells."

"Apparently that plan changed," Rex said.

Ogden stood up behind him. "It's true," he said.

Roberta turned to Cronos. "Is it?" She stepped forward, into his line of sight. "Is it true?"

Cronos ignored her. "I always knew you were weak, Ogden, that you would never see this through to the end. That's why I insisted we make the process simple. So that you would be expendable."

As he raised his gun and tried to sight Ogden, I spread out my arms and said, "No!"

Roberta moved closer to Cronos, partially blocking whatever shot he thought he had. "Is it true? You're planning on killing all the Plants?"

"Of course!" he snapped. "It's the only way to accomplish our goals."

"But…so many people."

He glared at her. "Precisely. Millions of people bent on oppressing chimeras, making us less than human. CLAD's mission is to put an end to that oppression. This is how we accomplish that. Once and for all."

She took a step back, away from him. "I never agreed to that."

Cronos spun on her and snarled, "You swore an oath!"

She shook her head. "Not to that."

He took a step toward her. "To *me*." His head whipped around toward Ogden again. Toward me. "Jimi," he said. "I don't want to shoot you, but I will. You know that, right?"

Looking down the barrel of his gun, I felt a strange sensation on my neck and realized it was the hairs standing up. I was terrified.

Then Roberta abruptly raised her gun, as well. At Cronos.

Rex raised his arms and shouted, "*No!*"

But Roberta fired, a single shot, the sound of it deafening as it echoed off the brick walls.

Cronos spun on her once again, with a roar, and backhanded her across the face with such force she landed several feet away.

As Cronos went after her, I heard Claudia's dart gun spitting over my shoulder, and I raised mine, as well. The darts were so small, it was hard to track them. They seemed to be hitting him, but then falling to the floor, like they couldn't penetrate his clothing.

In three strides, he was standing over Roberta.

She raised her gun, and snarled, "Get back!"

But he kept going, and she fired, holding the trigger, releasing a dense spray of bullets, even as he kicked the weapon out of her hand.

Bullets pinged and ricocheted off the brick walls. One of the big stained-glass windows disintegrated, a few large pieces and thousands of tiny jagged shards of multicolored glass raining like gemstones down onto the floor, and down the outside of the tower. Through the opening, I could see the Philadelphia skyline, and at the center of it, the tallest building in the city: Wells Tower.

Cronos kicked Roberta in the ribs, and she groaned, then curled up on the floor, unconscious.

He tensed, as if he was going to kick her again.

"*No!*" Rex thundered again, running toward them. "That's enough!"

Cronos stumbled slightly and dropped his gun. I thought maybe a few darts that stuck had penetrated his clothing, after all. I turned to see if Ogden was working on adapting the malware, and if not, to tell him that now would be a good time. But he was lying on the floor bleeding from his upper arm. Claudia, kneeling next to him, tore off the bloody sleeve of his shirt, revealing a round bullet hole. She looked up at me. "Give me a hand here."

"Oh, Ogden!" I said as I went over. "You've been shot."

Almost like an echo, I heard Rex's voice saying the same thing. "You've been shot."

Kneeling next to Ogden, putting pressure on the wound while Claudia tried to bind it, I glanced back toward Rex and saw Cronos turning around, revealing three red splotches on his midsection, rapidly growing and spreading down his front. He looked down at his wounds then back up at Rex.

"Yes, I have." Cronos turned and looked down at Roberta. "Traitor!"

He moved to kick her again, but Rex shoved him away. "I said that's enough."

Cronos stumbled again, but violently shoved Rex back. "Don't you touch me."

"Del," Rex said. "You're hurt. We need to get you fixed up. And then we need your help to stop Howard Wells."

"This isn't hurt, *Leo*!" he snapped. "You don't know the meaning of 'hurt.' This is nothing compared to the pain I've been through. You wouldn't be standing here if you'd been through what I have. But I'm better than you. Always have been. Stronger. Faster. Braver."

He gave Rex another shove, and Rex stumbled back but didn't fall.

"And you dare to tell me you need my help to stop Wells?! He *was* stopped. That problem was fixed. He'd soon be gone if you hadn't gotten in the way."

"We can stop him without killing millions of innocent people."

Cronos laughed at that. "'Innocent people…'"

"Look," Rex said, in a soothing voice. "We all want the same thing here."

"You don't know what I want," Cronos said, turning slightly, then hauling off with a mighty but clumsy swing at Rex, who ducked away from it easily. As Cronos stumbled to regain his footing, he glanced for a moment at me. "Or maybe you do."

Rex followed his gaze, and as he did, Cronos lashed out again, this time connecting with Rex's jaw, sending him staggering sideways.

"*Stop it!*" I yelled.

Rex spun out of his stagger with a thunderous punch of his own, a loud crack as he connected with Cronos's chin.

Cronos's head whipped to the side, then immediately snapped back. He gave Rex a dazed and deranged grin. "That's what I'm talking about."

Cronos took another swing, and Rex evaded it and snuck a punch to Cronos's gut, below the bullet holes. Cronos groaned, then growled.

I winced. "Enough, dammit!" I shouted out, getting to my feet.

"Keep the pressure on, Jimi," Claudia said, grabbing my sleeve.

Ogden draped his good arm over his face. "Oh, man, that hurts."

Cronos laughed again, thick and wet. "I see you've got a little bit of that killer instinct after all, don't you, Leo?" He tried to kick Rex in the knee, but Rex skipped out of the way and punched him under his arm.

"We don't have to do this," Rex said.

"Careful, though," Cronos said. "You don't want to be too much of a killer. Jimi isn't crazy about the murdering type. She prefers peaceful little weaklings."

"Del, what the hell are you talking about?" I demanded.

Claudia grabbed my wrist and pushed my hand more firmly against Ogden's arm. "Don't let go," she snapped, annoyed, as she fumbled with the tourniquet she was trying to tie.

Ogden groaned in pain.

"You know it's true," Cronos replied. "You could never be…friends… with someone capable of making the tough decisions, of doing the dirty work that needs to be done."

"Del!" I called out from my place on the floor. "This isn't about you or me or Rex. Don't you understand?"

"This isn't about any of us," Rex said, straightening up out of his fighting stance. "It's bigger than that. It's about all of us."

Cronos ignored me and stalked toward Rex. "You don't get to decide what this is about," he snarled.

"Okay, done!" Claudia said, sitting back.

I shot to my feet and ran toward Rex and Cronos, the dart gun in my hand, sticky with Ogden's blood.

I didn't know how many darts I had left, and Cronos was covered from head to toe in fabric that was apparently dart-proof, if not bullet-proof. Roberta groaned on the floor, and I thought about getting her gun, since I knew it would work—but I didn't want to kill Del. I didn't want to kill anyone. And I didn't want him to call my bluff, either.

As I approached, Cronos roared and threw himself at Rex. Blood seeped from his stomach as he grabbed Rex around the throat and they both stumbled toward the gaping hole where the window had been.

"Del! Stop it!" I pleaded, but he continued to ignore me, driving Rex back, their feet shuffling through the broken glass that littered the floor, perilously close to the opening in the wall.

"Del, you're *badly* hurt," I said. "We need to get you help."

"There's not enough help in the world for me," he said, his voice sounding sluggish. "Not in *this* world."

"There is," I said. "Doc Guzman can help."

"Patch . . . patch me up so I can go to prison?" He laughed, bitterly, easing up for just a moment. Rex grabbed at Cronos's hand, trying to pry it away from his neck. "You've seen what the nonks do to us out here, Jimi, out in the open. Can you imagine what they'd be like in prison?" Then he slammed Rex against the brick wall, next to the hole where the window had been, and Rex went slack, dazed by the blow.

I continued to approach them. Over the past several months, I had found myself shooting dart guns more than I ever would have expected, and by that point I felt surprisingly comfortable with them. But still, I knew this would be a tough shot. I raised the dart gun, took a deep breath, and said, quietly, "Del, look at me."

His shoulders sagged slightly, but his hands remained rigid as he turned his head.

I aimed and pulled the trigger.

Almost instantaneously, Cronos let go of Rex and stepped away, clamping both hands over his right eye.

Rex slid down the wall, but stopped himself halfway down, bracing himself as he coughed his throat back into shape.

"Ouch! Dammit, Jimi!" Cronos said, almost whining, sounding for a moment just like Del. He pulled his hands away from his eye and held up the dart pinched between his thumb and forefinger. "You shot me in the eye," he said.

He flicked away the dart and tore off his hood, and I saw that he was smiling. "Hell of a shot, actually," he said, with a crooked grin that betrayed a mouth full of blood.

He laughed softly, and through the blood, through the terrible scars and the multiple splices, through everything else that had transpired to transform him, I saw my friend Del. I saw all the phases and ages, all the iterations we'd gone through together over the years as we tried to figure out who we were, who we were going to be, all the way back to when we were little kids, before his mom died, before my dad died, back to when life was simple and good. Or at least, back to before we had discovered it wasn't.

For an instant, I smiled at the memories. "It's okay, Del," I said soothingly, walking slowly toward him. "It's okay."

"You're right," he said. "I know it is."

His eyes started to roll up in his head, and it seemed like he might drop on the spot. But he gave his head a vigorous shake and stayed on his feet. With what seemed like a great effort, he took an uneasy step backward, then another one, his feet leaving a trail of blood.

"Del?" I called out, not wanting to spook him, but concerned that he was moving toward the expanse of open sky behind him.

"I'm sorry, Leo," he called out, smiling now, not sarcastic, but for real. It was a little-kid smile, one I hadn't seen on him in years. Rex looked up, confused. "I'm happy for you two, you know that? Seriously. Jimi... I'm glad you're with him. He probably loves you more than I ever could have." He staggered back another step, closer to the ragged hole in the wall.

"Del!" I said more forcefully. "Be careful now."

"Do you remember that day in the playground, Jimi?" he asked. "Out in the zurbs, when we were little. Those big kids came and messed with us?"

"I do," I said, soothingly. "And you led them away from me, so they'd leave me alone. You saved me, Del."

It was true. We were seven or eight, visiting family friends, when a bunch of teenage bullies attacked us at a park. Del and Leo were both beaten up pretty bad; in fact Leo ended up in the hospital, then his parents moved him away. It was the last time I saw him until I met him again as Rex. I had been knocked unconscious, but it could have been a lot worse for me if Del hadn't led the bullies away from me.

Cronos glanced over at Rex and smiled sadly. "I didn't save you, Jimi. Little Leo Byron did. I ran away, but tiny as he was, Leo went back and drew them away from you." He shook his head. "Even then he was a better friend to you than I could ever be."

It was a defining moment of my childhood, and it had become part of the bedrock of my friendship with Del. I tried not to think about this sudden revision of personal history right then, tried not to be distracted by it, but it shook me deeply.

I looked at Rex and our eyes met, and I just wanted to run to him and hold him. But I turned back to Cronos.

"That doesn't matter," I said. "We were kids. What matters now is stopping Howard Wells and getting you to Doc Guzman. He can fix you up. It'll all be okay."

He looked down at his blood-soaked chest, the three glistening bullet holes. "No," he said softly. "It's too late for doctors. Too late for salamander splices and regeneration. But you're right." He smiled. "It will all be okay," he said, repeating my words back to me in a singsong voice as he swung his leg back again. But he'd run out of floor, and this time, his foot was through the window, dangling in the open air. I moved toward him, but he put up a hand. "Stay back!"

He coughed, and a cascade of blood fell from his mouth. He wiped it with his forearm, then he gazed across the room, at Ogden's Wellplant setup. "Do what you're going to do, Jimi." He steadied himself with a gloved hand on the raw brick edge of the opening as the breeze tugged at his clothing. "It'll all be okay," he said again, this time almost tauntingly, throwing it back at me, such an obvious falsehood.

His eyes closed, but I got the sense it was less the effects of the dart or the enormous loss of blood from the bullet wounds, and more the crushing weariness of his life in this world—his *lives* in this world, each of them filled with betrayal and disappointment and alienation. He opened his eyes halfway again, and I saw something in them, something alien and unfamiliar. It took me a second to recognize it as relief. "It'll all be okay," he said once more.

"Del?" I said, then I realized what he was doing. "*No!*" I screamed.

As I ran to him, he looked me in the eye, and then he stepped back, out into the empty space. He spread his arms and fell. He dropped from sight for an instant, but as I ran up to the opening and slid to my knees, we regained eye contact one last time as he fell.

He got smaller and smaller, as if he was shrinking away to nothing. But he didn't. He hit the rubble hard, with a heavy thud. Then he was still.

"Del, no…" I said, shaking my head, horrified, retching but unable to look away. Maybe subconsciously I expected him to get up and disappear, so he could return one more time. But he didn't.

Rex appeared at my elbow, looking aghast. "Jimi, I'm so sorry," he said, his voice hoarse. He put an arm around my waist, solid and reassuring, holding me back from the edge.

I hugged his arm to me, holding it in place as he eased me away from the window. I turned in his embrace and wrapped my arms around him, squeezing as tight as I could.

I'd said goodbye to Del so many times, mourned his death so many times, it felt like his actual passing was somehow overdue. I was crushed with sorrow, but as much as I felt the pain of his passing, I also felt that, in some way, we had just exorcised his ghost, had freed his trapped spirit to go on to whatever comes next.

I'd never much believed in an afterlife, but I wanted so badly to believe in one right then. And I wondered, if I ever got there, and Del was there, too, which Del would it be? The Del I'd grown up with? Or would it be Tamil, or Cronos?

Ogden groaned, and Rex and I both turned to look at him.

"Oh, Jimi…I…" Claudia said, looking small and vulnerable. She put her hand over her mouth.

I nodded as she came over and hugged us both. The tightness in my throat rendering me silent, as well. After a few seconds, I managed to ask, "How's Ogden?"

"He's holding up," Claudia said, wiping her eyes, pulling herself together. "Needs a doctor but I think he'll be okay for the time being."

Ogden gave me a feeble thumbs-up.

"Good," I said, wiping my eyes, too. "Then we better get to work before we run out of time."

"Actually," she said, pointing at the apparatus, "there's a problem."

The four metal arms that had been holding the Wellplant in place were wildly out of place, each one of them still holding a tiny piece of the Wellplant.

"Oh no!" Rex said, running over and looking helplessly down onto the bits and pieces of circuit boards and crystals and housing that littered the floor.

I turned to Ogden. "Can we upload the malware without a Wellplant?"

Ogden winced as he lifted himself up onto one elbow. "I don't know. We need some kind of node to access the network, but I don't know what else would work, other than a Wellplant."

"Then we need to get one. Where did this one come from?"

He shook his head. "It was defective. A reject. I stole it when I was working at Wellplant, brought it home and fixed it. The only way we could possibly get another one in time would be to rip it out of someone's head. But apart from killing them, that would also damage the Wellplant." He thought for a second, then said, "Wait, I do know where there's another node, a computer we can use to access the network."

All three of us responded simultaneously: "Where?"

Ogden pointed, out through the jagged hole in the brick wall, at Wells Tower.

FORTY-NINE

Even before we left the RCA building, I could tell the situation in the city had deteriorated in the short time we'd been in there. As we packed up the equipment Ogden needed to bring, we could see across the river, twice as many plumes of smoke were rising into the sky as there had been just an hour earlier. Some were black and sooty and definitely not just brush fires. Drones and copters buzzed around Wells Tower like bees wondering who kicked their hive.

Ogden was handing me a gadget to put in the backpack, a signal optimizer, when a huge commercial jet went by, startlingly close, flying low over the river and surrounded by a pair of military jets and a cloud of police drones. I didn't know what that was about, but I knew it couldn't be good.

We both looked over, so distracted we almost muffed the handoff. As the optimizer began to slip from our grasps, we both grabbed it.

"Eesh," he said. "Let's not drop that. We can't do any of this without it."

I slipped it carefully into the backpack.

When everything was packed up and ready to go, I walked right up to the hole in the wall and looked down. Del was still there. Still twisted and broken and dead.

Rex came up behind me and put his arm around my shoulder. "We need to go," he said.

I nodded. I thought I should say a few words, or at least think a few words. But nothing came to mind that I hadn't already said or thought.

"Goodbye, Del," I whispered. As we turned and walked back to where the equipment was stacked, I vowed that if we survived whatever happened next, we'd come back and get Del's body, make sure he got a decent funeral.

Ogden was carrying his tablet in his good hand. Everything else was packed into two duffle bags, which Claudia and Rex grabbed, and the backpack, which I carefully slipped over my shoulder.

Before we left, we checked on Roberta. She was breathing well and seemed fine apart from being unconscious. There didn't seem to be much we could do for her, but Claudia gently moved her into a stable position on her side, and slid an old, folded canvas under her head as a makeshift pillow. On our way out, we checked on Zak, too. He seemed fine as well, sleeping off the effects of the darts. If things worked out, we'd come back to make sure they were okay. If things didn't, it wouldn't much matter.

As we loaded up the car, Ogden winced in pain with each movement, but Claudia's bandage seemed to have stopped the bleeding.

"There's a couple of different ways to get into the tower that I know of," he said as Claudia drove. "Maintenance staff has a couple of 'smoke exits,' as they call them—fire exits with jammed locks and bypassed alarm sensors so they can sneak in and out undetected to take their smoke breaks. The first one is between some dumpsters on Cuthbert Street, the little alley that actually runs through the base of Wells Tower. The second one is in the parking garage that stretches under the whole building. On the first level down, the green level, there's a service door tucked into a corner near the entrance ramp. You wouldn't notice it if you weren't looking for it. That's how we get in."

The Wellplant network terminal was on the ninety-eighth floor, one floor down from Wells's penthouse office. The plan for getting up there involved the bullet guns and dart guns we had packed in the bags with Ogden's electronics. And a lot of luck.

It wasn't much of a plan.

Rex and I sat in the back, and he looked out the rear window as we drove, taking in the troubled sky filled with smoke and copters and drones with flashing lights, probably making the same observations that I had made from the tower. Things were messy.

As we turned onto the overpass that crossed over the bridge traffic we were about to merge with, Claudia muttered, "That's just great."

Below us, traffic at the toll plaza was a solid mass, backed up from where the six or eight toll lanes merged down to the single lane that was actually open across the bridge. Traffic was not at a standstill—not with the Smartdrive systems in charge—but instead of the usual seamless blending of lanes, the merge was more like a slow-motion zipper.

We all looked behind us, even Ogden, and all grunted or sighed in disappointment: we were already hemmed in by the cars behind us, meaning there was no chance of backing up and trying a different route, even if there was one.

Claudia turned to Ogden. "You doing okay?"

He nodded. "It hurts, but not too bad."

The clock on the dash showed 3:17, which should have left us enough time to get there before 4:00 p.m., when Operation Wellspring was supposed to be set in motion. But the way things were going, I was starting to worry. I could just imagine billions of people dying in an extinction-level pandemic because we got stuck in traffic.

Eventually, we made it through the toll plaza, merged onto the one lane open, and were moving across the bridge at a respectable speed.

Ahead of us, a mass of emergency vehicles was clustered around a couple of dented cars in the closed lanes. As we drove past, a pair of paramedics in hazmat suits and breathers were loading a body bag on a stretcher into the back of an ambulance.

"Weird," Rex said under his breath, watching them. "The cars are hardly damaged."

He was right. The cars were askew, but barely scratched. Just past them, at the side of the bridge, a second pair of paramedics were bent over a young woman sitting on the curb, her face red as she coughed uncontrollably.

"I don't think it was the collision that killed them," I said softly as we both turned in our seats to watch the scene shrink behind us. I wondered for a moment if this was what it was like when the first pandemic was starting, the one that took my dad. It suddenly occurred to me with great urgency that I needed to call my mom. Maybe Trudy, too. And Kevin, for that matter.

I didn't want to dwell on it, but depending on how things went down, this might be my last chance to talk to them at all.

"I need to call my mom," I whispered to him.

He squeezed my hand back and nodded, acknowledging me but not agreeing. And he was right. Even if we passed a pay phone, we didn't have time to stop.

It occurred to me for the first time that if this had happened a year ago, I might have been in great danger, and my family, as well. Before Del ran away to get spliced, before I met Rex—or re-met him—and before I became friends with Claudia and Sly and Ruth and Pell, I didn't know any chimeras. Hadn't even met any. If Wells had released his super-flu then, it might have killed me and my entire family.

I was already grateful for how Del had inadvertently brought these amazing people into my life. But I realized that if we failed to stop Wells's plan to release his virus, Del could end up having inadvertently saved my life, as well.

The radio announcer recited a roundup of headlines, including updates on the brush fires and the spreading influenza outbreak, and the anonymous allegations that Wells Life Sciences was to blame.

Several members of Congress were calling for hearings to look into the matter. No one had seen Wells in person in days. There were rumors that the stress was getting to him and talk about how the situation could torpedo his presidential campaign.

The traffic report warned us to avoid the bridge, just as we were finally getting off it. We were diverted off the Vine Street Smartway, which cuts across the city, and dumped with a thousand other cars into the tight grid of streets, a third of which seemed to be closed.

"What the hell is going on out here?" Claudia asked, annoyed.

We weren't far from the apartment hives I'd run past the day before.

As we inched through an intersection, I looked down the cross street and saw that it was closed off a couple of blocks away, clogged with yellow tape, a cluster of workers in hazmat suits and a handful of health department vehicles with their lights flashing.

"Pretty sure it's the flu," I said.

Claudia turned and looked at me. "Do you think this is all from that one chicken?"

"I have no idea," I said, thinking that if it was, we might be doomed even if we succeeded in stopping the broader release.

"I...I think it is," Ogden said. "I'd been reading the alerts...coming over the Wellplant. Last time I checked, right before you all arrived, there'd been no indication of any intentional releases."

The car in front of us turned, and Claudia hit the accelerator a little bit harder.

I felt the urge again, stronger, to call my mom.

The clock on the dash now showed 3:30. We had half an hour. I guess I'd call her when we were done, if I was still alive.

We had outrun the bridge traffic, but we still had plenty of police cordons and detours to navigate, and plenty of other cars trying to make their way around them, too. Traffic seemed to be thickening and slowing again.

Eventually, we got stuck at a light a block away from Wells Tower. The light was green but we were going nowhere because the idiots on the cross street had blocked the grid.

"Okay, that's it," Claudia said, pulling over into an illegal spot, a loading zone. She turned to Ogden. "Can you walk from here?"

He sat up and looked around, getting his bearings. "Yeah, no problem."

She turned to Rex and me. "At this point, I think it'll be quicker on foot."

We both nodded.

"It's an illegal spot," Rex said.

Claudia snorted. "Whatever way this ends, I imagine parking tickets will be the least of my worries."

FIFTY

Ogden winced as he got out of the car, but once we were walking, he seemed okay. Claudia found one of her dad's windbreakers in the trunk and draped it over Ogden to cover his bloody shirt.

As we turned the corner, one side of the Wells Tower appeared ahead of us. It was such a prominent part of the skyline, I saw it all the time, but rarely up close. The curves that from a distance made it look like a cluster of smaller cylindrical towers appeared from the ground more like an undulating wall of reflective glass, distorting everything, like a massive funhouse mirror.

As we walked down 8th Street toward Arch, one of the entrances came into view, cordoned off with caution tape and patrolled by three heavily armed guards in biohazard gear with the Wellplant Corporation logo on it. Outside the tape, police and health department types stood next to a cluster of city vehicles, half with flashing orange lights, the other half flashing red and blue. A small crowd had gathered across the street, pointing and staring.

"Whoa," Claudia said under her breath.

We snuck glances as we walked past, trying not look too interested or suspicions. We were close to the Levline hub, several bus terminals, and countless hotels, so our duffel bags and backpacks shouldn't have raised any suspicions, but the fact that inside them was a small arsenal and all the electronic equipment needed to crash the global Wellplant network made us a little jumpy.

"That could complicate things," Rex said, nodding back at the commotion we'd just passed.

"A lockdown could make getting inside a bit trickier," Ogden said, "But if the building has been cleared, that'll make it easier to do what we came to do without thousands of office workers getting in the way."

He pointed ahead, at a shadowy rectangular hole cut into the curved glass. "That's where we're going. Cuthbert Street."

To our left, Cuthbert was a narrow street lined with dumpsters and service entrances, but as it plunged through the base of the tower to our right, it turned into a dank, gloomy tunnel—a stark contrast to the elegant exterior of the building. *And a more honest portrayal of the true nature of Wells Corporation*, I thought.

As we got closer to the tunnel, we saw a single strip of yellow police tape stretched across it.

"It's taped off," I said.

"I see it," Ogden said. "Doesn't seem to be anyone guarding it, though."

As he said it, a pair of cops turned off of Market Street, coming toward us on foot.

"Crap," Ogden said.

"Slow down," I said. "Let them pass us before we reach the tunnel."

We all slowed down, trying to be subtle about it. I bent down and pretended to tie my shoelaces and the others stood around waiting for me. I kept my head down and took long enough that the cops should have passed us, but they didn't. When I looked up, I saw that they had paused in front of us.

"You kids lost?" one of them said with a friendly smile. He was an older guy with ruddy skin, a big gut, and a walrus mustache. The other cop was expressionless. He had light-brown skin and was taller, thinner, and younger than his partner. Nestled between his shades and the brim of his police hat was a Wellplant. He seemed to be staring at me, so I put my hand above my eyes, shading them from the sun, and hopefully hiding my face from whatever facial recognition the Wellplant might provide.

"No sir, officer," I said.

I felt a moment of relief as Officer Wellplant looked away from me, then I realized he was staring at Ogden, who was pale and sweaty and out of it.

"You feeling okay, son?" he asked in a tone that sounded more suspicious than concerned.

They both took a step back, and I realized they were afraid he might have the flu. I liked the idea of them keeping their distance, but worried about them putting Ogden in quarantine.

Ogden smiled and shook his head. "Yeah, I'm fine. Drank a little too much last night is all."

Officer Wellplant continued to stare at him. "You did, huh? And how old are you?"

Ogden grinned. "Twenty-one, as of yesterday."

Officer Walrus chuckled. "Happy birthday, then."

Officer Wellplant said, "Do you have any ID?"

Ogden shook his head. "Nope. But now that I'm twenty-one, I'll be getting some."

Officer Wellplant turned his attention back to me, and I lowered my head, squinting and shielding my eyes again.

"What's with all the police and everything?" Claudia asked, hooking her thumb back the way we had just come.

"Quarantine," said Officer Walrus, his face grim. "Looks like we might have another flu outbreak on our hands." He pointed up at the tower. "They've sealed off the building and turned the fifth floor into a makeshift infectious-disease ward."

I was shocked that Wellplant Corporation would be so hard hit, but then I remembered that Wells's immunity wasn't contagious, so it didn't spread to those who didn't have Wellplants. And with Wells's stance on chimeras, I doubt many of his employees had much interaction with them.

"What's with all the guns?" she asked.

"People don't like to be quarantined," Officer Walrus said with a shrug. "Anyway, be careful out here, okay? And keep your distance from this place, until things settle down."

"There's a curfew in effect," said Officer Wellplant, pointing at us. "Seven p.m. Make sure you're home by then."

Officer Walrus smiled flatly as if he was running out of patience with his partner. I was reminded of Agent Ralphs and her partner, and I thought how much of a drag it must be to be stuck with some uptight, humorless Plant all day.

"Yes, sir," Claudia said with a smile so sweet I couldn't imagine anyone falling for it. But maybe that was just because I knew her.

Officer Walrus smiled back, like he was a believer. "Okay, stay out of trouble, okay?"

"Will do, officer," Rex said.

As the two cops turned and walked away, it occurred to me that while Officer Wellplant was immune, his partner was probably still at risk of the flu. I coughed silently into my hand and called out, "Thanks, officer!"

As they turned around again, I stepped up to Officer Walrus, flashing the same kind of stupid sweet smile Claudia had given him, and stuck out my hand to shake his. He frowned down at it for a second, maybe taken aback by the gesture in general, or maybe, ironically, afraid of catching the flu. Then he shrugged and smiled. "You're welcome," he said, pumping my hand once.

I turned and ran back to the others.

"We don't really have time for pleasantries," Claudia said quietly as we walked on.

"I know," I said. "Sorry."

Rex gave me a wink and a smile, letting me know he understood.

I looked back and saw Officer Wellplant looking back, as well, but when we got to Cuthbert Street, a few seconds later, the two cops had turned the corner.

We made sure no one else was around, and then, without a word, we ducked under the tape and into the shadows.

It was at least ten degrees cooler in the tunnel, and it smelled musty and dusty. Ogden took the lead, inspecting the blank, unmarked doors that ran along the wall to our left. The dim lights in the ceiling didn't seem to make much of a difference. As we walked, it grew darker, but our eyes adjusted. I glanced behind us, toward 8th Street. From the darkness, it looked like a blazing furnace.

A third of the way down the tunnel, Ogden stepped between two dumpsters and tried a steel door, but it was locked. "It should be right around here," he said. We followed him down the sidewalk twenty feet to another door set between two more dumpsters. This one was locked, too.

As we approached the third door, he pointed at it and said, "Here it is." There was a little more room between these dumpsters. A brick leaned next to the door, ready to prop it open, and next to it, a conspicuous pile of empty vape canisters.

"Yuck," Claudia said, making a face.

Ogden was reaching for the door when he turned toward her and frowned. "Oh no," he said, snatching his hand back away from the door.

The rest of us turned and saw the same two cops, silhouetted against the sunlight out on 8th Street. Officer Wellplant shined a blindingly bright military-style flashlight at us. We all raised our hands to shield our eyes as he demanded, "What are you kids doing?"

As they started coming toward us, Claudia said *"Run!"*

FIFTY-ONE

Rex pushed over a stack of boxes, slowing the cops down enough that we got a decent head start. Ogden managed to keep up with the rest of us, but in his condition, I knew he wouldn't be able to for long. Glancing back, I saw that Officer Walrus wasn't going to be able to keep it up, either. He was already struggling, falling behind. But his partner was fast and determined, and he seemed to be running directly at me.

Rex and Claudia and Ogden were angling toward the sidewalk on the right-hand side of the street. On a hunch, I angled toward the left, and sure enough Officer Wellplant changed course to follow me.

It occurred to me that we probably had more firepower than they did, but apart from the fact that we'd have to stop to get our weapons out and they were much better trained than we were, the last thing I wanted was to start shooting people, or starting a gunfight when we should be up in the tower shutting down the network.

Then I had another idea. I was scared, but I knew the important thing was for Ogden to get inside and do what he needed to do. I wasn't actually all that essential to the plan. So when we ran out of the tunnel and into the sunlight on 9th Street and the others all turned the corner, I kept going straight.

Rex called out, "Jimi!"

I called back, "Keep going!"

I figured if Officer Wellplant stayed after me, I'd lead him away from the others. If he went after them, I'd try to dart him. When I looked back, Officer Wellplant was still coming after me. Officer Walrus was stopped in the tunnel, bent at the waist trying to catch his breath.

I slowed down for half a block, letting Officer Wellplant stay close enough that he wouldn't give up and go after the others. Then I put on some speed.

I started sweating as soon as we left the coolness of the tunnel. Now it was pouring off me. After a block, Officer Wellplant was still coming, and I wondered why. We hadn't done anything, other than sneak past the police tape. And why me instead of the others? I thought back to that moment during his speech when Howard Wells looked directly at me, and all the other Plants did, as well.

The next time I looked back, he was gaining on me. And even more distressing, another cop with a Wellplant had joined the chase. To my horror, as I watched, yet another Plant joined them, a woman in a business suit. Maybe she was a plainclothes detective or whatever, but I got the sense that she wasn't a cop at all. Which meant that she wasn't responding to a call for backup over police radio. She was there because of her Wellplant.

I pictured a thousand Plants chasing me through the city, like a horde of fast zombies, but I knew that if they were all after me, they'd catch me before there were more than a dozen. I imagined them approaching from all sides at that very moment panic tried to assert itself, but I knew if I was to have a chance of getting away, I needed to stay calm and focus.

Approaching 10th Street, I considered my next move. I didn't want to lead the Plants back to Rex and Ogden and Claudia, but if I was planning on rejoining them somehow, I couldn't just keep running farther and farther away from them, either. I decided I would turn on 10th Street, start to circle back toward the tower and the parking garage, where the other secret entrance was. If I could lose my pursuers on the way, great, and if not, I'd just keep running. Hopefully, Ogden would succeed in shutting down the network without me, and the Plants would all stop chasing me then.

I moved to turn sharply around the corner, but what I saw made me stop so abruptly, I almost went sprawling, and probably came close to blowing out my ankle.

At least a dozen Plants were running toward me from the right. Turning the other way, I saw three more approaching from the left.

I cursed and kept running straight, following Cuthbert Street as it tunneled under another building. Up ahead, the tunnel opened out onto 11th Street, where Cuthbert Street ended. Across 11th, I could see the Reading Terminal Market. It was a historic indoor market under an ancient defunct railroad terminal and one of my favorite spots in the city, a maze of tightly packed stalls and storefronts, always jammed with tourists and locals, with nine or ten entrances to choose from.

Halfway through the tunnel, I glanced behind me and saw ten pursuers now outlined against the sunlit street, with several new ones turning the corner to join them. As I turned back ahead, a figure stepped out in to street in front of me. He looked big and strong, an Asian man in his thirties wearing a business suit.

I cursed again, trying to keep my fear at bay, and ran directly at him. I remembered Stan, rolling and tumbling like a trained athlete, and I wondered what tricks this guy might have ready. I was a good runner, but evasive maneuvers weren't really my thing.

As I approached, he spread his arms wide and smiled. I lowered my right shoulder and angled right, then pivoted left. As he went for me, I pivoted right again and arched my back as I spun around him.

I crossed the street, stunned that I had somehow managed to get past him, and pulled the heavy old glass door open just enough for me and my backpack to slip inside.

The first thing to hit me was the smell—kind of gross, kind of delectable, hundreds of different foods combined with centuries of people and a very old building. The second thing to hit me was that it was practically empty. There was no crowd to get lost in or to slow down my pursuers.

Recalculating on my feet, I zigzagged through the stalls. If I wasn't being chased by a murderous horde of Plants, it might have been fun, running through the wide-open aisles that were usually so densely packed. But this wasn't fun. I was terrified, and not seeing any pursuers when I looked behind me barely lessened that terror.

I passed a souvenir stall with a rack of windbreakers and sweatshirts on display: Liberty Bells, sports logos and other touristy graphics. I grabbed a windbreaker and a cap as I ran, putting on the cap and pulling the windbreaker over my backpack as I darted through the exit onto 12th Street.

I immediately slowed to a leisurely pace. My legs were grateful, but every other fiber of my body wanted to keep running. I crossed 12th and walked slowly past a shoe store with an impressive selection of hideous boots in the window. As three Plants burst onto the street behind me, I ducked into the shop.

I watched them through the window as they looked up and down the street, searching for me.

The store was very trendy, pricier than I could afford and edgier than I could pull off—so edgy that the sales rep who asked me if I needed any help was a chimera. I glanced out the window and saw that the three Plants were still out on the sidewalk, talking.

"Do you have these in an eight?" I said, grabbing the least hideous boots I could find on the New Arrivals rack.

She gave me an unpleasant look as she took them, presumably thinking that even with twenty percent off, it was unlikely I could afford $400 boots.

And she was right.

As she went into the back to check, the three Plants went back inside the market and I slipped out onto the street. I felt bad for wasting the sales clerk's time, but I was trying to stay alive and helping to save the world. And frankly, she'd been kind of rude.

I hurried down the street while trying to look like I wasn't hurrying. It was 3:40, which meant there were only twenty minutes left until "Operation Wellspring." Hopefully, Rex and Claudia and Ogden were already up in Wells Tower, shutting down the entire network. I wondered if I should even bother trying to help them, or if the best thing I could do would be to keep drawing any possible Plant pursuers away from them. As I puzzled over that, I circled back around to the parking garage.

With every step, the backpack slapped heavily against my spine, hard enough to distract me. While I was stopped at an intersection, I pulled the backpack around to the front so I could tighten the strap. And while I was doing that, I remembered why the backpack was so heavy.

"No, no, no, no," I said, tugging open the zipper, then quickly tugging it closed, hoping no one else on the street had seen the signal optimizer, which Ogden said was essential for the plan to work, or the dart gun for that matter. I looked at my watch again—3:45, only fifteen minutes left, and now I knew I had a critical component with me. I needed to be there or else the whole plan was going to fail.

Putting my trust in Smartdrive, I darted into the street, and as traffic screeched to a halt, I ran.

Wells Tower loomed a block away, dominating the sky above me. At its base, I saw the entrance to the underground parking garage, and the sign that said, NO PEDESTRIANS—CARS ONLY. *Whatever*, I thought, as I ran down it anyway.

The service door was supposed to be near the bottom of the ramp. I was already going fast, and the slope propelled me even faster down the spiral ramp. My eyes still hadn't adjusted to the relative darkness, and when I rounded a curve I almost ran into the gate before I even saw it. I tried to stop but couldn't, so instead I jumped over it. I landed okay, but my momentum sent me sprawling onto the floor between two hulking transit vans.

I skinned both knees and the palms of my hands, but the fall might have saved my life. While I was on the floor, I looked to my right and saw, under one of the vans, a bright green door, and in front of it, a pair of shiny black shoes, cop shoes, and they were walking slowly around the other van, coming my way.

I scooted over behind one of the tires in case the cop looked under the van. As his footsteps grew closer, I eased open the zipper and pulled out the dart gun. I held it up and waited, wondering if I was about to die, and wishing I had called my mom like I wanted to.

The first thing I saw as he stepped out from behind the van was his gun—a bullet gun, not a dart gun—held in two hands out front of him. As he crept forward, I saw the peak of his hat, then the badge on the front of his uniform and the Wellplant above his eye. He stood motionless, listening, processing.

I didn't want to rush the shot, but I didn't want him to see me, either. I held my breath, not making a sound. Finally, he took another step, and I fired, two darts, and landed both of them on the side of his neck. He slapped his hand over them, then turned and glared at me. He raised his gun, aiming it at my head. I fought the urge to try to climb under the van, knowing it would only make my death humiliating as well as tragic.

He smiled, as if he recognized me, then he pitched forward and toppled like a tree. I scrambled out of the way, so he didn't land on me, and he hit the cement floor, face-first, with a wet smack and a metallic crunch. His shades smashed into pieces, and blood trickled out of his nose. I couldn't see the fate of his Wellplant.

I raised myself into a crouch and was about to run over to the green door when I heard more footsteps approaching—two sets, maybe three. I crept farther back, against the wall, and as the footsteps grew closer and closer, I squeezed between the front of the van and the wall, keeping the van between me and them.

The footsteps came to a halt and shadows spilled across the wall to my right and across the cop on the floor. I slid around to the far side of the van and crept toward the back with my dart gun raised. I paused at the rear fender and took a breath, preparing to jump out and dart them all in the back, then jump back and try to stay hidden and hope they joined their comrade on the floor before they had a chance to kill me.

But when I jumped out, my finger on the trigger, I wasn't looking at their backs, I was looking at their faces, and they were looking at me. I was so keyed up that I fired anyway, but managed to raise the gun a little higher at the last second. As a trio of darts flew over their heads, Rex, Ogden, and Claudia all shouted, "*Jimi!*"

FIFTY-TWO

Rex grabbed me by the shoulders and pulled me tight, wrapping me in his arms.

Claudia gave me an affectionate poke in the ribs. "Man, I thought for *sure* they'd gotten you."

I gave Rex a quick kiss then pushed him away. "What are you guys still doing out here? We're running out of time!"

"I know, I know," Rex said. He pointed at the cop on the floor. "We were trying to get past this guy."

"Oh," I said, vaguely relieved to know I hadn't led the cop to them. "Okay." I turned to Ogden and pointed at the green door. "Is this the place?" It wasn't until then that I got a good look at him: sweaty and gray with dark rings under his eyes. "Whoa, are you okay?"

He closed his eyes and nodded as he shuffled over toward the door. "I didn't think I'd be doing so much running around…but I'll be alright. Come on, let's go."

As we followed him toward the green door, Claudia snorted. "Um . . 'H4H Forever'? You have a change of heart?"

"What are you talking about?" I said.

Rex snorted. "Your jacket. Going deep undercover, are you?"

Even Ogden grinned at me as I took off the jacket I'd swiped from the tourist shop and looked at the back, which was plastered with the H4H logo and H4H4EVER in bold letters.

"Ugh," I said, realizing maybe that was why the woman in the shoe store had been giving me such an attitude. I balled up the jacket and threw it into a nearby trash can.

The green door didn't have a handle, but Ogden picked at the edge with his fingernails, then his fingertips, and then he pulled it open.

We followed him inside, down a dank, concrete-and-cinderblock corridor, through a dirty boiler room filled with massive machines and a loud wash of noise, then down another corridor to an elevator.

Ogden pushed the call button, and the door opened immediately. It was a freight elevator, and as we got on, Ogden pressed 8. "We have to change elevators to get up to the ninety-seventh floor," he said. "That cop said the quarantine was set up on the fifth floor, so I figured we should switch above that."

Then he closed his eyes and leaned against the dirty pads hanging against the wall.

I looked at Rex and Claudia and tipped my head at Ogden questioningly. They both shrugged, their faces grim.

"I'm fine," Ogden said without opening his eyes. "Well, I'll *be* fine."

The rest of us watched the numbers on the display counting up—1, 2, 3, 4. When it showed 5, I heard people, lots of them, talking and coughing and moaning. Ogden opened his eyes, and all four of us exchanged glances. I pictured an open-plan office and rows and rows of cots filled with deathly ill people being cared for by workers in biohazard suits. Then I pictured armed guards stationed by the elevator, maybe noticing as we ascended past them and wondering who we were, asking their superiors about it, warning them so they would be expecting us.

The elevator came to a stop with a loud *ding*. The doors opened and we stepped out into a nondescript office: cream-colored walls, beige carpet, gray cubicle dividers, and inoffensive art prints in pastel shades lining the walls. Apart from the background hum of climate control, the only sound came from our feet on the carpet and the rustle of our clothes as we followed Ogden to another bank of elevators.

He pressed the button and we waited in silence. Above each elevator door, a display revealed what floor each car was on. To the left of us, the display showed 22, then it changed to 21, then 20. As it came closer to us, I scanned the other displays, to see if any of them were moving toward the 12th floor, but they all stayed where they were.

The elevator arrived with another gong-like tone, and we all got on. It was a lot nicer than the freight elevator, with polished wood—or a convincing fake—and brass accents.

Ogden hit the button for the 147th floor, and after the doors closed, he said, "The tech suite is up on 148, but to be safe, I figure we should get off one floor below and take the steps up—in case anyone is in there."

We nodded our understanding, and he resumed his eyes-closed resting against the wall as the elevator hurled us into the sky. It was a smooth ride, but I knew how high we were going and how fast we had to be moving to get there.

There was an instant of near weightlessness as we decelerated, then the doors opened with another *ding*. This floor was almost identical to the twelfth, except that the cubicles were larger and there were fewer of them. And the view, which I could only see from a distance, looked spectacular.

Ogden led us to a door set in the far wall. We followed him through it and up a flight of concrete steps to another door, this one with a security panel. He didn't seem bothered. He opened the duffel bag Claudia was carrying and pulled out a fabric tool kit and a can of liquid nitrogen.

"Excuse me," she said, but he ignored her, spraying the liquid nitrogen onto the security keypad on the wall, and the lock mechanism on the door next to it. It steamed and crackled, but he kept spraying, letting the cold really sink in. Then he jammed a slender screwdriver into the gap between the keypad and the bolt. Holding it in place, he turned to Rex and said, "Can you give that a whack?"

Rex gave it a sharp jab with the side of his fist, and several inches of the door and the frame surrounding the lock shattered, raining bits of metal and concrete and plastic circuitry onto the floor.

Ogden put the can and the screwdriver back into the duffle and pulled the door open.

We were at the end of a little alcove that opened onto another open-plan floor. There was a desk at the front, and next to it, a thick glass-composite wall, four or five feet tall, running to our right. Beyond the partition was a wide space with white walls and pale gray carpet, open and airy, with high ceilings. Windows took up an entire wall, looking onto the city and, from this height, a good bit of the surrounding countryside, as well. There was a row of desks to our left, but the focus of the room was an enormous, reinforced composite glass cube, twenty feet high, twenty feet on each side. A door of the same material was set into it. To the left of the door was another security panel, and to the right, suspended in the glass composite, delicate chrome letters spelled TECH SUITE.

Ogden reached into Claudia's duffle bag again, and pulled out the liquid nitrogen and started spraying the glass all around the lock. "What's the time?"

"Three fifty-one," Rex said, his voice tight with stress.

Ogden looked over at him, mildly alarmed. "Cutting it close." He kept spraying for another few seconds, as more and more frost built up on the glass. Then he put the can back in the duffle and took out a small hammer. He stood at arms' length from the door and gave the glass under the locking mechanism a solid whack. The area he had sprayed, all around the lock, shattered and fell away, pattering onto the carpet. The lock stayed attached to the door frame and the security panel, and Ogden pushed the whole assemblage open and walked in, beckoning us to follow.

Inside, there were two long work benches. One had a basic workstation, but the other had an assortment of crazy-high-tech computers—crystal-based, gel-based, glass chambers full of liquids or glowing plasma. Stuff I couldn't even identify. At the end of the table, connected to everything else by a bundle of thick cables, was a large black metal mesh cage, with stacks of computer servers inside, humming and whirring and sparkling with blinking blue, red, and orange lights.

"How the hell are you going to hack into that?" Claudia said.

Ogden was looking even worse than before, but he managed a smile. "That cage holds the quantum servers that run all the in-house computing for the entire tower. Those on the bench are next-gen experimental—5Q quantum, DNA gel phase, 4D crystals. But remember, the Wellplant network is distributed—there is no central computer. So we only need to hack into that." He turned and pointed at a very basic desktop computer, sitting on the other long table. "It's barely even a computer, more like an access port they use to push the software upgrades."

He took the backpack off my back and gingerly removed the signal optimizer and put it on the table next to the terminal. Claudia helped him unpack the rest, the two of them talking in hushed tones, using jargon I didn't understand.

We had six minutes to save civilization as we knew it, but Rex and I were just in the way. We walked back out through the door, crunching over the glass on the carpet, and sat on one of the desks facing the cube.

"I was worried about you," Rex said, putting his arm around me.

I leaned into him and laughed. "I'm *still* worried about me. About you, too. If this doesn't work…" My voice trailed off as my throat constricted.

"I know," he said softly, holding me tighter.

"Even if it does work, though, what then? We're trying to take down the most sophisticated computer network the world has ever known. And even without the second part of the malware, people are going to get hurt, and we're going to be held responsible. We're also taking on the most powerful tycoon the world has ever known, a man who could still end up as president. I can't see him just saying, 'Okay, well done. You guys win.'"

He took a breath and opened his mouth as if he was going to say something, but instead he stayed quiet and nodded.

I heard a quiet curse and looked over to see Claudia fiddling with two cables, apparently trying to disconnect them. She called over, "Hey, big guy, can you give us a hand over here?"

"Duty calls," Rex said. He took his arm from around my shoulder and gave my thigh a squeeze as he pushed himself off from the desk and crunched his way back into the cube.

Through the windows, I could see plumes of smoke still rising into the sky, contributing to the haze that hung in the air. I put my hands behind me, and as I leaned back against the desk, I noticed that two lights on the phones were lit. Apparently, the phones were still working.

Doesn't hurt to try, I told myself, as I picked up the handset, pushed a button, and got a dial tone. My hands shook as I punched in my mom's phone number. There was of course the possibility that someone might listen in, but this was important, and it wasn't like I was about to say anything sensitive. On the second ring, someone answered.

"Hello?"

"Aunt Trudy?"

"Ohmygodohmygodjimithankgodyou'reokay!"

"Yeah, I'm fine Aunt Trudy," I said.

Before I could say anything else, Mom was on the line. "Jimi? Is that you? Are you okay?"

"I'm fine, Mom, I—"

"Do you know how worried we've been?"

Rex emerged from the cube, looking at me in quizzical disbelief.

I smiled at him and shrugged. "Mom," I said. "I've only been gone since this morning."

"Yes, in the middle of a public health disaster! And there's a curfew." She started crying. "Jimi, this is serious. They're saying it could be worse than…worse than before." She sobbed once, then got herself under control. "Kevin's school is in lockdown. You need to get home, Jimi. Now. This instant. Where are you, anyway?…Caller ID says you're at…Wells *Tower*? What are you doing *there*?"

For some reason, I started laughing. I couldn't help it. It was a perfectly reasonable question, but the answer was totally ridiculous.

Claudia pushed the door open and stuck her head out. "He's tapped into the main signal. He just has to optimize our signal and tweak the phase to compensate for the different architecture between this terminal and the Wellplant we were using before." Then she noticed I was on the phone and she turned to Rex. "Who's she talking to?"

Rex flashed a bashful grin. "Her mom."

"Tell her I said hi," Ogden called out, not taking his eyes off his work.

"I'll be home soon, Mom," I said into the phone. "But in the meantime, I have to tell you something important…something Dymphna told me."

"*Dymphna?!* What are you talking about, Jimi? You told the FBI you hadn't spoken to her! You talked to *Dymphna?*"

"I lied, Mom. Sorry, but I had to."

"Why?"

"I'll tell you later, but here's the thing," I said. "You don't have to worry about the flu, or about me or Kevin or Trudy. Any of us. Dymphna—well, it's a long story. I'll tell you that later, too. But the chimeras have a virus that makes them immune to the flu, so they can't catch it, and the immunity virus is highly contagious, so everyone they encounter is immune, too."

"What are you talking about? Jimi, you explain yourself right now!"

And that's when the elevator dinged.

For a fraction of a second, the four of us looked up, then over toward the elevators.

"Mom, I love you," I said. "I gotta go."

As I hung up the phone, I heard her saying, "Jimi, wait…"

Then the elevator doors opened, and we all scrambled back into the cube.

FIFTY-THREE

Inside the cube, we hunkered down behind the table and dumped all the weapons out of the bags. Claudia snatched up one of the two rifles. Rex raised an eyebrow at me, asking if I wanted the other one. I grabbed the dart gun instead, switching out the cartridge for a full one. Rex nodded and picked up the other rifle.

Left on the floor were a couple of spare magazines, one for a rifle and two for a dart gun, plus another dart gun, and a pair of what I was pretty sure were hedgehogs, basically spiny little grenades that fired a cloud of fast-acting, short-duration tranquilizer darts. I'd only ever seen them in Holovid movies.

Rex and I peered over the table toward the alcove where the elevators were.

Behind us, Claudia said, "Oh, shit."

I glanced back and saw her bending over Ogden, who was slumped over the keyboard.

"Is he okay?" I whispered.

She had her hand on his neck. "He's alive, but unconscious." She looked alarmed. "His pulse is really fast."

"Did he upload the malware?" Rex asked.

She gently moved him to the side, off the keyboard. The screen said OPTIMIZING SIGNAL PHASE…PLEASE WAIT. She shook her head. "It's still optimizing."

We had three minutes to go.

A second *ding* came from the elevator area, followed by the sound of another door opening and the rumble of what sounded like a hundred pairs of boots on the floor. A fraction of a second later, a dozen commandoes in full tactical gear erupted from around the corner, bristling with weapons, all diving into rolls and coming out of them running flat out.

One of them had a cast on his arm and he seemed to tumble more than roll. Instead of coming out if it on his feet, he crashed into one of the desks and ended up in a tangled heap with a cord around his foot.

The others all had their handguns out, firing as they ran. The bullets slammed into the glass, chipping it, splintering it, but not penetrating it.

Claudia ran to the door, but I called out, "No! Stay on that!" Behind her the screen flashed, saying SIGNAL PHASE OPTIMIZATION COMPLETE. CONTINUE? [Y] OR N

She nodded and slapped the ENTER key. The screen said UPLOADING...

Rex leveled his rifle through the gap around the lock and fired, hitting one of the commandoes and slowing them down, but not dropping them. He fired again and hit another with the same result. There were too many of them, they were covered with armor, and they were coming too fast. Almost as alarming was the fact that Rex was firing actual bullets. Shooting to kill. It brought home to me how serious, how real, how life-or-death this whole situation was.

I grabbed one of the hedgehogs and pushed the door open a few inches. The hedgehog had a red button with a clear cover over it. Trying desperately to remember how they were used in the movies, I thumbed open the cover and pressed the button, then tossed it through the opening.

"Get back!" I cried, as I jumped back from the door.

Rex said, "What?"

The hedgehog bounced across the floor into the middle of the attackers, then seemingly vanished with a small flash and a puff of smoke.

For a moment, the commandoes kept coming, a wedge of black Kevlar and high-tech weaponry. Then, the wedge dissolved as they all stumbled and fell, like a drunken pantomime of their earlier precision. They all hit the floor, and then there was stillness, except for the one guy under the desk groaning and trying to extricate himself from the tangle of cords.

Rex grinned at me and said, "Good job." Then his eyes rolled up and he crumpled to the floor. I grabbed him as he fell, and he took me with him.

Landing on top of him on the floor, I saw half a dozen tiny darts embedded in his shoulder.

"Dammit, no!" I said, grabbing his shirt and shaking him, plucking the darts from his shoulder.

Claudia looked at us. "What's going on over there?"

I cursed myself out loud. "I accidentally darted Rex."

Claudia came over. "Do you need a hand?"

"No," I said. "You keep working on that. Is it almost done?"

"Still uploading."

I dragged Rex back from the door, and as Claudia was headed back to the computer terminal, a gun went off outside the cube. A bullet hit the glass with a loud thud, followed by the dull tone of reverberating glass. The shot had come from the guy who'd been tangled in cords, and who was now climbing out from under the desk. He fired again.

Claudia stuck her gun through the hole in the door and returned fire. The phone on the desk above him flipped into the air, spraying bits of plastic and metal. The guy cried out, "Ouch! Son of a—!" and threw himself out into the open.

He seemed to realize where he was and looked up, straight at us. That was the first time I got a good look at him. Claudia was about to fire again, but I put my hand on her arm to stop her. I put my face near the hole where the security panel used to be and called out, "Stan? Is that you?"

He looked scared and confused, but it was him all right. He had a greenish yellow bruise under the red skin around his Wellplant. He fired wildly at us, them dove behind the glass wall in front of the elevator bank. "What did you do to them?" he demanded, looking down at the bodies littering the floor.

"They're just darted," I called back. "They'll be okay."

"More than I can say for you!" he shouted, standing up and firing three more shots. Each bullet slammed harmlessly into the thick glass.

"Stan!" I called to him. "Why are you doing this?"

"Ha!" he spat back, bitterly. "Because..." He paused, sounding momentarily lost. "Because...You know why!" Then he stood and fired another shot.

"I don't, Stan. I really don't," I said.

He screwed up his face, as if he didn't quite understand what I was saying, but suspected he didn't like it. He shook his head, and his forehead creased, like he was thinking hard.

Then the elevator dinged again, and his eyes went wide with terror. "Oh no," he said, and he stood up straight and started firing again—*blam, blam, blam*—the glass humming with reverberations. He looked behind him, toward the elevators, his attention, his fear, solely focused on whoever had just stepped off.

I glanced back at Claudia, and she replied with an uneasy shrug.

Stan said, "I...I..."

A voice I recognized said, "Quiet."

Stan backed away, as if trying to escape the shadow that fell across him. Then the figure casting it came into view.

Howard Wells.

FIFTY-FOUR

Wells looked…different. His teeth were still stupid white, and his skin was still gloriously fake-tanned. But his handsome features were distorted. His forehead seemed swollen, distended around his Wellplant, and his eyes were slightly skewed and bulging, one of them smudged bright red. But he still emanated power, even more than before, like some sort of comic book evil genius about to shed his human form.

"Holy crap," Claudia whispered. Wells's head whipped around, as if, impossibly, he had heard her. I was relieved to see that she had already swiveled the computer screen away from him, and even more relieved to see that the screen now said, UPLOAD COMPLETE. EXECUTE? [Y] OR N.

I caught Claudia's eye and nodded at the screen. She glanced down and tapped ENTER.

When I turned back, Wells was grinning at us, a terrible grimace that radiated a kind of dangerous insanity I'd never witnessed before.

"Jimi Corcoran," he said. "We've been thinking it's time we had a talk with you. Face-to-face."

Wells's use of "we" was chilling. I didn't know if I was talking to Wells or to everyone with a Wellplant, or if I was actually talking to whatever the Wellplant network had become, if it was human at all.

Stan said, "Sir—"

Wells cut him off, his head whipping around as he thundered, "SHUT UP!…You will know if we want you to speak."

Stan looked away, his eye twitching. He seemed so confused he was almost in tears.

Wells's head swiveled back toward me. He smiled, and it was horrific. "You might think we don't have much in common, Jimi Corcoran. But you'd be wrong. We're a big fan of yours, you know. We've been watching you these past few months. You've been a thorn in our side, but an impressive one. You remind us of your aunt when she was young. She was an amazing woman."

"Yes, she was," I shouted through the hole. "It's a shame you killed her."

He laughed sadly and shook his head. "You're wrong there. We didn't have her killed. She meant far too much to us, to the *world*. We had always held out hope she would come around, see the error of her ways, and the righteousness of ours. No, it was those maniacs in CLAD who killed her. Her death is a tragedy, a crime."

"It *was* a tragedy and a crime," I said. "But it was your people, and no one else, who murdered her. I saw it happen."

Stan turned to look at me, still confused, like he didn't understand what was going on. Wells's eyes darkened.

"By whom?" Wells demanded, his voice low and dangerous.

I hated Stan Grainger. He had shot Del, killing him, as far as he knew. He had killed Dymphna. And I truly did wish he was dead. But I did not want to kill him, and I could see in Wells's face that that's what would happen if I told him. Maybe I felt some sympathy for Stan, because of all he had been through, how damaged he was. I knew that to some extent, the hatred he put out there in the world was at its core a form of mental illness. And maybe it had something to do with how confused he seemed right now, how vulnerable. Or maybe it was just because I didn't want to kill. I didn't want to be a murderer, however justified.

But it didn't matter, because right then Stan looked up like he'd just had a brilliant idea and said, "I did it. I killed her."

Wells's face darkened further as he turned to Stan. "Who are you?"

Stan looked around, nervously. "I'm…I'm Stanley Grainger, sir."

Wells's distended brow wrinkled and furrowed, his eyes all but disappearing in the shadow. "You killed Dymphna Corcoran?"

"Um…yes, sir, but—"

"Why did we not know this?"

Stan reached a trembling hand to his forehead. "My, um, my Wellplant. I think it's malfunctioning."

Wells grabbed Stan by the throat, pulling him closer so he could examine the Wellplant. "You broke it," Wells said, his voice indignant, his breath rapid and loud.

"I guess so, sir," Stan said, his voice muffled by Wells's grip. "But I didn't—"

"Enough!" Wells snapped at him. "This miracle is wasted on you. You're unworthy of it."

Before I even knew what was happening, Wells, still holding Stan's throat with one hand, grasped Stan's Wellplant between the thumb and forefinger of his other hand and twisted and pulled at the same time. Stan made a sound like he was stifling a sneeze, then the Wellplant came free with a wrenching, tearing sound, trailing wires and blood and bits of flesh.

I screamed. Claudia did, too.

Stan's eyes rolled back into his head as Wells dropped him to the floor, disgusted, then Wells shook off the Wellplant and put it in his breast pocket. Blood dribbled down his jacket. He looked up at me and said, "There. We have avenged Dymphna's murder."

He seemed like he was waiting for a response from me, like he was expecting praise or thanks. But I was speechless, unable to respond at all.

"The planet can't continue on as it is," he said, with a false sparkle in his eye and a poor imitation of earnestness in his voice. "We all know it. But this thing you're trying to stop, it can change that. We recovered data from a gel phase drive left at the vertical farm in Camden. We know what Dymphna was up to, with her little virus that makes all your mixie friends immune. And that's fine. Whatever. It's a big planet, there will be lots of resources for everyone who's left. I'm saving the world for both of us, for those with splices and those with Wellplants."

"What, so you can enslave more chimeras?" I said. "Hunt them? Work them to death in mines?"

Before he could reply, a trio of black helicopters roared past the window, close. Everyone looked over at them for a moment, then they were gone, the sound of the motors fading but not disappearing.

The sparkle in Wells's eyes disappeared, replaced by anger before they went dull and emotionless. "I don't know what you're hoping to accomplish here," he said flatly. "You can't simply blow up a single node and bring down the network. It isn't built that way. It doesn't work like that."

I glanced back at Claudia, at the computer screen. It said EXECUTION COMPLETE. PROPAGATING.

I looked back at Wells. "You're insane," I said.

He laughed, a big, genuine belly laugh, like he really thought that was funny. "Well, it's an insane world."

"You're a murderer."

He shook his head and sighed, like he was disappointed in me. "Everyone's a murderer. You, your friends. Everyone who takes a breath on this Earth. Anyone who eats food and drinks water is taking air and food and water from someone else. Everybody is a murderer. We're just being practical about it. Systematic. Logical. Smart. But make no mistake: Life is murder."

He laughed again. "But that's okay. Everybody dies, too. People say 'murder' like it's a bad word, a tragedy, like the people being murdered weren't going to die before long anyway. But everybody dies. Or at least everybody has so far. I have some ideas that could change that in the next few years, but I digress. You think you're being merciful, but what good is saving billions of lives that will end before long anyway, at the expense of the entire planet, the cost of the trillions of lives that could one day be lived if we stop destroying the Earth right now?"

"And it's up to you to decide who lives or dies?" I said, my voice bitter with sarcasm.

"You could do a lot worse." He tapped his Wellplant once again. "We're very, very smart." He laughed again, then stopped abruptly. "Look, child, we don't want to kill you. You really do remind us of Dymphna, before she ruined herself. We don't even want to kill your friends, here, not if you don't want us to. But the world can't keep going the way it's going. And as we've just explained, you're not doing anyone any favors saving a few billion now if it means the sacrifice of the trillions of lives yet to come, if it means the end of humanity. What a crime that would be. Especially when, really, we're just getting started."

His eye twitched and he looked concerned for a moment, like he'd heard a noise that shouldn't be there, or caught a whiff of smoke.

Outside the cube, one of the guards on the floor groaned and stirred. Then another one did, too. Suddenly, they were all stirring.

Wells smiled. He bent down and pulled Stan's rifle from his dead shoulder, then took another one from one of his still-unconscious guards. "Well, we'd love to chat some more, but we have a feeling we're not going to change your mind and we have an important matter to attend to in"—he looked at his watch—"one minute."

I glanced back at Claudia and she shook her head. The screen still said PROPAGATING....

I jumped as a sound tore through the air, like a jackhammer crossed with a buzz saw. Wells fired both guns on automatic, one in each hand, concentrating the two streams of bullets onto the same dime-sized spot on the glass. The sound was horrendous, and it got worse as the cube began to resonate, much louder than before. I covered my ears against the noise, as the glass started to groan. The whole time he was firing, neither stream of bullets wavered the slightest bit, both of them grinding and chipping away at that one spot, dropping a thin cascade of glass chips and dust.

I dragged Rex away from the glass walls, toward the center of the cube.

Mercifully, one of Wells's guns ran out of ammunition, then the other one did, too. But not before a crack formed, arcing from the bullet hole almost to the corner of the wall. Another crack appeared on the other side of the hole, and two more splintered from that one.

Wells laughed, standing there in a cloud of gun smoke as he replaced the magazines. More of his guards were starting to wake up.

I put the second hedgehog in my pocket and grabbed Rex's rifle, the dart gun still in my other hand. I turned to Claudia. "Anything?"

She was similarly armed, her face grim. "Not if they're still coming at us."

I looked past her at the screen. Still propagating.

Wells fired again, a single bullet, and this time the glass shattered, all four sides of the cube disintegrating simultaneously and falling to the floor in a shower of crystals. Luckily, the ceiling stayed up, swaying erratically on the cables it hung from.

Wells grinned as his men got to their feet and brushed themselves off, raised their rifles, and began marching toward us.

Claudia and I stepped back, into the center of what used to be the cube and was now a square-shaped outline of glass shards. I held the hedgehog behind my back, my thumb resting on the red button guard. Without the glass walls, there would be nothing to protect us from the darts, but if the hedgehog stopped them, too, then hopefully by the time we all woke up, Ogden's malware would have done its thing. Hopefully, we'd wake up in a world where the Wellplant network had been crashed.

"Put down your guns," Wells said as his men marched toward us.

I flicked the button guard open with my thumb, and I was about to press it and tell Claudia to drop when I heard a stampede of feet, just like when Wells's men arrived. Only this time it was accompanied by a woman's voice, forceful and familiar, saying, *"FBI! Drop your weapons!"*

As Wells's commandos stopped and turned to see who was behind them, roughly twenty FBI agents in black tactical gear emerged from the direction of the stairwell. Balaclavas covered their faces, and they looked ready for action with their rifles raised. The agent at the front held her badge up high with one hand, pulling off her balaclava with the other. It was Agent Ralphs.

The agent standing next to her pulled his mask off, too. Agent Scanlon.

"I said, drop your weapons, *now*!" Ralphs repeated. Scanlon seemed oddly content to let her do the talking.

The commandos looked to Wells for an answer about what to do, but he refused to look at them, as if he was unable to acknowledge that his plan had fallen apart.

I felt a moment of relief that the cavalry had arrived to save the day, to stop the end of the world and arrest the guy trying to end it. And I might have felt kind of smug when I looked at Howard Wells, expecting to see in his face the crushing defeat of his crazy plot being thwarted, or at least to see it blank and affectless because it was mostly controlled by a machine. But his smile looked as smug as I felt. Then I didn't feel so smug anymore.

The balaclavas the agents wore covered their faces except for a horizontal oval that revealed their eyes, and, on half of them, their Wellplants.

Howard Wells's smile broadened into a grin.

"Ralphs!" I shouted. "Look out!"

It was all I had time to say, but even as I said it, all the agents with Wellplants swiveled to point their guns at the non-spiked agents. Before the targeted agents could even react, Wells laughed and shouted, *"Fire!"*

FIFTY-FIVE

No one fired. Wells stood there in silence with a big stupid grin on his face. Behind him, nobody moved a muscle. Except for Agent Ralphs, that is. She sprang into action, pushing Scanlon's gun up out of the way so it was pointed at the ceiling, then kicking out his knee and punching him in the throat.

I'm pretty sure it wasn't until Scanlon was crumpled on the floor that Ralphs realized he was immobilized. But I'm not positive. He'd been pretty annoying, and I imagine she might have built up enough serious resentments to want to take advantage of the situation and get a few in there. But who knows?

Even the agents without Wellplants seemed frozen in place, stunned that their comrades would turn on them like that.

I looked at Claudia, who was so transfixed by the spectacle that part of me wondered if somehow she'd been frozen, too. But when she saw me looking, she adjusted the screen so I could see it: PROPAGATION COMPLETE. SYSTEM REBOOTING. THIS MAY TAKE SOME TIME.

She grinned and said, "Without a moment to spare." Then her grin faded as she hurried over to Ogden. I hurried over to Rex, whose eyelids fluttered as he groaned.

Ralphs came up to me and said, "You need to tell me what the hell just happened here."

Behind her, the agents who didn't have Wellplants were milling about, fascinated by the immobility of the agents with Wellplants, and maybe emboldened by it. They poked them and prodded them, blowing on their faces, even tickling them, trying to get them to move or respond, until Ralphs snapped at them, "Knock it off. Disarm them and restrain them, until we know what just happened."

I turned to Claudia and asked, "How's he doing?"

"Alive," she said. "But not good."

Rex let out a loud sigh, like he might be waking up soon.

"Okay," I said, turning to Ralphs. "We'll tell you everything, although you might not believe it. But first, our friend needs a doctor. Now."

"The medical team is on its way up," she told me, then she called out over her shoulder. "Simmons, Hickman, we need first aid over here."

A pair of FBI agents came over and attended to Ogden and Rex.

Claudia stepped back and said, "I need to call my mom and dad." As she looked around for a phone, Ralphs raised a hand to stop her.

"We shut down the Wellplant network," I said, distracting Ralphs as Claudia lifted the handset of a phone on one of the desks and punched in a number.

Ralphs whipped her head around. "*What?* How? Why?" she demanded, as the medical team arrived, a dozen figures in biohazard suits, fanning out through the room. One of them went straight to Ogden, another came over to Rex.

"I'll explain everything later," I said, reluctantly stepping away from Rex to give the medic space to work. "Howard Wells, or whatever he's turned into"—we both looked at him, standing there immobile with his face distended and insane—"he's behind the super-flu, but what we're dealing with now was just an accidental release." I left out the part about us being the ones who accidentally released it. "The big release was supposed to be happening now, right now. That's what we prevented by crashing the Wellplant network."

"Wait." She held up a hand. "Why would he do that?"

"He wanted to wipe out most of the world's population to preserve the planet's resources for those who were left.... People with Wellplants."

"What? That's insane!"

"I know. But…" I gestured toward Howard Wells, still standing there with that same crazed grin on his face. "It sounds nuts and it is. And there's a lot more to figure out. But right now, everyone with a Wellplant, all the world leaders and first responders, they're all frozen like that. You need to let people know what's happening so they can figure out how to respond."

"Uh, okay, yeah," she said, confused and momentarily overwhelmed. As she took out a pad and started making notes, I gave her a super-condensed recap of what Wells had been planning, how the flu was already out, and how people could get immunity via Dymphna's virus.

Struggling to keep up, she looked at me, confused. "How the hell do you know about all this?"

I didn't hesitate. "Dymphna Corcoran told me."

Her eyes hardened. "I thought you said you hadn't had any contact with her."

I shrugged. "I lied."

That's when Rex woke up, looking around and blinking his eyes, disoriented.

The medic stepped away from him. "He's fine," she said. "He'll be okay in a minute."

Ralphs pointed her pen at me and opened her mouth to speak, but I cut her off. I told her about Roberta and Zak, back at the RCA building. And Cronos. "That's all you need to know, right now. We'll talk more later, but that's what's urgent. You need to get on all that *now*."

In the space of a second, she frowned, glared, looked at her notepad, nodded, then turned and started barking orders using acronyms like CDC, WHO, CIA, and NSA, delegating the tasks I had just given her.

Rex looked up and said, "What did I miss?"

Before I answered, I kissed him, long and hard, and as we kissed, the magnitude sank in of what had just happened, and what just hadn't. So many emotions ran through me. I was scared of what was going to come next, of the trouble we all might face for crashing the Wellplant network, whatever damage that might have caused, might continue to cause, plus the fact that the flu was already out there.

But at the same time, I knew that whatever bad there was to come was better than the alternative. The worst had been averted. Close on the heels of that hope came grief, for Dymphna and Del, Reverend Calkin and the others, even Stan, whose life I mourned as much as his death. It was all so sad.

I held the kiss because I wanted to, because I was desperately relieved that Rex was okay and also because I needed time to get my emotions under some semblance of control.

When we finally parted, I helped Rex to his feet and we looked at the chaos surrounding us. The cube was gone, reduced to shards. The office was shot to pieces. To our left was the new Wellplant sculpture garden: Howard Wells, along with dozens of his commandoes and the FBI agents, all standing there immobilized, except for their rhythmic breathing and occasional blinking. To our right, the windows looked east over the city and across the river to New Jersey. With all the smoke, the blinking lights and the dense, frenetic drone and copter traffic, it seemed like a war zone.

"So...I guess we stopped them?" Rex asked.

"Yes," I said. "We did."

"Looks like a lot of work to do out there."

"Yeah, it does."

We stood there looking out at it for a few minutes, then an agent I didn't know walked up to us, an African American woman whose tag said MUNROE. "Jimi Corcoran?" she said.

"Yeah?"

"Your mother is downstairs, waiting outside. She's, um, kind of agitated."

Rex laughed. "That was fast."

"She saw the caller ID when I called," I told him. "She must have left as soon as we got off the phone." *And driven at twice the speed limit.*

"We can't release you, yet," Munroe said, "but I can escort you down if you want to see her."

"Thanks," I said. "That would be great."

As we followed Munroe toward the elevator, the medical team was just starting to load the immobilized Plants onto stretchers: wheeling the stretchers up to them upright, strapping them in place, and then tilting the stretchers back.

I wondered if the Plants could see us, hear us. I knew the malware had frozen their motor functions, but I imagine their senses still worked.

They were edging a stretcher up behind Howard Wells, when I stopped in front of him.

I also didn't know how much of him was left in there anymore, and how much was the network. At the end, he wasn't saying "I" or "me" or "my," he was saying "we," and "us," and "ours." But the network was down now. If he was in there, he was in there alone.

I stepped closer and looked into his eyes. "I don't know how much of this was on you, and how much was your…your creation, but I want you to know, it didn't work. And I'm nothing like you. Neither was Dymphna. We have *nothing* in common with you. She was disgusted by you, by what you'd become. She told me so herself." I shook my head. "You had such gifts—intellect and wealth and power. You could have made the world a better place. You could have fixed what was broken, made sure there was enough for everyone. But instead you made it worse, trying to kill billions to make sure there was plenty for you and your chosen few. And using hatred and fear to do it."

As they tilted him back, I leaned over him, making sure his eyes were on me. "Dymphna was about love and compassion," I said. "And that's what triumphed. That's why you lost."

FIFTY-SIX

The destruction of the world as we knew it had been stopped, or at least postponed. But it wasn't really a time for celebration. The climate was still a mess, and as Howard Wells himself said, perverse as it was, by thwarting his plot—which was ghastly and terrible and *needed* to be thwarted—we had also thwarted the closest thing there was to a concrete plan to fix it. And while we had prevented the widespread release of Wells's super-flu, what was already out there was tearing through the population.

Philadelphia had been one of the hardest-hit places in the first big flu pandemic, back in 1918, and it was the hardest hit this time, too. Even with the news blasting out the message that contact with chimeras would make people immune, it took weeks for Dymphna's chimera virus to outpace Wells's super-flu and choke off its supply of fresh victims. In that time, millions of people got sick, and many of them died.

People died from the Wellplant crash, too, and everyone involved faced weeks of tough questioning. This was not like after Pitman or Omnicare, a couple of stern interviews and then that's that. We were held in custody for weeks—me, Rex, Claudia, and Ogden, plus Roberta, Sly, and Dara; and, from what I heard, Martin and Gary and Audrey and the rest of the Chimerica council, as well.

Around the world, folks with Wellplants were gathered into special hospital wards set aside to care for them. After a week or so, one by one, they began to snap out of their comas or fugues or standby modes or whatever, and they acknowledged the horrors of what they had almost done, and expressed gratitude at having been prevented from doing it. They also described being passengers in their own bodies, in their own brains, as their humanity, their individuality, was overwhelmed by a superior force. It was only then that the heat on us began to let up, and it was recognized—unofficially, of course—how essential our actions had been. But Marcella DeWitt made sure I got it in writing that there were no arrests, or anything like that, on my record.

Having been temporarily freed from their implants, most of the Plants realized how much they had been changed by their Wellplants, controlled by them. They had them removed voluntarily, despite the clear risks of doing so. Chris Bembry, as one of the newest Plants, had a fairly easy recovery. After a few months of physical and occupational therapy, he was pretty much back to his old self.

Wells, as the earliest adopter, had the hardest road ahead of him. He regained the ability to walk and talk, but his brain had grown so dependent on his Wellplant that he was left terribly impaired. Still, he insisted he made the right choice in having it removed. For the first time since he implanted the prototype, he was free to be his true self. That would be the extent of his freedom, probably for the rest of his life. He was charged with dozens of crimes, multiple counts of each, some I'd never even heard of. He pled guilty to pretty much all of them. Some thought that was proof he was too mentally impaired to stand trial or advocate on his own behalf. Others said it was because his Wellplant itself provided overwhelming physical evidence of his crimes. But even spending the rest of his life in jail, he said, he was freer than he had been in decades.

Not surprisingly, he was not elected president.

The government declared Wellplants unsafe and issued a recall, which was wending its way through the courts, opposed by the handful of people who wanted to keep their Wellplants.

Many questions remain unanswered about what exactly happened with the Wellplant network. *Had* the network become a sentient being? And if so, what happened to it? Could it remain sentient once detached from all those brains, or were those brains an essential part of the network?

The U.S. government confiscated all the removed Wellplants in America, to study them, they said. Other countries followed suit, prompting another wave of lawsuits, this time in the international courts, about state secrets, intellectual property rights, and national defense. People were seriously freaking out about what the Wellplant network had become and who got to keep what pieces were left of it.

Claudia became obsessed with the whole thing, convinced that the Feds had merely changed the signal phase to separate the confiscated devices from the few still implanted. She suspected the military had reassembled the rest of the network, to try to duplicate the effect. Ogden shared her obsession. We'd have to see if they ended up sharing anything else, but I think they'd bonded a bit during all the excitement. I knew personally how powerful that could be.

As word spread about the immunity virus, people who had never met a chimera went out of their way to do so. For the most part, people with splices were good sports about it, especially once it came to light that this was all part of Dymphna's plan, and that she was, essentially, the mother of chimeras.

Pictures showed up in the news of chimeras taking shifts standing on street corners holding up signs that offered FREE HUGS AND HANDSHAKES.

There were, unfortunately, a few incidents of assault, of chimera-haters figuring they could have contact with chimeras by punching and kicking instead of hugging and shaking hands. But, whether it was because of the immunity virus or the fall of Howard Wells or the fact that a bunch of chimeras had saved the world—with a little help from their nonk friend Jimi—people largely moved past the whole chimera-hating thing.

As more non-spliced people got to know chimeras—and began to understand the many reasons a person might choose to get spliced—they learned to respect chimeras for the individual humans they were. Just like I had done, less than a year earlier.

Humans for Humanity all but disappeared, except for a tiny core group. The same was true of The Church of the Eternal Truth. Their membership and attendance collapsed, and within a few months they had to sell their church and move to a tiny storefront more befitting of their hate-spouting fringiness.

In a nice twist, the church property itself was bought by St. Peter's Church, where Reverend Calkin had been the pastor. The congregation renounced their opposition to people with splices and their affiliation with H4H.

Within a few months of the shutdown, the Genetic Heritage Act was overturned in the courts. It had become so widely reviled that no one even appealed the ruling. All the similar state and federal proposals were quietly abandoned and allowed to die, with the focus diverted to regulating splicing, making sure it was safe for those who wanted to pursue it.

During that time, Doc Guzman initiated an appeal process to get his medical license reinstated and was optimistic about the outcome. He was also hired by the University of Pennsylvania medical school to resume his research, teach a course, and maybe, down the road, create a department on chimeric medicine—which he hoped would become part of a global movement in the healthcare industry to acknowledge that they had abdicated their responsibility and failed people with splices, and that they needed to expand their expertise and their openness to treating everyone, regardless of splices or spikes or whatever other flavors of transhumanism were coming down the pike.

With Cronos gone, CLAD withered and died, as well. I think even the people who agreed with everything CLAD had tried to do ended up distancing themselves from the group.

Chimerica, similarly, found itself without a leader—and in their case, also without a secret mandate. The governing council issued a statement saying that they were going to spend the next year re-visioning, determining what their mission was going to be, and inviting all those who had been a part of Chimerica, or supporters of it, to weigh in. I spoke briefly to Martin before he headed back to Canada, and he said they would be meeting with facilitators and organizational experts bimonthly for the foreseeable future. Better him than me.

Weather wise, that summer ended up being the worst on record for brush fires, droughts, and superstorms. Maybe it was that, or maybe it was partly the wake-up call of Wells's plot and the realization that if the smartest and most powerful person in the world was ready to take such drastic action, however crazy, maybe the rest of us could get together and finally come up with a plan that was a little more sane, but by the end of the summer, the United Nations announced a new round of talks, and the twelve countries with the largest economies in the world issued a joint declaration on climate change that committed to zero carbon emissions, a tripled investment in remediation, and a trade embargo on all countries that did not join them.

Who knows, maybe this time it would work. And maybe it wouldn't be too late.

By the time we were done with all the interrogations and investigations, it was mid-October. Even with everything else going on, including the start of senior year, I managed to put in my hours with DeWitt after school and I continued to learn a lot from her, as a lawyer and as a person.

I'd applied early to Temple University and got in that month, pre-law. I was looking forward to living on my own, but I decided I would probably commute from home for the first year or two. Campus housing was expensive, and it wasn't like I'd be getting an athletic scholarship, like Kevin. More important, though, I knew I'd put my mom through a lot over the past year, and I figured she might want to have me close for a while.

By then she might be just as excited about me moving out as I was.

I was shocked when Rex told me that he had been accepted by Temple, as well. I didn't know he had even applied, or that he'd taken and passed his General Educational Development test, which was equivalent to a high school diploma. He was delaying his admission for a year, so we could start together in the fall.

There was a time when Del and I had planned on going to Temple together. I was touched that Rex and I would be going together, instead, but also careful not to put too much pressure or expectation on it. A year was a long time, and we were young. But I was optimistic. For the life of me, I couldn't see myself getting sick of Rex or growing apart from him, ever. He assures me he feels the same way about me, and I believe him.

Don't get me wrong, there were some adjustments to be made. For the first time, we were free to let our relationship progress and deepen without the constant backdrop of crisis and drama and secrets. I went to school and did my homework. Rex worked for Jerry and read voraciously. And we spent a lot of time together, just being.

Sometimes I'd get antsy, expecting something crazy intense to happen, to sweep us up. But it didn't, not right away. And that was really, really nice.

In late October, Camden County finally released Del's remains. With Stan dead, there'd been no family to claim him, but it took a while because there were jurisdictional squabbles between the federal and local agencies that had been trying to track down Cronos. It wasn't that they wanted his body—they didn't—but they didn't know exactly how to process it. It was a bit of a mess.

Luckily, Mom took it on herself to negotiate all the red tape, so I wasn't actually aware of the details until much later. She thought they would be painful for me, and she was right, they would have been. Del had dealt with so much trouble during his life, and even months later, I found it really upsetting that trouble seemed to follow him in death, too.

Mom paid for Del's cremation, too, and she and Trudy helped me decide what to do with the ashes. It took a while. I wanted it to be somewhere he'd been happy, but Del hadn't been happy anywhere in a long time—except maybe at our house, our kitchen table, our sofa. With that in mind, I briefly considered just keeping the ashes, but I decided that was morbid.

In the end, I had to go way back to our childhood, when Del's mom was still alive and Stan hadn't gone off the rails. And my dad was alive, too. We were five or six, and Mom and Dad took all of us—me, Del, Leo, our friend Nina, plus Kevin and a couple of his friends—to the Wissahickon Gorge. We played in the creek and ran around the trails, then hiked all the way up to the top of what seemed like a mountain back then. Del climbed up on this outcrop and spread out his arms and beat his chest and danced around, grinning like a maniac the whole time. He wouldn't come down until my parents made the rest of us pretend we were leaving without him. It was the happiest I ever saw him.

It took Rex and me weeks to find that spot again. But searching for it gave us an excuse to go hiking in the woods a couple of times a week. That time was special, too—somber but peaceful. As we wandered the woods, we shared memories of when we were little. And of Del. Later, I would realize it was the process of remembering him that was the real goodbye.

Finally, we found the spot. The years since we'd been there had changed it quite a bit, but we both recognized it immediately.

A week later, we had the ceremony. It was quiet and simple. Mom and Trudy were there, and all our friends came out, even Doc Guzman and Jerry. None of them had gotten to know Del all that well, but I appreciated their presence. Even Kevin came up from school for the weekend. He'd known Del, of course, as a kid, but he was there for me, too, and it meant a lot.

I reached out to Roberta, Ogden, and Zak, the only people I'd really known from CLAD, but none of them showed up. I totally understood, too. They were dealing with their own fallout, processing things their own way. And this wasn't about Cronos. It was about Del.

I said a few words that I don't remember now, but I do remember that they felt right. Then I climbed up on the rock and scattered his ashes, and we watched as they slowly drifted away through the trees.

Claudia's mom and dad hosted the reception afterward, because their house was just across the gorge. It was very sweet, especially since Chris was still recovering—the whole family was still recovering, really. It didn't last long and soon it was just me and Rex, and Mom, Trudy, and Kevin, along with Claudia, of course. We didn't stay much beyond that, either. I guess we were still recovering, too.

━━ ━━ ━━

Two weeks later, the federal government released Dymphna's body, as well. They had confiscated it to run all sorts of tests, trying to learn all they could from the splices she had given herself. We couldn't get too mad about the protracted scientific process, because that's probably what Dymphna would have wanted.

St. Peter's offered to host the funeral in their brand-new megachurch, but Dymphna had a will, and—in addition to leaving the bulk of her substantial estate to fund E4E and Chimerica, with a bit each for Mom and Trudy and Kevin and me—she left specific instructions for a green funeral.

Her body was placed in a casket of woven bamboo and buried atop a hill in the woods overlooking a lovely creek, not unlike Del's rock. Trudy wept when she saw the place. Apparently, Grandma and Grandad had taken her and Dymphna and my dad camping there when they were little.

It was in the middle of nowhere, out in the zurbs, but word had gotten around, both about the funeral and about how Dymphna had saved humanity from Wells's plot. In addition to all of our family and friends, and Dymphna's comrades from Chimerica—some of whom she'd known for decades—several thousand other chimeras came out to pay their respects. Some of them might have been there for me, too, faces I recognized from Pitman and Omnicare, even people I just knew to say hi to at the coffee shop.

It was a lovely ceremony; sad, but not without moments of joy. Autumn leaves swirled around us as people sang songs and recited poems, all of them chosen by Dymphna. Audrey was the officiant, and afterward, people were invited to come up and say a few words. They did, too—dozens and dozens of them, so many that even at just a minute or two each, it took quite a long time. But it was perfect, especially for me—by the time the last person spoke, I felt like I had gotten to know Dymphna even better. Mom and Trudy and I were overwhelmed. Even Kevin was choked up.

And then it was over.

The crowd dissipated, many leaving without a word to any of us—I guess not wanting to overwhelm us. They paid their respects to Dymphna, and then they faded away.

By the time we spoke to each person waiting to speak to us, everyone else was gone. Jerry hosted the reception at the coffee shop, and he and Ruth and Pell left early to help set up. Trudy went with them. I think she welcomed the excuse to get away.

As Mom and Kevin and Rex and I walked back to the car, a cold breeze kicked up, rustling the leaves. I heard a Lev train race by in the distance, and I realized we weren't in the middle of nowhere, after all. It occurred to me then that it was almost exactly a year ago that Del had run off to get spliced. I felt an instant of vertigo as I considered how much my life had changed, how much the *world* had changed, since that day.

Rex had his arm around my shoulder, and he slipped it down around my waist, supporting me. "You okay?" he murmured, not loud enough for anyone else to hear.

I smiled up at him. "Yeah," I said. "I am."

Mom drove and Kevin sat up front with her. Rex and I sat in the back. I knew the reception was going to be nice, and I wanted to go—knew I had to go—but I also knew we were all exhausted. I snuggled up next to Rex and he rested his chin on my head.

As we got out of the car a block down from the coffee shop, I could sense that Mom wanted to talk to me. Rex seemed to pick up on it, too, and as we walked along the sidewalk, he paced alongside Kevin, and asked him about college.

As Mom and I lagged behind, she ran her fingertips up and down my back, something she used to do when I was little. "He's a sweetheart, that Rex," she said.

"Yeah." I smiled. "He really is."

We walked in silence for another few moments, long enough that I was starting to wonder if that was all she wanted to say. Then she stopped, and I did, too. We both turned to look at each other.

"Jimi," she said. "I don't know what your plans are going forward, but I just…If you decide you want to get spliced, I just want you to know, I'll…I'll support you in that. In whatever. I'll always love you, no matter what you do."

She started to cry, and I did, too. It had been an emotional day, but I was touched by the sentiment, and touched by the reality, too.

"Thanks, Mom," I said. Then I smiled. "I'll keep you posted."

We hugged and resumed walking.

Frankly, I didn't know if I would ever get spliced. Sometimes I thought about it, but I didn't feel compelled, and it seemed like the kind of thing you should only do if you felt strongly about it, not on a whim.

Rex loved me just how I was, and it occurred to me that I did, too—I loved him, but I loved me, too. I teared up again at the thought of it, at the realization that I was happy with who I was. Who I had become. Who I was still becoming.

Up ahead, Rex opened the door to the coffee shop. Kevin walked in, but Rex waited for me with a smile on his face.

Maybe I would get spliced someday, and maybe I wouldn't. But it was comforting to know that I had a mom who wouldn't reject me if I did, and that perhaps, in some tiny way, I had helped shape a world that wouldn't reject me, either.

ACKNOWLEDGMENTS

One of the challenges of writing acknowledgments to the third book in a trilogy is trying not to be repetitive. So many of the people whose help was essential to this book were already acknowledged in the first or second book. So, to everyone I have already thanked—my wife, Elizabeth; my agent, Stacia Decker; my editor, Kelly Loughman, and everyone at Holiday House; all the librarians, booksellers, bloggers, and reviewers who have supported *Spliced* and *Splintered*; everyone who helped my research for those books; and all the authors whose friendship and community has been so essential to retaining my sanity (more or less)—I thank you all once again, for all you have done, and all that you will likely do in the future, for me and my books, and to make the world more of a place I want to inhabit.

But there are other folks out there who I haven't yet thanked. Kate Moretti is not only a brilliant thriller author, she is also a scientist and her help was invaluable in figuring out some of the infectious disease aspects of the book. Denise Weintraut and the New Jersey Council of Teachers of English have been enormously supportive, as has the Free Library of Philadelphia, and the Montgomery County Library and Information Network Consortium.

I have previously thanked my cohosts on The Liars Club Oddcast, but I'd also like to thank the scores of authors who have come on the podcast as guests, who have shared their time and their knowledge and their charming selves. I've learned a tremendous amount from them and treasure the opportunity to speak with so many phenomenally talented (and often hilarious) authors. I am a better writer for their wisdom and their generosity with it.

More than anyone else, however, I'd like to thank the readers out there who have embraced *Spliced* and *Splintered*, and who will hopefully embrace *Spiked* as well, those who have come with me on this journey so far, and those who will now accompany me on what is, for now at least, that journey's last leg. I hope they enjoy reading *Spiked* as much as I enjoyed working on it.

My goal in writing these books was to write an entertaining arc of stories populated by compelling and believable characters, and to explore some of the technologies that I believe are on our horizon. More important, though, I wanted to address some of the unfortunate aspects of human behavior that are increasingly a part of our day-to-day reality, and some of the heroic aspects of humanity that are fortunately rising to meet that challenge. This is an exciting time in many ways, both good and bad. For many people, it seems as though for perhaps the first time they have the opportunity to be seen for who they really are. There are others, unfortunately, who feel threatened or frightened by that progress, who seek to turn back the clock. While it may seem at times that the forces of closed-mindedness are advancing, are winning, the arc of history ultimately bends toward acceptance and tolerance and love, and I am thankful for all those who are out there fighting to make that true. This book, all my books, are for them.